Tales Told By The Kathaakaar

Traditional tales, fables and sagas

from the Indian tradition.

Compiled, Adapted & Edited by Clive Gilson

Tales from the World's Firesides

Book 1 in Part 5 of the series: Central and Southern Asia

Tales Told By The Kathaakaar, edited by Clive Gilson,

Solitude, Bath, UK

www.clivegilson.com

Printed by IngramSpark

ISBN: 978-1-915081-25-4

I have edited Clive Gilson's books for over a decade now – he's prolific and can turn his hand to many genres. poetry, short fiction, contemporary novels, folklore, and science fiction – and the common theme is that none of them ever fails to take my breath away. There's something in each story that is either memorably poignant, hauntingly unnerving, or sidesplittingly funny.

Lorna Howarth, *The Write Factor*

Tales From The World's Firesides is a grand project. I've collected "000's of traditional texts as part of other projects, and while many of the original texts are available through channels like Project Gutenberg, some of the narratives can be hard to read by modern readers, & so the Fireside project was born. Put simply, I collect, collate & adapt traditional tales from around the world & publish them as a modern archive. *Part 5* covers Central and Southern Asia. I'm not laying any claim to insight or specialist knowledge, but these collections are born out of my love of storytelling & I hope that you'll share my affection for traditional tales, myths & legends.

Interior image: Harisankar Sahoo from Pixabay

Cover image Dee from Pixabay

CONTENTS

ORIGINAL FICTION BY CLIVE GILSON

- Songs of Bliss
- Out of the Walled Garden
- The Mechanic's Curse
- The Insomniac Booth
- A Solitude of Stars

AS EDITOR – *FIRESIDE TALES – Part 1, Europe*

- Tales From the Land of Dragons
- Tales From the Land of The Brave
- Tales From the Land of Saints And Scholars
- Tales From the Land of Hope And Glory
- Tales From Lands of Snow and Ice
- Tales From the Viking Isles
- Tales From the Forest Lands
- Tales From the Old Norse
- More Tales About Saints and Scholars
- More Tales About Hope and Glory
- More Tales About Snow and Ice
- Tales From the Land of Rabbits
- Tales Told by Bulls and Wolves
- Tales of Fire and Bronze
- Tales From the Land of the Strigoi
- Tales Told by the Wind Mother
- Tales from Gallia
- Tales from Germania

EDITOR – *FIRESIDE TALES – Part 2, North America*

- Okaraxta - Tales from The Great Plains
- Tibik-Kìzis – Tales from The Great Lakes & Canada
- Jóhonaa'éí –Tales from America's Southwest
- Qugaaĝix̂ - First Nation Tales from Alaska & The Arctic
- Karahkwa - First Nation Tales from America's Eastern States
- Pot-Likker - Folklore, Fairy Tales, and Settler Stories from America

EDITOR – *FIRESIDE TALES – Part 3, Africa*

- Arokin Tales – Folklore & Fairy Tales from West Africa
- Hadithi Tales – Folklore & Fairy Tales from East Africa
- Inkathaso Tales – Folklore & Fairy Tales from Southern Africa
- Tarubadur Tales – Folklore & Fairy Tales from North Africa
- Elephant And Frog – Folklore from Central Africa

EDITOR – *FIRESIDE TALES – Part 4, Middle East*

- Tales From The Meddahs – Turkish Folk & Fairy Tales
- Tales From The Hakawati – Arabic Folk & Fairy Tales
- Tales Told By Balebos & Gusan – Jewish & Armenian Folk & Fairy Tales

Preface

I've been collecting and telling stories for a couple of decades now, having had several of my own fictional works published in recent years. My particular focus is on short story writing in the realms of magical realities and science fiction fantasies.

I've always drawn heavily on traditional folk and fairy tales, and in so doing have amassed a digital collection of many thousands of these tales from around the world. It has been one of my long-standing ambitions to gather these stories together and to create a library of tales that tell the stories of places and peoples from all corners of our world.

One of the main motivations for me in undertaking the project is to collect and tell stories that otherwise might be lost or, at best, be forgotten by predominantly English-speaking readers. Given that a lot of my sources are from early collectors, particularly covering works produced in the late eighteenth century, throughout the nineteenth century, and in the early years of the twentieth century, I do make every effort to adapt stories for a modern reader. Early collectors had a different world view to many of us today, and often expressed views about race and gender, for example, that we find difficult to reconcile in the early years of the twenty-first century. I try, although with varying degrees of success, to update these stories with sensitivity while trying to stay as true to the original spirit of each story as I can.

I also want to assure readers that I try hard not to comment on or appropriate originating cultures. It is almost certainly true that the early collectors of these tales, with their then prevalent world views, have made assumptions about the originating cultures that have given us these tales. I hope that you'll accept my mission to preserve these tales, however and wherever I find them, as just that. I have, therefore, made sure that every story has a full attribution, covering both the original collector / writer and the collection title that this version has been adapted from, as well as having notes about publishers and other relevant and, I hope, interesting source data. Wherever possible I have added a cultural or indigenous attribution as well, although for some of the titles, the country-based theme is obvious.

This volume, *Tales Told By The Kathaakaar*, is the first in a set of collections covering indigenous tales from what we in Europe know now as Central and Southern Asia, an area that actually covers a whole host of nations and storytelling traditions. *Tales Told By The Kathaakaar* collects together a group of generic Indian tales. I hope to delve a little more deeply into regional Indian storytelling in future collections.

I've long wanted to put this collection together. Having spent time in the western states of India, I have a basic sense of the depth of history and culture of the region. Historical study also shows us how Indian culture has flourished for many thousands of years. For me that depth is reflected in the fact that Indian folklore encompasses a wide range of themes, including mythology, religion, history, morality, and cultural traditions. The stories in this collection often reflect the rich tapestry of Indian society and its many diverse cultures, languages, and regions.

Many Indian folk tales and legends are imbued with moral and ethical lessons designed to impart wisdom and guidance to listeners. These stories often feature characters who must navigate complex moral dilemmas and make choices that reflect virtues such as honesty, kindness, and humility.

Indian folk tales and legends also play a significant role in preserving and transmitting that cultural heritage. They reflect the values, beliefs, customs, and traditions of Indian society, serving as a window into the collective identity of its people. While there are obvious regional and cultural differences across India, it is the case that a fair proportion of Indian folklore is heavily influenced by Hindu mythology, with many stories featuring gods, goddesses, demons, and mythical creatures. These tales often explore the cosmic battles between good and evil, the nature of karma, and the cyclical nature of existence.

Of course, India is a vast and diverse country, and its folklore reflects the distinct regional cultures and languages found across the subcontinent. Each region has its own unique repertoire of folk tales, legends, and fairy tales, contributing to the rich mosaic of Indian folklore. Overall, I find that Indian folk tales, legends, and fairy tales are characterized by their diversity, moral complexity, mythological richness, and cultural significance, making them an integral part of India's literary and cultural heritage.

As for the Fireside Tales project, these collections will grow over coming years to tell lost and forgotten tales from every continent, and even then, I'll just be scratching the surface of the world's lore and love. That's the great gift in storytelling. Since the first of our ancestors sat around in a cave, contemplating an ape's place in the world, we have, as a species, continued to tell each other stories of magic and cunning and caution and love. All those years ago, when I began to read through tales from the Celts, tales from Indonesia, tales from Africa and the Far East, tales from everywhere, one of the things that struck me clearly was just how similar are our roots. We share characters and characteristics. The nature of these tales is so similar underneath the local camouflage. Human beings clearly share a storytelling heritage so much deeper than the world that we see superficially as always having been just as it is now.

These tales were originally told by firelight as a way of preserving histories and educating both adult and child. These tales form part of our shared heritage, witches, warts, fantastic beasts, and all. They can be dark and violent. They can be sweet and loving. They are we and we are they in so many ways. I've loved reading and re-reading these stories. I hope that you do too.

Clive

Bath 2024

The King and the Hawk

This story has been adapted from a tale originally told by Kate Douglas Wiggin and Nora Archibald Smith in The Talking Beasts, published in 1911 by Houghton Mifflin Company. The fables in The Talking Beasts are engaging and entertaining, with whimsical characters and imaginative settings. Through these tales, Wiggin and Smith aimed to stimulate the imagination of children while also instilling important values that promote character development and moral growth.

It is related that in ancient times there was a King fond of hunting. He was ever giving reins to the courser of his desire in the pursuit of game, and was always casting the lasso of gladness over the neck of sport. Now this King had a Hawk, who at a single flight could bring down a pebble from the peak of the Caucasus, and in terror of whose claws the constellation Aquila kept himself in the green nest of the sky, and the King had a prodigious fondness for this Hawk and always cared for it with his own hands.

It happened one day that the Monarch, holding the Hawk on his hand, had gone to the chase. A stag leapt up before him and he galloped after it with the utmost eagerness. But he did not succeed in catching it, and became separated from his retinue and servants, and though some of them followed him, the King rode so hotly that the morning breeze could not have reached the dust he raised.

Meantime the fire of his thirst was kindled, and the intense desire to drink overcame the King. He galloped his steed in every direction in search of water until he reached the skirt of a mountain, and beheld that from its summit limpid water was trickling. The King drew forth a cup which he had in his quiver, and riding under the mountain filled the cup with that water, which fell drop by drop. As he was about to take a draught, the Hawk made a blow with his wing, and spilled all the water in the goblet. The King was vexed at this action, but held the cup a second time under the rock, until it was brim full. He then raised it to his lips again, and again the Hawk made a movement and overthrew the cup. The King, made angry and impatient by thirst, dashed the Hawk on the ground and killed it.

Shortly after one of the king's stirrup-holders came up and saw the Hawk dead, and the Monarch with a raging thirst. He then undid a water-vessel from his saddle-cord and washed the cup clean, and was about to give the King a drink. The latter bade him ascend the mountain, as he still wanted the pure water which trickled from the rock, and could not wait to collect it in the cup, drop by drop. The stirrup-holder ascended the mountain and saw a spring giving out a drop at a time with a great pauses in between drops. A huge serpent lay dead on the margin of the fountain, and as the heat of the sun had taken effect upon it, the serpent's poisonous saliva mixed with the water of that mountain, and it trickled drop by drop down the rock.

The stirrup-holder was overcome with horror, and came down from the mountain bewildered, and told the King what he had seen, and gave the King a cup of cold water from his water-vessel. The latter raised the cup to his lips, and his eyes overflowed with tears. The attendant asked the reason of his weeping. The King drew a sigh from his anguished heart and relating in full the story of the Hawk and the spilling of the water in the cup, said, "I grieve for the death of the Hawk, and bemoan my own deed in that. Without inquiry I have deprived a creature, so dear to me, of life."

The attendant replied, "This Hawk protected you from a great peril, and has established a claim to the gratitude of all the people of this country. It would have been better if the King had not been precipitate in slaying it, and had quenched the fire of wrath with the water of mildness."

The King replied, "I repent of this unseemly action, but my repentance is now unavailing, and the wound of this sorrow cannot be healed by any salve.

This story is related in order that it may be known that many such incidents have occurred where, through the disastrous results of precipitation, men have fallen into the whirlpool of repentance.

A Cat, a Mouse, a Lizard and an Owl

This story has been adapted from a tale originally told by Siddha Mohana Mitra and Nancy Bell in Hindu Tales from the Sanskrit, published in 1919 by MacMillan and Company, London & Canada. The book features a selection of stories drawn from classical Sanskrit literature, including the Panchatantra, Hitopadesha, and other traditional sources. The Panchatantra and Hitopadesha are two of the most famous collections of Indian fables and moral stories. They are believed to have originated over two millennia ago and have been passed down through generations. These tales are often characterized by their use of animal characters to convey moral lessons and practical wisdom.

CHAPTER I

This is the story of four creatures, none of whom loved each other, who lived in the same banyan tree in a forest in India. Banyan trees are very beautiful and very useful, and get their name from the fact that "banians," as merchants are called in India, often gather together in their shade to sell their goods. Banyan trees grow to a very great height, spreading their branches out so widely that many people can stand beneath them. From those branches roots spring forth, which, when they reach the ground, pierce it, and look like, columns holding up a roof. If you have never seen a banyan tree, you can easily find a picture of one, and when you have done so, you will understand that a great many creatures can live in one without seeing much of each other.

In an especially fine banyan tree, outside the walls of a town called Vidisa, a cat, an owl, a lizard and a mouse, had all taken up their abode. The cat lived in a big hole in the trunk some little distance from the ground, where she could sleep very cosily, curled up out of sight with her head resting on her forepaws, feeling perfectly safe from harm, for no other creature, she thought, could possibly discover her hiding-place.

The owl roosted in a mass of foliage at the top of the tree, near the nest in which his wife had brought up their children, before those children flew away to seek mates for themselves. He too felt pretty secure as long as he remained up there, but he had seen the cat prowling about below him more than once, and was very sure that, if she should happen to catch sight of him when he was off his guard seeking his prey and obliged to give all his attention to what he was doing, she might spring out upon him and kill him. Cats do not generally attack such big birds as owls, but they will sometimes kill a mother sitting in her nest, as well as the little ones, if the father is too far off to protect them.

The lizard loved to lie and bask in the sunshine, catching the flies on which he lived, lying so still that they did not notice him, and darting out his long tongue suddenly to suck them into his mouth. Yet he hid from the owl and the cat, because he knew full well that, tough though he was, they would gobble him up if they happened to be hungry. He made his home amongst the roots on the south side of the tree where it was hottest.

The mouse had his hole on the other side amongst damp moss and dead leaves. The mouse was in constant fear of the cat and the owl. He knew that both of them could see in the dark, and he would have no chance of escape if they once caught sight of him.

CHAPTER II

The lizard and the mouse could only get food in daylight, but the lizard did not have to go far for the flies on which he lived, whilst the mouse had a very dangerous journey to take to his favourite feeding place. This was a barley field a short distance from the banyan tree, where he loved to nibble the full ears, running up the stalks to get at them. The mouse was the only one of the four creatures in the banyan tree who did not feed on others, for, like the rest of his family, he was a vegetarian, that is to say, he ate nothing but vegetables and fruit.

Now the cat knew full well how fond the mouse was of the barley-field, and she used to keep watch amongst the tall stems, creeping stealthily about with her tail in the air and her green eyes glistening, expecting any moment to see the poor little mouse darting hastily along. The cat never dreamt that any danger could come to her, and she trod down the barley, making quite a clear path through it. She was quite wrong in thinking herself so safe, for that path got her into very serious trouble.

It so happened that a hunter, whose great delight was to kill wild creatures, and who was very clever in finding them, noticing every little thing which could show him where they had passed by, came one day into the barley-field. He spied the path directly and cried, "Ha, ha! Some wild animal has been here, not a very big one; let's have a look for the footprints!" So he stooped down to the ground, and very soon saw the marks of pussy's feet. "A cat, I do believe," he said to himself, "spoiling the barley she doesn't want to eat herself. I'll soon pay her out."

The hunter waited until the evening lest the creature should see what he was going to do, and then in the twilight he set snares all over the barley-field. A snare, you know, is a string with a slip-knot at the end of it, and if an animal puts his head or one of his paws into this slip-knot and goes on without noticing it, the string is pulled tight and the poor creature cannot get free.

CHAPTER III

Exactly what the hunter expected happened. The cat came as usual to watch for the mouse, and caught sight of him running across the end of the path. Puss dashed after him, and just as she thought she really had got him this time, she found herself caught by the neck, for she had put her head into one of the snares. She was nearly strangled and could scarcely even mew. The mouse was so close that he heard the feeble mew, and in a terrible fright, thinking the cat was after him, he peeped through the stems of the barley to make sure which way to run to get away from her. Imagine his delight when he saw his enemy in such trouble and quite unable to do him any harm!

Now it so happened that the owl and the lizard were also in the barley-field, not very far away from the cat, and they too saw the distress their hated enemy was in. They also caught sight of the little mouse peeping through the barley, and the owl thought to himself, "I'll have you, my little friend, now puss cannot do me any harm."

The lizard, meanwhile, darted away into the sunshine, feeling glad that the cat and the owl were neither of them now likely to trouble their heads about him. The owl flew quietly to a tree hard by to watch what would happen, feeling so sure of having the mouse for his dinner that he was in no hurry to catch him.

CHAPTER IV

The mouse, small and helpless though he was, was a wise little creature. He saw the owl fly up into the tree, and knew quite well that if he did not take care he would serve as dinner to that great strong bird. He knew too that, if he went within reach of the claws of the cat, he would suffer for it. "How I do wish," he thought to himself, "I could make friends with the cat, now she is in distress, and get her to promise not to hurt me if ever she gets free. As long as I am near the cat, the owl will not dare to come after me."

As he thought and thought, his eyes got brighter and brighter, and at last he decided what he would do. He had, you see, kept his presence of mind, that is to say, he did not let his fear of the cat or the owl prevent him from thinking clearly. He now ventured forth from amongst the barley, and coming near enough to the cat for her to see him quite clearly, but not near enough for her to reach him with her claws, or far enough away for the owl to get him without danger from those terrible claws, he said to the cat in a queer little squeaky voice, "Dear Puss, I do not like to see you in such a fix. It is true we have never been exactly friends, but I have always looked up to you as a strong and noble enemy. If you will promise never to do me any harm, I will do my best to help you. I have very sharp teeth, and I might perhaps be able to nibble through the string round your beautiful neck and set you free. What do you think about it?"

CHAPTER V

When the cat heard what the mouse said, she could hardly believe her ears. She was of course ready to promise anything to anyone who would help her, so she said at once, "You dear little mouse, to wish to help me. If only you will nibble through that string which is killing me, I promise that I will always love you, always be your friend, and however hungry I may be, I will starve rather than hurt your tender little body."

On hearing this, the mouse, without hesitating a moment, climbed up on to the cat's back, and cuddled down in the soft fur near her neck, feeling very safe and warm there. The owl would certainly not attack him there, he thought, and the cat could not possibly hurt him. It was one thing to pounce down on a defenceless little creature running on the ground amongst the barley, quite another to try and snatch him from the very neck of a cat.

The cat of course expected the mouse to begin to nibble through the string at once, and became very uneasy when she felt the little creature nestle down as if to go to sleep, instead of helping her. Poor Pussy could not turn her head so as to see the mouse without drawing the string tighter, and she did not dare to speak angrily lest she should offend him. "My dear little friend," she said, "don't you think it is high time to keep your promise and set me free?"

Hearing this, the mouse pretended to bite the string, but took care not to do so really, and the cat waited and waited, getting more miserable every minute. All through the long night the same thing went on. The mouse took a little nap now and then, and the cat got weaker and weaker. "Oh," she thought to herself, "if only I could get free, the first thing I would do would be to gobble up that horrid little mouse."

The moon rose, the stars came out, the wind murmured amongst the branches of the banyan tree, making the unfortunate cat long to be safe in her cosy home in the trunk. The cries of the wild animals which prowl about at night seeking their food were heard, and the cat feared one of them might find her and kill her. A mother tiger perhaps would snatch her, and take her to her hungry cubs, hidden away in the deep forest, or a bird of prey might swoop down on her and grip her in his terrible claws. Again and again she entreated the mouse to be quick, promising that, if only he would set her at liberty, she would never, never, never forget it or do any harm to her beloved friend.

CHAPTER VI

It was not until the moon had set and the light of the dawn had put out the light of the stars that the mouse, made any real effort to help the cat. By this time the hunter who had set the snare came to see if he had caught the cat, and the poor cat, seeing him in the distance, became so wild with terror that she nearly killed herself in the struggle to get away.

"Keep still! keep still," cried the mouse, "and I will really save you."

Then with a few quick bites with his sharp teeth he cut through the string, and the next moment the cat was hidden amongst the barley, and the mouse was running off in the opposite direction, determined to keep well out of sight of the creature he had kept in such misery for so many hours. Full well he knew that all the cat's promises would be forgotten, and that she would eat him up if she could catch him. The owl too flew away, and the lizard went off to hunt flies in the sunshine, and there was not a sign of any of the four inhabitants of the banyan tree when the hunter reached the snare. He was very much surprised and puzzled to find the string hanging loose in two pieces, and no sign of there having been anything caught in it, except two white hairs lying on the ground close to the trap. He had a good look round, and then went home without having found out anything.

When the hunter was quite out of sight, the cat came forth from the barley, and hastened back to her beloved home in the banyan tree. On her way there she spied the mouse also hurrying along in the same direction, and at first she felt inclined to hunt him and eat him then and there. On second thoughts however she decided to try and keep friends with him, because he might help her again if she got caught a second time. So she took no notice of the mouse until the next day, when she climbed down the tree and went to the roots in which she knew the mouse was hidden. There she began to purr as loud as she could, to show the mouse she was in a good humour, and called out, "Dear good little mouse, come out of your hole and let me tell you how very, very grateful I am to you for saving my life. There is nothing in the world I will not do for you, if you will only be friends with me."

The mouse only squeaked in answer to this speech, and took very good care not to show himself, till he was quite sure the cat was gone beyond reach of him. He stayed quietly in his hole, and only ventured forth after he had heard the cat climb up into the tree again. "It is all very well," thought the mouse, "to pretend to make friends with an enemy when that enemy is helpless, but I should indeed be a silly mouse to trust a cat when she is free to kill me."

The cat made a good many other efforts to be friends with the mouse, but they were all unsuccessful. In the end the owl caught the mouse, and the cat killed the lizard. The owl and the cat both lived for the rest of their lives in the banyan tree, and died in the end at a good old age.

Story Of The King Who Would Be Stronger Than Fate

This story has been adapted from a tale originally told by Andrew Lang in The Brown Fairy Book, published in 1904 by Longmans, Green And Co., London And New York. Andrew Lang's Coloured Fairy Books were a series of twelve collections of fairy tales and folk stories from around the world, edited and compiled by Scottish author Andrew Lang. The first volume, The Blue Fairy Book, was published in 1889, followed by eleven more volumes, each with a different colour in the title, such as The Red Fairy Book, The Green Fairy Book, and so on, concluding with The Lilac Fairy Book in 1910.

Once upon a time, far away in the east country, there lived a king who loved hunting so much that, when once there was a deer in sight, he was careless of his own safety. Indeed, he often became quite separated from his nobles and attendants, and in fact was particularly fond of lonely adventures. Another of his favourite amusements was to give out that he was not well, and could not be seen, and then, with the knowledge only of his faithful Grand Vizier, to disguise himself as a pedlar, load a donkey with cheap wares, and travel about. In this way he found out what the common people said about him, and how his judges and governors fulfilled their duties.

One day his queen presented him with a baby daughter as beautiful as the dawn, and the king himself was so happy and delighted that, for a whole week, he forgot to hunt, and spent the time in public and private rejoicing.

Not long afterwards, however, he went out after some deer which were to be found in a far corner of his forests. In the course of the beat his dogs disturbed a beautiful snow-white stag, and directly he saw it the king determined that he would have it at any cost. So he put the spurs to his horse, and followed it as hard as he could gallop. Of course all his attendants followed at the best speed that they could manage, but the king was so splendidly mounted, and the stag was so swift, that, at the end of an hour, the king found that only his favourite hound and himself were in the chase; all the rest were far, far behind and out of sight.

Nothing daunted, however, he went on and on, till he perceived that he was entering a valley with great rocky mountains on all sides, and that his horse was getting very tired and trembled at every stride. Worse than all evening was already drawing on, and the sun would soon set. In vain had he sent arrow after arrow at the beautiful stag. Every shot fell short, or went wide of the mark, and at last, just as darkness was setting in, he lost sight altogether of the beast. By this time his horse could hardly move from fatigue, his hound staggered panting along beside him, he was far away amongst mountains where he had never been before, and had quite missed his way, and not a human creature or dwelling was in sight.

All this was very discouraging, but the king would not have minded if he had not lost that beautiful stag. That troubled him a good deal, but he never worried over what he could not help, so he got down from his horse, slipped his arm through the bridle, and led the animal along the rough path in hopes of discovering some shepherd's hut, or, at least, a cave or shelter under some rock, where he might pass the night.

Presently he heard the sound of rushing water, and made towards it. He toiled over a steep rocky shoulder of a hill, and there, just below him, was a stream dashing down a precipitous glen, and, almost beneath his feet, twinkling and flickering from the level of the torrent, was a dim light as of a lamp. The king with his horse and hound made his way towards this light, sliding and stumbling down a steep, stony path. At the bottom the king found a narrow grassy ledge by the brink of the stream, across which the light from a rude lantern in the mount of a cave shed a broad beam of uncertain light. At the edge of the stream sat an old hermit with a long white beard, who neither spoke nor moved as the king approached, but sat throwing into the stream dry leaves which lay scattered about the ground near him.

"Peace be upon you," said the king, giving the usual country salutation.

"And upon you peace," answered the hermit, but still he never looked up, nor stopped what he was doing.

For a minute or two the king stood watching him. He noticed that the hermit threw two leaves in at a time, and watched them attentively. Sometimes both were carried rapidly down by the stream. Sometimes only one leaf was carried off, and the other, after whirling slowly round and round on the edge of the current, would come circling back on an eddy to the hermit's feet. At other times both leaves were held in the backward eddy, and failed to reach the main current of the noisy stream.

"What are you doing?" asked the king at last, and the hermit replied that he was reading the fates of men .Every one's fate, he said, was settled from the beginning, and, whatever it were, there was no escape from it. The king laughed.

"I care little," he said, "what my fate may be, but I should be curious to know the fate of my little daughter."

"I cannot say," answered the hermit.

"Do you not know, then?" demanded the king.

"I might know," returned the hermit, "but it is not always wisdom to know much."

But the king was not content with this reply, and began to press the old man to say what he knew, which for a long time he would not do. At last, however, the king urged him so greatly that he said, "The king's daughter will marry the son of a poor slave-girl called Puruna, who belongs to the king of the land of the north. There is no escaping from Fate."

The king was wild with anger at hearing these words, but he was also very tired, so he only laughed, and answered that he hoped there would be a way out of such a fate. Then he asked if the hermit could shelter him and his beasts for the night, and the hermit said "Yes", so, very soon the king had watered and tethered his horse, and, after a supper of bread and parched peas, lay down in the cave, with the hound at his feet, and tried to go to sleep. But instead of sleeping he only lay awake and thought of the hermit's prophecy, and the more he thought of it the angrier he felt, until he gnashed his teeth and declared that it should never, never come true.

Morning came, and the king got up, pale and sulky, and, after learning from the hermit which path to take, was soon mounted and found his way home without much difficulty. Directly he reached his palace he wrote a letter to the king of the land of the north, begging him, as a favour, to sell him his slave girl Puruna and her son, and saying that, if he consented, he would send a messenger to receive them at the river which divided the kingdoms.

For five days he awaited the reply, and hardly slept or ate, but was as cross as could be all the time. On the fifth day his messenger returned with a letter to say that the king of the land of the north would not sell, but he would give, the king the slave girl and her son. The king was overjoyed. He sent for his Grand Vizier and told him that he was going on one of his lonely expeditions, and that the Vizier must invent some excuse to account for his absence. Next he disguised himself as an ordinary messenger, mounted a swift camel, and sped away to the place where the slave girl was to be handed over to him. When he got there he gave the messengers who brought her a letter of thanks and a handsome present for their master and rewards for themselves, and then without delay he took the poor woman and her tiny baby-boy up on to his camel and rode off to a wild desert.

After riding for a day and a night, almost without stopping, he came to a great cave where he made the woman dismount, and, taking her and the baby into the cave, he drew his sword and with one blow chopped her head off. But although his anger made him cruel enough for anything so dreadful, the king felt that he could not turn his great sword on the helpless baby, who he was sure must soon die in this solitary place without its mother, so he left it in the cave where it was, and, mounting his camel, rode home as fast as he could.

Now, in a small village in his kingdom there lived an old widow who had no children or relations of any kind. She made her living mostly by selling the milk of a flock of goats, but she was very, very poor, and not very strong, and often used to wonder how she would live if she got too weak or ill to attend to her goats. Every morning she drove the goats out into the desert to graze on the shrubs and bushes which grew there, and every evening they came home of themselves to be milked and to be shut up safely for the night

One evening the old woman was astonished to find that her very best nanny-goat returned without a drop of milk. She thought that some naughty boy or girl was playing a trick upon her and had caught the goat on its way home and stolen all the milk. But when evening after evening the goat remained almost dry she determined to find out who the thief was. So the next day she followed the goats at a distance and watched them while they grazed.

At length, in the afternoon, the old woman noticed this particular nanny-goat stealing off by herself away from the herd and she at once went after her. On and on the goat walked for some way, and then disappeared into a cave in the rocks. The old woman followed the goat into the cave and then, what should she see but the animal giving her milk to a little boy-baby, whilst on the ground near by lay the sad remains of the baby's dead mother!

Wondering and frightened, the old woman thought at last that this little baby might be a son to her in her old age, and that he would grow up and in time to come be her comfort and support. So she carried home the baby to her hut, and next day she took a spade to the cave and dug a grave where she buried the poor mother.

Years passed by, and the baby grew up into a find handsome lad, as daring as he was beautiful, and as industrious as he was brave. One day, when the boy, whom the old woman had named Nur Mahomed, was about seventeen years old, he was coming from his day's work in the fields, when he saw a strange donkey eating the cabbages in the garden which surrounded their little cottage. Seizing a big stick, he began to beat the intruder and to drive him out of his garden. A neighbour passing by called out to him saying. "Hi! I say! Why are you beating the pedlar's donkey like that?"

"The pedlar should keep him from eating my cabbages," said Nur Mahomed. "If he comes this evening here again I'll cut off his tail for him!"

Whereupon he went off indoors, whistling cheerfully. It happened that this neighbour was one of those people who make mischief by talking too much, so, meeting the pedlar in the 'serai,' or inn, that evening, he told him what had occurred, and added, "Yes, and the young spitfire said that if beating the donkey would not do, he would beat you also, and cut your nose off for a thief!"

A few days later, the pedlar having moved on, two men appeared in the village inquiring who it was who had threatened to ill-treat and to murder an innocent pedlar. They declared that the pedlar, in fear of his life, had complained to the king, and that they had been sent to bring the lawless person who had said these things before the king himself. Of course they soon found out about the donkey eating Nur Mahomed's cabbages, and about the young man's hot words, but although the lad assured them that he had never said anything about murdering anyone, they replied they were ordered to arrest him, and bring him to take his trial before the king. So, in spite of his protests, and the wails of his mother, he was carried off, and in due time brought before the king. Of course Nur Mahomed never guessed that the supposed pedlar happened to have been the king himself, although nobody knew it.

But as he was very angry at what he had been told, he declared that he was going to make an example of this young man, and intended to teach him that even poor travelling pedlars could get justice in his country, and be protected from such lawlessness. However, just as he was going to pronounce some very heavy sentence, there was a stir in the court, and up came Nur Mahomed's old mother, weeping and lamenting, and begging to be heard. The king ordered her to speak, and she began to plead for the boy, declaring how good he was, and how he was the support of her old age, and if he were put in prison she would die. The king asked her who she was. She replied that she was his mother.

"His mother?" said the king. "You are too old, surely, to have so young a son!"

Then the old woman, in her fright and distress, confessed the whole story of how she found the baby, and how she rescued and brought him up, and ended by beseeching the king for mercy.

It is easy to guess how, as the story came out, the king looked blacker and blacker, and grimmer and grimmer, until at last he was half fainting with rage and astonishment. This, then, was the baby he had left to die, after cruelly murdering his mother! Surely fate might have spared him this! He wished he had sufficient excuse to put the boy to death, for the old hermit's prophecy came back to him as strongly as ever, and yet the young man had done nothing bad enough to deserve such a punishment. Everyone would call him a tyrant if he were to give such an order, so he dared not try it!

At length he collected himself enough to say, "If this young man enlists in my army I will let him off. We have need of such as him, and a little discipline will do him good."

Still the old woman pleaded that she could not live without her son, and was nearly as terrified at the idea of his becoming a soldier as she was at the thought of his being put in prison. But at length the king, determined to get the youth into his clutches, pacified her by promising her a pension large enough to keep her in comfort, and Nur Mahomed, to his own great delight, was duly enrolled in the king's army.

As a soldier Nur Mahomed seemed to be in luck. He was rather surprised, but much pleased, to find that he was always one of those chosen when any difficult or dangerous enterprise was afoot, and, although he had the narrowest escapes on some occasions, still, the very desperateness of the situations in which he found himself gave him special chances of displaying his courage. And as he was also modest and generous, he became a favourite with his officers and his comrades.

Thus it was not very surprising that, before very long, he became enrolled amongst the picked men of the king's bodyguard. The fact is, that the king had hoped to have got him killed in some fight or another, but, seeing that, on the contrary, he throve on hard knocks, he was now determined to try more direct and desperate methods.

One day, soon after Nur Mahomed had entered the bodyguard, he was selected to be one of the soldiers told to escort the king through the city. The procession was marching on quite smoothly, when a man, armed with a dagger, rushed out of an alley straight towards the king. Nur Mahomed, who was the nearest of the guards, threw himself in the way, and received the stab that had been apparently intended for the king. Luckily the blow was a hurried one, and the dagger glanced on his breastbone, so that, although he received a severe wound, his youth and strength quickly got the better of it. The king was, of course, obliged to take some notice of this brave deed, and as a reward made him one of his own attendants.

After this the strange adventures the young man passed through were endless. Officers of the bodyguard were often sent on all sorts of secret and difficult errands, and such errands had a curious way of becoming necessary when Nur Mahomed was on duty. Once, while he was taking a journey, a foot-bridge gave way under him. Once he was attacked by armed robbers. On another occasion a rock rolled down upon him in a mountain pass. A heavy stone coping fell from a roof at his feet in a narrow city alley. Altogether, Nur Mahomed began to think that, somewhere or other, he had made an enemy, but he was light-hearted, and the thought did not much trouble him. He escaped somehow every time, and felt amused rather than anxious about the next adventure.

It was the custom of that city that the officer for the day of the palace guards should receive all his food direct from the king's kitchen. One day, when Nur Mahomed's turn came to be on duty, he was just sitting down to a delicious stew that had been sent in from the palace, when one of those gaunt, hungry dogs, which, in eastern countries, run about the streets, poked his nose in at the open guard-room door, and looked at Nur Mahomed with his mouth watering and nostrils sniffing the air. The kind-hearted young man picked out a lump of meat, went to the door, and threw it outside to him. The dog pounced upon it, and gulped it down greedily, and was just turning to go, when it staggered, fell, rolled over, and died. Nur Mahomed, who had been lazily watching him, stood still for a moment, then he came back whistling softly. He gathered up the rest of his dinner and carefully wrapped it up to carry away and bury somewhere, and then he sent back the empty plates.

How furious the king was when, at the next morning's durbar, Nur Mahomed appeared before him fresh, alert and smiling as usual. The king was determined, however, to try once more, and bidding the young man come into his presence that evening, gave orders that he was to carry a secret despatch to the governor of a distant province. "Make your preparations at once," added he, "and be ready to start in the morning. I myself will deliver you the papers at the last moment."

Now this province was four or five days' journey from the palace, and the governor of it was the most faithful servant the king had. He could be silent as the grave, and prided himself on his obedience. Whilst he was an old and tried servant of the king's, his wife had been almost a mother to the young princess ever since the queen had died some years before. It happened that, a little before this time, the princess had been sent away for her health to another remote province, and whilst she was there her old friend, the governor's wife, had begged her to come and stay with them as soon as she could.

The princess accepted gladly, and was actually staying in the governor's house at the very time when the king made up his mind to send Nur Mahomed there with the mysterious despatch.

According to orders Nur Mahomed presented himself early the next morning at the king's private apartments. His best horse was saddled, food placed in his saddle-bag, and with some money tied up in his waist-band, he was ready to start. The king handed over to him a sealed packet, desiring him to give it himself only into the hands of the governor, and to no one else. Nur Mahomed hid it carefully in his turban, swung himself into the saddle, and five minutes later rode out of the city gates, and set out on his long journey.

The weather was very hot, but Nur Mahomed thought that the sooner his precious letter was delivered the better; so that, by dint of riding most of each night and resting only in the hottest part of the day, he found himself, by noon on the third day, approaching the town which was his final destination.

Not a soul was to be seen anywhere, and Nur Mahomed, stiff, dry, thirsty, and tired, looked longingly over the wall into the gardens, and marked the fountains, the green grass, the shady apricot orchards, and giant mulberry trees, and wished he were there.

At length he reached the castle gates, and was at once admitted, as he was in the uniform of the king's bodyguard. The governor was resting, the soldier said, and could not see him until the evening. So Nur Mahomed handed over his horse to an attendant, and wandered down into the lovely gardens he had seen from the road, and sat down in the shade to rest himself. He flung himself on his back and watched the birds twittering and chattering in the trees above him. Through the branches he could see great patches of sky where the kites wheeled and circled incessantly, crying out with their shrill whistling. Bees buzzed over the flowers with a soothing sound, and in a few minutes Nur Mahomed was fast asleep.

Every day, through the heat of the afternoon, the governor, and his wife also, used to lie down for two or three hours in their own rooms, and so, for the matter of that, did most people in the palace. But the princess, like many other girls, was restless, and preferred to wander about the garden, rather than rest on a pile of soft cushions. What a torment her stout old attendants and servants sometime thought her when she insisted on staying awake, and making them chatter or do something, when they could hardly keep their eyes open! Sometimes, however, the princess would pretend to go to sleep, and then, after all her women had gladly followed her example, she would get up and go out by herself, her veil hanging loosely about her. If she was discovered her old hostess scolded her severely, but the princess only laughed, and did the same thing next time.

This very afternoon the princess had left all her women asleep, and, after trying in vain to amuse herself indoors, she had slipped out into the great garden, and rambled about in all her favourite nooks and corners, feeling quite safe as there was not a creature to be seen. Suddenly, on turning a corner, she stopped in surprise, for before her lay a man fast asleep! In her hurry she had almost tripped over him. But there he was, a young man, tanned and dusty with travel, in the uniform of an officer of the king's guard.

One of the few faults of this lovely princess was a devouring curiosity, and she lived such an idle life that she had plenty of time to be curious. Out of one of the folds of this young man's turban there peeped the corner of a letter! She wondered what the letter was, and whom it was for! She drew her veil a little closer, and stole across on tip-toe and caught hold of the corner of the letter. Then she pulled it a little, and just a little more! A great big seal came into view, which she saw to be her father's, and at the sight of it she paused for a minute half ashamed of what she was doing. But the pleasure of taking a letter which was not meant for her was more than she could resist, and in another moment it was in her hand. All at once she remembered that it would be death to this poor officer if he lost the letter, and that at all hazards she must put it back again. But this was not so easy, and, moreover, the letter in her hand burnt her with longing to read it, and see what was inside. She examined the seal. It was sticky with being exposed to the hot sun, and with a very little effort it parted from the paper. The letter was open and she read it!

And this was what was written: 'Behead the messenger who brings this letter secretly and at once. Ask no questions.'

The girl grew pale. What a shame, she thought. Then she decided that she could not let a handsome young fellow like that be beheaded, but how to prevent it was not quite clear at the moment. Some plan must be invented, and she wished to lock herself in where no one could interrupt her, as might easily happen in the garden. So she crept softly to her room, and took a piece of paper and wrote upon it: 'Marry the messenger who brings this letter to the princess openly at once. Ask no questions.' And even contrived to work the seals off the original letter and to fix them to this, so that no one could tell, unless they examined it closely, that it had ever been opened. Then she slipped back, shaking with fear and excitement, to where the young officer still lay asleep, thrust the letter into the fold of his turban, and hurried back to her room. It was done!

Late in the afternoon Nur Mahomed woke, and, making sure that the precious despatch was still safe, went off to get ready for his audience with the governor. As soon as he was ushered into his presence he took the letter from his turban and placed it in the governor's hands according to orders. When he had read it the governor was certainly a little astonished, but he was told in the letter to 'ask no questions,' and he knew how to obey orders. He sent for his wife and told her to get the princess ready to be married at once.

"Nonsense!" said his wife, "what in the world do you mean?"

"These are the king's commands," he answered. "Go and do as I bid you. The letter says, 'at once,' and 'ask no questions.' The marriage, therefore, must take place this evening."

In vain his wife urged every objection, but the more she argued, the more determined was her husband. "I know how to obey orders," he said, "and these are as plain as the nose on my face!"

So the princess was summoned, and, somewhat to their surprise, she seemed to take the news very calmly. Next Nur Mahomed was informed, and he was greatly startled, but of course he could but be delighted at the great and unexpected honour which he thought the king had done him. Then all the castle was turned upside down, and when the news spread in the town, that too was turned upside down. Everybody ran everywhere, and tried to do everything at once, and, in the middle of it all, the old governor went about with his hair standing on end, muttering something about 'obeying orders.'

And so the marriage was celebrated, and there was a great feast in the castle, and another in the soldiers' barracks, and illuminations all over the town and in the beautiful gardens. And all the people declared that such a wonderful sight had never been seen, and talked about it to the ends of their lives.

The next day the governor despatched the princess and her bridegroom to the king, with a troop of horsemen, splendidly dressed, and he sent a mounted messenger on before them, with a letter giving the account of the marriage to the king.

When the king got the governor's letter, he grew so red in the face that everyone thought he was going to have apoplexy. They were all very anxious to know what had happened, but he rushed off and locked himself into a room, where he ramped and raved until he was tired. Then, after a while, he began to think he had better make the best of it, especially as the old governor had been clever enough to send him back his letter, and the king was pretty sure that this was in the princess's handwriting. He was fond of his daughter, and though she had behaved badly, he did not wish to cut her head off, and he did not want people to know the truth because it would make him look foolish. In fact, the more he considered the matter, the more he felt that he would be wise to put a good face on it, and to let people suppose that he had really brought about the marriage of his own free will.

So, when the young couple arrived, the king received them with all state, and gave his son-in-law a province to govern. Nur Mahomed soon proved himself as able and honourable a governor as he was a brave soldier, and, when the old king died, he became king in his place, and reigned long and happily.

Nur Mahomed's old mother lived for a long time in her fake son's palace, and died in peace. The princess, his wife, although she had got her husband by a trick, found that she could not trick him, and so she never tried, but busied herself in teaching her children and scolding her maids. As for the old hermit, no trace of him was ever discovered, but the cave is there, and the leaves lie thick in front of it to this day.

The Triumph Of Truth

This story has been adapted from a tale originally told by Katharine Pyle in Tales Of Folk And Fairies, published in 1929 by Little, Brown And Company, Boston. Tales of Folk and Fairies is renowned for its timeless storytelling, whimsical characters, and beautiful illustrations.

There was once a Rajah who was both young and handsome, and yet he had never married. One time this Rajah, whose name was Chundun, found himself obliged to make a long journey. He took with him attendants and horsemen, and also his Vizier. This Vizier was a very wise man, so wise that nothing was hidden from him.

In a certain far-off part of the kingdom the Rajah saw a fine garden, and so beautiful was it that he stopped to admire it. He was surprised to see growing in the midst of it a small bingal tree that bore a number of fine bingals, but not a single leaf.

"This is a very curious thing, and I do not understand it," said Chundun Rajah to his Vizier. "Why does this tree bear such fine and perfect fruit, and yet it has not a single leaf?"

"I could tell you the meaning," said the Vizier, "but I fear that if I did you would not believe me and would have me punished for telling a lie."

"That could never be," answered the Rajah, "I know you to be a very truthful man and wise above all others. Whatever you tell me I shall believe."

"Then this is the meaning of it," said the Vizier. "The gardener who has charge of this garden has one daughter. Her name is Guzra Bai, and she is very beautiful. If you will count the bingals you will find there are twenty-and-one. Whoever marries the gardener's daughter will have twenty-one children, twenty boys and one girl."

Chundun Rajah was very much surprised at what his Vizier said. "I should like to see this Guzra Bai," he said.

"You can very easily see her," answered the Vizier. "Early every morning she comes into the garden to play among the flowers. If you come here early and hide you can see her without frightening her, as you would do if you went to her home."

The Rajah was pleased with this suggestion, and early the next morning he came to the garden and hid himself behind a flowering bush. It was not long before he saw the girl playing about among the flowers, and she was so very beautiful the Rajah at once fell in love with her. He determined to make her his Ranee, but he did not speak to her or show himself to her then for fear of frightening her. He determined to go to the gardener's house that evening and tell him he wished his daughter for a wife.

As he had determined, so he did. That very evening, accompanied only by his Vizier, he went to the gardener's house and knocked upon the door.

"Who is there?" asked the gardener from within.

"It is I, the Rajah," answered Chundun. "Open the door, for I wish to speak with you."

The gardener laughed. "That is a likely story," he said. "Why should the Rajah come to my poor hut? No, no; you are someone who wishes to play a trick on me, but you shall not succeed. I will not let you in."

"But it is indeed Chundun Rajah," called the Vizier. "Open the door that he may speak with you."

When the gardener heard the Vizier's voice he came and opened the door a crack, but still he only half believed what they told him. Imagine how amazed he was to see that it was indeed the Rajah who stood there in all his magnificence with his Vizier beside him. The poor man was terrified, fearing Chundun would be angry, but the Rajah spoke to him graciously.

"Do not be afraid," he said. "Call your daughter that I may speak with her, for it is she whom I wish to see."

The girl was hiding (for she was afraid) and would not come until her father took her hand and drew her forward.

When the Rajah saw her now, this second time, she seemed to him even more beautiful than at first. He was filled with joy and wonder.

"Now I will tell you why I have come here," he said. "I wish to take Guzra Bai for my wife."

At first the gardener would not believe him, but when he found the Rajah did indeed mean what he said he turned to his daughter. "If the girl is willing you shall have her," he said, "but I will not force her to marry even a Rajah."

The girl was still afraid, yet she could not but love the Rajah, so handsome was he, and so kind and gracious was his manner. She gave her consent, and the gardener was overjoyed at the honour that had come to him and his daughter.

Chundun and the beautiful Guzra Bai were married soon after in the gardener's house, and then the Rajah and his new Ranee rode away together.

Now Chundun Rajah's mother, the old Ranee, was of a very proud and jealous nature. When she found her son had married a common girl, the daughter of a gardener, and that Chundun thought of nothing but his bride and her beauty, she was very angry. She determined to rid herself of Guzra Bai in some way or other. But Chundun watched over his young Ranee so carefully that for a long time the old Queen could find no chance to harm her.

But after a while the Rajah found it was again necessary for him to go on a long journey. Just before he set out he gave Guzra Bai a little golden bell. "If any danger should threaten or harm befall you, ring this bell," he said. "Wherever I am I shall hear it and be with you at once, even though I return from the farthest part of my kingdom."

No sooner had he gone than Guzra Bai began to wonder whether indeed it were possible that he could hear the bell at any distance and return to her. She wondered and wondered until, at last, her curiosity grew so great that she could not resist from ringing it.

No sooner had it sounded than the Rajah stood before her. "What has happened?" he asked. "Why did you call me?"

"Nothing has happened," answered Guzra Bai, "but it did not seem to me possible that you could really hear the bell so far away, and I could not resist from trying it."

"Very well," said the Rajah. "Now you know that it is true, so do not call me again unless you have need of me."

Again he went away, and Guzra Bai sat and thought and thought about the golden bell. At last she rang it again. At once the Rajah stood before her.

"Oh, my dear husband, please forgive me," cried Guzra Bai. "It seemed so wonderful I thought I must have dreamed that the bell could bring you back."

"Guzra Bai, do not be so foolish," said her husband. "I will forgive you this time, but do not call me again unless you have need of me." And he went away.

Again and for the third time Guzra Bai rang the bell, and the Rajah appeared.

"Why do you call me again?" he asked. "Is it again for nothing, or has something happened to you?"

"Nothing has happened," answered Guzra Bai, "only somehow I felt so frightened that I wanted you near me."

"Guzra Bai, I am away on affairs of state," said the Rajah. "If you call me in this way when you have no need of me, I shall soon refuse to answer the bell. Remember this and do not call me again without reason."

And for the third time the Rajah went away and left her.

Soon after this the young Ranee had twenty-one beautiful children, twenty sons and one daughter.

When the old Queen heard of this she was more jealous than ever. "When the Rajah returns and sees all these children," she thought to herself, "he will be so delighted that he will love Guzra Bai more dearly than ever, and nothing I can do will ever separate them." She then began to plan within herself as to how she could get rid of the children before the Rajah's return.

She sent for the nurse who had charge of the babies, and who was as wicked as herself. "If you can rid me of these children, I will give you a lac (100,000) of gold pieces," she said. "Only it must be done in such a way that the Rajah will lay all the blame on Guzra Bai."

"That can be done," answered the nurse. "I will throw the children out on the ash heaps, where they will soon perish, and I will put stones in their places. Then when the Rajah returns we will tell him Guzra Bai is a wicked sorceress, who has changed her children into stones."

The old Ranee was pleased with this plan and said that she herself would go with the nurse and see that it was carried out.

Guzra Bai looked from her window and saw the old Queen coming with the nurse, and at once she was afraid. She was sure they intended some harm to her or the children. She seized the golden bell and rang and rang it, but Chundun did not come. She had called him back so often for no reason at all that this time he did not believe she really needed him.

The nurse and the old Ranee carried away the children, as they had planned, and threw them on the ash heaps and brought twenty-one large stones that they put in their places.

When Chundun Rajah returned from his journey the old Ranee met him, weeping and tearing her hair. "Alas, alas!" she cried. "Why did you marry a sorceress and bring such terrible misfortune upon us all!"

"What misfortune?" asked the Rajah. "What do you mean?"

His mother then told him that while he was away Guzra Bai had had twenty-one beautiful children, but she had turned them all into stones.

Chundun Rajah was thunderstruck. He called the wicked nurse and questioned her. She repeated what the old Ranee had already told him and also showed him the stones.

Then the Rajah believed them. He still loved Guzra Bai too much to put her to death, but he had her imprisoned in a high tower, and would not see her nor speak with her.

But meanwhile the little children who had been thrown out on the ash heap were being well taken care of. A large rat, of the kind called Bandicote, had heard them crying and had taken pity on them. She drew them down into her hole, which was close by and where they would be safe. She then called twenty of her friends together. She told them who the children were and where she had found them, and the twenty agreed to help her take care of the little ones. Each rat was to have the care of one of the little boys and to bring him suitable food, and the old Bandicote who had found them would care for the little girl.

This was done, and so well were the children fed that they grew rapidly. Before long they were large enough to leave the rat hole and go out to play among the ash heaps, but at night they always returned to the hole. The old Bandicote warned them that if they saw anyone coming they must at once hide in the hole, and under no circumstances must anyone see them.

The little boys were always careful to do this, but the little girl was very curious. Now it so happened that one day the wicked nurse came past the ash heaps. The little boys saw her coming and ran back into the hole to hide. But the little girl lingered until the nurse was quite close to her before she ran away.

The nurse went to the old Ranee, and said, "Do you know, I believe those children are still alive? I believe they are living in a rat hole near the ash heap, for I saw a pretty little girl playing there among the ashes, and when I came close to her she ran down into the largest rat hole and hid."

The Ranee was very much troubled when she heard this, for if it were true, as she thought it might be, she feared the Rajah would hear about it and inquire into the matter. "What shall I do?" she asked the nurse.

"Send out and have the ground dug over and filled in," the nurse replied. "In this way, if any of the children are hidden there, they will be covered over and smothered, and you will also kill the rats that have been harbouring them."

The Ranee at once sent for workmen and bade them go out to the rat holes and dig and fill them in, and the children and the rats would certainly have been smothered just as the nurse had planned, only luckily the old mother rat was hiding nearby and overheard what was said. She at once hastened home and told her friends what was going to happen, and they all made their escape before the workmen arrived. She also took the children out of the hole and hid them under the steps that led down into an old unused well. There were twenty-one steps, and she hid one child under each step. She told them not to utter a sound whatever happened, and then she and her friends ran away and left them.

Presently the workmen came with their tools and began to fill in the rat holes. The little daughter of the head workman had come with him, and while he and his fellows were at work the little girl amused herself by running up and down the steps into the well. Every time she trod upon a step it pinched the child who lay under it. The little boys made no sound when they were pinched, but lay as still as stones, but every time the child trod on the step under which the Princess lay she sighed, and the third time she felt the pinch she cried out, "Have pity on me and tread more lightly. I too am a little girl like you!"

The workman's daughter was very much frightened when she heard the voice. She ran to her father and told him the steps had spoken to her.

The workman thought this a strange thing. He at once went to the old Ranee and told her he dared no longer work near the well, for he believed a witch or a demon lived there under the steps, and he repeated what his little daughter had told him.

The wicked nurse was with the Ranee when the workman came to her. As soon as he had gone, the nurse said, "I am sure some of those children must still be alive. They must have escaped from the rat holes and be hiding under the steps. If we send out there we will probably find them."

The Ranee was frightened at the thought they might still be alive. She ordered some servants to come with her, and she and the nurse went out to look for the children.

But when the little girl had cried out the little boys were afraid some harm might follow, and prayed that they might be changed into trees, so that if anyone came to search for them they might not find them.

Their prayers were answered. The twenty little boys were changed into twenty little banyan trees that stood in a circle, and the little girl was changed into a rose-bush that stood in the midst of the circle and was full of red and white roses.

The old Ranee and the nurse and the servants came to the well and searched under every step, but no one was there, so they went away again.

All might now have been well, but the workman's mischievous little daughter chanced to come by that way again. At once she espied the banyan trees and the rose-bush. "It is a curious thing that I never saw these trees before," she thought. "I will gather a bunch of roses."

She ran past the banyan trees without giving them a thought and began to break the flowers from the rose-tree. At once a shiver ran through the tree, and it cried to her in a pitiful voice, "Oh, oh, you are hurting me. Do not break my branches, I pray of you. I am a little girl, too, and can suffer just as you might."

The child ran back to her father and caught him by the hand. "Oh, I am frightened!" she cried. "I went to gather some roses from the rose-tree, and it spoke to me;" and she told him what the rose-tree had said.

At once the workman went off and repeated to the Ranee what his little daughter had told him, and the Queen gave him a piece of gold and sent him away, bidding him keep what he had heard a secret.

Then she called the wicked nurse to her and repeated the workman's story. "What had we better do now?" she asked.

"My advice is that you give orders to have all the trees cut down and burned," said the nurse. "In this way you will rid yourself of the children altogether."

This advice seemed good to the Ranee. She sent men and had the trees cut down and thrown in a heap to burn.

But heaven had pity on the children, and just as the men were about to set fire to the heap a heavy rainstorm arose and put out the fire.

Then the river rose over its banks, and swept the little trees down on its flood, far, far away to a jungle where no one lived. Here they were washed ashore and at once took on their real shapes again.

The children lived there in the jungle safely for twelve years, and the brothers grew up tall and straight and handsome, and the sister was like the new moon in her beauty, so slim and white and shining was she.

The brothers wove a hut of branches to shelter their sister, and every day ten of them went out hunting in the forest, and ten of them stayed at home to care for her. But one day it chanced they all wished to go hunting together, so they put their sister up in a high tree where she would be safe from the beasts of the forest, and then they went away and left her there alone.

The twenty brothers went on and on through the jungle, farther than they had ever gone before, and so came at last to an open space among the trees, and there was a hut.

"Who can be living here?" said one of the brothers.

"Let us knock and see," cried another.

The Princes knocked at the door and immediately it was opened to them by a great, wicked-looking Rakshas. She had only one red eye in the middle of her forehead, her grey hair hung in a tangled mat over her shoulders, and she was dressed in dirty rags.

When the Rakshas saw the brothers she was filled with fury.

She considered all the jungle belonged to her, and she was not willing that anyone else should come there. Her one eye flashed fire, and she seized a stick and began beating the Princes, and each one, as she struck him, was turned into a crow. She then drove them away and went back into her hut and closed the door.

The twenty crows flew back through the forest, cawing mournfully. When they came to the tree where their sister sat they gathered about her, trying to make her understand that they were her brothers.

At first the Princess was frightened by the crows, but when she saw there were tears in their eyes, and when she counted them and found there were exactly twenty, she guessed what had happened, and that some wicked enchantment had changed her brothers into this shape. Then she wept over them and smoothed their feathers tenderly.

After this the sister lived up in the tree, and the crows brought her food every day and rested around her in the branches at night, so that no harm should come to her.

Sometime after this a young Rajah came into that very jungle to hunt. In some way he became separated from his attendants and wandered deeper and deeper into the forest, until at length he came to the tree where the Princess sat. He threw himself down beneath the tree to rest. Hearing a sound of wings above him the Rajah looked up and was amazed to see a beautiful girl sitting there among the branches with a flock of crows about her.

The Rajah climbed the tree and brought the girl down, while the crows circled about his head, cawing hoarsely.

"Tell me, beautiful one, who are you? And how come you here in the depths of the jungle?" asked the Rajah.

Weeping, the Princess told him all her story except that the crows were her brothers. She let him believe that her brothers had gone off hunting and had never returned.

"Do not weep anymore," said the Rajah. "You shall come home with me and be my Ranee, and I will have no other but you alone."

When the Princess heard this she smiled, for the Rajah was very handsome, and already she loved him.

She was very glad to go with him and be his wife. "But my crows must go with me," she said, "for they have fed me for many long days and have been my only companions."

To this the Rajah willingly consented, and he took her home with him to the palace, and the crows circled about above them, following closely all the way.

When the old Rajah and Ranee (the young Rajah's father and mother) saw what a very beautiful girl he had brought back with him from the jungle they gladly welcomed her as a daughter-in-law.

The young Ranee would have been very happy now in her new life, for she loved her husband dearly, but always the thought of her brothers was like a weight upon her heart. She had a number of trees planted outside her windows so that her brothers might rest there close to her. She cooked rice for them herself and fed them with her own hands, and often she sat under the trees and stroked them and talked to them while her tears fell upon their glossy feathers.

After a while the young Ranee had a son, and he was called Ramchundra. He grew up straight and tall, and he was the joy of his mother's eyes.

One day, when he was fourteen years old, and big and strong for his age, he sat in the garden with his mother. The crows flew down about them, and she began to caress and talk to them as usual. "Ah, my dear ones!" she cried, "how sad is your fate! If I could but release you, how happy I should be."

"Mother," said the boy, "I can plainly see that these crows are not ordinary birds. Tell me where they come from, and why you weep over them and talk to them as you do?"

At first his mother would not tell him, but in the end she related to him the whole story of who she was, and how she and her brothers had come to the jungle and had lived there happily enough until they were changed into crows, and then of how the Rajah had found her and brought her home with him to the palace.

"I can easily see," said Ramchundra, when she had ended the tale, "that my uncles must have met a Rakshas somewhere in the forest and have been enchanted. Tell me exactly where the tree was, the tree where you lived, and what kind it was?"

The Ranee told him.

"And in which direction did your brothers go when they left you?"

This also his mother told him. "Why do you ask me these questions, my son?" she asked.

"I wish to know," said Ramchundra, "for some day I intend to set out and find that Rakshas and force her to free my uncles from her enchantment and change them back to their natural shapes again."

His mother was terrified when she heard this, but she said very little to him, hoping he would soon forget about it and not enter into such a dangerous adventure.

Not long afterward Ramchundra went to his father and said, "Father, I am no longer a child. Give me your permission to ride out into the world and see it for myself."

The Rajah was willing for him to do this and asked what attendants his son would take with him.

"I wish for no attendants," answered Ramchundra. "Give me only a horse, and a groom to take care of it."

The Rajah gave his son the handsomest horse in his stables and also a well-mounted groom to ride with him. Ramchundra, however, only allowed the groom to go with him as far as the edge of the jungle, and then he sent him back home again with both the horses.

The Prince went on and on through the forest for a long distance until, at last, he came to a tree that he felt sure was the one his mother had told him of. From there he set forth in the same direction she told him his uncles had taken. He went on and on, ever deeper and deeper into the forest, until he came to a miserable looking hut. The door was open, and he looked in. There lay an ugly old hag fast asleep. She had only one eye in the middle of her forehead, and her grey hair was tangled and matted and fell over her face. The Prince entered in very softly, and sitting down beside her, he began to rub her head. He suspected that this was the Rakshas who had bewitched his uncles, and it was indeed she.

Presently the old woman awoke. "My pretty lad," she said, "you have a kind heart. Stay with me here and help me, for I am very old and feeble, as you see, and I cannot very well look out for myself."

This she said not because she really was old or feeble, but because she was lazy and wanted a servant to wait on her.

"Gladly will I stay," answered the lad, "and what I can do to serve you, that I will do."

So the Prince stayed there as the Rakshas' servant. He served her hand and foot, and every day she made him sit down and rub her head.

One day, while he was rubbing her head and she was in a good humour he said to her, "Mother, why do you keep all those little jars of water standing along the wall? Let me throw out the water so that we may make some use of the jars."

"Do not touch them," cried the Rakshas. "That water is very powerful. One drop of it can break the strongest enchantment, and if anyone has been bewitched, that water has power to bring him back to his own shape again."

"And why do you keep that crooked stick behind the door? Tomorrow I shall break it up to build a fire."

"Do not touch it," cried the hag. "I have but to wave that stick, and I can conjure up a mountain, a forest, or a river just as I wish, and all in the twinkling of an eye."

The Prince said nothing to that, but went on rubbing her head. Presently he began to talk again. "Your hair is in a dreadful tangle, mother," he said. "Let me get a comb and comb it out."

"Do not dare!" screamed the Rakshas. "One hair of my head has the power to set the whole jungle in flames."

Ramchundra again was silent and went on rubbing her head, and after a while the old Rakshas fell asleep and snored till the hut shook with her snoring.

Then, very quietly, the Prince arose. He plucked a hair from the old hag's head without awakening her, he took a flask of the magic water and the staff from behind the door, and set out as fast as he could go in the direction of the palace.

It was not long before he heard the Rakshas coming through the jungle after him, for she had awakened and found him gone.

Nearer and nearer she came, and then the Prince turned and waved the crooked stick. At once a river rolled between him and the Rakshas.

Without pause the Rakshas plunged into the river and struck out boldly, and soon she reached the other side.

On she came again close after Ramchundra. Again he turned and waved the staff. At once a thick screen of trees sprang up between him and the hag. The Rakshas brushed them aside this way and that as though they had been nothing but twigs.

On she came, and again the Prince waved the staff. A high mountain arose, but the Rakshas climbed it, and it did not take her long to do this.

Now she was so close that Ramchundra could hear her panting, but the edge of the jungle had been reached. He turned and cast the Rakshas' hair behind him. Immediately the whole jungle burst into fire, and the Rakshas was burned up in the flames.

Soon after the Prince reached the palace and hastened out into the garden. There sat his mother weeping, with the crows gathered about her. When she saw Ramchundra she sprang to her feet with a scream of joy and ran to him and took him in her arms.

"My son, my son! I thought you had perished!" she cried. "Did you meet the Rakshas?"

"Not only did I meet her, but I have slain her and brought back with me that which will restore my uncles to their proper shapes," answered the Prince.

He then dipped his fingers into the jar he carried and sprinkled the magic water over the crows. At once the enchantment was broken, and the twenty Princes stood there, tall and handsome, in their own proper shapes.

The Ranee made haste to lead them to her husband and told him the whole story. The Rajah could not wonder enough when he understood that the Princes were his wife's brothers, and were the crows she had brought home with her.

He at once ordered a magnificent feast to be prepared and a day of rejoicing to be held throughout all the kingdom.

Many Rajahs from far and near were invited to the feast, and among those who came was the father of the Ranee and her brothers, but he never suspected, as he looked upon them, that they were his children.

Before they sat down to the feast the young Ranee said to him, "Where is your wife Guzra Bai? Why has she not come with you? We had expected to see her here?"

The Rajah was surprised that the young Ranee should know his wife's name, but he made some excuse as to why Guzra Bai was not there.

Then the young Rajah said, "Send for her, I beg of you, for the feast cannot begin till she is here."

The older Rajah was still more surprised at this. He could not think anyone was really concerned about Guzra Bai, and he feared the young Rajah wished, for some reason, to quarrel with him. But he agreed to send for his wife, and messengers were at once dispatched to bring Guzra Bai to the palace.

No sooner had she come than the young Ranee began to weep, and she and the Princes gathered about their mother. Then they told the Rajah the whole story of how his mother and the nurse had sought to destroy Guzra Bai and her children, and how they had been saved, and had now come to safety and great honour.

The Rajah was overcome with joy when he found that Guzra Bai was innocent. He prayed her to forgive him, and this she did, and all was joy and happiness.

As for the old Ranee, she was shut up in the tower where Guzra Bai had lived for so many years, but the old nurse was killed as befitted such a wicked woman.

Kupti And Imani

This story has been adapted from a tale originally told by Andrew Lang in The Olive Fairy Book, published in 1907 by Longmans, Green And Co., London And New York. Andrew Lang's Coloured Fairy Books were a series of twelve collections of fairy tales and folk stories from around the world, edited and compiled by Scottish author Andrew Lang. The first volume, The Blue Fairy Book, was published in 1889, followed by eleven more volumes, each with a different colour in the title, such as The Red Fairy Book, The Green Fairy Book, and so on, concluding with The Lilac Fairy Book in 1910. This story was based on a story originally told by Major Campbell, Feroshepore, and it is a story from The Punjab.

Once there was a king who had two daughters, and their names were Kupti and Imani. He loved them both very much, and spent hours in talking to them, and one day he said to Kupti, the elder, "Are you satisfied to leave your life and fortune in my hands?"

"Yes," answered the princess, surprised at the question. "In whose hands should I leave them, if not in yours?"

But when he asked his younger daughter Imani the same question, she replied, "No, indeed! If I had the chance I would make my own fortune."

At this answer the king was very displeased, and said, "You are too young to know the meaning of your words. But, be it so. I will give you the chance of gratifying your wish."

Then he sent for an old lame fakir who lived in a tumbledown hut on the outskirts of the city, and when he had presented himself, the king said, "No doubt, as you are very old and nearly crippled, you would be glad of some young person to live with you and serve you, so I will send you my younger daughter. She wants to earn her living, and she can do so with you."

Of course the old fakir had not a word to say, or, if he had, he was really too astonished and troubled to say it, but the young princess went off with him smiling, and tripped along quite gaily, whilst he hobbled home with her in perplexed silence.

Directly they got to the hut the fakir began to think what he could arrange for the princess's comfort, but after all he was a fakir, and his house was bare except for one bedstead, two old cooking pots and an earthen jar for water, and one cannot get much comfort out of those things.

However, the princess soon ended his perplexity by asking, "Have you any money?"

"I have a penny somewhere," replied the fakir.

"Very well," rejoined the princess, "give me the penny and go out and borrow me a spinning-wheel and a loom."

After much seeking the fakir found the penny and started on his errand, whilst the princess went off shopping. First she bought a farthing's worth of oil, and then she bought three farthings' worth of flax. When she got back with her purchases she set the old man on the bedstead and rubbed his crippled leg with the oil for an hour. Then she sat down to the spinning-wheel and spun and spun all night long whilst the old man slept, until, in the morning, she had spun the finest thread that ever was seen. Next she went to the loom and wove and wove until by the evening she had woven a beautiful silver cloth.

"Now," she said to the fakir, "go into the market-place and sell my cloth whilst I rest."

"And what am I to ask for it?" said the old man.

"Two gold pieces," replied the princess.

So the fakir hobbled away, and stood in the market-place to sell the cloth. Presently the elder princess drove by, and when she saw the cloth she stopped and asked the price.

"Two gold pieces," said the fakir. And the princess gladly paid them, after which the old fakir hobbled home with the money. As she had done before so Imani did again day after day. Always she spent a penny upon oil and flax, always she tended the old man's lame limb, and spun and wove the most beautiful cloths and sold them at high prices. Gradually the city became famous for her beautiful stuffs, the old fakir's lame leg became straighter and stronger, and the hole under the floor of the hut where they kept their money became fuller and fuller of gold pieces.

At last, one day, the princess said, "'I really think we have got enough to live in greater comfort.

She sent for builders, and they built a beautiful house for her and the old fakir, and in all the city there was none finer except the king's palace. Presently this reached the ears of the king, and when he inquired whose it was they told him that it belonged to his daughter.

"Well," exclaimed the king, "she said that she would make her own fortune, and somehow or other she seems to have done it!"

A little while after this, business took the king to another country, and before he went he asked his elder daughter what she would like him to bring her back as a gift.

"A necklace of rubies," answered she. And then the king thought he would like to ask Imani too; so he sent a messenger to find out what sort of a present she wanted. The man happened to arrive just as she was trying to disentangle a knot in her loom, and bowing low before her, he said, "The king sends me to inquire what you wish him to bring you as a present from the country of Dûr?"

But Imani, who was only considering how she could best untie the knot without breaking the thread, replied, "Patience!" meaning that the messenger should wait till she was able to attend to him. But the messenger went off with this as an answer, and told the king that the only thing the princess Imani wanted was 'patience.'

"Oh!" said the king, "I don't know whether that's a thing to be bought at Dûr. I never had it myself, but if it is to be got I will buy it for her."

Next day the king departed on his journey, and when his business at Dûr was completed he bought for Kupti a beautiful ruby necklace. Then he said to a servant, "The princess Imani wants some patience. I did not know there was such a thing, but you must go to the market and inquire, and if any is to be sold, get it and bring it to me."

The servant saluted and left the king's presence. He walked about the market for some time crying, "Has anyone patience to sell?

patience to sell?" And some of the people mocked, and some (who had no patience) told him to go away and not be a fool, and some said, "The fellow's mad! As though one could buy or sell patience!"

At length it came to the ears of the king of Dûr that there was a madman in the market trying to buy patience. And the king laughed and said, "I should like to see that fellow, bring him here!"

And immediately his attendants went to seek the man, and brought him to the king, who asked, "What is this that you want?"

And the man replied, "Sire! I am bidden to ask for patience."

"Oh," said the king, "you must have a strange master! What does he want with it?"

"My master wants it as a present for his daughter Imani," replied the servant.

"Well," said the king, "I know of some patience which the young lady might have if she cares for it, but it is not to be bought."

Now the king's name was Subbar Khan, and Subbar means 'patience', but the messenger did not know that, or understand that he was making a joke. However, he declared that the princess Imani was not only young and beautiful, but also the cleverest, most industrious, and kindest-hearted of princesses, and he would have gone on explaining her virtues had not the king laughingly put up his hand and stopped him saying, "Well, well, wait a minute, and I will see what can be done."

With that he got up and went to his own apartments and took out a little casket. Into the casket he put a fan, and shutting it up carefully he brought it to the messenger and said, "Here is a casket. It has no lock nor key, and yet will open only to the touch of the person who needs its contents, and whoever opens it will obtain patience, but I can't tell whether it will be quite the kind of patience that is wanted."

And the servant bowed low, and took the casket, but when he asked what was to be paid, the king would take nothing. So he went away and gave the casket and an account of his adventures to his master.

As soon as their father got back to his country Kupti and Imani each got the presents he had brought for them. Imani was very surprised when the casket was brought to her by the hand of a messenger.

"But," she said, "what is this? I never asked for anything! Indeed I had no time, for the messenger ran away before I had unravelled my tangle."

But the servant declared that the casket was for her, so she took it with some curiosity, and brought it to the old fakir. The old man tried to open it, but in vain, so closely did the lid fit that it seemed to be quite immovable, and yet there was no lock, nor bolt, nor spring, nor anything apparently by which the casket was kept shut. When he was tired of trying he handed the casket to the princess, who hardly touched it before it opened quite easily, and there lay within a beautiful fan. With a cry of surprise and pleasure Imani took out the fan, and began to fan herself.

Hardly had she finished three strokes of the fan before there suddenly appeared from nowhere in particular, king Subbar Khan of Dûr! The princess gasped and rubbed her eyes, and the old fakir sat and gazed in such astonishment that for some minutes he could not speak. At length he said, "Who may you be, fair sir, if you please?"

"My name," said the king, "is Subbar Khan of Dûr. This lady," bowing to the princess, "has summoned me, and here I am!"

"I?" stammered the princess. "I have summoned you? I never saw or heard of you in my life before, so how could that be?"

Then the king told them how he had heard of a man in his own city of Dûr trying to buy patience, and how he had given him the fan in the casket.

"Both are magical," he added. "When anyone uses the fan, in three strokes of it I am with them. If they fold it and tap it on the table, in three taps I am at home again. The casket will not open to all, but you see it was this fair lady who asked for patience, and, as that is my name, here I am, very much at her service."

Now the princess Imani, being of a high spirit, was anxious to fold up the fan, and give the three taps which would send the king home again, but the old fakir was very pleased with his guest, and so in one way and another they spent quite a pleasant evening together before Subbar Khan took his leave.

After that he was often summoned, and as both the fakir and he were very fond of chess and were good players, they used to sit up half the night playing, and eventually a little room in the house began to be called the king's room, and whenever he stayed late he used to sleep there and go home again in the morning.

By-and-by it came to the ears of the princess Kupti that there was a rich and handsome young man visiting at her sister's house, and she was very jealous. So she went one day to pay Imani a visit, and pretended to be very affectionate, and interested in the house, and in the way in which Imani and the old fakir lived, and of their mysterious and royal visitor. As the sisters went from place to place, Kupti was shown Subbar Khan's room, and presently, making some excuse, she slipped in there by herself and swiftly spread under the sheet which lay upon the bed a quantity of very finely powdered and splintered glass which was poisoned, and which she had brought with her concealed in her clothes. Shortly afterwards she took leave of her sister, declaring that she could never forgive herself for not having come near her all this time, and that she would now begin to make amends for her neglect.

That very evening Subbar Khan came and sat up late with the old fakir playing chess as usual. Very tired, he at length bade him and the princess good-night and, as soon as he lay down on the bed, thousands of tiny, tiny splinters of poisoned glass ran into him. He could not think what the matter was, and started this way and that until he was pricked all over, and he felt as though he were burning from head to foot. But he never said a word, only he sat up all night in agony of body and in worse agony of mind to think that he should have been poisoned, as he guessed he was, in Imani's own house. In the morning, although he was nearly fainting, he still said nothing, and by means of the magic fan was duly transported home again. Then he sent for all the physicians and doctors in his kingdom, but none could make out what his illness was, and so he lingered on for weeks and weeks trying every remedy that anyone could devise, and passing sleepless nights and days of pain and fever and misery, until eventually he was at the point of death.

Meanwhile the princess Imani and the old fakir were much troubled because, although they waved the magic fan again and again, no Subbar Khan appeared, and they feared that he had tired of them, or that some evil fate had overtaken him. At last the princess was in such a miserable state of doubt and uncertainty that she determined to go herself to the kingdom of Dûr and see what the matter was. Disguising herself in man's clothes as a young fakir, she set out upon her journey alone and on foot, as a fakir should travel. One evening she found herself in a forest, and lay down under a great tree to pass the night. But she could not sleep for thinking of Subbar Khan, and wondering what had happened to him. Presently she heard two great monkeys talking to one another in the tree above her head.

"Good evening, brother," said one, "Where have you. Come from? What is the news?"

"I come from Dûr," said the other, "and the news is that the king is dying."

"Oh," said the first, "I'm sorry to hear that, for he is a master hand at slaying leopards and creatures that ought not to be allowed to live. What is the matter with him?"

"No man knows," replied the second monkey, "but the birds, who see all and carry all messages, say that he is dying of poisoned glass that Kupti the king's daughter spread upon his bed."

"Ah!" said the first monkey, "that is sad news, but if they only knew it, the berries of the very tree we sit in, steeped in hot water, will cure such a disease as that in three days at most."

"True!" said the other, "it's a pity that we can't tell some man of a medicine so simple, and so save a good man's life. But men are so silly. They go and shut themselves up in stuffy houses in stuffy cities instead of living in nice airy trees, and so they miss knowing all the best things."

Now when Imani heard that Subbar Khan was dying she began to weep silently, but as she listened she dried her tears and sat up, and as soon as daylight dawned over the forest she began to gather the berries from the tree until she had filled her cloth with a load of them. Then she walked on as fast as she could, and in two days reached the city of Dûr. The first thing she did was to pass through the market crying, "Medicine for sale! Are any ill that need my medicine?"

And presently one man said to his neighbour, "See, there is a young fakir with medicine for sale, perhaps he could do something for the king."

"Pooh!" replied the other, "where so many grey-beards have failed, how should a lad like that be of any use?"

"Still," said the first, "he might try." And he went up and spoke to Imani, and together they set out for the palace and announced that another doctor was come to try and cure the king.

After some delay Imani was admitted to the sick room, and, whilst she was so well disguised that the king did not recognize her, he was so wasted by illness that she hardly knew him. But she began at once, full of hope, by asking for some apartments all to herself and a pot in which to boil water. As soon as the water was heated she steeped some of her berries in it and gave the mixture to the king's attendants and told them to wash his body with it. The first washing did so much good that the king slept quietly all the night. Again the second day she did the same, and this time the king declared he was hungry, and called for food. After the third day he was quite well, only very weak from his long illness. On the fourth day he got up and sat upon his throne, and then sent messengers to fetch the physician who had cured him. When Imani appeared everyone marvelled that so young a man should be so clever a doctor, and the king wanted to give him immense presents of money and of all kinds of precious things. At first Imani would take nothing, but at last she said that, if she must be rewarded, she would ask for the king's signet ring and his handkerchief. So, as she would take nothing more, the king gave her his signet ring and his handkerchief, and she departed and travelled back to her own country as fast as she could.

A little while after her return, when she had related to the fakir all her adventures, they sent for Subbar Khan by means of the magic fan, and when he appeared they asked him why he had stayed away for so long. Then he told them all about his illness, and how he had been cured, and when he had finished the princess rose up and, opening a cabinet, brought out the ring and handkerchief, and said, laughing, "Are these the rewards you gave to your doctor?"

At that the king looked, and he recognised her, and understood in a moment all that had happened, and he jumped up and put the magic fan in his pocket, and declared that no one should send him away to his own country anymore unless Imani would come with him and be his wife. And so it was settled, and the old fakir and Imani went to the city of Dûr, where Imani was married to the king and lived happily ever after.

The Mouse and the Farmer

This story has been adapted from a tale originally told by W. H. D. Rouse in The Giant Crab and Other Tales from Old India, published in 1897 by David Nutt, London. The tales in the collection cover a wide range of themes, including adventure, morality, wisdom, and magic. Many of the stories feature talking animals, brave heroes, cunning tricksters, and mythical beings, offering readers a glimpse into the rich storytelling traditions of India.

Once upon a time there was a Mouse, who made his hole in a place where there were thousands and thousands of golden sovereigns buried in the ground. Now there was a Farmer who owned the land where this treasure was buried, but he did not know about it, or else of course he would have dug it up. He often noticed the little Mouse sitting with his head peeping out of the hole, but as he was a very kind Farmer, he never hurt the Mouse, and now and then when he was having his own dinner, he would throw the Mouse a bit of cheese.

The Mouse was very grateful to the Farmer, and wondered what he could do to show it. At last he thought of the treasure, for this Mouse was sensible enough to know that Farmers are very pleased to get a golden sovereign now and again. So one day, as the Farmer went by the hole, Mousie ran out with a golden sovereign in his mouth, and dropped it at the Farmer's feet. You can imagine how glad the Farmer was to see a golden sovereign. Indeed, it was the first one he had seen since the Corn Laws were abolished. So he thanked the Mouse, and went down to the village, and bought a beautiful piece of meat. After this every day the Mouse brought the Farmer a golden sovereign, and every day the Farmer gave him a big chunk of meat. Thus in a few weeks Mousie grew quite fat.

But the Farmer had a big black cat that used to prowl about watching for mice. It used never to notice the Farmer's own favourite Mouse while the Mouse was thin, but when he grew sleek and fat and shiny, Grimalkin (which was the Cat's name) lay in wait for him one day and pounced upon him. Poor little Mousie was terrified.

"Please don't kill me, Mr. Grimalkin!" said Mousie.

"Why not? I'm hungry and you are fat!"

"But, sir, if you eat me now, you'll be hungry tomorrow, won't you?"

"Of course I shall!" said Grimalkin.

"Well," said Mousie, who had suddenly thought of a plan, "if you will only let me go, I'll bring you a beautiful juicy piece of meat every day!"

This was a tempting offer for Grimalkin, who was a lazy Cat, and liked sitting by the fire, and licking himself all over, better than hunting for mice.

"All right," he said, "only if you leave out one day, you're a dead mouse!" Then, with a frightful spit, bristling up all his whiskers and eyebrows, Grimalkin ran away.

So next day, when the Farmer gave Mousie his dinner, Mousie carried it off to the black Cat, and the black Cat spat and swore and ate it up, and away ran Mousie trembling. But by degrees Mousie grew thinner and thinner, because Grimalkin always had his dinner, and soon he was nothing but skin and bone. Then the Farmer noticed how thin his Mouse had become, so one day he asked the Mouse whether he was ill.

"No," said Mousie, "I'm not ill."

"What is the matter, then?" asked the Farmer.

"I never get any dinner now," said Mousie, with tears running down over his nose, "because Grimalkin eats it all!" Then he told the Farmer about the bargain he had made with Grimalkin.

Now the Farmer had a beautiful piece of glass, with a hole in the middle. I think it was an inkstand, but I am not sure. So he took this piece of glass and put Mousie inside it, and turned it upside down upon the ground in front of Mousie's hole. "Now," he said, "next time Grimalkin comes for your dinner, tell him you have none for him, and see what will happen."

So next day up comes Grimalkin for his dinner, spitting and looking very fierce.

"Meat, meat!" says he to the Mouse.

"Get off, vile thief!" says Mousie, "I've no meat for the likes of you!"

At this Grimalkin could hardly believe his ears. He was in a rage, I can tell you, and, without stopping to think, pounced upon Mousie, and swallowed him, inkstand and all. You see, as it was all glass, Grimalkin did not know that there was any inkstand there, because he saw the Mouse through it.

Now cats can digest a good deal, but they can't digest a glass inkstand. So Grimalkin, when he had swallowed the Mouse and the inkstand, felt a pain inside, and this got worse and worse, until eventually he died. And then Mousie crept out of the inkstand, and crawled up through Grimalkin's throat, and went back to his hole again. And there he lived all his life in happiness, every day bringing a golden sovereign to the Farmer, who gave him every day a beautiful dinner of meat.

The Lion and the Crane

This story has been adapted from a tale originally told by Joseph Jacobs in Indian Fairy Tales, published in 1892 by David Nutt, London. Joseph Jacobs was a prolific collector and re-teller of folktales from different cultures. Indian Fairy Tales includes a diverse range of stories, featuring elements of magic, mythology, and adventure. Many of these tales have been passed down through oral tradition for generations, reflecting the cultural richness and diversity of India.

The Bodhisatta was at one time born in the region of Himavanta as a white crane. Now Brahmadatta was at that time reigning in Benares. Now it chanced that as a lion was eating meat a bone stuck in his throat. The throat became swollen, he could not take food, and the lion's suffering was terrible.

The crane seeing him, as he was perched on a tree looking for food, asked, "What ails you, friend?"

The lion told him why.

"I could free you from that bone, friend, but dare not enter your mouth for fear you might eat me."

"Don't be afraid, friend, I'll not eat you. Please save my life."

"Very well," said the crane, who then asked the lion lie down on his left side. But thinking to himself, 'Who knows what this fellow will do,' he placed a small stick upright between the lion's two jaws so that he could not close his mouth, and inserting his head inside the lion's mouth, struck one end of the bone with his beak. The bone dropped and fell out. As soon as he had caused the bone to fall, the crane got out of the lion's mouth, striking the stick with his beak so that it fell out, and then the crane settled on a branch.

The lion got well and one day was eating a buffalo he had killed. The crane thinking "I will sing to him," settled on a branch just over the lion, and in conversation spoke this first verse:

"A service have we done you

To the best of our ability,

King of the Beasts! Your Majesty!

What return shall we get from you?"

In reply the Lion spoke the second verse:

"As I feed on blood,

And always hunt for prey,

'Tis much that you are still alive

Having once been between my teeth."

Then in reply the crane said the two other verses:

"Ungrateful, doing no good,

Not doing as he would be done by,

In him there is no gratitude,

To serve him is useless."

"His friendship is not won

By the clearest good deed.

Better softly withdraw from him,

Neither envying nor abusing."

And having thus sung his song the crane flew away.

And when the great Teacher, Gautama the Buddha, told this tale, he used to add, "Now at that time the lion was Devadatta the Traitor, but the white crane was I myself."

Story of Wali Dad the Simple-Hearted

This story has been adapted from a tale originally told by Andrew Lang in The Brown Fairy Book, published in 1904 by Longmans, Green And Co., London And New York. Andrew Lang's Coloured Fairy Books were a series of twelve collections of fairy tales and folk stories from around the world, edited and compiled by Scottish author Andrew Lang. The first volume, The Blue Fairy Book, was published in 1889, followed by eleven more volumes, each with a different colour in the title, such as The Red Fairy Book, The Green Fairy Book, and so on, concluding with The Lilac Fairy Book in 1910.

Once upon a time there lived a poor old man whose name was Wali Dad Gunjay, or Wali Dad the Bald. He had no relations, but lived all by himself in a little mud hut some distance from any town, and made his living by cutting grass in the jungle, and selling it as fodder for horses. He only earned by this five halfpence a day, but he was a simple old man, and needed so little out of it, that he saved up one halfpenny daily, and spent the rest upon such food and clothing as he required.

In this way he lived for many years until, one night, he thought that he would count the money he had hidden away in the great earthen pot under the floor of his hut. So he set to work, and with much trouble he pulled the bag out on to the floor, and sat gazing in astonishment at the heap of coins which tumbled out of it. What should he do with them all? he wondered. But he never thought of spending the money on himself, because he was content to pass the rest of his days as he had been doing for ever so long, and he really had no desire for any greater comfort or luxury.

At last he threw all the money into an old sack, which he pushed under his bead, and then, rolled in his ragged old blanket, he went off to sleep.

Early next morning he staggered off with his sack of money to the shop of a jeweller, whom he knew in the town, and bargained with him for a beautiful little gold bracelet. With this carefully wrapped up in his cotton waistband he went to the house of a rich friend, who was a travelling merchant, and used to wander about with his camels and merchandise through many countries. Wali Dad was lucky enough to find him at home, so he sat down, and after a little talk he asked the merchant who was the most virtuous and beautiful lady he had ever met with. The merchant replied that the princess of Khaistan was renowned everywhere as well for the beauty of her person as for the kindness and generosity of her disposition.

"Then," said Wali Dad, "next time you go that way, give her this little bracelet, with the respectful compliments of one who admires virtue far more than he desires wealth."

With that he pulled the bracelet from his waistband, and handed it to his friend. The merchant was naturally much astonished, but said nothing, and made no objection to carrying out his friend's plan.

Time passed by, and at length the merchant arrived in the course of his travels at the capital of Khaistan. As soon as he had opportunity he presented himself at the palace, and sent in the bracelet, neatly packed in a little perfumed box provided by himself, giving at the same time the message entrusted to him by Wali Dad.

The princess could not think who could have bestowed this present on her, but she bade her servant to tell the merchant that if he would return, after he had finished his business in the city, she would give him her reply. In a few days, therefore, the merchant came back, and received from the princess a return present in the shape of a camel-load or rich silks, besides a present of money for himself. With these he set out on his journey.

Some months later he got home again from his journeyings, and proceeded to take Wali Dad the princess's present. Great was the perplexity of the good man to find a camel-load of silks tumbled at his door! What was he to do with these costly things? But, presently, after much thought, he begged the merchant to consider whether he did not know of some young prince to whom such treasures might be useful.

"Of course," cried the merchant, greatly amused. "from Delhi to Baghdad, and from Constantinople to Lucknow, I know them all, and there lives none worthier than the gallant and wealthy young prince of Nekabad."

"Very well, then, take the silks to him, with the blessing of an old man," said Wali Dad, much relieved to be rid of them.

So, the next time that the merchant journeyed that way he carried the silks with him, and in due course arrived at Nekabad, and sought an audience of the prince. When he was shown into his presence he produced the beautiful gift of silks that Wali Dad had sent, and begged the young man to accept them as a humble tribute to his worth and greatness. The prince was much touched by the generosity of the giver, and ordered, as a return present, twelve of the finest breed of horses for which his country was famous to be delivered over to the merchant, to whom also, before he took his leave, he gave a munificent reward for his services.

As before, the merchant at last arrived at home, and next day, he set out for Wali Dad's house with the twelve horses. When the old man saw them coming in the distance he said to himself, "Here's luck! A troop of horses coming! They are sure to want quantities of grass, and I shall sell all I have without having to drag it to market."

Thereupon he rushed off and cut grass as fast he could. When he got back, with as much grass as he could possibly carry, he was greatly discomfited to find that the horses were all for himself. At first he could not think what to do with them, but, after a little, a brilliant idea struck him! He gave two to the merchant, and begged him to take the rest to the princess of Khaistan, who was clearly the fittest person to possess such beautiful animals.

The merchant departed, laughing. But, true to his old friend's request, he took the horses with him on his next journey, and eventually presented them safely to the princess. This time the princess sent for the merchant, and questioned him about the giver. Now, the merchant was usually a most honest man, but he did not quite like to describe Wali Dad in his true light as an old man whose income was five halfpence a day, and who had hardly clothes to cover him. So he told her that his friend had heard stories of her beauty and goodness, and had longed to lay the best he had at her feet. The princess then took her father into her confidence, and begged him to advise her what courtesy she might return to one who persisted in making her such presents.

"Well," said the king, "you cannot refuse them, so the best thing you can do is to send this unknown friend at once a present so magnificent that he is not likely to be able to send you anything better, and so will be ashamed to send anything at all!" Then he ordered that, in place of each of the ten horses, two mules laden with silver should be returned by her.

Thus, in a few hours, the merchant found himself in charge of a splendid caravan, and he had to hire a number of armed men to defend it on the road against the robbers, and he was glad indeed to find himself back again in Wali Dad's hut.

"Well, now," cried Wali Dad, as he viewed all the wealth laid at his door, "I can well repay that kind prince for his magnificent present of horses, but to be sure you have been put to great expenses! Still, if you will accept six mules and their loads, and will take the rest straight to Nekabad, I shall thank you heartily."

The merchant felt handsomely repaid for his trouble, and wondered greatly how the matter would turn out. So he made no difficulty about it, and as soon as he could get things ready, he set out for Nekabad with this new and princely gift.

This time the prince, too, was embarrassed, and questioned the merchant closely. The merchant felt that his credit was at stake, and whilst inwardly determining that he would not carry the joke any further, could not help describing Wali Dad in such glowing terms that the old man would never have known himself had he heard them. The prince, like the king of Khaistan, determined that he would send in return a gift that would be truly royal, and which would perhaps prevent the unknown giver sending him anything more. So he made up a caravan on twenty splendid horses caparisoned in gold embroidered cloths, with fine Morocco saddles and silver bridles and stirrups, also twenty camels of the best breed, which had the speed of race-horses, and could swing along at a trot all day without getting tired, and, lastly, twenty elephants, with magnificent silver howdahs and coverings of silk embroidered with pearls. To take care of these animals the merchant hired a little army of men, and the troop made a great show as they travelled along.

When Wali Dad from a distance saw the cloud of dust which the caravan made, and the glitter of its appointments, he said to himself, "By Allah! Here's a grand crowd coming! Elephants, too! Grass will be selling well today!" And with that he hurried off to the jungle and cut grass as fast as he could. As soon as he got back he found the caravan had stopped at his door, and the merchant was waiting, a little anxiously, to tell him the news and to congratulate him upon his riches.

"Riches!" cried Wali Dad, "What has an old man like me with one foot in the grave to do with riches? That beautiful young princess, now! She'd be the one to enjoy all these fine things! Take for yourself two horses, two camels, and two elephants, with all their trappings, and present the rest to her."

The merchant at first objected to these remarks, and pointed out to Wali Dad that he was beginning to feel these embassies a little awkward. Of course he was himself richly repaid, so far as expenses went, but still he did not like going so often, and he was getting nervous. At length, however he consented to go once more, but he promised himself never to embark on another such enterprise.

So, after a few days' rest, the caravan started off once more for Khaistan.

The moment the king of Khaistan saw the gorgeous train of men and beasts entering his palace courtyard, he was so amazed that he hurried down in person to inquire about it, and became dumb when he heard that these also were a present from the princely Wali Dad, and were for the princess, his daughter. He went hastily off to her apartments, and said to her, "I tell you what it is, my dear, this man wants to marry you. That is the meaning of all these presents! There is nothing for it but that we go and pay him a visit in person. He must be a man of immense wealth, and as he is so devoted to you, perhaps you might do worse than marry him!"

The princess agreed with all that her father said, and orders were issued for vast numbers of elephants and camels, and gorgeous tents and flags, and litters for the ladies, and horses for the men, to be prepared without delay, as the king and princess were going to pay a visit to the great and munificent prince Wali Dad. The merchant, the king declared, was to guide the party.

The feelings of the poor merchant in this sore dilemma can hardly be imagined. Willingly would he have run away, but he was treated with so much hospitality as Wali Dad's representative, that he hardly got an instant's real peace, and never any opportunity of slipping away. In fact, after a few days, despair possessed him to such a degree that he made up his mind that all that happened was fate, and that escape was impossible, but he hoped devoutly some turn of fortune would reveal to him a way out of the difficulties which he had, with the best intentions, drawn upon himself.

On the seventh day they all started, amidst thunderous salutes from the ramparts of the city, and much dust, and cheering, and blaring of trumpets.

Day after day they moved on, and every day the poor merchant felt more ill and miserable. He lay awake nearly the whole of every night thinking over the situation. He wondered what kind of death the king would invent for him, and went through almost as much torture as he would have suffered if the king's executioners were already setting to work upon his neck.

At last they were only one day's march from Wali Dad's little mud home. Here a great encampment was made, and the merchant was sent on to tell Wali Dad that the King and Princess of Khaistan had arrived and were seeking an interview. When the merchant arrived he found the poor old man eating his evening meal of onions and dry bread, and when he told him of all that had happened he had not the heart to proceed to load him with the reproaches which rose to his tongue. For Wali Dad was overwhelmed with grief and shame for himself, for his friend, and for the name and honour of the princess, and he wept and plucked at his beard, and groaned most piteously. With tears he begged the merchant to detain them for one day by any kind of excuse he could think of, and to come in the morning to discuss what they should do.

As soon as the merchant was gone Wali Dad made up his mind that there was only one honourable way out of the shame and distress that he had created by his foolishness, and that was to kill himself. So, without stopping to ask any one's advice, he went off in the middle of the night to a place where the river wound along at the base of steep rocky cliffs of great height, and determined to throw himself down and put an end to his life. When he got to the place he drew back a few paces, took a little run, and at the very edge of that dreadful black gulf he stopped short! He could not do it!

From below, unseen in the blackness of the deep night shadows, the water roared and boiled round the jagged rocks. He could picture the place as he knew it, only ten times more pitiless and forbidding in the visionless darkness, for the wind soughed through the gorge with fearsome sighs, and rustlings and whisperings, and the bushes and grasses that grew in the ledges of the cliffs seemed to him like living creatures that danced and beckoned, shadowy and indistinct. An owl laughed 'Hoo! Hoo!' almost in his face, as he peered over the edge of the gulf, and the old man threw himself back in a perspiration of horror. He was afraid! He drew back shuddering, and covering his face in his hands he wept aloud.

Presently he was aware of a gentle radiance that shed itself before him. Surely morning was not already coming to hasten and reveal his disgrace! He took his hands from before his face, and saw before him two lovely beings whom his instinct told him were not mortal, but were Peris from Paradise.

"Why do you weep, old man?" said one, in a voice as clear and musical as that of the bulbul.

"I weep for shame," replied he.

"What are you doing here?" questioned the other.

"I came here to die," said Wali Dad. And as they questioned him, he confessed all his story.

Then the first stepped forward and laid a hand upon his shoulder, and Wali Dad began to feel that something strange was happening to him. His old cotton rags of clothes were changed to beautiful linen and embroidered cloth. On his hard, bare feet were warm, soft shoes, and on his head a great jewelled turban. Round his neck there lay a heavy golden chain, and the little old bent sickle, which he cut grass with, and which hung in his waistband, had turned into a gorgeous scimitar, whose ivory hilt gleamed in the pale light like snow in moonlight.

As he stood wondering, like a man in a dream, the other peri waved her hand and bade him turn and see, and, there before him a noble gateway stood open. And up an avenue of giant place trees the peris led him, dumb with amazement. At the end of the avenue, on the very spot where his hut had stood, a gorgeous palace appeared, ablaze with myriads of lights. Its great porticoes and verandahs were occupied by hurrying servants, and guards paced to and fro and saluted him respectfully as he drew near, along mossy walks and through sweeping grassy lawns where fountains were playing and flowers scented the air. Wali Dad stood stunned and helpless.

"Fear not," said one of the peris. "Go to your house, and learn that God rewards the simple-hearted."

With these words they both disappeared and left him. He walked on, thinking still that he must be dreaming. Very soon he retired to rest in a splendid room, far grander than anything he had ever dreamed of. When morning dawned he woke, and found that the palace, and himself, and his servants were all real, and that he was not dreaming after all!

If he was dumbfounded, the merchant, who was ushered into his presence soon after sunrise, was much more so. He told Wali Dad that he had not slept all night, and by the first streak of daylight had started to seek out his friend. And what a search he had had! A great stretch of wild jungle country had, in the night, been changed into parks and gardens, and if it had not been for some of Wali Dad's new servants, who found him and brought him to the palace, he would have fled away under the impression that his trouble had sent him crazy, and that all he saw was only imagination.

Then Wali Dad told the merchant all that had happened. By his advice he sent an invitation to the king and princess of Khaistan to come and be his guests, together with all their retinue and servants, down to the very humblest in the camp.

For three nights and days a great feast was held in honour of the royal guests. Every evening the king and his nobles were served on golden plates and from golden cups, and the smaller people on silver plates and from silver cups, and each evening each guest was requested to keep the places and cups that they had used as a remembrance of the occasion. Never had anything so splendid been seen. Besides the great dinners, there were sports and hunting, and dances, and amusements of all sorts.

On the fourth day the king of Khaistan took his host aside, and asked him whether it was true, as he had suspected, that he wished to marry his daughter. But Wali Dad, after thanking him very much for the compliment, said that he had never dreamed of so great an honour, and that he was far too old and ugly for so fair a lady, but he begged the king to stay with him until he could send for the Prince of Nekabad, who was a most excellent, brave, and honourable young man, and would surely be delighted to try to win the hand of the beautiful princess.

To this the king agreed, and Wali Dad sent the merchant to Nekabad, with a number of attendants, and with such handsome presents that the prince came at once, fell head over ears in love with the princess, and married her at Wali Dad's palace amidst a fresh outburst of rejoicings.

And now the King of Khaistan and the Prince and Princess of Nekabad, each went back to their own country, and Wali Dad lived to a good old age, befriending all who were in trouble and preserving, in his prosperity, the simple-hearted and generous nature that he had when he was only Wali Dad Gunjay, the grass cutter.

The Talking Thrush

This story has been adapted from a tale originally told by William Crooke and W. H. D. Rouse in The Talking Thrush, published in 1899 by E. P. Dutton, New York. Their version of this story is based on an original telling by Káshi Prasád at the village school, Bhingá, district, Bahráich, Oudh.

A CERTAIN man had a garden, and in his garden he sowed cotton seeds. By-and-by the cotton seeds grew up into a cotton bush, with big brown pods upon it. These pods burst open when they are ripe, and you can see the fluffy white cotton bulging all white out of the pods. There was a Thrush in this garden, and the Thrush thought within herself how nice and soft the cotton looked. She plucked out some of it to line her nest with, and never before was her sleep so soft as it was on that bed of cotton.

Now this Thrush had a clever head, so she thought something more might be done with cotton besides lining a nest. In her flights abroad she used often to pass by the door of a Cotton-carder. The Cotton-carder had a thing like a bow, made of a piece of wood, and a thong of leather tying the ends together into a curve. He used to take the cotton, and pile it in a heap. Then he took the carding-bow, and twang-twang-twanged it among the heap of cotton, so that the fibres or threads of it became disentangled. Then he rolled it up into oblong balls, and sold it to other people, who made it into thread.

The Thrush often watched the Cotton-carder at work. Every day after dinner, she went to the cotton tree, and plucked out a fluff of cotton in her beak and hid it away. She went on doing this till at last she had quite a little heap of cotton all of her own. At least, it was not really her own, because she stole it, but then you cannot get policemen to take up a Thrush for stealing, and as men catch Thrushes and put them in a cage all for nothing, it is only fair the birds should have their turn.

When the heap of cotton was big enough, our Thrush flew to the house of the Cotton-carder, and sat down in front of him.

"Good day, Man," said the Thrush.

"Good day, Birdie," said the Cotton-carder. The Thrush was not a bit afraid, because she knew he was a kind man, who never caught little birds to put them in a cage. He liked better to hear them singing free in the woods.

"Man," said the Thrush, "I have a heap of beautiful cotton, and I'll tell you what. You shall have half of it, if you will card the rest and make it up into balls for me."

"That I will," said the man, "where is it?"

"If you will come with me," said the Thrush, "I'll show you."

So the Thrush flew in front, and the man followed after, and they came to the place where the hoard of cotton was hidden away. The man took the cotton home, and carded it, and made it into balls. Half of the cotton he took for his trouble, and the rest he gave back to the Thrush. He was so honest that he did not cheat even a bird, although he could easily have done so. For birds cannot count, and if you find a nest full of eggs, and take one or two, the mother-bird will never miss them, but if you take them all, the bird is unhappy.

Not far away from the Carder lived a Spinner. This man used to put a ball of cotton on a stick, and then he pulled out a bit of the cotton without breaking it, and tied it to another little stick with a weight on it. Then he twisted the weight, and set it a-spinning, and as it span, he held the cotton ball in one hand, and pulled out the cotton with the other, working it between finger and thumb to keep it fine. Thus the spindle went on spinning, and the cotton went on twisting, until it was twisted into thread. That is why the man was called a Spinner. It looks very easy to do, when you can do it, but it is really very hard to do well.

To this Spinner the Thrush came, and after bidding him good day, she said, "Mr. Spinner, I have some balls of cotton ready to spin into thread. Will you spin one half of them into thread for me, if I give you the other half?"

"That I will," said Mr. Spinner, and away they went to find the cotton balls, Thrush first and Spinner following.

In a very few days the Spinner had spun all the cotton into the finest thread. Then he took a pair of scales, and weighed it into two equal parts (he was an honest man, too). Half he kept for himself, and the other half he gave to the Thrush.

The next thing this clever Thrush did was to fly to the house of a Weaver. The Weaver used to buy thread, and fasten a number of threads to a wooden frame, called a loom, which was made of two upright posts, with another bar fastened across the top. The threads were hung to the cross-bar, and a little stone was tied to the bottom of each, to keep it steady. Then the Weaver wound some more thread around a long stick called a shuttle, and the shuttle he pushed in front of one thread and behind the next, until it had gone right across the whole of the threads, in and out. Then he pushed it back in the same way, and after a bit, the upright threads and the cross-threads were woven together and made a piece of cloth.

The Thrush flew down to the Weaver, and they made the same bargain as before. The Weaver wove all the thread into pieces of cloth, and half he kept for himself, but the other half he returned to the Thrush.

So now the Thrush had some beautiful cloth, and I dare say you wonder what she wanted it for. As you have not been inquisitive, I will tell you. She wanted clothes to dress herself. The Thrush had noticed that men and women walking about wore clothes, and being an ambitious Thrush, and eager to rise in the world, she felt it would not be proper to go about without any clothes on. So she now went to a Tailor, and said to him, "Good Mr. Tailor, I have some pieces of very fine cloth, and I should be much obliged if you would make a part of it into clothes for me. You shall have one half of the cloth for your trouble."

The Tailor was very glad of this job, as times were slack. So he took the cloth, and at once set to work. Half of it he made into a beautiful dress for the Thrush, with a skirt and jacket, and sleeves in the latest fashion, and as there was a little cloth left over, and he was an honest Tailor, he made her also a pretty little hat to put on her head.

Then the Thrush was indeed delighted, and felt there was little more to desire in the world. She put on her skirt, and her jacket with fashionable sleeves, and the little hat, and looked at her image in a river, and was mightily pleased with herself. Now she became so vain that nothing would do, but she must show herself to the King.

So she flew and flew, and away she flew, until she came to the King's palace. Into the King's palace she flew, and into the great hall where the King sat and the Queen and all the courtiers. There was a peg high up on the wall, and the Thrush perched on this peg, and began to sing.

"Oh, look there!" cried the Queen, who was the first to see this wonderful sight, "see, a Thrush in a jacket and skirt and a pretty hat!"

Everybody looked at the Thrush singing on her peg, and clapped their hands.

"Come here, Birdie," said the King, "and show the Queen your pretty clothes."

The Thrush felt highly flattered, and flew down upon the table, and took off her jacket to show the Queen. Then she flew back to her peg, and watched to see what would happen.

The Queen turned over the jacket in her hand, and laughed. Then she folded it up, and put it in her pocket.

"Give me my jacket!" twittered the Thrush. "I shall catch cold, and besides, it is not proper for a lady to be seen without a jacket."

Then they all laughed, and the King said, "Come here, Mistress Thrush, and you shall have your jacket."

Down flew the Thrush upon the table again, but the King caught her, and held her fast.

"Let me go!" squeaked the Thrush, struggling to get free.

But the King would not let her go. I am afraid that although he was a King, he was not so honest as the Carder or the Spinner, and cared less for his word than the Weaver and the Tailor.

"Greedy King," said the Thrush, "to covet my little jacket!"

"I covet more than your jacket," said the King, "I covet you, and I am going to chop you up into little bits."

Then he began to chop her up into bits. As she was being chopped up, the Thrush said, "The King snips and cuts like a Tailor, but he is not so honest!"

When the King had finished chopping her up, he began to wash the pieces. And each piece, as he washed it, called out, "The King scours and scrubs like a washerwoman, but he is not so honest!"

Then the King put the pieces of the Thrush into a frying-pan with oil, and began to fry them. But the pieces went on calling out, "The King is like a cook, frying and sputtering, but he is not so honest!"

When she was fried, the King ate her up. From within the body of the King still the Thrush kept calling out, "I am inside the King! It is just like the inside of any other man, only not so honest!"

The King became like a walking musical-box, and he did not like it at all, but it was his own fault. Wherever he went, everybody heard the Thrush crying out from inside the King, "Just like any other man, only not so honest!" Everybody that heard this began to despise the King.

At last the King could stand it no longer. He sent for his doctor, and said, "Doctor, you must cut this talking bird out of me."

"Your majesty will die, if I do," said the Doctor.

"I shall die if you don't," answered the King, "for I cannot endure being made a fool of."

So there was nothing for it. The Doctor took his knives, and made a hole in the King, and pulled out the Thrush. Strange to say, the pieces of the Thrush had all joined together again, and away she flew, but her beautiful clothes were all gone. However, it was a lesson she never forgot, and after that, she slept in her nest of soft cotton, and never again tried to mimic her betters. As for the King, he died, and a good riddance too. His son became king in his stead, and all life-long he remembered his father's miserable death, and kept all his promises to men, and beasts, and birds.

The Mouse and the Frog

This story has been adapted from a tale originally told by Kate Douglas Wiggin and Nora Archibald Smith in The Talking Beasts, published in 1911 by Houghton Mifflin Company. The fables in The Talking Beasts are engaging and entertaining, with whimsical characters and imaginative settings. Through these tales, Wiggin and Smith aimed to stimulate the imagination of children while also instilling important values that promote character development and moral growth.

Once upon a time, there was a Mouse who lived near a fountain, making its home at the base of a tree. Nearby, a Frog spent its days in the water, occasionally coming to the edge of the pool to enjoy the air. One day, the Frog, feeling particularly melodious, started singing in what it believed to be a beautiful, nightingale-like tone.

Hearing the commotion, the Mouse, who was busy chanting in its own corner, was intrigued and came out to investigate. Impressed by the Frog's performance, the Mouse clapped and nodded in approval, which pleased the Frog. This led to the two becoming fast friends, sharing stories and tales with each other.

As time passed, the Mouse expressed a desire to confide a secret and share a grief with the Frog, but found it challenging due to the noise of the water and other frogs. They brainstormed a solution, and they tied a string between them so that when one needed the other's attention, they could signal by shaking the string.

Their friendship flourished with this arrangement until one unfortunate day when a Crow swooped down unexpectedly, seizing the Mouse in its beak. The string attached to the Mouse's leg inadvertently pulled the Frog from the water, leaving it hanging upside down as the Crow flew off with its prey.

Onlookers commented on the unusual sight, joking about the Frog's misfortune of associating with a Mouse. In response, the Frog lamented that it wasn't the Crow's typical prey, but rather the consequence of associating across species, warning against such friendships.

The moral of the story: Beware of associating with those different from yourself, lest you find yourself entangled in their misfortunes, like the Frog on the string of calamity.

Dorani

This story has been adapted from a tale originally told by Andrew Lang in The Olive Fairy Book, published in 1907 by Longmans, Green And Co., London And New York. Andrew Lang's Coloured Fairy Books were a series of twelve collections of fairy tales and folk stories from around the world, edited and compiled by Scottish author Andrew Lang. The first volume, The Blue Fairy Book, was published in 1889, followed by eleven more volumes, each with a different colour in the title, such as The Red Fairy Book, The Green Fairy Book, and so on, concluding with The Lilac Fairy Book in 1910. This story was based on a story originally told by Major Campbell, Feroshepore

Once upon a time there lived in a city of Hindustan a seller of scents and essences, who had a very beautiful daughter named Dorani. This maiden had a friend who was a fairy, and the two were high in favour with Indra, the king of fairyland, because they were able to sing so sweetly and dance so deftly that no one in the kingdom could equal them for grace and beauty. Dorani had the loveliest hair in the world, for it was like spun gold, and the smell of it was like the smell of fresh roses. But her locks were so long and thick that the weight of it was often unbearable, and one day she cut off a shining tress, and wrapping it in a large leaf, threw it in the river which ran just below her window.

Now it happened that the king's son was out hunting, and had gone down to the river to drink, when there floated towards him a folded leaf, from which came a perfume of roses. The prince, with idle curiosity, took a step into the water and caught the leaf as it was sailing by. He opened it, and within he found a lock of hair like spun gold, and from which came a faint, exquisite odour.

When the prince reached home that day he looked so sad and was so quiet that his father wondered if any ill had befallen him, and asked what the matter was. Then the youth took from his breast the tress of hair which he had found in the river, and holding it up to the light, replied, "See, my father, was ever hair like this? Unless I may win and marry the maiden that owns that lock I must die!"

So the king immediately sent heralds throughout all his dominions to search for the damsel with hair like spun gold, and at last he learned that she was the daughter of the scent-seller. The object of the herald's mission was quickly noised abroad, and Dorani heard of it with the rest, and, one day, she said to her father, "If the hair is mine, and the king requires me to marry his son, I must do so, but, remember, you must tell him that if, after the wedding, I stay all day at the palace, every night will be spent in my old home."

The old man listened to her with amazement, but answered nothing, as he knew she was wiser than he. Of course the hair was Dorani's, and heralds soon returned and informed the king, their master, who summoned the scent-seller, and told him that he wished for his daughter to be given in marriage to the prince. The father bowed his head three times to the ground, and replied, "Your highness is our lord, and all that you bid us we will do. The maiden asks this only.

That if, after the wedding, she stays all day at the palace, she may go back each night to her father's house.'

The king thought this a very strange request, but said to himself it was, after all, his son's affair, and the girl would surely soon get tired of going to and fro. So he made no difficulty, and everything was speedily arranged and the wedding was celebrated with great rejoicings.

At first, the condition attaching to his wedding with the lovely Dorani troubled the prince very little, for he thought that he would at least see his bride all day. But, to his dismay, he found that she would do nothing but sit the whole time upon a stool with her head bowed forward upon her knees, and he could never persuade her to say a single word. Each evening she was carried in a palanquin to her father's house, and each morning she was brought back soon after daybreak, and yet never a sound passed her lips, nor did she show by any sign that she saw, or heard, or heeded her husband.

One evening the prince, very unhappy and troubled, was wandering in an old and beautiful garden near the palace. The gardener was a very aged man, who had served the prince's great grandfather, and when he saw the prince he came and bowed himself to him, and said, "Child, child! Why do you look so sad? What is the matter?"

Then the prince replied, "I am sad, old friend, because I have married a wife as lovely as the stars, but she will not speak to me, and I know not what to do. Night after night she leaves me for her father's house, and day after day she sits in mine as though turned to stone, and utters no word, whatever I may do or say."

The old man stood thinking for a moment, and then he hobbled off to his own cottage. A little later he came back to the prince with five or six small packets, which he placed in his hands and said,

"Tomorrow, when your bride leaves the palace, sprinkle the powder from one of these packets upon your body, and while seeing clearly, you will become yourself invisible. More I cannot do for you, but may all go well!"

And the prince thanked him, and put the packets carefully away in his turban.

The next night, when Dorani left for her father's house in her palanquin, the prince took out a packet of the magic powder and sprinkled it over himself, and then hurried after her. He soon found that, as the old man had promised, he was invisible to everyone, although he felt as usual, and could see all that passed. He speedily overtook the palanquin and walked beside it to the scent-seller's dwelling. There it was set down, and, when his bride, closely veiled, left it and entered the house, he, too, entered unperceived.

At the first door Dorani removed one veil; then she entered another doorway at the end of a passage where she removed another veil; next she mounted the stairs, and at the door of the women's quarters removed a third veil. After this she proceeded to her own room where were set two large basins, one of attar of roses and one of water; in these she washed herself, and afterwards called for food. A servant brought her a bowl of curds, which she ate hastily, and then arrayed herself in a robe of silver, and wound about her strings of pearls, while a wreath of roses crowned her hair. When fully dressed, she seated herself upon a four-legged stool over which was a canopy with silken curtains, which she drew around her, and then called out, "Fly, stool, to the palace of Rajah Indra."

Instantly the stool rose in the air, and the invisible prince, who had watched all these proceedings with great wonder, seized it by one leg as it flew away, and found himself being borne through the air at a rapid rate.

In a short while they arrived at the house of the fairy who, as I told you before, was the favourite friend of Dorani. The fairy stood waiting on the threshold, as beautifully dressed as Dorani herself was, and when the stool stopped at her door she cried in astonishment, "Why, the stool is flying all crooked today! What is the reason of that, I wonder? I suspect that you have been talking to your husband, and so it will not fly straight."

But Dorani declared that she had not spoken one word to him, and she couldn't think why the stool flew as if weighed down at one side. The fairy still looked doubtful, but made no answer, and took her seat beside Dorani, the prince again holding tightly one leg. Then the stool flew on through the air until it came to the palace of Indra the Rajah.

All through the night the women sang and danced before the Rajah Indra, whilst a magic lute played of itself the most bewitching music; till the prince, who sat watching it all, was quite entranced. Just before dawn the Rajah gave the signal to cease, and again the two women seated themselves on the stool, and, with the prince clinging to the leg, it flew back to earth, and bore Dorani and her husband safely to the scent-seller's shop. Here the prince hurried away by himself past Dorani's palanquin with its sleepy bearers, straight on to the palace, and, as he passed the threshold of his own rooms he became visible again. Then he lay down upon a couch and waited for Dorani's arrival.

As soon as she arrived she took a seat and remained as silent as usual, with her head bowed on her knees. For a while not a sound was heard, but presently the prince said, "I dreamed a curious dream last night, and as it was all about you I am going to tell it you, although you heed nothing."

The girl, indeed, took no notice of his words, but in spite of that he proceeded to relate every single thing that had happened the evening before, leaving out no detail of all that he had seen or heard. And when he praised her singing, and his voice shook a little, Dorani just looked at him, but she said nothing, though, in her own mind, she was filled with wonder. 'What a dream!' she thought. 'Could it have been a dream? How could he have learnt in a dream all she had done or said?' Still she kept silent, only she looked that once at the prince, and then remained all day as before, with her head bowed upon her knees.

When night came the prince again made himself invisible and followed her. The same things happened again as had happened before, but Dorani sang better than ever. In the morning the prince a told Dorani a second all that she had done, pretending that he had dreamt of it. Directly he had finished Dorani gazed at him, and said, "Is it true that you dreamt this, or were you really there?"

"I was there," answered the prince.

"But why do you follow me?" asked the girl.

"Because," replied the prince, "I love you, and to be with you is happiness."

This time Dorani's eyelids quivered, but she said no more, and was silent the rest of the day. However, in the evening, just as she was stepping into her palanquin, she said to the prince, "If you love me, prove it by not following me tonight."

And so the prince did as she wished, and stayed at home.

That evening the magic stool flew so unsteadily that they could hardly keep their seats, and at last the fairy exclaimed, "There is only one reason that it should jerk like this! You have been talking to your husband!"

And Dorani replied, "Yes, I have spoken. Oh, yes, I have spoken!" But no more would she say.

That night Dorani sang so marvellously that at the end the Rajah Indra rose up and vowed that she might ask what she would and he would give it to her. At first she was silent, but, when he pressed her, she answered, "Give me the magic lute."

The Rajah, when he heard this, was displeased with himself for having made so rash a promise, because this lute he valued above all his possessions. But as he had promised, so he must perform, and with an ill grace he handed it to her.

"You must never come here again," he said, "for, once having asked so much, how will you in future be content with smaller gifts?"

Dorani bowed her head silently as she took the lute, and passed with the fairy out of the great gate, where the stool awaited them. More unsteadily than before, it flew back to earth.

When Dorani got to the palace that morning she asked the prince whether he had dreamt again. He laughed with happiness, for this time she had spoken to him of her own free will, and he replied, "No, but I begin to dream now…not of what has happened in the past, but of what may happen in the future."

That day Dorani sat very quietly, but she answered the prince when he spoke to her, and when evening fell, and with it the time for her departure, she still sat on. Then the prince came close to her and said softly, "Are you not going to your house, Dorani?"

At that she rose and threw herself weeping into his arms, whispering gently, "Never again, my lord, never again would I leave you!"

So the prince won his beautiful bride, and though they neither of them dealt any further with fairies and their magic, they learnt more daily of the magic of love, which one may still learn, although fairy magic has fled away.

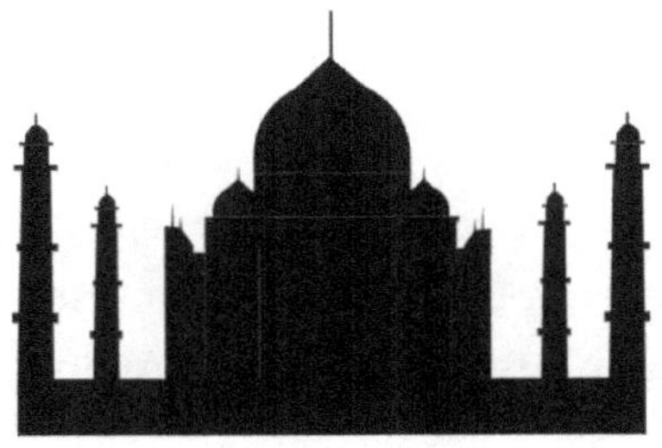

Raja Rasalu

This story has been adapted from a tale originally told by Penrhyn Wingfield Coussens in The Jade Story Book; Stories From The Orient, published in 1922 by Duffield And Company, New York. One of the notable aspects of The Jade Story Book is Coussens' engaging narrative style, which brings the characters and settings to life while staying true to the spirit of the original tales.

Once there lived a great Rajah, whose name was Salabhan, and he had a Queen, by name Lona, who, though she wept and prayed at many a shrine, had never a child to gladden her eyes. After a long time, however, a son was promised to her.

Queen Lona returned to the palace, and when the time for the birth of the promised son drew nigh, she inquired of three Jogis who came begging to her gate, what the child's fate would be, and the youngest of them answered and said, "Oh, Queen! The child will be a boy, and he will live to be a great man. But for twelve years you must not look upon his face, for if either you or his father see it before the twelve years are past, you will surely die! This is what you must do: As soon as the child is born you must send him away to a cellar underneath the ground, and never let him see the light of day for twelve years. After they are over he may come forth, bathe in the river, put on new clothes, and visit you. His name shall be Rajah Rasalu, and he shall be known far and wide."

So, when a fair young Prince was in due time born, his parents hid him away in an underground palace, with nurses and servants, and everything else a king's son might desire. And with him they sent a young colt, born the same day, and sword, spear, and shield, against the day when Rajah Rasalu should go forth into the world.

So there the child lived, playing with his colt, and talking to his parrot, but when the twelfth year began the lad's heart leaped up with desire for change, and he loved to listen to the sounds of life which came to him in his palace-prison from the outside world.

"I must go and see where the voices come from!" he said, and when his nurses told him he must not go for one year more, he only laughed aloud, saying, "Nay! I stay no longer here for any man!"

Then he saddled his Arab horse Bhanur, put on his shining armour, and rode forth into the world, but, mindful of what his nurses had often told him, when he came to the river, he dismounted, and going into the water, washed himself and his clothes.

Then, clean of raiment, fair of face, and brave of heart, he rode on his way until he reached his father's city. There he sat down to rest awhile by a well, where the women were drawing water in earthern pitchers. Now, as they passed him, their full pitchers poised upon their heads, the gay young Prince flung stones at the earthern vessels, and broke them all. Then the women, drenched with water, went weeping and wailing to the palace, complaining to the King that a mighty young Prince in shining armour, with a parrot on his wrist and a gallant steed beside him, sat by the well, and broke their pitchers.

Now, as soon as Rajah Salabhan heard this he guessed at once that it was Prince Rasalu come forth before the time, and, mindful of the Jogis' words that he would die if he looked on his son's face before twelve years were past, he did not dare to send his guards to seize the offender and bring him to be judged. So he bade the women be comforted, and take pitchers of iron and brass, giving new ones from the treasury to those who did not possess any of their own.

But when Prince Rasalu saw the women returning to the well with pitchers of iron and brass, he laughed to himself, and drew his mighty bow till the sharp-pointed arrows pierced the metal vessels as though they had been clay.

Yet still the King did not send for him, so he mounted his steed and set off in the pride of his youth and strength to the palace. He strode into the audience hall, where his father sat trembling, and saluted him with all reverence, but Rajah Salabhan, in fear of his life, turned his back hastily and never said a word in reply.

Then Prince Rasalu called scornfully to him across the hall "I came to greet you, King, and not to harm you! What have I done that you should turn away? Sceptre and empire have no power to charm me. I go to seek a worthier prize than they!"

Then he strode away, full of bitterness and anger, but as he passed under the palace windows, he heard his mother weeping, and the sound softened his heart, so that his wrath died down, and a great loneliness fell upon him, because he was spurned by both father and mother. So he cried sorrowfully:

"Oh, heart crown'd with grief, have you nothing

But tears for your son?

And you mother of mine? Give one thought

To my life just begun!"

And Queen Lona answered through her tears:

"Yea! Mother am I, though I weep,

So hold this word for sure,

Go, reign king of all men, but keep

Your heart good and pure!"

So Rajah Rasalu was comforted, and began to make ready for fortune. He took with him his horse Bhanur and his parrot, both of whom had lived with him since he was born.

So they made a goodly company, and Queen Lona, when she saw them going, watched them from her window till she saw nothing but a cloud of dust on the horizon; then she bowed her head on her hands and wept, saying:

"Oh! Son who ne'er gladdened mine eyes,

Let the cloud of your going arise,

Dim the sunlight and darken the day;

For the mother whose son is away

Is as dust!"

Rasalu had started off to play chaupur with King Sarkap. And as he journeyed there came a fierce storm of thunder and lightning, so that he sought shelter, but found no shelter save an old graveyard, where a headless corpse lay upon the ground. So lonesome was it that even the corpse seemed company, and Rasalu, sitting down beside it, said:

"There is no one here, nor far nor near,

Save this breathless corpse so cold and grim;

Would God he might come to life again,

'Twould be less lonely to talk to him."

And immediately the headless corpse arose and sat beside Rajah Rasalu. And he, nothing astonished, said to it:

"The storm beats fierce and loud

The clouds rise thick in the West;

What ails your grave and shroud,

Oh, corpse! That you cannot rest?"

Then the headless corpse replied:

"On earth I was even as you,

My turban awry like a king,

My head with the highest, I say.

Having my fun and my fling,

Fighting my foes like a brave,

Living my life with a swing.

And, now I am dead,

Sins, heavy as lead,

Will give me no rest in my grave!"

So the night passed on, dark and dreary, while Rasalu sat in the graveyard and talked to the headless corpse. Now when morning broke and Rasalu said he must continue his journey, the headless corpse asked him where he was going, and when he said, "To play chaupur with King Sarkap," the corpse begged him to give up the idea, saying, "I am King Sarkap's brother, and I know his ways. Every day before breakfast he cuts off the heads of two or three men just to amuse himself. One day no one else was at hand, so he cut off mine, and he will surely cut off yours on one pretence or another. However, if you are determined to go and play chaupur with him, take some of the bones from this graveyard, and make your dice out of them, and then the enchanted dice with which my brother plays will lose their virtue. Otherwise he will always win."

So Rasalu took some of the bones lying about, and fashioned them into dice, and these he put into his pocket. Then, bidding adieu to the headless corpse, he went on his way to play chaupur with the king.

Now, as Rajah Rasalu, tender-hearted and strong, journeyed along to play chaupur with the king, he came to a burning forest, and a voice rose from the fire, saying, "Oh, traveler! Save me from the fire!"

Then the Prince turned towards the burning forest, and the voice was the voice of a tiny cricket. Nevertheless, Rasalu, tender-hearted and strong, snatched it from the fire and set it at liberty. Then the little creature, full of gratitude, pulled out one of its feelers, and giving it to its preserver, said, "Keep this, and should you ever be in trouble, put it into the fire, and instantly I will come to your aid."

The Prince smiled, saying, "What help could you give me?" Nevertheless, he kept the feeler and went on his way.

Now, when he reached the city of King Sarkap, seventy maidens, daughters of the king, came out to meet him. They were seventy fair maidens, merry and careless, full of smiles and laughter, but one, the youngest of them all, when she saw the gallant young Prince riding on Bhanur, going gayly to his doom, was filled with pity, and called to him, saying:

"Fair Prince, on the charger so grey,

Turn back! Turn back!

Or lower your lance for the fray;

Your head will be forfeit today!

Do you love life? Then, stranger, I pray,

Turn back! Turn back!"

But he, smiling at the maiden, answered lightly:

"Fair maiden, I come from afar,

Sworn conqueror in love and in war!

King Sarkap my coming will rue,

His head in four pieces I'll hew;

Then forth as a bridegroom I'll ride,

With you, little maid, as my bride!"

Now when Rasalu replied so gallantly, the maiden looked in his face, and seeing how fair he was, and how brave and strong, she straightway fell in love with him, and would gladly have followed him through the world.

But the other sixty-nine maidens, being jealous, laughed scornfully at her, saying, "Not so fast, oh gallant warrior! If you would marry our sister you must first do our bidding, for you will be our younger brother."

"Fair sisters!" said Rasalu gayly, "give me my task and I will perform it."

So the sixty-nine maidens mixed a hundred-weight of millet seed with a hundred-weight of sand, and giving it to Rasalu, bade him separate the seed from the sand.

Then he thought of the cricket, and drawing the feeler from his pocket, thrust it into the fire. And immediately there was a whirring noise in the air, and a great flight of crickets alighted beside him, and amongst them the cricket whose life he had saved.

Then Rasalu said, "Separate the millet seed from the sand."

"Is that all?" said the cricket. "Had I known how small a job you wanted me to do, I would not have assembled so many of my brethren."

With that the flight of crickets set to work, and in one night they separated the seed from the sand.

Now when the sixty-nine fair maidens, daughters of the king, saw that Rasalu had performed his task, they set him another, bidding him swing them all, one by one, in their swings, until they were tired.

Whereupon he laughed, saying, "There are seventy of you, counting my little bride yonder, and I am not going to spend my life swinging girls! Why, by the time I have given each of you a swing, the first will be wanting another! No! If you want a swing, get in, all seventy of you, and then I'll see what can be done."

So the seventy maidens climbed into one swing, and Rajah Rasalu, standing in his shining armour, fastened the ropes to his mighty bow, and drew it up to its fullest bent. Then he let go, and like an arrow the swing shot into the air, with its burden of seventy fair maidens, merry and careless, full of smiles and laughter.

But as it swung back again, Rasalu, standing there in his shining armour, drew his sharp sword and severed the ropes. Then the seventy fair maidens fell to the ground headlong, and some were bruised and some were broken, but the only one who escaped unhurt was the maiden who loved Rasalu, for she fell out last, on the top of the others, and so came to no harm.

After this, Rasalu strode on fifteen paces, till he came to the seventy drums, that everyone who came to play chaupur with the king had to beat in turn, and he beat them so loudly that he broke them all. Then he came to the seventy gongs, all in a row, and he hammered them so hard that they cracked to pieces.

Seeing this, the youngest Princess, who was the only one who could run, fled to her father, the king, in a great fright, saying:

"A mighty Prince, Sarkap, making havoc rides along.

He swung us, seventy maidens fair, and threw us out headlong

He broke the drums you placed there,

And the gongs, too, in his pride,

Sure, he will kill you, father mine, and take me for his bride!"

But King Sarkap replied scornfully:

"Silly maiden, your words make a lot

Of a very small matter;

For fear of my valour, I say,

His armour will clatter.

As soon as I've eaten my bread

I'll go forth and cut off his head!"

Notwithstanding these brave and boastful words he was in reality very much afraid, having heard of Rasalu's renown. And learning that he was stopping at the house of an old woman in the city, till the hour of playing chaupur arrived, Sarkap sent slaves to him with trays of sweetmeats and fruit, as to an honoured guest. But the food was poisoned.

Now, when the slaves brought the trays to Rajah Rasalu, he rose up haughtily, saying, "Go tell your master I have nothing to do with him in friendship. I am his sworn enemy, and I eat not of his salt!"

So saying, he threw the sweetmeats to Rajah Sarkap's dog, which had followed the slaves, and the dog died.

Then Rasalu was very angry, and said bitterly, "Go back to Sarkap, slaves. And tell him that Rasalu deems it no act of bravery to kill even an enemy by treachery."

Now, when evening came, Rajah Rasalu went forth to play chaupur with King Sarkap, and as he passed some potters' kilns he saw a cat wandering about restlessly; so he asked what ailed her, that she never stood still, and she replied, "My kittens are in an unbaked pot in the kiln yonder. It has just been set alight, and my children will be baked alive; therefore I cannot rest!"

Her words moved the heart of Rajah Rasalu, and going to the potter, he asked him to sell the kiln as it was, but the potter replied that he could not settle a fair price till the pots were burned, as he could not tell how many would come out whole. Nevertheless, after some bargaining, he consented at last to sell the kiln, and Rasalu, having searched all the pots, restored the kittens to their mother, and she in gratitude for his mercy, gave him one of them, saying, "Put it in your pocket, for it will help you when you are in difficulties." So Rajah Rasalu put the kitten in his pocket, and went to play chaupur with the king.

Now, before they sat down to play, Rajah Sarkap fixed his stakes. On the first game, they would play for his kingdom, on the second, the wealth of the whole world, and on the third, his own head. So, likewise, Rajah Rasalu fixed his stakes, they being on the first game, his arms, on the second, his horse, and on the third, his own head.

Then they began to play, and it fell to Rasalu's lot to make the first move. Now he, forgetful of the dead man's warning, played with the dice given him by Rajah Sarkap, besides which, Sarkap let loose his famous rat, Dhol Rajah, and it ran about the board, upsetting the chaupur pieces on the sly, so that Rasalu lost the first game, and gave up his shining armour.

Then the second game began, and once more Dhol Rajah, the rat, upset the pieces, and Rasalu, losing the game, gave up his faithful steed. Then Bhanur, the Arab steed, who stood by, found voice, and cried to his master:

"Sea-born am I, bought with much gold;

Dear Prince! Trust me now as of old.

I'll carry you far from these wiles,

My flight, all unspurr'd, will be swift as a bird,

For thousands and thousands of miles!

Or if needs you must stay;

Before the next game you play

Place your hand in your pocket, I pray!"

Hearing this, Rajah Sarkap frowned, and bade his slaves remove Bhanur, the Arab steed, since he gave his master advice in the game. Now, when the slaves came to lead the faithful steed away, Rasalu could not refrain from tears, thinking over the long years during which Bhanur, the Arab steed, had been his companion. But the horse cried out again:

"Weep not, dear Prince! I shall not eat my bread

Of stranger hands, nor to strange stall be led.

Take your right hand, and place it as I said."

These words roused some recollection in Rasalu's mind, and when, just at this moment, the kitten in his pocket began to struggle, he remembered all about the warning, and the dice made from dead men's bones. Then his heart rose up once more, and he called boldly to Rajah Sarkap, "Leave my horse and arms here for the present. Time enough to take them away when you have won my head!"

Now, Rajah Sarkap, seeing Rasalu's confident bearing, began to be afraid, and ordered all the women of his palace to come forth in their gayest attire and stand before Rasalu, so as to distract his attention from the game. But he never even looked at them, and drawing the dice from his pocket, said to Sarkap, "We have played with your dice all this time. Now we will play with mine."

Then the kitten went and sat at the window through which the rat Dhol Rajah used to come, and the game began.

After a while, Sarkap, seeing Rajah Rasalu was winning, called to his rat, but when Dhol Rajah saw the kitten he was afraid, and would not go farther. So Rasalu won, and took back his arms. Next he played for his horse, and once more Rajah Sarkap called for his rat, but Dhol Rajah, seeing the kitten keeping watch, was afraid. So Rasalu won the second stake, and took back Bhanur, the Arab steed.

Then Sarkap brought all his skill to bear on the third and last game, saying:

"Oh, moulded pieces! Favour me today!

Forsooth this is a man with whom I play.

No paltry risk, but life and death at stake;

As Sarkap does, so do, for Sarkap's sake!"

But Rasalu answered back:

"Oh, moulded pieces! Favour me today!

Forsooth it is a man with whom I play.

No paltry risk, but life and death at stake;

As Heaven does, so do, for Heaven's sake!"

So they began to play, whilst the women stood round in a circle, and the kitten watched Dhol Rajah, from the window. Then Sarkap lost, first his kingdom, then the wealth of the whole world, and lastly his head.

Just then, a servant came in to announce the birth of a daughter to Rajah Sarkap, and he, overcome by misfortunes, said, "Kill her at once! For she has been born in an evil moment, and has brought her father ill luck!"

But Rasalu rose up in his shining armour, tender-hearted and strong, saying, "Not so, O King! She has done no evil. Give me this child to wife, and if you will vow, by all you hold sacred, never again to play chaupur for another's head, I will spare yours now!"

Then Sarkap vowed a solemn vow never to play for another's head, and after that he took a fresh mango branch, and the new-born babe, and placing them on a golden dish, gave them to Rasalu.

Now, as he left the palace, carrying with him the new-born babe and the mango branch, he met a band of prisoners, and they called out to him:

"A royal hawk are you, O King, the rest

But timid wild-fowl. Grant us our request,

Unloose these chains, and live forever blest!"

And Rajah Rasalu listened to them, and bade King Sarkap set them at liberty.

Then he went to the Murti Hills, and placed the new-born babe, Kokilan, in an underground palace, and planted the mango branch at the door, saying, "In twelve years the mango tree will blossom; then will I return and marry Kokilan."

And after twelve years, the mango tree began to flower, and Raja Rasalu married the Princess Kokilan, who he won from Sarkap when he played chaupur with the king.

The Fox and the Drum

This story has been adapted from a tale originally told by Kate Douglas Wiggin and Nora Archibald Smith in The Talking Beasts, published in 1911 by Houghton Mifflin Company. The fables in The Talking Beasts are engaging and entertaining, with whimsical characters and imaginative settings. Through these tales, Wiggin and Smith aimed to stimulate the imagination of children while also instilling important values that promote character development and moral growth.

Once, a Fox was wandering across a moor, eagerly searching for something to eat. Eventually, he arrived at the base of a tree where a drum hung from one of the branches. Whenever the wind blew, the branch would strike the drum, creating a loud noise.

Spotting a domestic fowl nearby, the Fox decided to lay in wait, hoping to make her his meal. Suddenly, he heard the sound of the drum, which piqued his interest even more. Thinking that such a loud noise must come from a large and meaty source, he approached the tree.

However, the fowl, alerted by the noise, fled, forcing the Fox to climb the tree in pursuit of the prey up in the tree. After much effort, he managed to tear open the drum, only to find it empty except for a skin and a piece of wood. Regret filled his heart as he realized he had wasted his time chasing after an illusion.

The moral of the story is clear: appearances can be deceiving, and it's better to focus on substance rather than mere semblance.

Loudly ever sounds the labour,

But in vain, within is nought:

Art you wise, for substance labour,

Semblance will avail you nought.

The Timid Hare And The Flight Of The Beasts

This story has been adapted from a tale originally told by Laure Claire Foucher in Stories to Read or Tell from Fairy Tales and Folklore, published in 1917 by Moffat, Yard And Company, New York. Stories to Read or Tell from Fairy Tales and Folklore collects stories featuring folk tales from various countries, including Japan, Germany, Ireland, India and Russia.

Once upon a time when Brahmadatta reigned in Benares, the Bodhisatta came to life as a young lion. And when fully grown he lived in a wood. At this same time there was near the Western Ocean a grove of palms mixed with vilva trees. A certain hare lived here beneath a palm sapling, at the foot of a vilva tree.

One day this hare after feeding came and lay down beneath a young palm tree. And the thought struck him, "If this earth should be destroyed, what would become of me?" And at this very moment a ripe vilva fruit fell on a palm leaf. At the sound of it, the hare thought, "This solid earth is collapsing," and starting up he fled without so much as looking behind him.

Another saw him scampering off as if frightened to death, and asked the cause of his panic flight. "Pray, don't ask me," he said.

The other hare cried, "Pray, sir, what is it?" and kept running after him.

Then the hare stopped a moment and without looking back he said, "The earth here is breaking up." And at this the second hare ran after the other. And so first one and then another hare caught sight of him running, and joined in the chase till one hundred thousand hares all took flight together. They were seen by a deer, a boar, an elk, a buffalo, a wild ox, a rhinoceros, a tiger, a lion, and an elephant. And when they asked what it meant and were told that the earth was breaking up, they too took flight. So by degrees this host of animals extended to the length of a full mile.

When the Bodhisatta saw this headlong flight of the animals, and heard that the cause of it was that the earth was coming to an end, he thought, "The earth is nowhere coming to an end. Surely it must be some sound which was misunderstood by them. And if I don't make a great effort, they will surely perish. I will save their lives."

So with the speed of a lion he got before them to the foot of a mountain, and lion-like roared three times. They were terribly frightened at the lion, and stopped in their flight, stood huddled together. The lion went in amongst them and asked why they were running away.

"The earth is collapsing," they answered.

"Who saw it collapsing?" he said.

"The elephants know all about it," they replied.

He asked the elephants. "We don't know," they said, "the lions know."

But the lions said, "We don't know; the tigers know."

The tigers said, "The rhinoceroses know."

The rhinoceroses said, "The wild oxen know."

The wild oxen, "The buffaloes."

The buffaloes, "The elks."

The elks, "The boars."

The boars, "The deer."

The deer said, "We don't know; the hares know."

When the hares were questioned, they pointed to one particular hare and said, "This one told us."

So the Bodhisatta asked, "Is it true, sir, that the earth is breaking up?"

"Yes, sir, I saw it," said the hare.

"Where," he asked, "were you living when you saw it?"

"Near the ocean, sir, in a grove of palms mixed with vilva trees. For as I was lying beneath the shade of a palm sapling at the foot of a vilva tree, I thought, 'If this earth should break up, where shall I go?' And at that very moment I heard the sound of breaking up of the earth, and I fled."

The lion thought, "A ripe vilva fruit evidently must have fallen on a palm leaf and made a 'thud,' and this hare jumped to the conclusion that the earth was coming to an end, and ran away. I will find out the exact truth about it."

So he reassured the herd of animals, and said, "I will take the hare and go find out exactly whether the earth is coming to an end or not, in the place pointed out by him. Until I return stay here."

Then, placing the hare on his back, he sprang forward with the speed of a lion, and putting the hare down in a palm grove, he said, "Come, show us the place you meant."

"I dare not, my lord," said the hare.

"Come, don't be afraid," said the lion.

The hare, not venturing to go near the vilva tree, stood afar off and cried, "Yonder, sir, is the place of dreadful sounds," and so saying, he repeated the first stanza:

"From the spot where I did dwell

Issued forth a fearful 'thud';

What it was I could not tell,

Nor what caused it understood."

After hearing what the hare said, the lion went to the foot of the vilva tree, and saw the spot where the hare had been lying beneath the shade of the palm tree, and the ripe vilva fruit that fell on the palm leaf, and having carefully ascertained that the earth had not broken up, he placed the hare on his back and with the speed of a lion soon came again to the herd of beasts.

Then he told them the whole story, and said, "Don't be afraid." And having thus reassured the herd of beasts, he let them go.

If it had not been for the Bodhisatta at that time, all the beasts would have rushed into the sea and perished. It was all owing to the Bodhisatta that they escaped death.

Alarmed at sound of fallen fruit,

A hare once ran away;

The other beasts all followed suit,

Moved by that hare's dismay.

They hastened not to view the scene,

But lent a willing ear

To idle gossip, and were clean

Distraught with foolish fear.

They who to Wisdom's calm delight

And Virtue's heights attain,

Though ill example should invite,

Such panic fear disdain.

These three stanzas were inspired by Perfect Wisdom.

The Sagacious Snake

This story has been substantially adapted from a tale originally told by Kate Douglas Wiggin and Nora Archibald Smith in The Talking Beasts, published in 1911 by Houghton Mifflin Company. The fables in The Talking Beasts are engaging and entertaining, with whimsical characters and imaginative settings. Through these tales, Wiggin and Smith aimed to stimulate the imagination of children while also instilling important values that promote character development and moral growth.

As the ravages of time gnawed away at his once formidable frame, the Snake found himself ensnared by the cruel grip of age. Once a formidable predator, now reduced to a feeble state, he struggled to pursue his prey, his once sharp instincts dulled by the passing years. In the shadow of his former glory, he found himself adrift, lost in the labyrinth of his own dwindling strength, unsure of how to secure his next meal.

In the depths of his despair, the Snake reflected upon the folly of youth, realizing that the vigour of days gone by could never be reclaimed. Instead, he turned his gaze towards the uncertain horizon of the future, acknowledging the wisdom accrued through the passage of time. With a newfound resolve, he vowed to chart a course guided by prudence and restraint, seeking sustenance without causing harm to others.

Seeking solace by the edge of a spring, the Snake encountered a community of frogs, led by a powerful monarch revered by all. Casting himself down in the dust, the Snake bemoaned his fate to a sympathetic frog, recounting the tragedy that had befallen him. His confession reached the ears of the Frog King, who approached him with curiosity, eager to unravel the mystery of the Snake's plight.

With solemn humility, the Snake confessed his misdeed, admitting that his insatiable greed had led to a fateful encounter with tragedy. In his pursuit of a single frog, he had inadvertently brought about the death of an innocent child, invoking the wrath of a vengeful holy man who cursed him to serve as the humble steed of the Frog King. Bound by fate to fulfil this unlikely role, the Snake submitted to his new station, accepting it as the will of a higher power.

Embracing his role as the Frog King's loyal steed, the Snake humbly accepted his daily ration of frogs, acknowledging the symbiotic relationship between them. Despite the indignity of his servitude, he found solace in the knowledge that his obedience brought him sustenance and shelter from the harsh realities of the world.

In the end, the tale of the Snake and the Frog King serves as a testament to the power of humility and courtesy in overcoming adversity. Where brute force and conflict may fail, kindness and humility have the power to disarm even the most bitter of enemies, paving the way for reconciliation and mutual benefit in the face of adversity.

The Pious Wolf

This story has been adapted from a tale originally told by W. H. D. Rouse in The Giant Crab and Other Tales from Old India, published in 1897 by David Nutt, London. The tales in the collection cover a wide range of themes, including adventure, morality, wisdom, and magic. Many of the stories feature talking animals, brave heroes, cunning tricksters, and mythical beings, offering readers a glimpse into the rich storytelling traditions of India.

Once there was a flood, and there was a large rock with a Wolf sleeping on the top. The water came pouring around the rock, and when the Wolf awoke he found himself imprisoned, with no way of getting off, and nothing to eat.

"Hm!" he said to himself, "here I am, caught fast sure enough, and here I shall have to stay yet awhile. Nothing to eat, either! Well," he thought, after a pause, "it is Friday today, when people say you ought to fast. Suppose I keep a holy fast today? A capital idea!" So he crossed his paws, and pretended to pray, and thought himself very good and pious to be fasting.

A fairy saw this, and heard what he said, and she thought she would just see how much was real and how much was sham. So she changed herself into the shape of a pretty little Kid, and jumped down out of the air on to the rock.

The Wolf opened an eye to see what the noise could be, and there was a tender little Kid, standing on the rock. He forgot his prayers in a minute.

"Aha!" he said. "A Kid! I can keep my Friday fast tomorrow. Now for the Kid!" He smacked his lips, and jumped at the Kid.

But the Kid jumped away, and, try as he would, he could not come near it. You know it was the fairy, and the fairy did not let herself be caught.

After trying to catch the Kid for some time the Wolf lay down again. "After all," he said, "it is Friday, and perhaps I had best keep my fast today."

"You humbug!" said the fairy, who had gone back to her proper shape, "you are a nice creature to pretend that you are keeping fast! You fast because you can't help it, not because you are really good. As a punishment, you shall stay on this rock till next Friday, and fast for a week!"

So saying, she opened her wings and flew far away.

A Crow is a Crow for Ever

This story has been adapted from a tale originally told by William Crooke and W. H. D. Rouse in The Talking Thrush, published in 1899 by E. P. Dutton, New York. Their version of this story is based on an original telling by Sáhib Rám, Brahman, of Nardauli, Etah district.

THERE once was a very learned Bishop, who was very fond of bird's-nesting. One day he saw a fine large nest up in an elm-tree, and when he had climbed up he saw that it was full of young Crow-chicks. One of these chicks had such a winsome appearance, that the Bishop put him inside his hat, and took him home to the Palace.

In due time the Crow grew up, and as he heard around him continually the Bishop and his friends talking divinity, by degrees he became quite clever in divinity himself. He knew all the kings of Israel and Judah, and the cities of refuge, so that at last there was no question in a divinity paper he could not answer. Indeed, once when the examining Chaplain was ill, the Crow did his work for him.

The fame of this learned Crow spread far and wide, until eventually it reached the King's ears. Now the Bishop had been expecting this all along, and ever since he found the young Crow he had been training him for a purpose. I am sorry to say he was rather a greedy man, and as he hoped to get something out of the King by the means of this Crow, he trained him to fly towards anything that shone bright, such as gold and silver.

"When the King asks me to show off my Crow," he thought, "I will ask as a price anything the Crow may choose, and then doubtless he will fly to the King's crown, and I shall be King!"

At the first all fell out as he hoped for. The King sent word to say he wanted to see the Crow. He was sitting in the garden, with his gold crown on, and all his courtiers around him, and then asked to hear him say all the kings of Israel and Judah.

"With pleasure, sire," said the Bishop, "if your Majesty will deign to grant him what he chooses for a reward. He has been well taught, and will not work for nothing."

"By all means," said the King, "let him choose his reward, and I will give it."

Then the Bishop took his Crow out of his hat, and the Crow said all the kings of Israel and Judah quite right, forwards and backwards, without a single mistake. The King was delighted: he could not have done as much.

"And now, sire," said the Bishop, "I will let him go, and tell him to choose his own prize."

So the Bishop let the Crow loose. The Crow was flying straight for the King's crown, when all on a sudden what should he spy but a dead cat! He turned off on the instant, and down he swooped on the dead cat. You know Crows eat dead things and offal, and this Crow liked a dead cat for dinner better than a gold crown.

The King laughed, and the courtiers roared with merriment.

"Bishop," said the King when he had done laughing, "your Crow is easily pleased, it seems! Well, he has chosen his reward, and by my royal beard, he shall have it. Ha, ha, ha!"

But the Bishop felt very rueful indeed. All his pains and trouble were lost, and he had nothing to show for it! He shook his head and went away, singing to himself a little chant he made up on the spot, all out of his own head:

"I kept my Crow in a lovely cage,

And taught him wisdom's holy page;

But still 'tis true, whatever he may know,

A dirty Crow is a dirty Crow."

The Maid Of Jhalnagor

This story has been adapted from a tale originally told by Edmund Mitchell in Tales Of Destiny, published in 1913 by Constable And Company Ltd, London.

Well, since you would have it so, listen to the story of Rukpur Singh, hereditary chief of Jhalnagor, mansabdar of five hundred men, captain of the bodyguard of Akbar the Great, King of Kings, Lord of the Earth.

"This day in the Hall of Assembly, in the presence of the great Padishah himself, we have listened to the arguments of men of diverse faiths. It is well. As Akbar, the Most High, himself has said, all religions are good; each man has the god or gods of his fathers; let there be no obstacle placed against worshipping the divine power in any manner that seems fit. That is both wisdom and justice. That is why I, a Hindu, a Rajput, one of the twice born, can serve my lord, the Moslem Emperor Akbar, with loyalty of heart and of sword that no man may question."

At these words the captain of the bodyguard touched the jewelled hilt of his scimitar lying on the cushion by his side. He glanced around, as if to see whether anyone present dared to question the fidelity he had professed. But there was neither movement nor remark among his listeners, and with a disdainful little smile of self-complacency he resumed.

"During today's discussion, in the spirit of tolerance that Akbar teaches to all of us, we Rajputs have had to listen to severe upbraiding. We are accused of inhumanity because in our homes a female child may be done away with at birth, lawfully and without dishonour. It is so, and I shall not dispute the fact itself. Nor shall I defend the practice except to point out that a woman more or less in the world does not matter, that the babe suffers no pain and knows no ill, that had she lived it might have been to a life of widowhood if courage were wanting to choose the suttee, and therefore to long days of shame and sorrow.

"Furthermore, it has to be remembered that the marriage of one of our daughters costs much money. According to the rules of our caste and the customs of our race, the ceremony must be worthy of the parents and of the position they occupy; all of the district must be feasted, and no matter that the expense is grievous it must be borne. To some who are rich the money thus spent is of no account. But to others who are poor yet proud, and all Rajputs are proud, a wedding that is seemly for a daughter of the house may mean poverty and ruin for the father and brothers for twenty years to follow. In certain circumstances this misfortune cannot be thought of. The honour of the race, the very safety of a whole clan, may depend on rigid economy as a provision against danger. So it may be both right and wise for an infant daughter to be put painlessly to her death. Such was the doctrine my father taught me, and his name is blessed."

The speaker dropped his eyes, folded his hands across his breast, and for a full minute remained in silent meditation. When at last he looked up again, there had come over the usually stern and haughty face a wonderful glow of kindliness, and his voice took a softer modulation.

"However, know this, my friends, that in my zenana at Jhalnagor there are little girls, three, and more will be welcome should the divine Krishna send them. Three little daughters have I, all born of my wife Lakmibai, the jewel of Jhalnagor. With sons also am I blessed. We have two brave little boys, of whom I may well be proud. But I do not love them more than my daughters, nor would I change any one daughter for a son. This I say out of the truth of my heart, and in no wise because fortune has been kind to me and mine, and has given us such prosperity that there is a fit dower for each daughter without my treasury knowing the loss.

"So when the learned mullah from Stamboul denounced infanticide, I was one with him in sympathy, for my inclination is to cherish with love and care every female child the gods send.

"Now would you hear how a Rajput came to this manner of thinking? My story is that of a little maid. Listen. It happened just five years ago.

* * * * *

"Under the firm and just rule of our master Akbar there has been peace for many years in our part of the world. Except when, as now, I come to Fathpur-Sikri for my yearly month of service in providing part of the Emperor's bodyguard, I live quietly among my own people. The soil around our villages is tilled, our shopkeepers buy and sell, we worship in our temples, and we are happy, for no enemy comes to disturb the peace of our beautiful little valley of Jhalnagor embosomed among the hills.

"One day it happened that I had gone on a hunting trip with a party of my friends. In the early dawn we had descended from the fort on

124

the hilltop which is my home and the rallying-place for my clan. Ours is a small clan, numbering but a few thousands, but nobly born as any tribe in Rajputana, brave and of honour unsullied, men who have never yet given a daughter to the harem of a Moslem."

The features of the Rajput flashed with pride. His brother-at-arms, the Afghan, met the defiant look, and said, with a quiet smile, "There are many Rajput women wed to Moslem lords."

"Yes, but not Rajput women of Jhalnagor. They would have died first. In fact, many of them did so prefer to die when the Moslem host first swept over our land. In the hour of defeat, against overwhelming numbers, within the citadel of Jhalnagor the women of my race, refusing to accept dishonour, bared their bosoms to the spears of those they loved, husbands, brothers, and fathers, and so they died."

With hands outstretched and eyes upraised in rapt pride and reverence for the deeds of his ancestors, again the Rajput fell into momentary silence.

"The story of the little maid." It was the voice of the physician recalling the narrator to his task.

"Yes, the story of the little maid," resumed the Rajput. "As I have said, we had gone to the hunt one morning, a party of twelve, riding on three elephants. For we were in pursuit of a tiger, a destroyer of men, which the villagers had marked down in a patch of jungle by the river side. Of the hunt I need say nothing; we killed the tiger, and, with the huge, striped body slung across the neck of my elephant, we were returning home. It was toward evening, for we had rested in the forest during the heat of the day.

"We were just entering the narrow gorge that leads to the fort on the hill, when, right on the pathway before me, I saw the prone figure of a child. My elephant's feet were almost upon it before the sage brute himself stopped and trumpeted a warning to us in the howdah. With the tiger's body occupying the place where the mahout was wont to ride, the latter was walking, and he, too, had not noticed the tiny bundle of bright yellow clothing lying on the road.

"Glancing down, I beheld a little girl with her forehead touching the dust. At my calling she arose, and spread her hands across her breast.

"'Listen, O chief, to my warning, listen, O my lord,' she called out in a shrill tone of supplication. I had already observed that her face was one of great beauty, although that of just a little child, but six or seven years old.

"The other two elephants had halted behind mine, and some of the party had descended. But at the approach of these men the maid shrank away, and, keeping her eyes fixed in my direction, she continued to address me, "'Listen to my words, O chief, and be saved from death.'

"In another moment I had sprung to the ground. As I advanced the child ran toward me, absolutely fearless. Taking her in my arms, I sat down by the roadside. Close to my breast she nestled, and, with sobs and tears now, told me her story.

"A robber band was in the nullah, less than a mile further along, fully a hundred strong, fierce men and murderers. They had already slain the father and the mother of the little maid. They were humble woodcutters, and I had known them well. They were poor, but of my own people, and instantly in my heart I vowed that I would be avenged.

"The little girl, Brenda her name, as she told me in her childish way of confidence, had hidden in the brushwood all day, trembling and afraid. But at last she divined that the men had come to lay an ambush for me, for as the afternoon advanced they disposed themselves among bushes and behind trees, also in the hut of her dead parents. Even now the assassins were waiting for me, for the girl had seen our party ride forth in the early morning, and she knew that I had not yet returned.

"With wonderful intuition for a child so tender in years, the thought came to her that I was to be assailed, she stole down the gorge, moving cautiously through the undergrowth, and waited at the spot we found her to give me warning.

"The child had described to me the leader of the gang, and I had immediately recognized Gunesh Tanti, accursed son of a pig, a robber from across the desert of Sindh, who had more than once ravaged peaceful villages of Rajputana. He would know that I had treasure in the fort, and of an instant I could read his wily plan. Moving through the country, he had doubtless heard a day or two before of this projected expedition of mine for the killing of the man-eating tiger. So he had designed to slay me on my homeward way, and, the deed accomplished, would rely on gaining access to the citadel by loading his ruffians into the howdahs of my elephants. Once over the drawbridge and within the portcullised gateway, his murderous scheme might have been easy, for my score of men-at-arms on duty would have been taken by surprise and so at a disadvantage.

"But knowing now the danger, I laughed in my beard, for Gunesh Tanti, this human tiger and slayer of innocent men, just as had been the tiger now slung across the back of my elephant, was fairly delivered into my hand. He who had come to trap me was himself entrapped. And thanks all to this little maid of the glen! At the thought, I patted her soft cheek with my hand, and in response she smiled up into my eyes with wondrous trust and winsomeness.

"Our party, as I have said, numbered twelve, this without counting the three mahouts, lithe and active men, and brave as any one of us. The neck of the gorge was narrow, and for a hundred yards on either side there were steep precipices down which rocks could be tumbled on fleeing men. By a goat path over the hillside the fort could be reached by one sure of foot and knowing the way. Such a lad was of our party, a cousin of my own, who could race with the deer.

"In a few minutes he had girded his loins and was on his mission, disappearing over the crest of the almost perpendicular crag up which he had clambered. He was to warn the garrison, turn out every man and boy fully armed, and bid them to sweep down on the ambushed robbers. The mothers and the maidens would hold the fort. No other garrison, when once on the alert, was needed for such an enemy."

Again the Rajput smiled proudly, but the silence of intent listening was unbroken, and he continued, "The firing of a matchlock was to be our signal that my men held the upper end of the pass, and were descending on our enemies. Meanwhile, my immediate followers prepared the rocks above the narrow neck of the defile and got them ready for instant rolling down. To this last task four of our number were deputed. The others abided with me. Our plan was to block the narrow passage by ranging the elephants abreast of each other, and, so that the animals themselves might not be stampeded by the unexpected din of battle, we chained their forelegs, first each animal separately, and then the middle one to his comrades on either side.

"At last all our preparations were completed, the huge beasts in line, my companions mounted into the howdahs. I alone remained on foot, I and the little woodcutters' daughter, standing by my side, holding trustfully to my hand, and no longer weeping.

"'You must come with me, my almond-sweet,' I said, as I raised the child in my arms, and passed her up into the howdah of my own elephant, the central one. Then I myself clambered aloft. The tiger's corpse had been flung to the ground, and our three mahouts sat in their proper places, iron goads in hand, ready to perform their task of keeping the elephants under control.

"At last, after a tense period of waiting, the welcome report of the matchlock reverberated from among the hills.

"The fight does not really concern my story," said the Rajput, grimly. "It is sufficient to say that Gunesh Tanti and all his band perished to a man. Some were slain by the swords of my horsemen charging down the pass, some crushed by the falling rocks, some of the last survivors, who flung themselves desperately against our living barrier, dying on our handpikes or being trampled underfoot by the elephants. Not one of more than five score men lived to carry back the tale of death to the robber haunts from where they had come.

"On our side some lives were lost, seven in all, but this is the penalty that brave men have to pay in the doing of righteous deeds. Their memory is honoured.

"As for the little maid, I had nested her in the best-protected corner of the howdah, and in the thick of the fray, when a shower of arrows had fallen upon us, I had covered her tiny form with my shield. But during the final hand-to-hand fight, when all was din and turmoil with the shouting of the men and the angry trumpeting of the elephants, I had not paid her any special heed. From her lips came no sound to attract my attention, no cry of fear, nor wailing murmur.

"But at the end I looked for the little child, lifting the shield that had partly guarded her. She met my gaze with a smile. But straightway I noticed that an arrow, descending almost perpendicularly, had pierced her soft little arm, and transfixed it to her side. Yet had she not cried out, nor even now, when I was tending her, did she whimper.

"I drew forth the arrow, breaking it in two, so as to let the shaft pass through the arm. Although blood flowed freely, I saw at a glance that the wound in the body was a mere puncture, and also that on the limb only a piercing of the flesh. Therefore her hurt was not serious, although of a certainty painful, and terrifying too for a child so young. But even now not one word of complaint did she utter. She kept her sweet smile on me. Brave little maid!

"Tearing a length of cambric from my turban, I had bound both arm and tender breast, and readjusted the sari of yellow-dyed cotton that formed her simple garment. And now she reposed, happy and contented, in my arms. I remained in the howdah, while my companions cut off the heads of the robbers, and loaded these trophies of victory on one of the other elephants, so that a triumphal pile might be made in the courtyard of the citadel. Then, with the tiger replaced on the neck of my own elephant, we moved for home, a group of fifty horsemen now forming our escort. The headless bodies of our enemies were left as fitting spoil for the jackals and the vultures, the latter of whom, scenting the carrion, were already beginning to drop down, it might seem, from the blue vault of heaven.

"By the time we gained the fortress the dusk was gathering. Across the drawbridge, promptly lowered at the sound of our joyful shouting, I saw my wife standing beside the big carronade that commanded the roadway up the hill. The smoking match was in her hand, but at sight of me she stooped and smothered in the dust the spark that would have dealt out death to the robbers had they ever gained a near approach. Descending from my elephant, I greeted her and thanked her for the courage of herself and all the other women, our loved ones.

"Then my friends above handed down gently into my arms the form of the little maid. At sight of my wife's sweet and kindly countenance the eyes of the child were lighted with joyousness. But with a quick motion my wife drew her veil completely over her features. Before this was done, however, I had caught a strange look in her face, a look of mingled surprise and terror. At the same moment her old attendant and confidant, Rakaya, flung herself at my feet, and began to babble for my forgiveness.

"'What does this mean?' I asked, glancing in profound amazement from the woman's prostrate form up into my wife's eyes. There again I read the strangely troubled expression. Puzzled, yet restraining my curiosity before the others gathered around, I placed the wounded child in my wife's arms, and, with a gesture to signify that she and Rakaya were to follow, I led the way to the women's quarters.

"Once within the zenana, I told my story briefly: how the little damsel of the glen had saved me from certain death, and then, through danger and through pain, had been brave as the noblest-born Rajput maid could be. After this recital, I commended the child to my wife's affections, bidding her love the orphan as she would a daughter.

"Then my wife, the jewel of Jhalnagor, was suffused with great joy. Hugging the child to her motherly bosom, she exclaimed, "'Oh, my lord, I have a confession to make, but now you will forgive me. Do you remember our first-born babe?'

"My brow darkened. I felt the hot flush of shame on my cheeks. For our first-born had been a girl, and I, disappointed and aggrieved, because I was then strongly under the influence of my father's teachings, proud of my family's position and wealth, and fearful to be impoverished in the future, had given the word that the babe must die. This in spite of my wife's pitiful tears and pleadings. And it was not the memory of the deed itself that made me now ashamed, but the memory of those tears and of how I had repelled her. Through the intervening years I had tried never to think of this painful episode, and, with two little boys playing at my knee, had well-nigh forgotten the first child that had come. Mention of the dead and buried past now made me resentful.

"'Why do you speak thus?' I asked, angrily.

"'Because, my lord,' exclaimed my wife, dropping on her knees at my feet, yet with the little child still pressed to her breast, and drawing me down to her with her free hand, so that we were all three close together, 'because, oh, my lord, in our arms now this very moment is our first-born, our daughter. We spared her, Rakaya and I. We bribed Runjit, who is now dead, and to whom you gave the terrible orders, and Rakaya smuggled the babe safe away to the cottage of the woodcutters. Since then I have managed to see her sometimes by stealth, and have loved her, but I have never dared to clothe her in any but humble garments. She has worn no silks, no bangles, no jewels of any kind, lest suspicion should be aroused.'

"'Oh, great master, forgive your humble slave,' moaned the old crone, Rakaya, grovelling in a corner of the room.

"But to my wife only I paid heed. 'Can this be?' I murmured, surprised and deeply moved.

"'She is our very own, our little girl.' And back into my arms she placed the child, whose tresses I straightway fell to fondling, as her sweet, trustful eyes looked up into mine, beaming with love as if she had indeed long before divined in her heart that I was her father and her natural protector.

"'And, oh, my dear lord,' continued my wife, her eyes brimming with tears, you know now it was to save you that, in the mysterious workings of fate, this little child was saved.'"

The Rajput paused in his story, bending his head to hide the emotion that caused his lips to tremble. "A month later," he went on, softly, "a little sister was born to Brenda, and only last year a third daughter came to our home. And all, as I have said, are well beloved."

The speaker's face was now upraised. The soldierly sternness had gone out of it. His face shone only with paternal pride and love as he added, "Today Brenda, our first-born, is the light of my home, and a year from now she will be married to the Rajah of Jodhpur, to make the heart of that great and noble prince of the Rajputs happy for evermore."

And so ended the Rajput's tale.

There was silence for a time, broken at last by the voice of the ash-besprinkled devotee, "Allahu akbar! God is great! Over many things he gives his servants power."

The Beetle and the Silken Thread

This story has been adapted from a tale originally told by Siddha Mohana Mitra and Nancy Bell in Hindu Tales from the Sanskrit, published in 1919 by MacMillan and Company, London & Canada. The book features a selection of stories drawn from classical Sanskrit literature, including the Panchatantra, Hitopadesha, and other traditional sources.

CHAPTER I

The strange adventures related in the story of the Beetle and the Silken Thread took place in the town of Allahabad, "the City of God," so called because it is situated near the point of meeting of the two sacred rivers of India, the Ganges, which the Hindus lovingly call Mother Ganga because they believe its waters can wash away their sins, and the Jumna, which they consider scarcely less holy.

The ruler of Allahabad was a very selfish and hot-tempered Raja named Surya Pratap, signifying "Powerful as the Sun," who expected everybody to obey him without a moment's delay, and was ready to punish in a very cruel manner those who hesitated to do so. He would never listen to a word of explanation, or own that he had been mistaken, even when he knew full well that he was in the wrong. He had a mantri, that is to say, a chief vizier or officer, whom he greatly trusted, and really seemed to be fond of, for he liked to have him always near him. The vizier was called Dhairya-Sila, or "the Patient One," because he never lost his temper, no matter what provocation he received. He had a beautiful house, much money and many jewels, carriages to drive about in, noble horses to ride and many servants to wait upon him, all given to him by his master. But what he loved best of all was his faithful wife, Buddhi-Mati, or "the Sensible One," whom he had chosen for himself, and who would have died for him.

Many of the Raja's subjects were jealous of Dhairya-Sila, and constantly brought accusations against him, of none of which his master took any notice, except to punish those who tried to set him against his favourite. It really seemed as if nothing would ever bring harm to Dhairya-Sila, but he often told his wife that such good fortune was not likely to last, and that she must be prepared for a change before long.

It turned out that he was right. For one day Surya Pratap ordered him to do what he considered would be a shameful deed. He refused; telling his master that he was wrong to think of such a thing, and entreating him to give up his purpose. "All your life long," he said, "you will wish you had listened to me, for your conscience will never let you rest!"

On hearing these brave words, Surya Pratap flew into a terrible rage, summoned his guards, and ordered them to take Dhairya-Sila outside the city to a very lofty tower, and leave him at the top of it, without shelter from the sun and with nothing to eat or drink. The guards were at first afraid to touch the vizier, remembering how others had been punished for only speaking against him. Seeing their unwillingness, the Raja got more and more angry, but Dhairya-Sila himself kept quite calm, and said to the soldiers, "I go with you gladly. It is for the master to command and for me to obey."

CHAPTER II

The guards were relieved to find they need not drag the vizier away, for they admired his courage and felt sure that the Raja would soon find he could not get on without him. It might go hard with them if he suffered harm at their hands. So they only closed in about him, and holding himself very upright, Dhairya-Sila walked to the tower as if he were quite glad to go. In his heart however he knew full well that it would need all his skill to escape with his life.

When her husband did not come home at night, Buddhi-Mati was very much distressed. She guessed at once that something had gone wrong, and set forth to try and find out what had happened. This was easy enough, for as she crept along, with her veil closely held about her lest she should be recognised, she passed groups of people discussing the terrible fate that had befallen the favourite. She decided that she must wait until midnight, when the streets would be deserted and she could reach the tower unnoticed. It was almost dark when she got there, but in the dim light of the stars she made out the form of him she loved better than herself, leaning over the edge of the railing at the top.

"Is my dear lord still alive?" she whispered, "and is there anything I can do to help him?"

"You can do everything that is needed to help me," answered Dhairya-Sila quietly, "if you only obey every direction I give you. Do not for one moment suppose that I am in despair. I am more powerful even now than my master, who has but shown his weakness by attempting to harm me. Now listen to me. Come tomorrow night at this very hour, bringing with you the following things: first, a beetle, secondly, sixty yards of the finest silk thread, as thin as a spider's web, thirdly, sixty yards of cotton thread, as thin as you can get it, but very strong, fourthly, sixty yards of good stout twine, fifthly, sixty yards of rope, strong enough to carry my weight, and last, but certainly not least, one drop of the purest bees' honey."

CHAPTER III

Buddhi-Mati listened very attentively to these strange instructions, and began to ask questions about them. "Why do you want the beetle? Why do you want the honey?" and so on. But her husband checked her. "I have no strength to waste in explanations," he said. "Go home in peace, sleep well, and dream of me."

So the anxious wife went meekly away, and early the next day she set to work to obey the orders she had received. She had some trouble in obtaining fine enough silk, so very, very thin it had to be, like a spider's web, but the cotton, twine and rope were easily bought, and to her surprise she was not asked what she wanted them for. It took her a good while to choose the beetle. For though she had a vague kind of idea that the silk, the cotton, twine, and rope, were to help her husband get down from the tower, she could not imagine what share the beetle and the honey were to take. In the end she chose a very handsome, strong-looking, brilliantly coloured fellow who lived in the garden of her home and whom she knew to be fond of honey.

CHAPTER IV

All the time Buddhi-Mati was at work for her husband, she was thinking of him and looking forward to the happy day of his return home. She had such faith in him that she did not for a moment doubt that he would escape, but she was anxious about the future, feeling sure that the Raja would never forgive Dhairya-Sila for being wiser than himself. Exactly at the time fixed the faithful wife appeared at the foot of the tower, with all the things she had been told to bring with her.

"Is all well with my lord?" she whispered, as she gazed up through the darkness. "I have the silken thread as fine as gossamer, the cotton thread, the twine, the rope, the beetle and the honey."

"Yes," answered Dhairya-Sila, "all is still well with me. I have slept well, feeling confident that my dear one would bring all that is needed for my safety, but I dread the great heat of another day, and we must lose no time in getting away from this terrible tower. Now attend most carefully to all I bid you do, and remember not to speak loudly, or the sentries posted within hearing will take alarm and drive you away. First of all, tie the end of the silken thread round the middle of the beetle, leaving all its legs quite free. Then rub the drop of honey on its nose, and put the little creature on the wall, with its nose turned upwards towards me. It will smell the honey, but will not guess that it carries it itself, and it will crawl upwards in the hope of getting to the hive from which that honey came. Keep the rest of the silk firmly held, and gradually unwind it as the beetle climbs up. Mind you do not let it slip, for my very life depends on that slight link with you."

CHAPTER V

Buddhi-Mati, though her hands shook and her heart beat fast as she realized all that depended on her, kept the silk from becoming entangled, and when it was nearly all unwound, she heard her husband's voice saying to her, "Now tie the cotton thread to the end of the silk that you hold, and let it gradually unwind." She obeyed, fully understanding now what all these preparations were for.

When the little messenger of life reached the top of the tower, Dhairya-Sila took it up in his hand and very gently unfastened the silken thread from its body. Then he placed the beetle carefully in a fold of his turban, and began to pull the silken thread up very, very slowly, for if it had broken, his wonderful scheme would have come to an end. Presently he had the cotton thread in his fingers, and he broke off the silk, wound it up, and placed it too in his turban. It had done its duty well, and he would not throw it away.

"Half the work is done now," he whispered to his faithful wife. "You have all but saved me now. Take the twine and tie it to the end of the cotton thread."

Very happily Buddhi-Mati obeyed once more, and soon the cotton thread and twine were also laid aside, and the strong rope tied to the last was being quickly dragged up by the clever vizier, who knew that all fear of death from sunstroke or hunger was over. When he had all the rope on the tower, he fastened one end of it to the iron railing which ran round the platform on which he stood, and very quickly slid down to the bottom, where his wife was waiting for him, trembling with joy.

CHAPTER VI

After embracing his wife and thanking her for saving him, the vizier said to her, "Before we return home, let us give thanks to the great God who helped me in my need by putting into my head the device by which I escaped."

The happy pair then prostrated themselves on the ground, and in fervent words of gratitude expressed their sense of what the God they worshipped had done for them.

"And now," said Dhairya-Sila, "the next thing we have to do is to take the dear little beetle which was the instrument of my rescue back to the place it came from." And taking off his turban, he showed his wife the tiny creature lying in the soft folds.

Buddhi-Mati led her husband to the garden where she had found the beetle, and Dhairya-Sila laid it tenderly on the ground, fetched some food for it, such as he knew it loved, and there left it to take up its old way of life. The rest of the day he spent quietly in his own home with his wife, keeping out of sight of his servants, lest they should report his return to his master.

"You must never breathe a word to any one of how I escaped," Dhairya-Sila said, and his wife promised that she never would.

CHAPTER VII

All this time the Raja was feeling very unhappy, for he thought he had himself caused the death of the one man he could trust. He was too proud to let anybody know that he missed Dhairya-Sila, and was longing to send for him from the tower before it was too late. What then was his relief and surprise when a message was brought to him that the vizier was at the door of the palace and begged for an interview.

"Bring him in at once," cried Surya Pratap. And the next moment Dhairya-Sila stood before his master, his hands folded on his breast and his head bent in token of his submission. The attendants looked on, eager to know how he had got down from the tower, some of them anything but glad to see him back. The Raja took care not to show how delighted he was to see him, and pretending to be angry, he said, "How dare you come into my presence, and which of my subjects has ventured to help you to escape the death on the tower you so richly deserved?"

"None of your subjects, great and just and glorious ruler," replied Dhairya-Sila, "but the God who created us both, making you my master and me your humble servant. It was that God," he went on, "who saved me, knowing that I was indeed guiltless of any crime against you. I had not been long on the tower when help came to me in the form of a great and noble eagle, which appeared above me, hovering with outspread wings, as if about to swoop down upon me and tear me limb from limb. I trembled greatly, but I need have had no fear, for instead of harming me, the bird suddenly lifted me up in its talons and, flying rapidly through the air, landed me upon the balcony of my home and disappeared. Great indeed was the joy of my wife at my rescue from what seemed to be certain death, but I tore myself away from her embraces, to come and tell my lord how heaven had interfered to prove my innocence."

Fully believing that a miracle had taken place, Surya Pratap asked no more questions, but at once restored Dhairya-Sila to his old place as vizier, taking care not to ill-treat the man he believed to be under the special care of God. Though he certainly did not deserve it, the vizier prospered greatly all the rest of his life and as time went on he became the real ruler of the kingdom, for the Raja depended on his advice in everything. He grew richer and richer, but he was never really happy again, remembering the lie he had told to the master to whom he owed so much. Buddhi-Mati could never understand why he made up the story about the eagle, and urged him to tell the truth. She thought it was far more wonderful that a little beetle should have been the means of rescuing him, than that a strong bird should have done so, and she wanted everyone to know what a very clever husband she had. She kept her promise never to tell anyone what really happened, but the secret came out for all that. By the time it was known, however, Dhairya-Sila was so powerful that no one could harm him, and when he died his son took his place as vizier.

The Giant Crab

This story has been adapted from a tale originally told by W. H. D. Rouse in The Giant Crab and Other Tales from Old India, published in 1897 by David Nutt, London. The tales in the collection cover a wide range of themes, including adventure, morality, wisdom, and magic. Many of the stories feature talking animals, brave heroes, cunning tricksters, and mythical beings, offering readers a glimpse into the rich storytelling traditions of India.

Once upon a time there was a lake in the mountains, and in that lake lived a huge Crab. I daresay you have often seen crabs boiled, and put on a dish for you to eat, and perhaps at the seaside you have watched them sidling away at the bottom of a pool. Sometimes a boy or girl bathing in the sea gets a nip from a crab, and then there is squeaking and squealing. But our Crab was much larger than these. He was the largest Crab ever heard of. He was bigger than a dining-room table, and his claws were as big as an armchair. Fancy what it must be to have a nip from such claws as those!

Well, this huge Crab lived all alone in the lake. Now the different animals that lived in the wild mountains used to come to that lake to drink - deer and antelopes, foxes and wolves, lions and tigers and elephants. And whenever they came into the water to drink, the great

Crab was on the watch, and one of them at least never went up out of the water again. The Crab used to nip it with one of his huge claws and pull it under, and then the poor beast was drowned, and made a fine dinner for the big Crab.

This went on for a long time, and the Crab grew bigger and bigger every day, fattening on the animals that came there to drink. So at last all the animals were afraid to go near that lake. This was a pity, because there was very little water in the mountains, and the creatures did not know what to do when they were thirsty.

At last a great Elephant made up his mind to put an end to the Crab and his doings. So he and his wife agreed that they would lead a herd of elephants there to drink, and while the other elephants were drinking, they would look out for the Crab.

They did as they arranged. When the herd of elephants got to the lake, these two went in first, and kept farthest out in the water, watching for the Crab, and the others drank, and trumpeted, and washed themselves close inshore.

Soon they had had enough, and began to go out of the water, and then, sure enough, the Elephant felt a tremendous nip on the leg. The Crab had crawled up under the water and got him fast. He nodded to his wife, who bravely stayed by his side, and then she began, "Dear Mr. Crab!" she said, "please let my husband go!"

The Crab poked his eyes out of the water. You know a crab's eyes grow on a kind of little stalk, and this Crab was so big, that his eyes looked like two thick tree-trunks, with a cannon-ball on the top of each. Now this Crab was a great flirt, or rather he used to be a great flirt, but lately he had nobody to flirt with, because he had eaten up all the creatures that came near him. And Mrs. Elephant was a beautiful elephant, with a shiny brown skin, and elegant flapping ears, and a curly trunk, and two white tusks that twinkled when she smiled. So when the big Crab saw this beautiful elephant, he thought he would like to have a kiss, and he said in a wheedling tone, "Dear little Elephant! Will you give me a kiss?"

Then Mrs. Elephant pretended to be very pleased, and put her head on one side, and flapped her tail, and she looked so sweet and so tempting, that the Crab let go the other elephant, and began to crawl slowly towards her, waving his eyes about as he went.

All this while Mr. Elephant had been in great pain from the nip of the Crab's claw, but he had said nothing, for he was a very brave Elephant. But he did not mean to let his wife come to any harm; not he! It was all part of their trick. And as soon as he felt his leg free, he trumpeted loud and long, and jumped right upon the Crab's back!

Crack, crack, went the Crab's shell, for, big as he was, an elephant was too heavy for him to carry. Crack, crack, crack! The Elephant jumped up and down on his back, and in a very short time the Crab was crushed to mincemeat.

What rejoicing there was among the animals when they saw the Crab crushed to death! From far and near they came, and passed a vote of thanks to the Elephant and his wife, and made them King and Queen of all the animals in the mountains.

As for the Crab, there was nothing left of him but his claws, which were so hard that nothing could crack them, so they were left in the pool. And in the autumn there came a great flood that carried the claws down into the river, and the river carried them hundreds of miles away, to a great city where the King's sons found them, and made out of them two immense drums, which they always beat when they go to war, and the very sound of these drums is enough to frighten the enemy away.

Harisarman

This story has been adapted from a tale originally told by Hamilton Wright Mabie in Young Folks Treasury, Volume 2, published in 1909 by The University Society Inc, New York. Young Folks Treasury, Volume 2 was part of a larger collection of children's literature compiled and edited by Hamilton Wright Mabie, a renowned American essayist, editor, and critic.

There was in a certain village, a certain Brahman named Harisarman. He was poor and foolish and unhappy for want of employment, and he had very many children. He wandered about begging with his family, and at last he reached a certain city, and entered the service of a rich householder called Sthuladatta. His sons became keepers of Sthuladatta's cows and other property, and his wife a servant to him, and he himself lived near his house, performing the duty of an attendant. One day there was a feast on account of the marriage of the daughter of Sthuladatta, largely attended by many friends of the bridegroom and merry-makers. Harisarman hoped that he would be able to fill himself up to the throat with oil and flesh and other dainties, and get the same for his family, in the house of his patron. While he was anxiously expecting to be fed, no one thought of him.

Then he was distressed at getting nothing to eat, and he said to his wife at night, "It is owing to my poverty and stupidity that I am treated with such disrespect here, so I will pretend by means of an artifice to possess a knowledge of magic, so that I may become an object of respect to this Sthuladatta. So, when you get an opportunity, tell him that I possess magical knowledge."

He said this to her, and after turning the matter over in his mind, while people were asleep he took away from the house of Sthuladatta a horse on which his master's son-in-law rode. He placed it in concealment at some distance, and in the morning the friends of the bridegroom could not find the horse, though they searched in every direction.

Then, while Sthuladatta was distressed at the evil omen, and searching for the thieves who had carried off the horse, the wife of Harisarman came and said to him, "My husband is a wise man, skilled in astrology and magical sciences. He can get the horse back for you, so why not ask him?"

When Sthuladatta heard that, he called Harisarman, who said, "Yesterday I was forgotten, but today, now the horse is stolen, I am called to mind."

Sthuladatta then propitiated the Brahman with these words, "I forgot you, forgive me," and asked him to tell him who had taken away their horse.

Then Harisarman drew all kinds of pretended diagrams, and said, "The horse has been placed by thieves on the boundary line south from this place. It is concealed there, and before it is carried off to a distance, as it will be at close of day, go quickly and bring it home."

When they heard that, many men ran and brought the horse quickly, praising the discernment of Harisarman. Then Harisarman was honoured by all men as a sage, and dwelt there in happiness, honoured by Sthuladatta.

Now, as days went on, much treasure, both of gold and jewels, had been stolen by a thief from the palace of the King. As the thief was not known, the King quickly summoned Harisarman on account of his reputation for knowledge of magic. And he, when summoned, tried to gain time, and said, "I will tell you tomorrow," and then he was placed in a chamber by the King and carefully guarded. And he was sad because he had pretended to have knowledge.

Now, in that palace there was a maid named Jihva (which means Tongue), who, with the assistance of her brother, had stolen that treasure from the interior of the palace. She, being alarmed at Harisarman's knowledge, went at night and applied her ear to the door of that chamber in order to find out what he was about. And Harisarman, who was alone inside, was at that very moment blaming his own tongue, that had made a vain assumption of knowledge.

He said, "Oh, tongue, what is this that you have done through your greediness? Wicked one, you will soon receive punishment in full."

When Jihva heard this, she thought, in her terror, that she had been discovered by this wise man, and she managed to get in where he was, and, falling at his feet, she said to the supposed wizard, "Brahman, here I am, that Jihva whom you have discovered to be the thief of the treasure, and after I took it I buried it in the earth in a garden behind the palace, under a pomegranate tree. So spare me, and receive the small quantity of gold which is in my possession."

When Harisarman heard that, he said to her proudly, "Depart, I know all this. I know the past, present, and future, but I will not denounce you, a miserable creature that has implored my protection. But whatever gold is in your possession you must give back to me."

When he said this to the maid, she consented, and departed quickly. But Harisarman reflected in his astonishment, "Fate brings about, as if in sport, things impossible, for, when calamity was so near, who would have thought chance would have brought us success? While I was blaming my jihva, the thief Jihva suddenly flung herself at my feet. Secret crimes manifest themselves by means of fear."

Thus thinking, he passed the night happily in the chamber. And in the morning he brought the King, by some skilful parade of pretended knowledge, into the garden and led him up to the treasure, which was buried under the pomegranate tree, and said the thief had escaped with a part of it. Then the King was pleased, and gave him the revenue of many villages.

But the minister, named Devajnanin, whispered in the King's ear, "How can a man possess such knowledge unattainable by men without having studied the books of magic? You may be certain that this is a specimen of the way he makes a dishonest livelihood, by having a secret intelligence with thieves. It will be much better to test him by some new artifice."

Then the King of his own accord brought a covered pitcher into which he had thrown a frog, and said to Harisarman, "Brahman, if you can guess what there is in this pitcher, I will do you great honour today."

When the Brahman Harisarman heard that, he thought that his last hour had come, and he called to mind the pet name of "Froggie," which his father had given him in his childhood in sport, and, impelled by luck, he called to himself by his pet name, lamenting his hard fate, and suddenly called out, "This is a fine pitcher for you, Froggie. It will soon become the swift destroyer of your helpless self."

The people there, when they heard him say that, raised a shout of applause, because his speech chimed in so well with the object presented to him, and murmured, "Ah! A great sage. He even knows about the frog!"

Then the King, thinking that this was all due to knowledge of divination, was highly delighted, and gave Harisarman the revenue of more villages, with gold, an umbrella, and state carriages of all kinds. So Harisarman prospered in the world.

The Jackal that Lost his Tail

This story has been adapted from a tale originally told by William Crooke and W. H. D. Rouse in The Talking Thrush, published in 1899 by E. P. Dutton, New York. Their version of this story is based on an original telling by Parmanand Tiwári, a student at the Anglo-Sanskrit School, Mirzápur.

THERE was once a Farmer, who used to go out every morning to work in his field, and his wife used to bring him dinner at noon. One day, as the Farmer's wife was carrying out the dinner to the field, she met a Jackal, who said, "Where are you going?"

Said she, "To my husband, and this is his dinner."

Said the Jackal, "Give me some, or I will bite you."

So the woman had to give the Jackal some of this food. And when her husband saw it, he said, "What a small dinner you have brought me today!"

"A Jackal met me," replied his wife, "and threatened to bite me if I gave him none."

"All right," said the Farmer, "tomorrow I'll settle with that Jackal."

On the morrow, the Farmer's wife went after the plough, and the Farmer dressed up in her clothes and carried out the dinner. Again the Jackal appeared.

"Give me some of that," he said, "or I'll bite you."

"Yes, yes, good Mr. Jackal," said the man, "you shall have some, only don't bite me."

Then he set down the plate and the Jackal began to eat.

"Just scratch my back, you, woman," said the Jackal, "while I am eating my dinner."

"Yes, sir, yes, sir," said the man. He began gently to tickle and scratch the back of the Jackal, and in the middle of doing that he suddenly took out his knife, and slish, he cut off the Jackal's tail.

The Jackal jumped up and capered about. "Yow-ow-ow!" he went, "What has come to my tail? Oh dear! How shall I swish away the flies? Oh dear, how it hurts! Yow-ow-ow!" Away he scuttled, as fast as his legs could carry him.

When he got home, all the Jackals came round him, and asked what had become of his tail. The Jackal was ashamed to have lost his tail, which was a particularly long and fine tail, but he pretended to like it.

"Poor fellow!" said the Jackals, "where is your tail?"

"I had it cut off," said the Jackal, "and good riddance. It was always in my way. Why, I never could sit down in comfort, and now look here!" He sat down on the place where his tail used to be, and looked proudly round. "Now, you try!" he said.

They all tried, and found that their tails got underneath them when they sat, and it hurt their tails rather.

"We never thought of that before," they said, "we must get rid of these things. Who cut off yours?"

"A kind Farmer's wife," said the first Jackal. Then he told them where the Farmer's wife lived.

That evening, a knock came at the Farmer's door, as the Farmer and his wife were sitting at tea.

"Come in!" said the Farmer.

The door opened, and in trooped a number of Jackals. "Please, Mr. Farmer," said they, "we want you kindly to cut off our tails."

"Willingly," said the Farmer. He whipped out his knife, and in a jiffy slish, slish, slish, off came the Jackals' tails.

"Yow-ow-ow!" went the Jackals, capering about, "We didn't think it would hurt!" Away they went, and all the woods echoed that night with yowling and howling.

When they all got home, they found the first Jackal waiting for them. He laughed in their faces. "Now we're all alike," he said, "all in the same boat."

"Are we?" said the other Jackals, and set on him and tore him to pieces.

"Now we must have our revenge on the Farmer," said the Jackals when they had eaten up their friend. So next morning they scampered off to the Farmer's house.

The Farmer was out, and his wife was gathering fuel.

"Good morning, Mrs. Farmer," said the Jackals, "we have come to eat the Farmer for cutting our tails off."

"Ah, poor fellow," said the Farmer's wife, "he is dead. When he saw how it hurt you to have your tails cut off, he just lay down on the bed, and died of grief."

"That's unlucky," said the Jackals.

"But we are preparing the funeral feast," she went on, "you see I am now getting fuel for it. Will you give us the pleasure of your company to dinner?"

"Gladly," said the Jackals, "we should like to see the last of the poor fellow," then they ran away.

At dinner-time, they all came back, and found chairs put for them, and plates round the table, with the woman at one end.

"You can sit like Christians now," said the Farmer's wife, "so I have set you a chair apiece."

"Thanks," said the Jackals, "that is thoughtful."

"But I know," the Farmer's wife went on, "what quarrelsome creatures you are over your meat. Don't you think I had better tie you to your chairs, and then each will have to keep to his own plateful?"

"A good plan," the Jackals said, wagging their heads. They had now no tails to wag, and they had to wag something. So the Farmer's wife tied them tight to their chairs.

"But how shall we eat?" said the Jackals, who could not stir a paw.

"Oh, no fear for that, I'll feed you."

Then she brought out a steaming mess, and put it in the middle of the table. All the Jackals sniffed at the steam, and all their eyes were fixed greedily upon the meat. They began to struggle.

"Softly, softly, good Jackals!" said the Farmer's wife.

But what a surprise awaited the Jackals! They were so intent upon watching the Farmer's wife and the meat, that none of them heard the door open, and none of them saw the Farmer himself creep softly in, with a great club in his hand. The first news they had of it was crack, crack, crack!

All but three of the Jackals looked round, and they saw these three of their comrades with their heads smashed in, lolling back in the chairs. The Farmer held the club poised in the air. Down it came, crack, on the head of the fourth Jackal. Then all the others began yowling and struggling to get free, but in vain, for the cords held them fast, they could not stir, and in five minutes all the Jackals lay dead on the floor.

After that the Farmer ploughed in peace, and no one molested the Farmer's wife when she brought his dinner.

Rasalu, The Fakir, And The Giants

This story has been adapted from a tale originally told by Penrhyn Wingfield Coussens in The Jade Story Book; Stories From The Orient, published in 1922 by Duffield And Company, New York. One of the notable aspects of The Jade Story Book is Coussens' engaging narrative style, which brings the characters and settings to life while staying true to the spirit of the original tales.

There was once a fakir who had gained such a wide reputation for working wonders that Rájá Rasalu, King of Sialkot, determined to pay him a visit. So one day, accompanied by his retinue, he set out for the village of Tilláh, where the holy man dwelt.

The fakir's power was so great that he knew of the King's approach long before he reached the foot of the mountain on one side of which the village was situated, and he said to his disciples, "Rájá Rasalu is on his way here with the purpose of putting my knowledge to the test. He is the son of a Hindu, and therefore should know better. I have heard that his own power is very great, so I will first put him to the test."

His pupils agreed with him, but said that he should first change himself into some great animal, so that the King might not know him. The fakir then turned himself into a powerful tiger, and when Rasalu and his followers reached the house they saw this wild beast prowling round.

The King's attendants were stricken with fear, and said, "How great must be the power of this fakir when even tigers are under his sway! Let us return while we may!"

But the Rájá answered sternly, "A wise man will finish the enterprise upon which he starts, and only a fool will confess to failure." So he challenged the tiger, and said, "You are indeed a mighty full-grown tiger, but I am a Rájput, therefore let us fight."

Then the tiger uttered a terrific growl which was like the roar of an earthquake, and prepared to spring. But Rasalu fitted a magic arrow to his bow, and the fakir, knowing its power, immediately vanished.

The King entered the house of the famous fakir, whom he found in the midst of his pupils, and who at once rose and made a respectful bow to one who was more powerful than himself.

Rasalu said, "You are a pretty poor fakir to try to outwit me or anyone."

The fakir was irritated and ashamed, and he said, "O King, this is only the abode of poor holy men, and not Gangar, which is the home of the seven famous giants. If you would achieve renown, conquer these, for none will come to you for lording it over fakirs."

To this the Rájá replied, "O fakir, you taunt me. Now, as I am the descendant of the great King Bikrámájit, I make a vow never to return to my home until I have defeated the giants of whom you speak. Tell me how I may find them."

The fakir told him the way, and said, "I pray for your success, and this will come to you if you observe the two following conditions: First, do not draw sword, and next, kill no woman."

So Rájá Rasalu set out for Gangar. Now Gangar was the name also of the mightiest giant of all the seven, and the mountain which was named after him was full of enormous caverns, which were the homes of himself and of his comrades.

In a few days the King arrived, and began to ascend the mountain, but for a long time he searched in vain for the giants. At last he saw one of them carrying water towards the base of a rock and he challenged him. The giant roared so that the stones rattled together and rushed upon Rasalu, who at once fitted an arrow to his bow, let fly, and slew him.

The noise made by the giant roused the others, who came rushing out from their dens. But when they saw that it was King Rasalu who had come against them they were afraid, for they had heard of his might. Then one of them said, "We have been told of your power, but to know whether or not you are worthy to fight with us, let us see you pierce seven plates of iron with your arrow."

Then they set up seven plates of iron, and the King sent his arrow through them all. This wonderful feat filled them with dismay, and they at once turned and fled. But the King pursued them, bow in hand, and with the exception of one only, he slew them all with his invincible arrows.

Rasalu then saw that the remaining giant was a woman, and remembering the second direction of the fakir he put back the arrow which he had already fitted to his bow. He called out, "Stand, woman, I am King Rasalu, and you cannot escape me."

But the giantess replied, "You may indeed capture me, O King, but take notice that in this very country which you have invaded your head shall be smitten from your body."

She then disappeared within a mighty cavern just as Rasalu, urging his horse, made a leap over a great chasm in order to reach her.

The Rájá dismounted, but by this time the giantess was a long way within the mountain. Then he engraved his likeness on the face of the rock inside the entrance of the cave, which he closed by rolling a great stone over its mouth. Escape for her was impossible, and there she remains to this day. At times she endeavours to get out, but as soon as she catches sight of King Rasalu's likeness on the rock she rushes back, filled with dismay, and her roaring fills the villages around with dread.

The Snake Prince

This story has been adapted from a tale originally told by Andrew Lang in The Olive Fairy Book, published in 1907 by Longmans, Green And Co., London And New York. Andrew Lang's Coloured Fairy Books were a series of twelve collections of fairy tales and folk stories from around the world, edited and compiled by Scottish author Andrew Lang. The first volume, The Blue Fairy Book, was published in 1889, followed by eleven more volumes, each with a different colour in the title, such as The Red Fairy Book, The Green Fairy Book, and so on, concluding with The Lilac Fairy Book in 1910.

Once upon a time there lived by herself, in a city, an old woman who was desperately poor. One day she found that she had only a handful of flour left in the house, and no money to buy more nor hope of earning it. Carrying her little brass pot, very sadly she made her way down to the river to bathe and to obtain some water, thinking afterwards to come home and to make herself an unleavened cake of what flour she had left, and after that she did not know what was to become of her.

Whilst she was bathing she left her little brass pot on the riverbank covered with a cloth, to keep the inside nice and clean, but when she came up out of the river and took the cloth off to fill the pot with water, she saw inside it the glittering folds of a deadly snake. At once she popped the cloth again into the mouth of the pot and held it there, and then she said to herself, "Ah, kind death! I will take you home to my house, and there I will shake you out of my pot and you shall bite me and I will die, and then all my troubles will be ended."

With these sad thoughts in her mind the poor old woman hurried home, holding her cloth carefully in the mouth of the pot, and when she got home she shut all the doors and windows, and took away the cloth, and turned the pot upside down upon her hearthstone. What was her surprise to find that, instead of the deadly snake which she expected to see fall out of it, there fell out with a rattle and a clang a most magnificent necklace of flashing jewels!

For a few minutes she could hardly think or speak, but stood staring, and then with trembling hands she picked the necklace up, and folding it in the corner of her veil, she hurried off to the king's hall of public audience.

"A petition, O king!" she said. "A petition for your private ear alone!"

And when her prayer had been granted, and she found herself alone with the king, she shook out her veil at his feet, and there fell from it in glittering coils the splendid necklace. As soon as the king saw it he was filled with amazement and delight, and the more he looked at it the more he felt that he must possess it at once. So he gave the old woman five hundred silver pieces for it, and put it straightway into his pocket. Away she went full of happiness, for the money that the king had given her was enough to keep her for the rest of her life.

As soon as he could leave his business the king hurried off and showed his wife his prize, with which she was as pleased as he, if not more so, and, as soon as they had finished admiring the wonderful necklace, they locked it up in the great chest where the queen's jewellery was kept, the key to which hung always round the king's neck.

A short while afterwards, a neighbouring king sent a message to say that a most lovely girl baby had been born to him, and he invited his neighbours to come to a great feast in honour of the occasion. The queen told her husband that of course they must be present at the banquet, and she would wear the new necklace which he had given her. They had only a short time to prepare for the journey, and at the last moment the king went to the jewel chest to take out the necklace for his wife to wear, but he could see no necklace at all, only, in its place, a fat little boy baby crowing and shouting. The king was so astonished that he nearly fell backwards, but presently he found his voice, and called for his wife so loudly that she came running, thinking that the necklace must at least have been stolen.

"Look here! look!" cried the king, "Haven't we always longed for a son? And now heaven has sent us one!"

"What do you mean?" cried the queen. "Are you mad?"

"Mad? No, I hope not," shouted the king, dancing in excitement round the open chest. "Come here, and look! Look what we've got instead of that necklace!"

Just then the baby let out a great crow of joy, as though he would like to jump up and dance with the king, and the queen gave a cry of surprise, and ran up and looked into the chest.

"Oh!" she gasped, as she looked at the baby, "What a darling! Where could he have come from?'

"I'm sure I can't say," said the king. "All I know is that we locked up a necklace in the chest, and when I unlocked it just now there was no necklace, but a baby, and as fine a baby as ever was seen."

By this time the queen had the baby in her arms. "Oh, the blessed one!" she cried, "Fairer ornament for the bosom of a queen than any necklace that ever was wrought. Write," she continued, "write to our neighbour and say that we cannot come to his feast, for we have a feast of our own, and a baby of our own! Oh, happy day!"

So the visit was given up, and, in honour of the new baby, the bells of the city, and its guns, and its trumpets, and its people, small and great, had hardly any rest for a week, for there was such a ringing, and banging, and blaring, and such fireworks, and feasting, and rejoicing, and merry-making, as had never been seen before.

A few years went by, and, as the king's boy baby and his neighbour's girl baby grew and throve, the two kings arranged that as soon as they were old enough they should marry, and so, with much signing of papers and agreements, and wagging of wise heads, and stroking of grey beards, the compact was made, and signed, and sealed, and lay waiting for its fulfilment. And this too came to pass, for, as soon as the prince and princess were eighteen years of age, the kings agreed that it was time for the wedding, and the young prince journeyed away to the neighbouring kingdom for his bride, and was there married to her with great and renewed rejoicings.

Now, I must tell you that the old woman who had sold the king the necklace had been called in by him to be the nurse of the young prince, and although she loved her charge dearly, and was a most faithful servant, she could not help talking just a little, and so, by-and-by, it began to be rumoured that there was some magic about the young prince's birth, and the rumour of course had come in due time to the ears of the parents of the princess. So now that she was going to be the wife of the prince, her mother (who was curious, as many other people are) said to her daughter on the eve of the ceremony, "Remember that the first thing you must do is to find out what this story is about the prince. And in order to do it, you must not speak a word to him whatever he says until he asks you why you are silent; then you must ask him what the truth is about his magic birth, and until he tells you, you must not speak to him again."

And the princess promised that she would follow her mother's advice.

Therefore when they were married, and the prince spoke to his bride, she did not answer him. He could not think what the matter was, but even about her old home she would not utter a word. At last he asked why she would not speak, and then she said, "Tell me the secret of your birth."

Then the prince was very sad and displeased, and although she pressed him sorely he would not tell her, but always reply, "If I tell you, you will repent that ever you asked me."

For several months they lived together, and it was not such a happy time for either as it ought to have been, for the secret was still a secret, and lay between them like a cloud between the sun and the earth, making what should be fair, dull and sad.

At length the prince could bear it no longer; so he said to his wife one day, "At midnight I will tell you my secret if you still wish it, but you will repent it all your life." However, the princess was overjoyed that she had succeeded, and paid no attention to his warnings.

That night the prince ordered horses to be ready for the princess and himself a little before midnight. He placed her on one, and mounted the other himself, and they rode together down to the river to the place where the old woman had first found the snake in her brass pot. There the prince drew rein and said sadly, "Do you still insist that I should tell you my secret?"

And the princess answered "Yes."

"If I do," answered the prince, "remember that you will regret it all your life."

But the princess only replied, "Tell me!"

"Then," said the prince, "know that I am the son of the king of a far country, but by enchantment I was turned into a snake."

The word 'snake' was hardly out of his lips when he disappeared, and the princess heard a rustle and saw a ripple on the water, and in the faint moonlight she beheld a snake swimming into the river. Soon it disappeared and she was left alone. In vain she waited with beating heart for something to happen, and for the prince to come back to her. Nothing happened and no one came. Only the wind mourned through the trees on the riverbank, and the night birds cried, and a dog howled in the distance, and the river flowed black and silent beneath her.

In the morning they found her, weeping and dishevelled, on the riverbank, but no word could they learn from her or from anyone as to the fate of her husband. At her wish they built on the riverbank a little house of black stone, and there she lived in mourning, with a few servants and guards to watch over her.

A long, long time passed by, and still the princess lived in mourning for her prince, and saw no one, and went nowhere away from her house on the riverbank and the garden that surrounded it. One morning, when she woke up, she found a stain of fresh mud upon the carpet. She sent for the guards, who watched outside the house day and night, and asked them who had entered her room while she was asleep. They declared that no one could have entered, for they kept such careful watch that not even a bird could fly in without their knowledge, but none of them could explain the stain of mud.

The next morning, again, the princess found another stain of wet mud, and she questioned everyone most carefully, but none could say how the mud came there. The third night the princess determined to lie awake herself and watch, and, for fear that she might fall asleep, she cut her finger with a penknife and rubbed salt into the cut, that the pain of it might keep her from sleeping. So she lay awake, and at midnight she saw a snake come wriggling along the ground with some mud from the river in its mouth, and when it came near the bed, it reared up its head and dropped its muddy head on the bedclothes.

She was very frightened, but tried to control her fear, and called out, "Who are you, and what do you want here?"

And the snake answered, "I am the prince, your husband, and I have come to visit you." Then the princess began to weep, and the snake continued, "Alas! Did I not say that if I told you my secret you would repent it? And have you not repented?'

"Oh, indeed!" cried the poor princess, "I have repented it, and shall repent it all my life! Is there nothing I can do?"

And the snake answered, "Yes, there is one thing, if you dared to do it."

"Only tell me," said the princess, "and I will do anything!"

"Then," replied the snake, "on a certain night you must put a large bowl of milk and sugar in each of the four corners of this room. All the snakes in the river will come out to drink the milk, and the one that leads the way will be the queen of the snakes. You must stand in her way at the door, and say, 'Oh, Queen of Snakes, Queen of Snakes, give me back my husband!' and perhaps she will do it. But if you are frightened, and do not stop her, you will never see me again." And he glided away.

On the night specified by the snake, the princess got four large bowls of milk and sugar, and put one in each corner of the room, and stood in the doorway waiting. At midnight there was a great hissing and rustling from the direction of the river, and presently the ground appeared to be alive with horrible writhing forms of snakes, whose eyes glittered and forked tongues quivered as they moved on in the direction of the princess's house. Foremost among them was a huge, repulsive scaly creature that led the dreadful procession.

The guards were so terrified that they all ran away, but the princess stood in the doorway, as white as death, and with her hands clasped tight together for fear she should scream or faint, and fail to do her part. As they came closer and saw her in the way, all the snakes raised their horrid heads and swayed them to and fro, and looked at her with wicked beady eyes, while their breath seemed to poison the very air. Still the princess stood firm, and, when the leading snake was within a few feet of her, she cried, "Oh, Queen of Snakes, Queen of Snakes, give me back my husband!"

Then all the rustling, writhing crowd of snakes seemed to whisper to one another "Her husband? her husband?"

But the queen of snakes moved on until her head was almost in the princess's face, and her little eyes seemed to flash fire. And still the princess stood in the doorway and never moved, but cried again,

"Oh, Queen of Snakes, Queen of Snakes, give me back my husband!"

Then the queen of snakes replied, "Tomorrow you shall have him, tomorrow!'

When she heard these words and knew that she had conquered, the princess staggered from the door, and sank upon her bed and fainted. As in a dream, she saw that her room was full of snakes, all jostling and squabbling over the bowls of milk until it was finished. And then they went away.

In the morning the princess was up early, and took off the mourning dress which she had worn for five whole years, and put on gay and beautiful clothes. And she swept the house and cleaned it, and adorned it with garlands and nosegays of sweet flowers and ferns, and prepared it as though she were making ready for her wedding. And when night fell she lit up the woods and gardens with lanterns, and spread a table as for a feast, and lit in the house a thousand wax candles. Then she waited for her husband, not knowing in what shape he would appear. And at midnight there came striding from the river the prince, laughing, but with tears in his eyes, and she ran to meet him, and threw herself into his arms, crying and laughing too.

So the prince came home, and the next day they two went back to the palace, and the old king wept with joy to see them. And the bells, so long silent, were set a-ringing again, and the guns firing, and the trumpets blaring, and there was fresh feasting and rejoicing.

And the old woman who had been the prince's nurse became nurse to the prince's children. At least she was called 'nurse', though she was far too old to do anything for them but love them. Yet she still thought that she was useful, and knew that she was happy. And happy, indeed, were the prince and princess, who in due time became king and queen, and lived and ruled long and prosperously.

The Old Woman's Cat

This story has been adapted from a tale originally told by Kate Douglas Wiggin and Nora Archibald Smith in The Talking Beasts, published in 1911 by Houghton Mifflin Company. The fables in The Talking Beasts are engaging and entertaining, with whimsical characters and imaginative settings. Through these tales, Wiggin and Smith aimed to stimulate the imagination of children while also instilling important values that promote character development and moral growth.

In former times there lived an old woman in a state of extreme debility. She possessed a cot narrower than the heart of the ignorant and darker than the miser's grave, and a Cat was her companion, which had never seen, even in the mirror of imagination, the face of a loaf, nor had heard from friend or stranger the name of meat. It was content if occasionally it smelt the odour of a mouse from its hole, or saw the print of the foot of one on the surface of a board, and if, on some rare occasion, by the aid of good fortune one fell into its claws, it subsisted a whole week, more or less, on that amount of food.

And, inasmuch as the house of the old woman was the famine-year of that Cat, it was always miserable and thin, and from a distance appeared like an idea.

One day, through excessive weakness, it had, with the utmost difficulty, climbed on the top of the roof. While there it beheld a Cat which walked proudly on the wall of a neighbouring house, and, after the fashion of a destroying lion, advanced with measured steps, and from excessive fat lifted its feet slowly.

When the old woman's Cat witnessed this, it was amazed and exclaimed, "You there, enjoying such luxury, where are you from? It seems you've come from the banquet hall of the Khan of Khata. But why do you look so sleek and strong?"

The Neighbour-Cat replied, "I am the one who feasts on the Sultan's platter. Every morning, I'm at the king's court. When they lay out the invitation tray, I boldly seize some juicy meats and fine flour bread. That's how I spend my days, content until the next."

The old woman's Cat asked, "What's 'fat meat'? And how does fine flour bread taste? All my life, I've only known the old woman's broths and mouse flesh."

The Neighbour-Cat chuckled, "That's why you're no different from a spider. Your appearance is a disgrace to our kind. If you saw the Sultan's court and smelled those delicious foods, you'd transform yourself."

The old woman's Cat pleaded earnestly, "Oh brother, we're bound by neighbourhood and kinship. Why not take me with you this time? Maybe I'll find food through your luck."

Moved by the Cat's desperate plea, the Neighbour-Cat decided not to go to the feast without him. The old woman's Cat felt hopeful hearing this and came down from the roof to inform its owner.

The old woman cautioned the Cat, saying, "Dear companion, don't be swayed by worldly desires. Stay content where you are, for greed only leads to disappointment and emptiness."

But the Cat was fixated on the idea of the Sultan's delicacies. It ignored this advice. The very next day, the old woman's Cat, along with its neighbour, set out for the court. However, before reaching there, misfortune dashed its hopes, and here's what happened…

The day before had been chaotic with cats launching a full-scale assault on the table, creating a commotion that greatly irritated both the guests and their host. Consequently, the Sultan had ordered a squad of archers to lay in wait, ensuring that any cat bold enough to trespass onto the dining area would be met with swift and lethal consequences. For each cat daring enough to flaunt its impudence by venturing into the realm of audacity, the very first morsel it consumed would be met with a liver-piercing arrow.

Unaware of this dire circumstance, the old woman's Cat, driven by its instinctual attraction to the tantalizing aroma of the food, eagerly approached the table like a falcon homing in on its prey. Before it could even indulge in a hearty meal, however, the heart-wrenching agony of an arrow piercing its chest shattered its anticipation.

Oh, dear friend! The sweetness of honey cannot outweigh the pain of the sting. Sometimes, being content with simplicity is a far superior choice than chasing after extravagant desires.

The Monkey's Bargains

This story has been adapted from a tale originally told by William Crooke and W. H. D. Rouse in The Talking Thrush, published in 1899 by E. P. Dutton, New York. Their version of this story is based on an original telling by Rameswar-Puri, a teacher at the, Khairwá village school in Mirzápur district.

ONCE upon a time an old Woman was cooking, and she ran short of fuel. She was so anxious to keep up her fire, that she tore out the hairs of her head, and threw them upon the flame instead of fuel.

A Monkey came capering by, and saw the old Woman at her fire.

"Old Woman," said the Monkey, "why are you burning your hair? Do you want to be bald?"

"O Monkey!" said the old Woman, "I have no fuel, and my fire will go out."

"Shall I get you some fuel, mother?" said the Monkey.

"That's like your kind heart," said the old Woman. "Do get me some fuel, and receive an old Woman's blessing."

The Monkey scampered away to the woods, and brought back a large bundle of sticks. The old Woman piled the dry sticks on the fire, and made a fine blaze. She put on her cooking-plank, and made four cakes.

All this while, the Monkey sat on his tail, and watched her. But when the cakes were done, and gave forth a delightful odour, the Monkey got up on his hind legs, and began dancing and cutting all manner of capers round about the cakes.

"O Monkey," said the old Woman, "why do you caper and dance around my cakes?"

"I gave you fuel," said the Monkey, "and won't you give me a cake?"

It seems to me that she might have thought of that without being asked, but she did not, so the Monkey had to ask for it.

Well, the old Woman gave the Monkey one cake, and the Monkey took his cake in high glee, and capered away.

On the way, he passed by the house of a Potter, and at the door of the Potter's house sat the Potter's son, crying his eyes out.

"What is the matter, little boy?" asked the Monkey.

"I am very hungry," whimpered the Potter's son, "and I have nothing to eat."

"Will a cake be of any use?" asked the kind Monkey.

The Potter's little Boy stretched out his hand, and into his hand the Monkey put his cake. Then the little Boy stopped crying, and ate the cake, but he forgot to say thank you. Perhaps he had never been taught manners, but the Monkey felt sad, because that was not the kind of thing he was used to.

The Potter's little Boy then went into the shop, and brought out four little earthenware pots, and began to play with them. He took no more notice of the Monkey, now that he had eaten his cake, but when the Monkey saw these earthenware pots, he began to dance and cut capers round them, like mad.

"Why are you dancing round my pots?" asked the little Boy. "Are you going to break them, Monkey?"

The Monkey replied, capering about all the while:

"One old Woman, in a fix,

Made me go and gather sticks;

Then she gave me, for the sake

Of the fuel, one sweet cake.

That sweet cake to you I gave:

In return, one pot I crave."

The Potter's little Boy was very much afraid of this dancing and singing Monkey, and perhaps he was a little bit ashamed of his ingratitude, so he gave the Monkey one of his four pots.

Away capered the Monkey, in high glee, carrying his pot. By-and-by he came to a place, where was a Cowherd's wife making curds in a mortar.

"What an odd thing to do, Mrs. Cowherd," said the Monkey. "Have you a fancy for making curds in a mortar?"

"No," said the Cowherd's wife, "but I have nothing better to make my curds in."

"Here's a pot which will do better than a mortar to make curds in," said the Monkey, offering the pot which he had received from the little Boy.

"Thank you, kind Mr. Monkey," said the Cowherd's wife. She took the pot and made curds in it. She took out the curds from the pot, and put them ready for eating, and some butter beside them. The Monkey watched her, sitting upon his tail.

Then the Monkey got up off his tail, and began to dance and cut capers round the curds and the butter.

"Why are you dancing about my butter?" said the Cowherd's wife. "Do you want to spoil it?"

Then the Monkey began to sing, as he capered about:

"One old Woman, in a fix,

Made me go and gather sticks;

Then she gave me, for the sake

Of the fuel, one sweet cake.

Potter's son ate that, and he

Gave a pot instead to me.

Since to you I gave that pot,

Give me butter, will you not?"

The wife of the Cowherd was much pleased with this song, as she was fond of music. "If your kindness," she said, "had not already earned the butter, your pretty song would be worth it." Then she gave him a good lump of butter.

Off went the Monkey in high glee, capering along with the lump of butter wrapped up in a leaf. As he went, he came to another place, where a Cowherd was grazing his kine. The Cowherd was sitting down at that moment, and enjoying his dinner, which consisted of a hunk of dry bread.

"Why do you eat dry bread, Mr. Cowherd?" asked the Monkey. "Are you fasting?"

"I am eating dry bread," said the Cowherd, "because I have nothing to eat with it."

"What do you say to this?" said the Monkey, cutting a caper, and offering to the Cowherd his lump of butter, wrapped up in a leaf.

"Ah," said the Cowherd, "prime." Not another word said he, but spread the butter upon his dry bread, and set to, with much relish.

The Monkey sat on his tail, and watched the Cowherd eating his meal. When the meal was eaten, up jumped the Monkey, and began capering and dancing, hopping and skipping, round and round the herd of kine.

"Ah," said the Bumpkin, "what are you doing that for?" The Bumpkin was so ignorant that he thought the Monkey wanted to bewitch his cattle, and dry up all their milk.

The Monkey went on with his skips and capers, and as he capered, he sang this ditty:

"One old Woman, in a fix,

Made me go and get her sticks;

Then she gave me, for the sake

Of the fuel, one sweet cake.

Potter's son the sweet cake got,

Gave me, in return, one pot.

Cow-wife had the pot, and she

Butter gave instead to me.

This I gave to you just now:

Will you give me, please, one cow?"

"Ah," said the Bumpkin, "'spose I must." He was afraid of the Monkey's spells, and so he gave him a cow.

Away capered the Monkey, in high glee, leading his cow by a string. "I am indeed getting on in the world," he said.

By-and-by, what should he see coming along the road, but the King himself. The King was fastened to the shafts of a cart, which he was slowly dragging along, and jogging by the side of this cart was an ox, and upon the ox sat the Queen. This King had very simple tastes, and so had the Queen.

"O King," said the Monkey, "why are you dragging your cart with your own royal hands?"

"This is the reason, O Monkey!" said the King. "My ox died in the forest, and I drag the cart because this cart will not drag itself."

"Come, sire," said the Monkey, "I don't like to see a King doing draught-work. Take this cow of mine, and welcome."

"Thank you, good and faithful Monkey," said the King. He mopped his brow, and yoked in the cow.

The Monkey began to dance and caper, jump and skip, round the Queen.

"What is the matter, worthy Monkey?" asked the King.

The Monkey began his ditty:

"One old Woman, in a fix,

Made me go and gather sticks;

Then she gave me, for the sake

Of the fuel, one sweet cake.

Potter's son the sweet cake got,

Gave me in its place, one pot.

Cow-wife had the pot, and she

Butter gave instead to me.

Bumpkin ate the butter, then

Paid me with this cow again.

Keep the cow, but don't be mean:

All I ask for, is the Queen."

This seemed reasonable enough, so the King gave his Queen to the Monkey.

Away went the Monkey, capering along, and the Queen walked after (you see the King could not part with his ox as well as the Queen).

By-and-by they came to a Man sewing a button on to his shirt.

"Why, Man," said the Monkey, "why do you sew on your own buttons?"

"Because my wife is dead," said the Man.

"Here is a nice wife for you," said the Monkey. He gave the Queen to the Man. The Monkey then began his capers again, but all he could find to caper about, was a drum.

"You may have that drum, if you like," said the Man. "I only kept it because its voice reminded me of my wife, and now I have another."

"Thank you, thank you!" said the Monkey. "Now I am rich indeed!" Then he began to beat upon the drum, and sang:

"One old Woman, in a fix,

Made me go and gather sticks;

Then she gave me, for the sake

Of the fuel, one sweet cake.

Potter's son the sweet cake got,

Gave me in its place, one pot.

Cow-wife had the pot, and she

Butter gave instead to me.

Bumpkin ate the butter, then

Gave a cow to me again.

King took cow, but was not mean,

For he paid me with a Queen.

Now I have a drum, that's worth

More than any drum on earth.

You are worth a queen, my drum!

Rub-a-dub-dub, dhum dhum dhum!"

So the Monkey capered away into the forest in

high glee, beating upon his drum, and he

has never been heard of since.

The Monkey's Rebuke

This story has been adapted from a tale originally told by William Crooke and W. H. D. Rouse in The Talking Thrush, published in 1899 by E. P. Dutton, New York. Their version of this story is based on an original telling by Lálá Bhawání Dín, a teacher in Majhgáon district, Hamirpur..

IN a certain village, whose name I know (but I think I will keep it to myself), in this village, I say, there was once a Milkman. I daresay you know that a Milkman is a man who sells milk, but I have seen milkmen who also sell water. That is to say, they put water in the milk which they sell, and so they get more money than they deserve. This was the sort of Milkman that my story tells of, and he was worse than the more part of such tricksters, since he actually filled his pans only half full of milk, and the other half all water. The people of that village were so simple and honest, that they never dreamt their Milkman was cheating them, and if the milk did seem thin, all they did was to shake their heads, and say, "What a lot of water the cows do drink this hot weather!"

By watering his milk, this Milkman got together a great deal of money. Ten pounds it was, all in sixpences, because the villagers always bought sixpenny worth of milk a day.

When the Milkman had got ten pounds, that is to say, no less than four hundred silver sixpences, he thought he would go and try his tricks in another place, where there were more people to be cheated. So he put his four hundred silver sixpences in a bag, and set out.

After travelling a while, he came to a pond. He sat down by the pond to eat his breakfast, laying his bag of sixpences by his side, and after breakfast, he proceeded to wash his hands in the pond.

Now it so happened that this was the very pond where the Milkman came to water his milk. He came all this way out of the village because he did not want to be seen by the people of the village. But there was one who saw him, and that was a Monkey, who lived in a tree which overhung the pond. Many a time had this Monkey seen the Milkman pour water into the milk-cans, chuckling over the profit he was to make. This was a very worthy and well-educated Monkey, and he knew just as well as you or I know, that if you sell milk, you should put no water in it. When the Man stooped down to wash his hands in the pond, quietly, quietly down came the Monkey, swinging himself from branch to branch with his tail. Down he came to the ground, and picked up the bag of sixpences, and then up again to his perch in the tree.

The Monkey untied the mouth of the bag, and took out one sixpence, and, click! dropped it into the pond. The Milkman heard a tiny splash, but it did not trouble him, because he thought it was a nut or something that had fallen from the tree. Click! another sixpence. Click! went a third.

By this time the Milkman's hands were dry, and he looked round to pick up his bag and get going on his journey, but there was no bag! Click! click! went the sixpences all this while, and now the Milkman began to look around him. Before long he spied the Monkey sitting on a branch with his beloved bag, and, O horror, dropping sixpences, click, click, click, one after another into the pond.

"I say, you Monkey!" shouted he, "That's my bag! What are you doing? Bring me back my bag!"

"Not yet," said the Monkey, and went on dropping the sixpences, click, click, click!

The Milkman wept, the Milkman tore handfuls of hair out of his head, but the Monkey might have been made of stone for all the notice he took of the Milkman.

At last the Monkey had dropped two hundred sixpences into the pond. Then he tied up the mouth of the money-bag, and threw it down to the Milkman. "There, take your money," said the Monkey.

"And where's the rest of my money?" asked the Milkman, fuming with rage.

"You have all the money that is yours," said the Monkey. "Half of the money was the price of water from this pond, so to the pond I gave it."

The Milkman felt very much ashamed of himself, and went away, a sadder but a wiser man, and never again did he put water in his milk. And that is why I have not told you the name of the village where he lived, for now that he has turned over a new leaf, it would hardly be fair to rake up his old misdeeds against him.

Life's Secret

This story has been adapted from a tale originally told by Katharine Pyle in Tales Of Folk And Fairies, published in 1929 by Little, Brown And Company, Boston. Tales of Folk and Fairies is renowned for its timeless storytelling, whimsical characters, and beautiful illustrations.

In a far-off country there once lived a great Rajah who had two wives, one named Duo and the other Suo. Both these Ranees were beautiful, but Duo was of a harsh and cruel nature, while Suo was gentle and kind to all.

Though the Rajah had been married to his Ranees for some time they neither of them had any children, and this was a great grief to everyone. Daily prayers were offered up in the temples for the birth of a son to the Rajah, but the prayers remained unanswered.

One day a beggar, a holy man who had vowed to live in poverty, came to the palace asking for alms. Duo would have had him driven away, but Suo felt compassion for him. She gave him the alms he asked and bade him sit in the cool of the courtyard to rest.

The beggar thanked her and ate the food she gave him. Just before he left, he asked to speak to her in private. This favour Suo granted him. She stepped aside with him, and as it so happened this brought them directly under the windows of Duo's apartments.

"Great Ranee, you have been very kind to me," said the beggar, "and I wish to reward you. I know that for years you have desired to have a son, but that this wish has not been granted. Now listen! In the midst of the jungle over beyond the city there grows the most wonderful tree in all the world. Its trunk is silver, and its leaves are of gold. Once in every hundred years this tree bears a single crimson fruit. She who eats this fruit, whosoever she may be, shall, within a year, bear a son. This is that hundredth year, the year in which the tree bears fruit, and I have gathered that fruit and have it here."

So saying, the beggar drew from among his rags a piece of silk embroidered with strange figures. This he unfolded, and showed to the Ranee, lying within it, a strange fruit such as she had never seen before. It was pear shaped, and of such a vivid red that it seemed to pulse and glow with light.

Suo looked at it with wonder and awe.

"If you wish to have it, it is yours," the beggar continued. "But I must tell you one other thing. Whoever eats this fruit shall indeed bear a son, but he will not be as other children. His life will not be altogether within himself as with other people, for it will be bound up with an object quite outside of himself. If this object should fall into the hands of an enemy that enemy could, by willing it, bring upon him misfortune or even death, and this no matter how closely the child was watched and guarded. And now, knowing this, do you still wish to eat the fruit?"

"Yes, yes!" cried Suo.

"Then I will tell you what this object is and where it is to be found," said the beggar. He drew still closer to the Ranee and whispered in her ear, but though what he told her was so important Suo paid but little attention to it. She thought only of the fruit, and the happiness that might come to her if she ate it.

Now all the while the beggar had been talking to Suo, Duo had been seated at her window just above them, and she overheard all that was said. Only when the beggar came closer to Suo and whispered in her ear Duo could not hear what he said, though she leaned out as far as she could and strained her ears to listen. So, though she had learned that if Suo had a child its life would depend on some object outside of itself, she did not learn what that object was.

The beggar now gave the fruit to Suo, and she took it and ate all of it. Not one seed or bit of rind did she miss. After that she went back to her own apartments to dream upon the joy that might be coming to her.

Within the year, even as the beggar had promised, Suo bore a child, and this child was so large and strong and handsome that he was the wonder of all who saw him.

The Rajah was wild with joy. He could scarcely think or talk of anything but his son, and he showered gifts and caresses upon the happy mother. Duo was quite forgotten. He never even went near her apartments, and her heart was filled with jealousy and hatred toward Suo and the little prince Dalim Kumar, for so the child was named. Nothing would have given her more joy than to be able to injure them and bring sorrow and misfortune upon them.

Now as Dalim Kumar grew older he became very fond of a flock of pigeons that his father had given him, and he spent a great deal of time playing with them in the courtyard. They were so tame they would come at his call and light upon his head and shoulders. Sometimes they flew in through the windows of Duo's apartments which overlooked the courtyard. Duo scattered peas and grain on the floor for them, and they came and ate them. Then one day she caught two or three of them.

Soon after Dalim Kumar missed his pigeons and began calling them.

Duo leaned from her window. "Your pigeons are up here," she cried. "If you want them you must come up and get them."

Suo had forbidden her son to go to Duo's apartments, but he quite forgot this in his eagerness to regain his pets, and he at once ran up to the Ranee's apartments.

Duo took him by the wrist and drew him into her room. "You shall have your pigeons again," she said, "but first there is something you must tell me."

"What is it?" asked Dalim Kumar.

"I wish to know where your life lies and in what object it is bound up."

Dalim Kumar was very much surprised. "I do not know what you mean," he said. "My life lies within me, in my head and my body and my limbs, as it is with everyone."

"No, that is not so," said Duo. "Has your mother never told you that your life is bound up in something outside of yourself?"

"No, she has never told me that, and moreover I do not believe it."

"Nevertheless it is so," said Duo. "If you find out what this thing is, then come and tell me and you shall have your pigeons again, and if you do not do this I will wring their necks."

Dalim Kumar was greatly troubled at the thought of harm coming to his pigeons. "No, no! You must not do that," he cried. "I will go to my mother and find out what she knows, and if there is indeed truth in what you say I will come back at once and tell you the secret. But you must do nothing to my pigeons while I am gone."

To this Duo agreed. "There is another thing you must promise," she said. "You must not let your mother know I have asked you anything about your life. If you do I will wring your pigeons' necks even though you tell me the secret."

"I will not let her know," promised the boy, and then he hastened away to his mother's apartments. When he came to the door he began to walk slowly and with dragging steps. He entered in and threw himself down among some cushions and closed his eyes.

"What ails you, my son?" asked his mother. "Why do you sit there so quietly instead of playing about?"

"Nothing ails me now," answered the boy, "but there is something that I wish to know, and unless you tell me I am sure I shall be quite ill."

"What is it that you wish to know, my darling?"

"I wish to know where my life lies, and in what it is bound up," answered the boy.

When Suo heard this she was very much frightened.

"What do you mean?" she cried. "Who has been talking to you of your life?"

Then Dalim said what was not true, for he feared that harm might come to his pigeons. "No one has been talking to me," he said, "but I am sure that my life lies somewhere outside of me, and if you will not tell me about it I will neither eat nor drink, and then perhaps I may die."

At last Suo could withstand him no longer. "My son," she said, "it is as you have guessed. You are not as other children. Your life is bound up in some object outside of yourself, and if this object should fall into the hands of an enemy the greatest misfortunes might come upon you, and perhaps even death."

"And what is this object?" asked the boy.

Again Suo hesitated. Then she said, "The beggar told me that under the roots of that same tree that bore the fruit lies buried a golden necklace, and it is with that necklace that part of your life is bound up."

Now that Dalim Kumar knew the secret he was content, and smiled upon his mother and caressed her, and ate some of the sweetmeats she had prepared for him. Then he ran away to get his pigeons.

Duo was waiting for him impatiently. "Have you found out the secret of your life?" she demanded.

"Yes," answered the Prince. "It is bound up in a golden necklace that lies buried under the roots of a tree over in the jungle, a tree with a silver trunk and golden leaves. And now give me my pigeons."

Duo was very willing to do this, for she had no longer any use for them. She placed the cage in which she had put them in his hands and pushed him impatiently from the room.

As soon as the boy had gone the Ranee sent for a man upon whom she could depend and told him what she wished him to do. She wished him to go into the jungle and search until he found a tree with a silver trunk and golden leaves. He was then to dig down about its roots until he found a golden necklace that lay buried there. This necklace he was to bring to her, and in return for his services she would give him a lac of gold mohurs.

The man willingly agreed to do as she wished and at once set out into the jungle. After searching for some time he at last found the tree and began to dig about its roots.

Now at the very time this happened Dalim Kumar was with his mother playing about in her apartment. But no sooner did the man in the jungle begin to dig about the tree than the boy gave a cry and laid his hand upon his heart. At the same time he became very pale.

"What is the matter, my son?" cried his mother anxiously. "Are you ill?"

"I do not know what the matter is," answered the Prince, "but something threatens me."

His mother put her arm about him, and at the very moment she did so the man who had been digging found the necklace and picked it up, and at that the young Prince sank back senseless in his mother's arms.

The Ranee was terrified. She sent at once for the Rajah, and physicians were called in, but none of them could arouse the child nor could they tell what ailed him. He lay there among the cushions where they had placed him still breathing, but unconscious of all around him.

And so the boy lay all the while that the man with the necklace hidden in his bosom was on his way back from the jungle. But when he reached the apartments of Duo and gave the necklace into the hands of the evil Ranee, the breath went out from the Prince's body, and he became as one dead.

The Rajah was in despair. His grief was now as great as his joy had been when the child was born. He had a magnificent temple built in the most beautiful of all his gardens, and in this temple the body of

Dalim Kumar was laid. After this was done the Rajah commanded that the gates of the garden should be locked, and that no one but the gardeners should ever enter there on pain of death.

This command was carried out. The garden gates were kept locked, and no one entered but the men who went there in the daytime to prune the trees and water the flowers and keep the place in order. Not even Suo might go into the garden to mourn beside the body of her son.

But though everyone believed Dalim Kumar to be dead, such was not really the case. All day, while Duo wore the necklace, he lay without breath or sign of life, but in the evening, when the Ranee took the necklace off, he revived and returned to life. And this happened every night, for every night the Rajah came to visit Duo, and just before he came she always took the necklace off and hid it. She feared if he saw it he might wonder and question her about it.

The wicked Ranee was now satisfied and happy. She believed she had destroyed the young Prince, and with him the Rajah's love for Suo. For the Rajah now never went to Suo's apartments. He neither saw her nor spoke of her, for she only reminded him of his grief for his son.

Now the first time that Dalim Kumar awoke in the temple he was very much surprised to find himself alone in a strange place, and with no attendants around him. He arose and went out into the garden, and then at once he knew where he was, though the temple was new to him. He went to one gate after another of the garden, intending to go and return to the palace, but he found them all locked. The gardeners had gone away for the night, and before going they had securely fastened the gates, according to the Rajah's orders. The young prince called and called, but no one heard or answered.

Feeling hungry, he plucked some fruit and ate it, and after that he amused himself as best he could, playing about among the trees and flowers.

Toward morning he felt sleepy and returned to the temple. He lay down upon the couch, and later on, when Duo again put on the necklace, his breath left him, and he became as one dead.

As it had been that night, so it was also in the many nights that followed. In the evening the Prince revived and came out to play among the flowers, but with the coming of day he returned to the temple and lay down on the couch, and all appearance of life left him. After a time he became used to the strange life he led, and no longer wondered why he was left there alone and why no one came to seek him.

So year after year slipped by, and from a child the Prince became a youth, and in all that time he had seen no one, for the gardeners had always gone away before he returned to life.

Now there lived at this time, in a country far away, a woman who had one only child, a daughter named Surai Bai. This girl was so beautiful that she was the wonder of all who saw her. Her hair was as black as night, her eyes like stars, her teeth like pearls, and her lips as red as ripe pomegranates.

When this child was born it was foretold to her mother that she would sometime marry a Prince who was both alive and dead. This prophecy frightened the mother so much that as soon as her daughter was of a marriageable age she left her own country and journeyed away into a far land, taking the girl with her. She hoped that if she went far enough she might escape the fate that had been foretold for the child.

Journeying on from one place to another, she came at last to the city where Dalim Kumar's father reigned, and where the garden was, and the temple where the young prince lay.

It was toward evening when the mother and daughter reached the city, and it was necessary for them to find some shelter for the night. Surai Bai was weary, and her mother bade her sit down and rest by the gate of one of the palace gardens while she went farther to seek a lodging. As soon as she had found a place where they could stay she would return for the girl.

So Surai Bai seated herself beside the gate, and there her mother left her. But the mother had not been gone long when some noise farther up the street frightened the girl. She looked about for a place to hide, and it occurred to her that she might go into the garden and wait there. She tried the gate and found it unfastened, for by some chance one of the gardeners had forgotten to lock it that evening when he went away.

Surai Bai pushed the gate open and stepped inside, closing it behind her. When she looked about her, she was amazed at the beauty of the garden. The fruit trees were laden with fruits of every kind. There were winding paths and flowers and fountains, and in the midst of the garden was a temple shining with gold and wondrous colours.

Though daylight had faded the moon had arisen, and the garden was full of light. Surai Bai went over to the temple, wishing to examine it, but just as she reached the foot of the steps that led up to it a young man appeared above her at the door of the temple. It was Dalim Kumar, who had aroused again to life and was coming forth to breathe the air of the garden.

When he saw Surai Bai he stood amazed, not only at her beauty, which was so great, but because hers was the first face he had ever seen in the years he had spent in the garden. As for Surai Bai, never before had she beheld a youth so handsome, or with such a noble air, and as the two stood looking at each other they became filled with love for one another.

Presently Dalim Kumar came down the steps of the temple and took Surai Bai's hand. "Who are you, beautiful one?" he asked. "Where have you come from, and what is your name?"

"My name is Surai Bai," answered the girl, "and I come from another country far away. My mother left me sitting by the gate while she went to find a lodging for us, but some noise frightened me, and I ran in here to hide."

"That is a strange thing," said the Prince. "In all the years I have been living here, the gates have never been unlocked before."

"But do you live here alone?" asked the girl.

"Yes, all alone. Yours is the first face I have seen for years, and yet I am a Prince, and the son of a great Rajah."

"Then why are you here?"

"I am here because my life was bound up in a golden necklace that lay buried under the roots of a tree in the jungle. I told the secret to a Ranee who was my enemy, though I did not know it at the time. She must in some way have gained possession of the necklace, and now she is using it for my harm. All day I lie there in the temple as though dead. No sound reaches me, and nothing arouses me. Only at night can I arise and come forth. I, a great prince, am as one both dead and alive."

When Dalim Kumar pronounced these words Surai Bai could not refrain from giving a loud cry. She was overcome with amazement and confusion.

The Prince at once wished to know what had moved her so. "Why do you cry out and change colour?" he asked. "And why do you tremble and look at me so strangely?"

At first Surai Bai would not tell him, but he was so urgent in his questioning that finally she was obliged to recount to him the prophecy made at the time of her birth. She told him that it had been foretold of her that she was to marry a Prince who was both alive and dead.

Dalim Kumar listened to her attentively. "That is a strange thing," he said. "I do not suppose in all the world there is another prince beside myself who is both alive and dead. If this saying is true, it must be that I am the one you are to marry. If so, I am very happy, for already I love you, and if you will stay here with me we will be married by the ceremony of Grandharva, and I will be a true and loving husband to you."

To this Surai Bai willingly consented, for already she loved the prince so dearly that she felt she could not live without him. That very night she and the Prince presented each other with garlands of flowers, for that is the ceremony of Grandharva, and so they became man and wife.

After that they lived together in great happiness, and nothing could exceed their love for each other. By day, while Dalim Kumar lay lifeless in the temple, his bride slept also, and at evening they awoke and talked together and walked through the garden.

But after a while a son was born to the young couple, and after that Surai Bai was no longer gay and happy. Her look was sad, and often she stole away from Dalim Kumar to weep in secret.

The Prince was greatly troubled by this. At first he forbore to question her, but one day he followed her and finding her in tears, he said, "Tell me, why are you sad and downcast? Have you wearied of this garden, and are you lonely here, or is it that you no longer love me?"

"Dalim Kumar," answered the girl, "I love you as dearly as ever, and I am never lonely with you. As long as we had no child I was content to stay here in the garden and see no one. But now that we have a son I wish him to be seen by your people, and I wish them to know that he is the heir to the kingdom."

At this Dalim Kumar became very thoughtful. "My dear wife," he said, "you are right. Our son should be known as my heir, but everyone believes I died long ago when I was a child. If you went out among them with the boy and told them he was my son, they would laugh at you, and either think you were an impostor or that you were crazy. If we could but gain possession of the necklace, then I could go out from the garden with you, and if I showed myself to my people they would be obliged to believe."

"That is what I have thought also," said Surai Bai, "and it has been in my mind to ask you to give me permission to leave the garden for a while. If you do this I will try to gain entrance to the palace and the apartments of Duo. Then possibly I can find where she keeps the necklace at night, and I may be able to get possession of it."

Dalim Kumar eagerly agreed to this plan, and the very next day, while he lay unconscious in the temple, Surai Bai took the child and managed to steal out through one of the gates without being seen by any of the gardeners.

She at once sought out a shop in the city and bought for herself the dress of a hairdresser. Then, leading the child by the hand she made her way to the palace. She told the attendants there that she was very skilful in dressing the hair, and if they would take her to the Ranees she was sure she could please them.

After some hesitation the attendants agreed to do this, and led the way first to the apartments of Suo. When Surai Bai entered the room and saw her husband's mother sitting there thin and pale and grief-stricken, her heart yearned over her.

But Suo would not so much as look at the pretended hairdresser. "Why do you bring her here?" she asked. "I have no wish to look beautiful. My son is dead and my husband no longer loves me nor comes to me. Take her away and leave me alone with my sorrow."

The attendants motioned to Surai Bai to come away, and they led her across the palace to the apartments of Duo. Here all was bright and joyous. The beautiful Duo lay among the cushions, smiling to herself and playing with the necklace that hung about her neck. When she heard that the young woman they had brought to her was a skilled hairdresser, she sat up and beckoned Surai Bai to approach.

"Come!" she said. "Let us see how well you can dress my hair. The Rajah will be here before long, and I must be beautiful for him."

Surai Bai at once came behind Duo and began to arrange her hair. The child meanwhile kept close by her side. When Surai Bai had almost finished she managed to loosen the clasp of the necklace so that it slipped from Duo's neck and fell upon the floor.

This was as the pretended hairdresser had planned, and she had explained to her son beforehand that when the necklace fell he must pick it up and hold it tight, and yield it to no one. So now, no sooner did the necklace slip to the floor, than the child picked it up and twisted it tight around his fingers.

Duo was frightened. "Give me my necklace," cried she, and reaching over she tried to take it from the boy, but at this he began to scream so loudly that it seemed as though the whole palace must be aroused by his cries.

Duo drew back alarmed and bade the child be quiet. Then she turned to the pretended hairdresser. "Make him give me the necklace again," she demanded.

Surai Bai pretended to hesitate. "If I try to take it from him now," she said, "he might break it. Have patience, and let him keep it for a while, for he will soon tire of it. Then I can take it from him and bring it to you."

To this Duo was obliged to agree. It was growing late and she feared at any moment now the Rajah might come in and that he might notice the necklace in the child's hands and ask questions about it.

"Very well," she said. "Let him keep it for the present, but bring it back to me the first thing in the morning. If you neglect to do this you shall be severely punished, you and the child also."

The pretended hairdresser made a deep obeisance, and then departed, carrying the child who still held the necklace tightly clutched in his hands.

As soon as Surai Bai was outside of the palace she hastened away to the garden and found Dalim Kumar awaiting her at the gate.

"I know you have the necklace," he cried to her, "for I aroused while it was still day, and with such a feeling of life and joy as I have never felt before."

"Yes, it is here," said Surai Bai, and she took the necklace from the child and held it out to him.

Dalim Kumar gave a cry of joy. His hands trembled with eagerness as he grasped the necklace. "Oh, my dear wife," he cried, "you have saved me. I have now again become as other men and can claim what is my own. Come! Let us return to the palace and to my father and mother."

So, with the child on his arm, and leading Surai Bai by the hand, the Prince hastened back to the palace. But when he entered the gates no one knew him, for when they had last seen him he had been only a boy. They wondered to see a stranger enter in like a master, but his air was so noble, and his appearance so handsome that no one dared to stop him.

Dalim Kumar went at once to his mother's apartments, and though no one else had known him, she recognized him at once, even though he had become a man. She knew not what miracle had brought him back, but she fell upon his neck and kissed him, and wept aloud, so that all in the palace heard the sound of her weeping.

The Rajah was sent for in haste, and when he came Dalim Kumar quickly made himself known to his father. The Rajah's joy was no less than the Ranee's over the return of his son. Soon the news spread through all the palace, and there was great rejoicing. But Duo was filled with fear. She knew not what punishment would fall upon her for her evil doings, but she guessed the wrath of the Rajah would be great. So she fled away secretly, and for a long time she wandered about from place to place, miserable and afraid, and at last died in poverty as she deserved.

Dalim Kumar and his young wife lived in happiness forever after, and when the old Rajah died Dalim Kumar became Rajah in his stead, and his own son ruled after him.

The Story Of The Three Deaf Men

This story has been adapted from a tale originally told by Mrs. Howard Kingscote and Pandit Natêsá Sástrî in Tales Of The Sun, published in 1890 by H. Allen & Co., London and Calcutta. The book contains a selection of tales from Indian mythology and folklore, centred around the theme of the sun. These tales often revolve around various deities associated with the sun, such as Surya, the solar deity in Hinduism.

When any awkward blunder occurs from a person acting under a mistaken notion, there is a common proverb in Tamil to the effect that the matter ended like the story of the three deaf men (Muchchevidan kadaiyây mudindadu). The following is the story told to explain the allusion.

In a remote village there lived a husband and wife. Both of them were quite deaf. They had made this household arrangement, namely, to cook cabbage with tamarind and soup without tamarind one day, and cabbage without tamarind and soup with tamarind on the other. Thus on every alternate day the same dishes were repeated. One day, when taking his meal, the husband found the tamarind cabbage so very tasty that he wanted to have it also next day, and gave instructions to that effect. The deaf wife did not understand the order. According to the established rule she cooked cabbage without tamarind next day. The husband, when he sat down to his meal, found his order disregarded and, being enraged, threw the cabbage against the wall, and went out in a rage. The wife ate her fill, and prepared the next day's tamarind cabbage for her husband.

The husband went out, and sat down in a place where three roads crossed, to calm down his anger. At that time a shepherd happened to pass that way. He had lately lost a good cow and calf of his, and had been seeking them for some days. When he saw the deaf man sitting by the way, he took him for a soothsayer, and asked him to find out by his knowledge of Jôsyam where the cow was likely to be found. The herdsman, too, was very deaf, and the man, without hearing what he was saying, abused him, and wished to be left undisturbed.

In abusing him the husband stretched out his hand, pointing to the shepherd's face. This pointing the shepherd understood to indicate the direction where the lost cow and calf would be found. Thus thinking the poor shepherd went on in that direction, promising to present the soothsayer with the calf if he found it there with the cow. To his joy, and by mere chance, he found them. His delight knew no bounds.

"That is a capital soothsayer. Surely I must present him with the calf." So thought he to himself, and returned with them to the deaf man, and, pointing to the calf, requested him to accept it.

Now it unfortunately happened that the calf's tail was broken and crooked. The man thought the herdsman was blaming him unreasonably for having broken the calf's tail, while he knew nothing about it, and so, by a wave of his hand, denied the charge. This the shepherd mistook for a refusal of the calf, and a demand for the cow.

The shepherd said, "How very greedy you are! I promised you only the calf, and not the cow."

The husband said, "Never; I know nothing of either your cow or calf. I never broke the calf's tail. Some other must have done it."

Thus they quarrelled, without understanding each other, for a long time, when a third party happened to pass by. Understanding the cause of the dispute, and, desiring to profit by their stupidity, he interfered, and said in a loud voice, and yet so as not to be heard by the deaf husband, "Well, shepherd, you had better go away with the cow. These soothsayers are always greedy. Leave the calf with me, and I shall make him accept it."

The shepherd, much pleased to have secured the cow, walked home, leaving the calf with the third person. When the shepherd had gone, the passenger said to the deaf man, "You see how very unlawful it is for the shepherd to charge you with an offence which you never committed. It is always the case with shepherds. They are the biggest fools in the world! But never mind, so long as you have a friend in me. I shall somehow explain to him your innocence, and restore the calf to him."

The husband, much pleased, ran home to escape from the consequences of supposed guilt. At the expense of the stupidity and deafness of both, the third traveller walked home with the calf.

The husband, on his return, sat down to his dinner, and his wife served him the tamarind cabbage. He happened to put his finger to the place where the cabbage without tamarind had previously been served on the leaf. On applying it to his mouth, he found it so very sweet that he demanded that dish again. The wife replied to him that she had already emptied the pan. "Then at least bring me the cabbage that is sticking to the saucepan," said the husband, and the wife did accordingly.

Here ends the story. The latter portion is also said to be the explanation of a proverb that is prevalent in Tamil: "Sevuru kîraiyai valichchu pôdudi sunaiketta mûli," meaning, "O you feelingless deaf woman, give me at least the cabbage that is sticking to the saucepan." This proverb is applied to stubborn wives, who will have their own way, and do not obey their husbands submissively in unrefined society.

The Jogi's Punishment

This story has been adapted from a tale originally told by Andrew Lang in The Lilac Fairy Book, published in 1910 by Longmans, Green And Co., London And New York. Andrew Lang's Coloured Fairy Books were a series of twelve collections of fairy tales and folk stories from around the world, edited and compiled by Scottish author Andrew Lang. The first volume, The Blue Fairy Book, was published in 1889, followed by eleven more volumes, each with a different colour in the title, such as The Red Fairy Book, The Green Fairy Book, and so on, concluding with The Lilac Fairy Book in 1910. This story was based on a story originally told by Major Campbell, Feroshepore

Once upon a time there came to the ancient city of Rahmatabad a jogi, a Hindu holy man, of holy appearance, who took up his abode under a tree outside the city, where he would sit for days at a time fasting from food and drink, motionless except for the fingers that turned restlessly his string of beads. The fame of such holiness as this soon spread, and daily the citizens would flock to see him, eager to get his blessing, to watch his devotions, or to hear his teaching, if he were in the mood to speak. Very soon the Rajah himself heard of the jogi, and began regularly to visit him to seek his counsel and to ask his prayers that a son might be vouchsafed to him. Days passed by, and at last the Rajah became so possessed with the thought of the holy man that he determined if possible to get him all to himself. So he built in the neighbourhood a little shrine, with a room or two added to it, and a small courtyard closely walled up, and, when all was ready, asked the jogi to occupy it, and to receive no other visitors except himself and his queen and such pupils as the jogi might choose, who would hand down his teaching. To this the jogi consented, and thus he lived for some time upon the king's bounty, whilst the fame of his godliness grew day by day.

Now, although the Rajah of Rahmatabad had no son, he possessed a daughter, who as she grew up became the most beautiful creature that eye ever rested upon. Her father had long before betrothed her to the son of the neighbouring Rajah of Dilaram, but as yet she had not been married to him, and lived the quiet life proper to a maiden of her beauty and position. The princess had of course heard of the holy man and of his miracles and his fasting, and she was filled with curiosity to see and to speak to him, but this was difficult, since she was not allowed to go out except into the palace grounds, and then was always closely guarded. However, at length she found an opportunity, and made her way one evening alone to the hermit's shrine.

Unhappily, the hermit was not really as holy as he seemed, for no sooner did he see the princess than he fell in love with her wonderful beauty, and began to plot in his heart how he could win her for his wife. But the maiden was not only beautiful, but she was also shrewd, and as soon as she read in the glance of the jogi the love that filled his soul, she sprang to her feet, and, gathering her veil about her, ran from the place as fast as she could. The jogi tried to follow, but he was no match for her, so, beside himself with rage at finding that he could not overtake her, he flung at her a lance, which wounded her in the leg. The brave princess stooped for a second to pluck the lance out of the wound, and then ran on until she found herself safe at home again. There she bathed and bound up the wound secretly, and told no one how naughty she had been, for she knew that her father would punish her severely.

Next day, when the king went to visit the jogi, the holy man would neither speak to nor look at him.

"What is the matter?" asked the king. "Won't you speak to me today?"

"I have nothing to say that you would care to hear," answered the jogi.

"Why?" said the king. "Surely you know that I value all that you say, whatever it may be."

But still the jogi sat with his face turned away, and the more the king pressed him the more silent and mysterious he became. At last, after much persuasion, he said, "Let me tell you, then, that there is in this city a creature which, if you do not put an end to it, will kill every single person in the place."

The king, who was easily frightened, grew pale. "What?" he gasped. "What is this dreadful thing? How am I to know it and to catch it? Only counsel me and help me, and I will do all that you advise."

"Ah!" replied the jogi, "it is indeed dreadful. It is in the shape of a beautiful girl, but it is really an evil spirit. Last evening it came to visit me, and when I looked upon it its beauty faded into hideousness, its teeth became horrible fangs, its eyes glared like coals of fire, great claws sprang from its slender fingers, and were I not what I am it might have consumed me."

The king could hardly speak from alarm, but at last he said, "How am I to distinguish this awful thing when I see it?"

"Search," said the jogi, "for a lovely girl with a lance wound in her leg, and when she is found secure her safely and come and tell me, and I will advise you what to do next."

Away hurried the king, and soon set all his soldiers scouring the country for a girl with a lance wound in her leg. For two days the search went on, and then it was somehow discovered that the only person with a lance wound in the leg was the princess herself. The king, greatly agitated, went off to tell the jogi, and to assure him that there must be some mistake. But of course the jogi was prepared for this, and had his answer ready.

"She is not really your daughter, who was stolen away at her birth, but an evil spirit that has taken her form," he said solemnly. "You can do what you like, but if you don't take my advice she will kill you all."

And so solemn he appeared, and so unshaken in his confidence, that the king's wisdom was blinded, and he declared that he would do whatever the jogi advised, and believe whatever he said. So the jogi directed him to send him secretly two carpenters, and when they arrived he set them to make a great chest, so cunningly jointed and put together that neither air nor water could penetrate it. There and then the chest was made, and, when it was ready, the jogi bade the king to bring the princess by night, and they two thrust the poor little maiden into the chest and fastened it down with long nails, and between them carried it to the river and pushed it out into the stream.

As soon as the jogi got back from this deed he called two of his pupils, and pretended that it had been revealed to him that there should be found floating on the river a chest with something of great price within it, and he bade them go and watch for it at such a place far down the stream, and when the chest came slowly along, bobbing and turning in the tide, they were to seize it and secretly and swiftly bring it to him, for he was now determined to put the princess to death himself. The pupils set off at once, wondering at the strangeness of their errand, and still more at the holiness of the jogi to whom such secrets were revealed.

It happened that, as the next morning was dawning, the gallant young prince of Dilaram was hunting by the banks of the river, with a great following of viziers, attendants, and huntsmen, and as he rode he saw floating on the river a large chest, which came slowly along, bobbing and turning in the tide. Raising himself in his saddle, he gave an order, and half a dozen men plunged into the water and drew the chest out on to the riverbank, where everyone crowded around to see what it could contain. The prince was certainly not the least curious among them, but he was a cautious young man, and, as he prepared to open the chest himself, he bade all but a few stand back, and these few to draw their swords, so as to be prepared in case the chest should hold some evil beast, or djinn, or giant. When all were ready and expectant, the prince with his dagger forced open the lid and flung it back, and there lay, living and breathing, the loveliest maiden he had ever seen in his life.

Although she was half stifled from her confinement in the chest, the princess speedily revived, and, when she was able to sit up, the prince began to question her as to who she was and how she came to be shut up in the chest and set afloat upon the water, and she, blushing and trembling to find herself in the presence of so many strangers, told him that she was the princess of Rahmatabad, and that she had been put into the chest by her own father.

When he on his part told her that he was the prince of Dilaram, the astonishment of the young people was unbounded to find that they, who had been betrothed without ever having seen one another, should have actually met for the first time in such strange circumstances. In fact, the prince was so moved by her beauty and modest ways that he called up his viziers and demanded to be married at once to this lovely lady who had so completely won his heart. And married they were then and there upon the riverbank, and went home to the prince's palace, where, when the story was told, they were welcomed by the old Rajah, the prince's father, and the remainder of the day was given over to feasting and rejoicing. But when the banquet was over, the bride told her husband that now, on the threshold of their married life, she had more to relate of her adventures than he had given her the opportunity to tell as yet, and then, without hiding anything, she informed him of all that happened to her from the time she had stolen out to visit the wicked jogi.

In the morning the prince called his chief vizier and ordered him to shut up in the chest in which the princess had been found a great monkey that lived chained up in the palace, and to take the chest back to the river and set it afloat once more and watch what became of it. So the monkey was caught and put into the chest, and some of the prince's servants took it down to the river and pushed it off into the water. Then they followed secretly a long way off to see what became of it.

Meanwhile the jogi's two pupils watched and watched for the chest until they were nearly tired of watching, and were beginning to wonder whether the jogi was right after all, when on the second day they spied the great chest coming floating on the river, slowly bobbing and turning in the tide, and instantly a great joy and exultation seized them, for they thought that here indeed was further proof of the wonderful wisdom of their master. With some difficulty they secured the chest, and carried it back as swiftly and secretly as possible to the jogi's house. As soon as they brought in the chest, the jogi, who had been getting very cross and impatient, told them to put it down, and to go outside whilst he opened the magic chest.

"And even if you hear cries and sounds, however alarming, you must on no account enter," said the jogi, walking over to a closet where lay the silken cord that was to strangle the princess.

And the two pupils did as they were told, and went outside and shut close all the doors. Presently they heard a great outcry within and the jogi's voice crying aloud for help, but they dared not enter, for had they not been told that whatever the noise, they must not come in? So they sat outside, waiting and wondering, and at last all grew still and quiet, and remained so for such a long time that they determined to enter and see if all was well. No sooner had they opened the door leading into the courtyard than they were nearly bowled over by a huge monkey that came leaping straight to the doorway and escaped past them into the open fields. Then they stepped into the room, and there they saw the jogi's body lying torn to pieces on the threshold of his dwelling!

Very soon the story spread, as stories will, and reached the ears of the princess and her husband, and when she knew that her enemy was dead she made her peace with her father.

The Sparrows and the Falcon

This story has been adapted from a tale originally told by Kate Douglas Wiggin and Nora Archibald Smith in The Talking Beasts, published in 1911 by Houghton Mifflin Company. The fables in The Talking Beasts are engaging and entertaining, with whimsical characters and imaginative settings. Through these tales, Wiggin and Smith aimed to stimulate the imagination of children while also instilling important values that promote character development and moral growth.

Two sparrows once built their nest on a tree branch, and they had enough water and grain to meet their needs. However, on a nearby mountain summit, there lived a falcon that would swiftly swoop down like lightning to snatch the weaker birds and devour them. Whenever the sparrows had young ones ready to leave the nest, the falcon would ambush them and take them away to feed its own chicks. The sparrows couldn't leave their nest due to their instinctive attachment to home, yet staying there was challenging because of the cruel falcon.

One day, when their young ones had grown feathers and wings and were strong enough to fly, the parents were delighted to see them attempting to take flight. But suddenly, they were overcome with worry as they remembered the threat of the falcon, and they began to lament their situation.

One of their children, who bore the signs of mature wisdom in his expression, noticed his parents' distress and asked them what was wrong. They told him about the falcon's attacks and how it had taken away their young ones.

The son responded, "There's a solution for every problem. If you work together to fend off this threat, we can likely avoid this calamity and ease your burden."

The sparrows found hope in his words. While one stayed to care for the young ones, the other set out to find help. Along the way, he decided that he would share his story with the first creature he encountered and seek a remedy for their sorrow.

As luck would have it, a salamander, emerging from a fiery mine, was wandering in the desert. When the sparrow spotted this unusual creature, he thought, 'This could be the answer! I'll confide in this remarkable bird and hope for a solution to our troubles.'

With great respect, he approached the salamander, exchanged greetings, and offered his assistance. The salamander, also courteous, noticed the sparrow's tired look and invited him to rest nearby. Then, he asked the sparrow to explain his problem so that he could do whatever was in his power to help.

The Sparrow spoke freely and presented his problems to the Salamander. His heart-breaking plight was so intense that even a rock, if told his story, would have shattered from the weight of his distress.

Upon hearing the sparrow's tale, the salamander felt a surge of compassion and declared, "Do not despair! Tonight, I will take action to destroy the falcon's dwelling, nest, and all within it. Show me where you live, and then return to your offspring until I come to you."

The sparrow clearly indicated his home to the salamander, leaving no room for doubt, and then joyfully flew back to his nest. As night fell, the salamander, accompanied by others of its kind, each carrying naphtha and brimstone, headed toward the falcon's nest under the guidance of the sparrow.

Unaware of the impending disaster, the falcon and its young had eaten their fill and fallen asleep. The salamanders poured naphtha and brimstone onto the nest and then retreated. The flames of justice descended upon the oppressors. Startled from their slumber of neglect, they and their home were swiftly reduced to ashes.

This tale serves to illustrate that anyone who endeavours to stand against an adversary, no matter how small or weak they may seem, while their foe is great and strong, can still hope for victory and triumph.

The Lambikin

This story has been adapted from a tale originally told by Joseph Jacobs in Indian Fairy Tales, published in 1892 by David Nutt, London. Joseph Jacobs was a prolific collector and re-teller of folktales from different cultures. Indian Fairy Tales includes a diverse range of stories, featuring elements of magic, mythology, and adventure. Many of these tales have been passed down through oral tradition for generations, reflecting the cultural richness and diversity of India.

Once upon a time there was a wee wee Lambikin, who frolicked about on his little tottery legs, and enjoyed himself amazingly.

Now one day he set off to visit his Granny, and was jumping with joy to think of all the good things he should get from her, when who should he meet but a Jackal, who looked at the tender young morsel and said, "Lambikin! Lambikin! I'll EAT YOU!"

But Lambikin only gave a little frisk and said:

"To Granny's house I go,

Where I shall fatter grow,

Then you can eat me so."

The Jackal thought this reasonable, and let Lambikin pass.

By-and-by Lambikin met a Vulture, and the Vulture, looking hungrily at the tender morsel before him, said, "Lambikin! Lambikin! I'll EAT YOU!"

But Lambikin only gave a little frisk, and said:

"To Granny's house I go,

Where I shall fatter grow,

Then you can eat me so."

The Vulture thought this reasonable, and let Lambikin pass.

And by-and-by he met a Tiger, and then a Wolf, and a Dog, and an Eagle, and all these, when they saw the tender little morsel, said, "Lambikin! Lambikin! I'll EAT YOU!"

But to all of them Lambikin replied, with a little frisk:

"To Granny's house I go,

Where I shall fatter grow,

Then you can eat me so."

At last he reached his Granny's house, and said, all in a great hurry, "Granny, dear, I've promised to get very fat, so, as people ought to keep their promises, please put me into the corn-bin at once."

So his Granny said he was a good boy, and put him into the corn-bin, and there the greedy little Lambikin stayed for seven days, and ate, and ate, and ate, until he could scarcely waddle, and his Granny said he was fat enough for anything, and must go home. But cunning little Lambikin said that would never do, for some animal would be sure to eat him on the way back, he was so plump and tender.

"I'll tell you what you must do," said Master Lambikin, "you must make a little drumikin out of the skin of my little brother who died, and then I can sit inside and trundle along nicely, for I'm as tight as a drum myself."

So his Granny made a nice little drumikin out of his brother's skin, with the wool inside, and Lambikin curled himself up snug and warm in the middle, and trundled away gaily. Soon he met with the Eagle, who called out, "Drumikin! Drumikin! Have you seen Lambikin?"

And Mr. Lambikin, curled up in his soft warm nest, replied:

"Fallen into the fire, and so will you

On little Drumikin. Tum-pa, tum-too!"

"How very annoying!" sighed the Eagle, thinking regretfully of the tender morsel he had let slip.

Meanwhile Lambikin trundled along, laughing to himself, and singing:

"Tum-pa, tum-too;

Tum-pa, tum-too!"

Every animal and bird he met asked him the same question: "Drumikin! Drumikin! Have you seen Lambikin?"

And to each of them the little slyboots replied:

"Fallen into the fire, and so will you

On little Drumikin. Tum-pa, tum too;

Tum-pa, tum-too; Tum-pa, tum-too!"

Then they all sighed to think of the tender little morsel they had let slip.

At last the Jackal came limping along, for all his sorry looks as sharp as a needle, and he too called out, "Drumikin! Drumikin! Have you seen Lambikin?"

And Lambikin, curled up in his snug little nest, replied gaily:

"Fallen into the fire, and so will you

On little Drumikin! Tum-pa..."

But he never got any further, for the Jackal recognised his voice at once, and cried, "Hello! You've turned yourself inside out, have you? Just you come out of that!"

Whereupon he tore open Drumikin and gobbled up Lambikin.

Muchie Lal

This story has been adapted from a tale originally told by Hamilton Wright Mabie in Young Folks Treasury, Volume 2, published in 1909 by The University Society Inc, New York. Young Folks Treasury, Volume 2 was part of a larger collection of children's literature compiled and edited by Hamilton Wright Mabie, a renowned American essayist, editor, and critic.

Once upon a time there were a Rajah and Ranee who had no children. Long had they wished and prayed that the gods would send them a son, but it was all in vain, for their prayers were not granted. One day a number of fish were brought into the royal kitchen to be cooked for the Rajah's dinner, and amongst them was one little fish that was not dead, but all the rest were dead. One of the palace maid-servants, seeing this, took the little fish and put him in a basin of water. Shortly afterward the Ranee saw him, and thinking him very pretty, kept him as a pet, and because she had no children she lavished all her affection on the fish and loved him as a son, and the people called him Muchie Rajah, the 'Fish Prince'.

In a little while Muchie Rajah had grown too long to live in the small basin, so they put him into a larger one, and then (when he grew too long for that) into a big tub. In time, however, Muchie Rajah became too large for even the big tub to hold him, so the Ranee had a tank made for him, in which he lived very happily, and twice a day she fed him with boiled rice. Now, though the people fancied Muchie Rajah was only a fish, this was not the case. He was, in truth, a young Rajah who had angered the gods, and been turned by them into a fish and thrown into the river as a punishment.

One morning, when the Ranee brought him his daily meal of boiled rice, Muchie Rajah called out to her and said, "Queen Mother, Queen Mother, I am so lonely here all by myself! Can you get me a wife?"

The Ranee promised to try, and sent messengers to all the people she knew, to ask if they would allow one of their children to marry her son, the Fish Prince. But they all answered, "We cannot give one of our dear little daughters to be devoured by a great fish, even though he is the Muchie Rajah and so high in your Majesty's favour."

At news of this the Ranee did not know what to do. She was so foolishly fond of Muchie Rajah, however, that she resolved to get him a wife at any cost. Again she sent out messengers, but this time she gave them a great bag containing a lac of gold mohurs, and said to them, "Go into every land until you find a wife for my Muchie Rajah, and to whoever will give you a child to be the Muchie Ranee you shall give this bag of gold mohurs."

The messengers started on their search, but for some time they were unsuccessful, for not even the beggars were to be tempted to sell their children, fearing the great fish would devour them. At last one day the messengers came to a village where there lived a Fakeer, who had lost his first wife and married again. His first wife had had one little daughter, and his second wife also had a daughter. As it happened, the Fakeer's second wife hated her little stepdaughter, always gave her the hardest work to do and the least food to eat, and tried by every means in her power to get her out of the way, in order that the child might not rival her own daughter.

When she heard of the errand on which the messengers had come, she sent for them when the Fakeer was out, and said to them, "Give me the bag of gold mohurs, and you shall take my little daughter to marry the Muchie Rajah." ("For," she thought to herself, "the great fish will certainly eat the girl, and she will thus trouble us no more.")

Then, turning to her stepdaughter, she said, "Go down to the river and wash your saree, that you may be fit to go with these people, who will take you to the Ranee's court."

At these words the poor girl went down to the river very sorrowful, for she saw no hope of escape, as her father was from home. As she knelt by the river-side, washing her saree and crying bitterly, some of her tears fell into the hole of an old Seven-headed Cobra, who lived on the river-bank. This Cobra was a very wise animal, and seeing the maiden, he put his head out of his hole, and said to her, "Little girl, why do you cry?"

"Oh, sir," she answered, "I am very unhappy, for my father is far from home, and my stepmother has sold me to the Ranee's people to be the wife of the Muchie Rajah, that great fish, and I know he will eat me up."

"Do not be afraid, my daughter," said the Cobra, "but take with you these three stones and tie them up in the corner of your saree," and so saying, he gave her three little round pebbles. "The Muchie Rajah, whose wife you are to be, is not really a fish, but a Rajah who has been enchanted. Your home will be a little room which the Ranee has had built in the tank wall. When you are taken there, wait and be sure you don't go to sleep, or the Muchie Rajah will certainly come and eat you up. But as you hear him coming rushing through the water, be prepared, and as soon as you see him, throw this first stone at him. He will then sink to the bottom of the tank. The second time he comes, throw the second stone, when the same thing will happen. The third time he comes, throw this third stone, and he will immediately resume his human shape."

So saying, the old Cobra dived down again into his hole. The Fakeer's daughter took the stones and determined to do as the Cobra had told her, though she hardly believed it would have the desired effect.

When she reached the palace the Ranee spoke kindly to her, and said to the messengers, "You have done your errand well. This is a dear little girl."

Then she ordered that she should be let down the side of the tank in a basket to a little room which had been prepared for her. When the Fakeer's daughter got there, she thought she had never seen such a pretty place in her life (for the Ranee had caused the little room to be very nicely decorated for the wife of her favourite), and she would have felt very happy away from her cruel stepmother and all the hard work she had been made to do, had it not been for the dark water that lay black and unfathomable below the door and the fear of the terrible Muchie Rajah.

After waiting some time she heard a rushing sound, and little waves came dashing against the threshold. Faster they came and faster, and the noise got louder and louder, until she saw a great fish's head above the water. Muchie Rajah was coming toward her open-mouthed. The Fakeer's daughter seized one of the stones that the Cobra had given her and threw it at him, and down he sank to the bottom of the tank. A second time he rose and came toward her, and she threw the second stone at him, and he again sank down. A third time he came more fiercely than before, when, seizing a third stone, she threw it with all her force. No sooner did it touch him than the spell was broken, and there, instead of a fish, swam a handsome young Prince. The poor little Fakeer's daughter was so startled that she began to cry. But the Prince said to her, "Pretty maiden, do not be frightened. You have rescued me from a horrible thraldom, and I can never thank you enough, but if you will be the Muchie Ranee, we will be married tomorrow." Then he sat down on the doorstep, thinking over his strange fate and watching for the dawn.

Early next morning several inquisitive people came to see if the Muchie Rajah had eaten up his poor little wife, as they feared he would. Imagine their astonishment, on looking over the tank wall, to see, not the Muchie Rajah, but a magnificent Prince! The news soon spread to the palace. Down came the Rajah, down came the Ranee, down came all their attendants. They dragged Muchie Rajah and the Fakeer's daughter up the side of the tank in a basket, and when they heard their story there were great and unparalleled rejoicings.

The Ranee said, "So I have indeed found a son at last!"

And the people were so delighted, so happy and so proud of the new Prince and Princess, that they covered all their path with damask from the tank to the palace, and cried to their fellows, "Come and see our new Prince and Princess! Were ever any so divinely beautiful? Come see a right royal couple, a pair of mortals like the gods!" And when they reached the palace the prince was married to the Fakeer's daughter.

There they lived very happily for some time. The Muchie Ranee's stepmother, hearing what had happened, came often to see her stepdaughter, and pretended to be delighted at her good fortune, and the Ranee was so good that she quite forgave all her stepmother's former cruelty, and always received her very kindly. At last, one day, the Muchie Ranee said to her husband, "It is a weary while since I saw my father. If you will give me leave, I should much like to visit my native village and see him again."

"Very well," he replied, "you may go. But do not stay away long, for there can be no happiness for me till you return."

So she went, and her father was delighted to see her, but her stepmother, though she pretended to be very kind, was in reality only glad to think she had got the Ranee into her power, and determined, if possible, never to allow her to return to the palace again. One day, therefore, she said to her own daughter, "It is hard that your stepsister should have become Ranee of all the land instead of being eaten up by the great fish, while we gained no more than a lac of gold mohurs. Do now as I bid you, that you may become Ranee in her stead." She then went on to instruct her that she must invite the Ranee down to the riverbank, and there beg her to let her try on her jewels, and while putting them on give her a push and drown her in the river.

The girl consented, and standing by the riverbank, said to her stepsister, "Sister, may I try on your jewels? How pretty they are!"

"Yes," said the Ranee, "and we shall be able to see in the river how they look."

So, undoing her necklaces, she clasped them round the other's neck. But while she was doing so her stepsister gave her a push, and she fell backward into the water. The girl watched to see that the body did not rise, and then, running back, said to her mother, "Mother, here are all the jewels, and she will trouble us no more."

But it happened that just when her stepsister pushed the Ranee into the river her old friend the Seven-headed Cobra chanced to be swimming across it, and seeing the little Ranee likely to be drowned, he carried her on his back until he reached his hole, into which he took her safely. Now this hole, in which the Cobra and his wife and all his little ones lived, had two entrances, the one under the water and leading to the river, and the other above water, leading out into the open fields. To this upper end of his hole the Cobra took the Muchie Ranee, where he and his wife took care of her, and there she lived with them for some time.

Meanwhile, the wicked Fakeer's wife, having dressed up her own daughter in all the Ranee's jewels, took her to the palace, and said to the Muchie Rajah, "See, I have brought your wife, my dear daughter, back safe and well."

The Rajah looked at her, and thought, 'This does not look like my wife.' However, the room was dark and the girl was cleverly disguised, and he thought he might be mistaken. Next day he said again, "My wife must be sadly changed or this cannot be she, for she was always bright and cheerful. She had pretty loving ways and merry words, while this woman never opens her lips." Still, he did not like to seem to mistrust his wife, and comforted himself by saying, "Perhaps she is tired with the long journey."

On the third day, however, he could bear the uncertainty no longer, and tearing off her jewels, saw, not the face of his own little wife, but another woman. Then he was very angry and turned her out of doors, saying, "Begone; since you are but the wretched tool of others, I spare your life."

But of the Fakeer's wife he said to his guards, "Fetch that woman here instantly, for unless she can tell me where my wife is, I will have her hanged."

It chanced, however, that the Fakeer's wife had heard of the Muchie Rajah having turned her daughter out of doors, so, fearing his anger, she hid herself, and was not to be found.

Meantime, the Muchie Ranee, not knowing how to get home, continued to live in the great Seven-headed Cobra's hole, and he and his wife and all his family were very kind to her, and loved her as if she had been one of them, and there her little son was born, and she called him Muchie Lal, after the Muchie Rajah, his father. Muchie Lal was a lovely child, merry and brave, and his playmates all day long were the young Cobras.

When he was about three years old a bangle-seller came by that way, and the Muchie Ranee bought some bangles from him and put them on her boy's wrists and ankles, but by the next day, in playing, he had broken them all. Then, seeing the bangle-seller, the Ranee called him again and bought some more, and so on every day until the bangle-seller got quite rich from selling so many bangles for the Muchie Lal, for the Cobra's hole was full of treasure, and he gave the Muchie Ranee as much money to spend every day as she liked. There was nothing she wished for that he did not give her, only he would not let her try to get home to her husband, which she wished more than all. When she asked him he would say, "No, I will not let you go. If your husband comes here and fetches you, it is well, but I will not allow you to wander in search of him through the land alone."

And so she was obliged to stay where she was.

All this time the poor Muchie Rajah was hunting in every part of the country for his wife, but he could learn no tidings of her. For grief and sorrow at losing her he had gone almost distracted, and did nothing but wander from place to place, crying, "She is gone! She is gone!"

Then, when he had long inquired without avail of all the people in her native village about her, he one day met a bangle-seller and said to him, "Where have you come from?"

The bangle-seller answered, "I have just been selling bangles to some people who live in a Cobra's hole in the river-bank."

"People! What people?" asked the Rajah.

"Why," answered the bangle-seller, "a woman and a child. The child is the most beautiful I ever saw. He is about three years old, and of course, running about, is always breaking his bangles and his mother buys him new ones every day."

"Do you know what the child's name is?" said the Rajah.

"Yes," answered the bangle-seller carelessly, "for the lady always calls him her Muchie Lal."

'Ah,' thought the Muchie Rajah, 'this must be my wife.' Then he said to him again, "Good bangle-seller, I would see these strange people of whom you speak. Can you take me there?"

"Not tonight," replied the bangle-seller, "daylight has gone, and we should only frighten them, but I shall be going there again tomorrow, and then you may come too. Meanwhile, come and rest at my house for the night, for you look faint and weary."

The Rajah consented. Next morning, however, very early, he woke the bangle-seller, saying, "Pray let us go now and see the people you spoke about yesterday."

"Stay," said the bangle-seller, "it is much too early. I never go till after breakfast."

So the Rajah had to wait till the bangle-seller was ready to go. At last they started off, and when they reached the Cobra's hole the first thing the Rajah saw was a fine little boy playing with the young Cobras.

As the bangle-seller came along, jingling his bangles, a gentle voice from inside the hole called out, "Come here, my Muchie Lal, and try on your bangles."

Then the Muchie Rajah, kneeling down at the mouth of the hole, said, "Oh, lady, show your beautiful face to me."

At the sound of his voice the Ranee ran out, crying, "Husband, husband! Have you found me again?"

And she told him how her sister had tried to drown her, and how the good Cobra had saved her life and taken care of her and her child. Then he said, "And will you now come home with me?"

And she told him how the Cobra would never let her go, and said, "I will first tell him of your coming, for he has been a father to me." So she called out, "Father Cobra, Father Cobra, my husband has come to fetch me. Will you let me go?"

"Yes," he said, "if your husband has come to fetch you, you may go."

And his wife said, "Farewell, dear lady, we are loath to lose you, for we have loved you as a daughter."

And all the little Cobras were very sorrowful to think that they must lose their playfellow, the young Prince. Then the Cobra gave the Muchie Rajah and the Muchie Ranee and Muchie Lal all the costliest gifts he could find in his treasure-house, and so they went home, where they lived very happy ever after.

The Mother-In-Law Became An Ass

This story has been adapted from a tale originally told by Mrs. Howard Kingscote and Pandit Natêsá Sástrî in Tales Of The Sun, published in 1890 by H. Allen & Co., London and Calcutta. The book contains a selection of tales from Indian mythology and folklore, centred around the theme of the sun. These tales often revolve around various deities associated with the sun, such as Surya, the solar deity in Hinduism.

Little by little the mother-in-law became an ass is a proverb among the Tamils, applied to those who day by day go downwards in their progress in study, position, or life, and based on the following story…

In a certain village their lived a Brâhman with his wife, mother, and mother-in-law. He was a very good man, and equally kind to all of them. His mother complained of nothing at his hands, but his wife was a very bad-tempered woman, and always troubled her mother-in-law by keeping her engaged in this work or that throughout the day, and giving her very little food in the evening. Owing to this the poor Brâhman's mother was almost dying of misery. On the other hand, the wife's own mother received very kind treatment, of course, at her daughter's hands, but the husband was so completely ruled by his wife, that he had no strength of mind to oppose her ill-treatment of his own mother.

One evening, just before sunset, the wife abused her mother-in-law with such fury, that the latter had to fly away to escape a thrashing. Full of misery she ran out of the village, but the sun had begun to set, and the darkness of night was fast overtaking her. So finding a ruined temple she entered it to pass the night there. It happened to be the abode of the village Kâlî (goddess), who used to come out every night at midnight to inspect her village. That night she perceived a woman, the mother of the poor Brâhman, lurking within her prâkâras (boundaries), and being a most benevolent Kâlî, called out to her, and asked her what made her so miserable that she should leave her home on such a dark night. The Brâhmanî told her story in a few words.

While she was speaking the cunning goddess was using her supernatural powers to see whether all she said was true or not, and finding it to be the truth, she thus replied in very soothing tones, "I pity your misery, mother, because your daughter-in-law troubles and vexes you when you have become old, and have no strength in your body. Now take this mango," and taking a ripe one from out her waist-band, she gave it to the old Brâhmanî with a smiling face. "Eat it, and you will soon become a young woman like your own daughter-in-law, and then she shall no longer trouble you."

Thus consoling the afflicted old woman, the kind-hearted Kâlî went away. The Brâhmanî lingered for the remainder of the night in the temple, and being a fond mother she did not like to eat the whole of the mango without giving a portion of it to her son.

Meanwhile, when her son returned home in the evening he found his mother absent, but his wife explained the matter to him, so as to throw the blame on the old woman, as she always did. As it was dark he had no chance of going out to search for her, so he waited for the daylight, and as soon as he saw the dawn, started to look for his mother. He had not walked far when to his joy he found her in the temple of Kâlî.

"How did you pass the cold night, my dearest mother?" he said. "What did you have for dinner? Wretch that I am to have got myself married to a cur. Forget all her faults, and return home."

His mother shed tears of joy and sorrow, and related her previous night's adventure, upon which he said, "Delay not even one nimisha (minute), but eat this fruit at once. I do not want any of it. I want you to become young and strong enough to stand that nasty cur's troubles, and that will be well and good."

So the mother ate up the divine fruit, and the son took her upon his shoulders and brought her home, on reaching which he placed her on the ground, when to his joy she was no longer an old woman, but a young girl of sixteen, and stronger than his own wife. The troublesome wife was now totally put down, and was powerless against so strong a mother-in-law.

She did not like the change at all, having to give up her habits of bullying, and so she argued to herself thus, "This jade of a mother-in-law became young through the fruit of the Kâlî, why should not my mother also do the same, if I instruct her and send her to the same temple."

So she instructed her mother as to the story she ought to give to the goddess and sent her there. Her old mother, agreeably to her daughter's injunctions, went to the temple, and on meeting with the goddess at midnight, gave a false story that she was being greatly ill-treated by her daughter-in-law, though, in truth, she had nothing of the kind to complain of. The goddess perceived the lie through her divine powers, but pretending to pity her, also gave her a fruit. Her daughter had instructed her not to eat it till next morning, and till she saw her son-in-law.

As soon as morning approached, the poor hen-pecked Brâhman was ordered by his wife to go to the temple and fetch his mother-in-law, as he had some time back fetched away his mother. He accordingly went, and invited her to come home. She wanted him to eat part of the fruit, as she had been instructed, but he refused, and so she swallowed it all, fully expecting to become young again on reaching home. Meanwhile her son-in-law took her on his shoulders and returned home, expecting, as his former experience had taught him, to see his mother-in-law also turn into a young woman.

He became anxious to see how the change came on, and halfway home he turned his head, and found such part of the burden on his shoulders as he could see, to be like parts of an ass, but he took this to be a mere preliminary stage towards youthful womanhood! Again he turned, and again he saw the same thing several times, and the more he looked the more his burden became like an ass, till at last when he reached home, his burden jumped down braying like an ass and ran away.

Thus the Kâlî, perceiving the evil intentions of the wife, disappointed her by turning her mother into an ass, but no one knew of it till she actually jumped down from the shoulders of her son-in-law.

This story is always cited as the explanation of the proverb quoted above – *'vara vara mâmi kaludai pôl ânâl'* – 'little by little the mother-in-law became an ass', to which is also commonly added *ûr varumbôdu ûlaiyida talaippattal,* or in English, 'as she approached the village, she began to bray'.

The Hermit, the Thief, and the Demon

This story has been adapted from a tale originally told by Kate Douglas Wiggin and Nora Archibald Smith in The Talking Beasts, published in 1911 by Houghton Mifflin Company. The fables in The Talking Beasts are engaging and entertaining, with whimsical characters and imaginative settings. Through these tales, Wiggin and Smith aimed to stimulate the imagination of children while also instilling important values that promote character development and moral growth.

It is said that there was a Hermit who lived in a remote area near Ahmedabad. He was known for his pure character, self-discipline, and virtue. He spent his mornings and evenings in devotion to the wise King (referring to God), and as a result, he distanced himself from worldly concerns. He was content with what he had and was free from worry.

One of his devoted followers learned of the Hermit's simple lifestyle and fasting. As a gesture of kindness, the disciple brought a young, healthy she-buffalo to the hermitage. This buffalo provided delicious milk, satisfying the Hermit's desires.

A thief saw what was happening and felt his hunger grow. He decided to head towards the hermit's cell. Accompanying him was a demon, disguised as a man. The thief asked the demon, "Who are you, and where are you going?"

The demon responded, "I am a demon taking on this human form. I am going to the hermitage of the recluse because many people in this area, inspired by his teachings, are turning away from sin, and our opportunities for temptation are dwindling. I want to seize the chance and kill him. That's my plan. Now, tell me about yourself. Who are you, and what brings you here?"

The thief replied, "I am a professional thief, constantly plotting how to steal from others and bring sorrow to their lives. Right now, I'm headed to the recluse's hermitage because I heard he has a valuable buffalo, and I intend to steal it for my own needs."

The demon nodded in agreement, saying, "Thank God for our shared purpose. Our common goal of harming him is enough to unite us, given our respective intentions."

They continued their journey and arrived at the hermit's cell at night. The hermit had already finished his daily prayers and had fallen asleep on his prayer mat. The thief realized that if the demon tried to kill the hermit, he might wake up and alert the neighbours, making it impossible to steal the buffalo. Similarly, the demon thought that if the thief tried to steal the buffalo, he would have to open the door, likely waking the hermit and delaying his plan to kill him. So, the demon proposed that he would first kill the hermit while the thief waited, and then the thief could steal the buffalo. But the thief insisted that he would steal the buffalo first, and then the demon could proceed with killing the hermit.

Their disagreement dragged on, and eventually, they began arguing loudly. Frustrated, the thief shouted to the hermit that there was a demon planning to kill him, while the demon yelled that there was a thief intending to steal his buffalo. The hermit woke up, alarmed by the commotion, and called out for help. The neighbours arrived, and both the thief and the demon fled. Thanks to their quarrel, the hermit's life and belongings remained safe.

In the end, it's unnecessary to resort to violence when enemies turn against each other.

The Cunning Crane and the Crab

This story has been adapted from a tale originally told by W. H. D. Rouse in The Giant Crab and Other Tales from Old India, published in 1897 by David Nutt, London. The tales in the collection cover a wide range of themes, including adventure, morality, wisdom, and magic. Many of the stories feature talking animals, brave heroes, cunning tricksters, and mythical beings, offering readers a glimpse into the rich storytelling traditions of India.

Once upon a time a number of fish lived in a little pool. It was all very well while there was rain, but when summer came, and it began to be very hot, the water dried up and got lower and lower, until there was hardly enough to hide the fish.

Now not far away there was a beautiful lake, always fresh and cool, for it lay under the shadow of great trees, and it was covered all over with water-lilies. And a Crane lived on the banks of this lake.

The Crane used to eat fish, when he could catch any, and one day, coming to the little pool, he saw all the fish gasping in it, and thought of a neat trick to get hold of them without trouble.

"Dear Fish," said the Crane, "I am so sorry to see you cooped up in this hole. I know a beautiful lake close by, deep and fresh and cool, and if you like I will carry you there."

The Fish did not know what to make of this, because never since the world began had a crane done a good turn to a fish. You see it is just as absurd to suppose that a crane would help fish, as to think that a cat would be kind to a mouse.

So they said to the Crane, "We don't believe you! What you want is to eat us."

This was just what the Crane did want, but he did not say so. "No, no!" he said. "I'm not so cruel as all that. I have eaten a fish now and then", he continued, for he saw it was of no use denying that, because they knew he had always eaten fish, "but I have plenty of other food, and it goes to my heart to see you here. In this hot water you will all be boiled fish before long!"

"That's true enough," said the Fish, "the water is hot."

Well, the end of it was, they persuaded an old Fish with one eye to go and see.

The Crane took the one-eyed Fish in his beak and put him in the lake, and when the one-eyed fish had seen that what the Crane said was true so far, he let the Crane carry him back again to tell the others.

The old Fish could not say enough to praise the lake. "It's ever so big," he said, "and deep and cool, just as the Crane said, and there are trees overshadowing it, and water-lilies are growing in the mud, and the whole of it is covered with fine fat flies! Ah, what a feast I have had!" And he rolled up his one eye at the thought of it.

Then all the Fish were eager to go, arguing about who should be first, for every Fish was anxious to get away from the hot pool. They came to the top of the water, all begging the Crane to take them to this beautiful lake.

"One at a time!" said the Crane. "I have only one beak, you know!" And he smiled to himself, for that beak was made to eat fish, not to carry them.

However, it was decided that as the one-eyed Fish had been so brave as to trust himself in the Crane's beak, before he knew what the truth was, he certainly deserved to go first.

So the Crane took the one-eyed Fish in his beak, and carried him over to the lake. But this time he did not drop the Fish in. Instead, he laid him in the cleft of a tree, and pecked his one eye out with his beak. Then he killed him, and ate him up, and dropped his bones at the foot of the tree.

By-and-by the Crane came back for another. "Now then, who's next?" asked the Crane. "Old One-eye is swimming about, as happy as a king!" He picked up another fish, and served him like the first, dropping his bones at the foot of the tree.

And so it went on, until in a few days the pool was empty. The cunning Crane had eaten every single one of the fish! He stood on the bank, peering into every hole, to see whether there might not be a little one left somewhere. There was one, surely! No, it was a Crab. 'Never mind', he thought, 'all's fish that comes to my net!'

So he invited the Crab to come with him to the lake.

"Why, how are you going to carry me?" asked the Crab.

"In my beak, to be sure!" replied the Crane.

"You might drop me," said the Crab, "and then I should split."

"Oh no, I promise I won't drop you!" said the Crane.

But the Crab had more sense than all the fish put together, and he did not believe in the Crane's friendship at all. So he still pretended to hesitate, and at last he said, "Well, I'll tell you what. I can hold on tighter with my claws than you can with your beak. I'll come, but you must let me hold on to your neck with my claws. Then I shall feel safe."

The Crane was so hungry that, without stopping to think, he agreed, and then the Crab got tight hold of his neck with his claws, and the Crane carried him towards the lake.

But after a while the Crab saw that he was being carried somewhere else, indeed to that tree where the Crane used to sit and eat the fish.

"Crane dear," he said, "aren't you going to put me in the lake?"

"Crane dear, indeed!" said the Crane, "do you suppose I was born to carry crabs about? Not I! Just look at that heap of bones under yon tree! Those are the bones of the fish that used to live in your pool. I ate them, and I'm going to eat you!"

"Are you, though!" said the Crab, and gave the Crane's neck a little nip.

Then the Crane saw what a fool he had been to let a Crab put a claw round his neck. He knew that the Crab could kill him if he liked, and he was frightened to death at the thought. People who try to deceive others often pay for it themselves, and that is what happened to the Crane.

"Dear Crab!" he said, with tears streaming from his eyes, "forgive me! I won't kill you, only let me go!"

"Just put me in the lake, then," said the Crab.

The Crane stepped down to the lakeside, and laid the Crab upon the mud. And the Crab, as soon as he felt himself safe, nipped off the Crane's head as clean as if it had been cut with a knife.

So perished the treacherous Crane, caught by his own trick. And the Crab lived happily in the beautiful lake for the rest of his life.

The Hermit's Daughter

This story has been adapted from a tale originally told by Siddha Mohana Mitra and Nancy Bell in Hindu Tales from the Sanskrit, published in 1919 by MacMillan and Company, London & Canada. The book features a selection of stories drawn from classical Sanskrit literature, including the Panchatantra, Hitopadesha, and other traditional sources.

CHAPTER I

Near a town in India called Ikshumati, on a beautiful wide river, with trees belonging to a great forest near its banks, there dwelt a holy man named Mana Kanaka, who spent a great part of his life praying to God. He had lost his wife when his only child, a lovely girl called Kadali-Garbha, was only a few months old. Kadali-Garbha was a very happy girl, with many friends in the woods round her home, not children like herself, but wild creatures, who knew she would not do them any harm. They loved her and she loved them. The birds were so tame that they would eat out of her hand, and the deer used to follow her about in the hope of getting the bread she carried in her pocket for them. Her father taught her all she knew, and that was a great deal, for she could read quite learned books in the ancient language of her native land.

Better even than what she found out in those books was what Mana Kanaka told her about the loving God of all gods who rules the world and all that live in it. Kadali-Garbha also learnt a great deal through her friendship with wild animals. She knew where the birds built their nests, where the baby deer were born, where the squirrels hid their nuts, and what food all the dwellers in the forest liked best. She helped her father to work in their garden in which all their own food was grown, and she loved to cook the fruit and vegetables for Mana Kanaka and herself. Her clothes were made of the bark of the trees in the forest, which she herself wove into thin, soft material suitable for wearing in a hot climate.

CHAPTER II

Kadali-Garbha never even thought about other children because she had not been used to having them with her. She was just as happy as the day was long, and never wished for any change. But when she was about sixteen something happened which quite altered her whole life. One day her father had gone into the forest to cut wood, and had left her alone. She had finished tidying the house, and got everything ready for the midday meal, and was sitting at the door of her home, reading to herself, with birds fluttering about her head and a pet doe lying beside her, when she heard the noise of a horse's feet approaching. She looked up, and there on the other side of the fence was a very handsome young man seated on a great black horse, which he had reined up when he caught sight of her. He looked at her without speaking, and she looked back at him with her big black eyes full of surprise at his sudden appearance. She made a beautiful picture, with the green creepers covering the hut behind her, and the doe, which had started up in fear of the horse, pressing against her.

The man was the king of the country, whose name was Dridha-Varman. He had been hunting and had got separated from his attendants. He was very much surprised to find anyone living in the very depths of the forest, and was going to ask the young girl who she was, when Kadali-Garbha saw her father coming along the path leading to his home. Jumping up, she ran to meet him, glad that he had come, for she had never before seen a young man and was as shy as any of the wild creatures of the woods. Now that Mana Kanaka was with her, she got over her fright, and felt quite safe, clinging to his arm as he and the king talked together.

CHAPTER III

Mana Kanaka knew at once that the man on the horse was the king, and a great fear entered his heart when he saw how Dridha-Varman looked at his beloved only child.

"Who are you, and who is that lovely girl?" asked the king.

Mana Kanaka answered, "I am only a humble woodcutter, and this is my only child, whose mother has long been dead."

"Her mother must have been a very lovely woman, if her daughter is like her," said the king. "Never before have I seen such perfect beauty."

"Her mother," replied Mana Kanaka, "was indeed what you say, and her soul was as beautiful as the body in which it dwelt all too short a time."

"I would have your daughter for my wife," said the king, "and if you will give her to me, she shall have no wish ungratified. She shall have servants to wait on her and other young girls to be her companions. She will wear beautiful clothes, eat the best of food, have as many horses and carriages as she wants, and have no work to do with her own hands."

CHAPTER IV

What Kadali-Garbha did was to cling closely to her father, hiding her face on his arm and whispering, "I will not leave you. Do not send me away from you, dear father."

Mana Kanaka stroked her hair, and said in a gentle voice, "But, dear child, your father is old, and must leave you soon. It is a great honour for his little girl to be chosen by the king for his bride. Do not be afraid, but look at him and see how handsome he is and how kind he looks."

Then Kadali-Garbha looked at the king, who smiled at her and looked so charming that her fear began to leave her. She still clung to her father, but no longer hid her face, and Mana Kanaka begged Kadali-Garbha to let him send her away, so that he might talk with the king alone about the wish he had expressed to marry her. The king consented to this, and Kadali-Garbha gladly ran away. But when she reached the door of her home, she looked back, and knew in her heart that she already loved the king and did not want him to go away.

It did not take long for the matter of the marriage to be settled. For Mana Kanaka, sad though he was to lose his dear only child, was glad that she should be a queen, and have someone to take care of her when he was gone. After this first visit to the little house in the forest the king came every day to see Kadali-Garbha, bringing all kinds of presents for her. She learnt to love him so much that she became as eager as he was for the wedding to be soon. When the day was fixed, the king sent several ladies of his court to dress the bride in clothes more beautiful that she had ever dreamt of, and in them she looked more lovely even than the first day her lover had seen her.

Now amongst these ladies was a very wise woman who could see what was going to happen, and she knew that there would be troubles for the young queen in the palace, because many would be jealous of her happiness. She was very much taken with the beautiful innocent girl, and wanted to help her so much that she managed to get her alone for a few minutes, when she said to her, "I want you to promise me something. It is to take this packet of mustard seeds, hide it in the bosom of your dress, and when you ride to the palace with your husband, strew the seed along the path as you go. You know how quickly mustard grows. Well, it will spring up soon, and if you want to come home again, you can easily find the way by following the green shoots. Alas, I fear they will not have time to wither before you need their help!"

Kadali-Garbha laughed when the wise woman talked about trouble coming to her. She was so happy, she could not believe she would want to come home again so soon. "My father can come to me when I want him," she said. "I need only tell my dear husband to send for him."

But for all that she took the packet of seeds and hid it in her dress.

CHAPTER V

After the wedding was over, the king mounted his beautiful horse, and bending down, took his young wife up before him. Holding her close to him with his right arm, he held the reins in his left hand, and away they went, soon leaving all the attendants far behind them, the queen scattering the mustard seed as she had promised to do. When they arrived at the palace there were great rejoicings, and everybody seemed charmed with the queen, who was full of eager interest in all that she saw.

For several weeks there was nobody in the wide world so happy and light-hearted as the bride. The king spent many hours a day with her, and was never tired of listening to all she had to tell him about her life in the forest with her father. Every day he gave her some fresh proof of his love, and he never refused to do anything she asked him to do. But presently a change came.

Amongst the ladies of the court there was a beautiful woman, who had hoped to be queen herself, and hated Kadali-Garbha so much that she made up her mind to get her into disgrace with the king. She asked first one powerful person and then another to help her, but everybody loved the queen, and the wicked woman began to be afraid that those she had told about her wish to harm her would warn the king. So she sought about for someone who did not know Kadali-Garbha, and suddenly remembered a wise woman named Asoka-Mala, who lived in a cave not far from the town, to whom many people used to go for advice in their difficulties. She went to this woman one night, and told her a long story in which there was not one word of truth. The young queen, she said, did not really love the king, and with the help of her father, who was a magician, she meant to poison him. How could this terrible thing be prevented, she asked, and she promised that if only Asoka-Mala would help to save Dridha-Varman, she would give her a great deal of money.

Asoka-Mala guessed at once that the story was not true, and that it was only because the woman was jealous of the beautiful young queen that she wished to hurt her. But she loved money very much. Instead therefore of at once refusing to have anything to do with the matter, she said, "Bring me fifty gold pieces now, and promise me another fifty when the queen is sent away from the palace, and I will tell you what to do."

The wicked woman promised all this at once. The very next night she brought the first fifty pieces of gold to the cave, and Asoka-Mala told her that she must get the barber, who saw the king alone every day, to tell him he had found out a secret about the queen. "You must tell the barber all you have already told me. But be very careful to give some proof of your story. For if you do not do so, you will only have wasted the fifty gold pieces you have already given to me, and, more than that, you will be terribly punished for trying to hurt the queen, whom everybody loves."

CHAPTER VI

The wicked woman went back to the palace, thinking all the way to herself, 'How can I get a proof of what is not true?' At last an idea came into her head. She knew that the queen loved to wander in the forest, and that she was not afraid of the wild creatures, but seemed to understand their language. She would tell the barber that Kadali-Garbha was a witch and knew the secrets of the woods, that she had been seen gathering wild herbs, some of them poisonous, and had been heard muttering strange words to herself as she did so.

Early the next morning the cruel woman went to see the barber, and promised him a reward if he would tell the king what she had found out about his wife. "He won't believe you at first," she said, "but you must go on telling him till he does. You are clever, enough," she added, "to make up something he will believe if what I have thought of is no good."

The barber, who had served the king for many years, would not at first agree to help to make him unhappy. But he too liked money very much, and in the end he promised to see what he could do if he was well paid for it. He was, as the wicked woman had said, clever enough, and he knew from long experience just how to talk to his master.

He began by asking the king if he had heard of the lovely woman who was sometimes seen by the woodmen wandering about alone in the forest, with wild creatures following her. Remembering how he had first seen Kadali-Garbha, Dridha-Varman at once guessed that she was the lovely woman. But he did not tell the barber so, for he was so proud of his dear wife's beauty that he liked to hear her praised, and wanted the man to go on talking about her. He just said, "What is she like? Is she tall or short, fair or dark?"

The barber answered the questions readily. Then he went on to say that it was easy to see that the lady was as clever as she was beautiful, for she knew not only all about animals but also about plants. "Every day," he said, "she gathers quantities of herbs, and I have been told she makes healing medicines of them. Some even go so far as to say she also makes poisons. But, for my part, I do not believe that. She is too beautiful to be wicked."

The king listened, and a tiny little doubt crept into his mind about his wife. She had never told him about the herbs she gathered, although she often chattered about her friends in the forest. Perhaps after all it was not Kadali-Garbha the barber was talking about. He would ask her if she knew anything about making medicines from herbs. He did so when they were alone together, and she said at once, "Oh, yes! My father taught me. But I have never made any since I was married."

"Are you sure?" asked the king, and she answered laughing, "Of course, I am. How could I be anything but sure? I have no need to think of medicine-making, now I am the queen."

Dridha-Varman said no more at the time. But he was troubled, and when the barber came again, he began at once to ask about the woman who had been seen in the woods. The wicked man was delighted, and made up a long story. He said one of the waiting women had told him of what she had seen. The woman, he said, had followed the lady home one day, and that home was not far from the palace. She had seen her bending over a fire above which hung a great sauce-pan full of water, into which she flung some of the herbs she had gathered, singing as she did so, in a strange language.

'Could it possibly be,' thought the king, 'that Kadali-Garbha had deceived him? Was she perhaps a witch after all?' He remembered that he really did not know who she was, or who her father was. He had loved her directly he saw her, just because she was so beautiful. What was he to do now? He was quite sure, from the description the barber had given of the woman in the forest, that she was his wife. He would watch her himself in future, and say nothing to her that would make her think he was doing so.

CHAPTER VII

Although the king said nothing to his wife about what the barber had told him, he could not treat her exactly as he did before he heard it, and she very soon began to wonder what she had done to vex him. The first thing she noticed was that one of the ladies of the court always followed her when she went into the forest. She did not like this, because she so dearly loved to be alone with the wild creatures, and they did not come to her when anyone else was near. She told the lady to go away, and she pretended to do so, but she only kept a little further off. And though the queen could no longer see her, she knew she was there, and so did the birds and the deer. This went on for a little time, and then Kadali-Garbha asked her husband to tell everyone that she was not to be disturbed when she went to see her friends in the forest.

"I am afraid," said the king, "that some harm will come to you. There are wild beasts in the depths of the wood who might hurt you. And what should I do if any harm came to my dear one?"

Kadali-Garbha was grieved when Dridha-Varman said this, for she knew it was not true, and she looked at him so sadly that he felt ashamed of having doubted her. All would perhaps have been well even now, if he had told her of the story he had heard about her, because then she could have proved that it was not true. But he did not do that. He only said, "I cannot let you be alone so far from home. Why not be content with the lovely gardens around the palace? If you still wish to go to the woods, I will send one of the game-keepers with you instead of the lady who has been watching you. Then he can protect you if any harmful creature should approach."

"If my lord does not wish me to be alone in the forest," answered the queen, "I will be content with the gardens. For no birds or animals would come near me if one of their enemies were with me. But," she added, as her eyes filled with tears, "will not my lord tell me why he no longer trusts his wife, who loves him with all her heart?"

The king was very much touched by what Kadali-Garbha said, but still could not make up his mind to tell her the truth. So he only embraced her fondly, and said she was a good little wife to be so ready to obey him. The queen went away very sadly, wondering to herself what she could do to prove to her dear lord that she loved him as much as ever. She took care never to go outside the palace gardens, but she longed very much for her old freedom, and began to grow pale and thin.

The wicked woman who had tried to do her harm was very much disappointed that she had only succeeded in making her unhappy; so she went again to Asoka-Mala, and promised her more money if only she would think of some plan to get the king to send his wife away.

The wise woman considered a long time, and then she said, "You must use the barber again. He goes from house to house, and he must tell the king that the beautiful woman, who used to roam about in the forest collecting herbs, has been seen there again in the dead of the night, when she could be sure no one would find out what she was doing."

Now it so happened that Kadali-Garbha was often unable to sleep because of her grief that the king did not love her so much as he used to do. One night she got so tired of lying awake that she got up very quietly, so as not to disturb her husband, and putting on her sari, she went out into the gardens, hoping that the fresh air might help her to sleep. Presently the king too woke up, and finding that his wife was no longer beside him, he became very uneasy, and was about to go and seek her, when she came back. He asked her where she had been, and she told him exactly what had happened, but she did not explain why she could not sleep.

CHAPTER VIII

When the barber was shaving the king the next morning, he told him he had heard that people were saying the beautiful woman had been seen again one night, gathering herbs and muttering to herself.

"They talk, my lord," said the man, "of your own name having been on her lips, and those who love and honour you are anxious for your safety. Maybe the woman is indeed a witch, who for some reason of her own will try to poison you."

Now Dridha-Varman remembered that Kadali-Garbha had left him the night before, 'and perhaps,' he thought, 'at other times when I was asleep.' He could scarcely wait until the barber had finished shaving him, so eager was he to find out the truth. He hurried to his wife's private room, but she was not there, and her ladies told him she had not been seen by them that day. This troubled him terribly, and he roused the whole palace to seek her. Messengers were soon hurrying to and fro, but not a trace of her could be found.

Dridha-Varman was now quite sure that the woman the barber had talked about was Kadali-Garbha, the wife he had so loved and trusted. 'Perhaps,' he thought, 'she has left poison in my food, and has gone away so as not to see me die.' He would neither eat nor drink, and he ordered all the ladies whose duty it was to wait on the queen to be locked up till she was found. Amongst them was the wicked woman who had done all the mischief because of her jealousy of the beautiful young queen, and very much she wished she had never tried to harm her.

CHAPTER IX

In her trouble about the loss of the king's love Kadali-Garbha longed for her father, for she felt sure he would be able to help her. So she determined to go to him. With the aid of the wise woman who had given her the packet of mustard seed, and who had been her best friend at court, she disguised herself as a messenger, and, mounted on a strong little pony, she sped along the path marked out by the young shoots of mustard, reaching her old home in the forest before the night fell. Great indeed was the joy of Mana Kanaka at the sight of his beloved child, and very soon she had poured out all her sorrow to him.

The hermit was at first very much enraged with his son-in-law for the way in which he had treated Kadali-Garbha, and declared that he would use all the powers he had to punish him. "Never," he said, "shall he see your dear face again, but I will go to him and call down on him all manner of misfortunes. You know not, dear child, I have never wished you to know, that I am a magician and can make the very beasts of the field and the winds of heaven obey me. I know full well who has made this mischief between you and your husband, and I will see that punishment overtakes them."

"No, no, father," cried Kadali-Garbha, "I will not have any harm done to my dear one, for I love him with all my heart. All I ask of you is to prove to him that I am innocent of whatever fault he thinks I have committed, and to make him love and trust me again."

It was hard work to persuade Mana Kanaka to promise not to harm the king, but in the end he yielded. Together the father and daughter rode back to the palace, and together they were brought before Dridha-Varman, who, in spite of the anger he had felt against his wife, was overjoyed to see her. When he looked at her clinging to Mana Kanaka's arm, as she had done the first time they met, all his old love returned, and he would have taken her in his arms and told her so before the whole court, if she had not drawn back.

It was Mana Kanaka who was the first to speak. Drawing himself up to his full height, and pointing to the king, he charged him with having broken his vow to love and protect his wife. "You have listened to lying tongues," he said, "and I will tell you to whom those tongues belong, that justice may be done to them."

Once more Kadali-Garbha interfered. "No, father," she said, "let their names be forgotten. Please only prove to my lord that I am his loving faithful wife, and I will be content."

"I need no proof," cried Dridha-Varman, "but lest others should follow their evil example, I will have vengeance on the slanderers. Name them, and their doom shall be indeed a terrible one."

Then Mana Kanaka told the king the whole sad story, and when it was ended the wicked woman who had first thought of injuring the queen, and the barber who had helped her, were sent for to hear their doom, which was to be shut up for the rest of their lives in prison. This was changed to two years only, because Kadali-Garbha was generous enough to plead for them. As for the third person in the plot, the old witch of the cave, not a word was said about her by anybody. Mana Kanaka knew well enough what her share in the matter had been, but magicians and witches are careful not to make enemies of each other, and so he held his peace.

Dridha-Varman was so grateful to his father-in-law for bringing his wife back to him, that he wanted him to stop at court, and said he would give him a very high position there. But Mana Kanaka refused every reward, declaring that he loved his little home in the forest better than the grand rooms he might have had in the palace.

"All I wish for," he said, "is my dear child's happiness. I hope you will never again listen to stories against your wife. If you do, you may be very sure that I shall hear of it, and next time I know that you have been unkind to her I will punish you as you deserve."

The king was obliged to let Mana Kanaka go, but after this he took Kadali-Garbha to see her father in the forest very often. When the queen had children of her own, their greatest treat was to go to the little home, in the depths of the wood. They too learnt to love animals, and had many pets, none of whom were kept in cages.

The Swan and the Paddy-Bird

This story has been adapted from a tale originally told by William Crooke and W. H. D. Rouse in The Talking Thrush, published in 1899 by E. P. Dutton, New York. Their version of this story is based on an original telling by Devi Dín, a student, and recorded by Badari Prasád of the school at Musanagar, Cawnpur district.

A WILD Swan was flying once to his home, when he paused to rest on a tree. This was a kind of tree you have most likely never seen. It was very tall, and had no branches upon it until you came to the top, but at the top was a large clump of green leaves, and bunches of cocoa-nuts hanging down.

It so happened that on this tree was the nest of a Paddy-bird. A Paddy-bird is a bird something like a heron, which feeds on fish and frogs. At the moment when the Swan perched upon the tree, this Paddy-bird was sitting demurely on the edge of a pond that was below the tree, watching the water for a rise. She had no fishing-rod, but when she saw a little fish or a frog swim past, out went her beak like a flash, and the fish was pierced. Then she ate the fish, or carried it off to her little ones in the nest.

When the Paddy-bird chanced to look round, she saw the Swan sitting upon her tree. She was frightened at this, thinking that perhaps it was some bird of prey, come to devour her chicks. So she left her fishing, and at once flew up to the top of the cocoa-nut tree. The Swan looked harmless enough when she came closer, so plucking up courage, the Paddy-bird thus addressed him, "Good-day, sir. May I ask who you are?"

"I am a Swan," said the other, "and I am on my way home, but as it is a hot day, I thought I would rest awhile on your tree. I hope you have no objection?"

"Welcome, my lord Swan, welcome!" said the Paddy-bird. "I only wish I could offer you entertainment. But I am ashamed to say that I have no food worth your taking. I am a poor bird, and you know we Paddy-birds eat only small fish and frogs, which your highness would hardly touch."

"Oh, never mind for that," answered the Swan, "thank you all the same, but I can find my own food on this tree of yours."

This set our Paddy-bird's heart all a-flutter, for what could he mean but her brood? However, all was well in a minute; when she saw the Swan go to one of the green cocoa-nuts hanging from the tree. You have seen, I suppose, three little soft places at the top of a cocoa-nut, which are holes in the shell filled up with pulp. The Swan pierced his bill through one of these holes, and drank the milk inside the cocoa-nut. Then he gave some of the milk to the Paddy-bird, and flew away.

This milk tasted very nice, and the Paddy-bird began to say to herself, "What a fool I have been all these years! Here am I, watching and waiting all day long for a frog, and nasty things they are too, and all this while there was plenty of delicious milk within a yard of my nest! Well, good-bye fish, and good-bye frogs, I have done with you now for ever."

The next time the Paddy-bird felt hungry, she flew to a cocoa-nut and began to peck at it. But she did not know the secret of the three little holes at the top of the cocoa-nut, so she pecked, and pecked, and got no further. At last she gathered all her strength, and gave a tremendous peck at the cocoa-nut. Snap! her bill broke off, and the blood ran out, and very soon the poor Paddy-bird had bled to death.

Next day, the Swan happened to fly by that way again, and coming to the tree, he found his friend the Paddy-bird lying dead on the ground, with her bill snapped off clean. He understood at once what had happened, and said to himself, "This is what comes of trying to do what one is not fit for. Let the cobbler stick to his last, or misfortune follows fast."

The Five Wise Words Of The Guru

This story has been adapted from a tale originally told by Andrew Lang in The Olive Fairy Book, published in 1907 by Longmans, Green And Co., London And New York. Andrew Lang's Coloured Fairy Books were a series of twelve collections of fairy tales and folk stories from around the world, edited and compiled by Scottish author Andrew Lang. The first volume, The Blue Fairy Book, was published in 1889, followed by eleven more volumes, each with a different colour in the title, such as The Red Fairy Book, The Green Fairy Book, and so on, concluding with The Lilac Fairy Book in 1910.

Once there lived a handsome young man named Ram Singh, who, though a favourite with everyone, was unhappy because he had a scold for a step-mother. All day long she went on talking, until the youth was driven so distracted that he determined to go away somewhere and seek his fortune. No sooner had he decided to leave his home than he made his plans, and the very next morning he started off with a few clothes in a wallet, and a little money in his pocket.

But there was one person in the village to whom he wished to say good-bye, and that was a wise old guru, or teacher, who had taught him much. So he turned his face first of all towards his master's hut, and before the sun was well up was knocking at his door. The old man received his pupil affectionately, but he was wise in reading faces, and saw at once that the youth was in trouble.

"My son," he said, "what is the matter?"

"Nothing, father," replied the young man, "but I have determined to go into the world and seek my fortune."

"Be advised," returned the guru, "and remain in your father's house. It is better to have half a loaf at home than to seek a whole one in distant countries."

But Ram Singh was in no mood to heed such advice, and very soon the old man ceased to press him.

"Well," he said at last, "if your mind is made up I suppose you must have your way. But listen carefully, and remember five parting counsels which I will give you, and if you keep these no evil shall befall you. First, always obey without question the orders of him whose service you enter. Second, never speak harshly or unkindly to anyone. Third, never lie. Fourth, never try to appear the equal of those above you in station, and fifth, wherever you go, if you meet those who read or teach from the holy books, stay and listen, if but for a few minutes, that you may be strengthened in the path of duty."

Then Ram Singh started out upon his journey, promising to bear in mind the old man's words.

After some days he came to a great city. He had spent all the money which he had at starting, and therefore resolved to look for work however humble it might be. Catching sight of a prosperous-looking merchant standing in front of a shop full of grain of all kinds, Ram Singh went up to him and asked whether he could give him anything to do. The merchant gazed at him so long that the young man began to lose heart, but at length he answered, "Yes, of course. There is a place waiting for you."

"What do you mean?" asked Ram Singh.

"Why," replied the other, "yesterday our Rajah's chief vizier dismissed his body servant and is wanting another. Now you are just the sort of person that he needs, for you are young and tall, and handsome, so I advise you to apply there."

Thanking the merchant for this advice, the young man set out at once for the vizier's house, and soon managed, thanks to his good looks and appearance, to be engaged as the great man's servant.

One day, soon after this, the Rajah of the place started on a journey and the chief vizier accompanied him. With them was an army of servants and attendants, soldiers, muleteers, camel-drivers, merchants with grain and stores for man and beast, singers to make entertainment by the way and musicians to accompany them, besides elephants, camels, horses, mules, ponies, donkeys, goats, and carts and wagons of every kind and description, so that it seemed more like a large town on the march than anything else.

Thus they travelled for several days, till they entered a country that was like a sea of sand, where the swirling dust floated in clouds, and men and beasts were half choked by it. Towards the close of that day they came to a village, and when the headmen hurried out to salute the Rajah and to pay him their respects, they began, with very long and serious faces, to explain that, whilst they and all that they had were of course at the disposal of the Rajah, the coming of so large a company had nevertheless put them into a dreadful difficulty because they had never a well nor spring of water in their country, and they had no water to give drink to such an army of men and beasts!

Great fear fell upon the host at the words of the headmen, but the Rajah merely told the vizier that he must get water somehow, and that settled the matter so far as he was concerned. The vizier sent off in haste for all the oldest men in the place, and began to question them as to whether there were no wells nearby.

They all looked helplessly at each other, and said nothing, but at length one old grey-beard replied, "'Truly, Sir Wazir, there is, within a mile or two of this village, a well which some former king made hundreds of years ago. It is, they say, great and inexhaustible, covered in by heavy stone-work and with a flight of steps leading down to the water in the very bowels of the earth, but no man ever goes near it because it is haunted by evil spirits, and it is known that whoever disappears down the well shall never be seen again.'

The vizier stroked his beard and considered a moment. Then he turned to Ram Singh who stood behind his chair.

"There is a proverb," he said, "that no man can be trusted until he has been tried. Go and get the Rajah and his people water from this well."

Then there flashed into Ram Singh's mind the first counsel of the old guru - 'Always obey without question the orders of him whose service you enter.' So he replied at once that he was ready, and left to prepare for his adventure. Two great brazen vessels he fastened to a mule, two lesser ones he bound upon his shoulders, and thus provided he set out, with the old villager for his guide. In a short time they came to a spot where some big trees towered above the barren country, whilst under their shadow lay the dome of an ancient building. This the guide pointed out as the well, but excused himself from going further as he was an old man and tired, and it was already nearly sunset, so that he must be returning home. So Ram Singh bade him farewell, and went on alone with the mule.

When he arrived at the trees, Ram Singh tied up his beast, lifted the vessels from his shoulder, and having found the opening of the well, descended by a flight of steps which led down into the darkness. The steps were broad white slabs of alabaster which gleamed in the shadows as he went lower and lower. All was very silent. Even the sound of his bare feet upon the pavements seemed to wake an echo in that lonely place, and when one of the vessels which he carried slipped and fell upon the steps it clanged so loudly that he jumped at the noise. Still he went on, until he eventually reached a wide pool of sweet water, and there he washed his jars with care before he filled them, and began to remount the steps with the lighter vessels, as the big ones were so heavy he could only take up one at a time. Suddenly, something moved above him, and looking up he saw a great giant standing on the stairway! In one hand he held clasped to his heart a dreadful looking mass of bones, in the other was a lamp which cast long shadows about the walls, and made him seem even more terrible than he really was.

"What do you think, O mortal," said the giant, "of my fair and lovely wife?" And he held the light towards the bones in his arms and looked lovingly at them.

Now I must tell you that this poor giant had had a very beautiful wife, whom he had loved dearly, but, when she died, her husband refused to believe in her death, and always carried her about long after she had become nothing but bones. Ram Singh of course did not know this, but there came to his mind the second wise saying of the guru, which forbade him to speak harshly or inconsiderately to others; so he replied, "Truly, sir, I am sure you could find nowhere such another."

"Ah, what eyes you have!" cried the delighted giant, "You at least can see! I do not know how often I have slain those who insulted her by saying she was but dried bones! You are a fine young man, and I will help you."

So saying, he laid down the bones with great tenderness, and snatching up the huge brass vessels, carried them up again, and replaced them with such ease that it was all done by the time that Ram Singh had reached the open air with the smaller ones.

"Now," said the giant, "you have pleased me, and you may ask of me one favour, and whatever you wish I will do it for you. Perhaps you would like me to show you where lies buried the treasure of dead kings?" he added eagerly.

But Ram Singh shook his head at the mention of buried wealth.

"The favour that I would ask," he said, "is that you will leave off haunting this well, so that men may go in and out and obtain water."

Perhaps the giant expected some favour more difficult to grant, for his face brightened, and he promised to depart at once, and as Ram Singh went off through the gathering darkness with his precious burden of water, he beheld the giant striding away with the bones of his dead wife in his arms.

Great was the wonder and rejoicing in the camp when Ram Singh returned with the water. He never said anything, however, about his adventure with the giant, but merely told the Rajah that there was nothing to prevent the well being used, and used it was, and nobody ever saw any more of the giant.

The Rajah was so pleased with the bearing of Ram Singh that he ordered the vizier to give the young man to him in exchange for one of his own servants. So Ram Singh became the Rajah's attendant, and as the days went by the king became more and more delighted with the youth because, mindful of the old guru's third counsel, he was always honest and spoke the truth. He grew in favour rapidly, until eventually the Rajah made him his treasurer, and thus he reached a high place in the court and had wealth and power in his hands.

Unluckily the Rajah had a brother who was a very bad man, and this brother thought that if he could win the young treasurer over to himself he might by this means manage to steal little by little any of the king's treasure which he needed. Then, with plenty of money, he could bribe the soldiers and some of the Rajah's counsellors, head a rebellion, dethrone and kill his brother, and reign himself instead. He was too wary, of course, to tell Ram Singh of all these wicked plans, but he began by flattering him whenever he saw him, and at last offered him his daughter in marriage.

But Ram Singh remembered the fourth counsel of the old guru – 'Never to try to appear the equal of those above him in station'. Therefore he respectfully declined the great honour of marrying a princess. Of course the prince, baffled at the very beginning of his enterprise, was furious, and determined to work Ram Singh's ruin, and entering the Rajah's presence he told him a story about Ram Singh having spoken insulting words of his sovereign and of his daughter. What it was all about nobody knew, and, as it was not true, the wicked prince did not know either, but the Rajah grew very angry and red in the face as he listened, and declared that until the treasurer's head was cut off neither he nor the princess nor his brother would eat or drink.

"But," he added, "I do not wish anyone to know that this was done by my desire, and anyone who mentions the subject will be severely punished." And with this the prince was forced to be content.

Then the Rajah sent for an officer of his guard, and told him to take some soldiers and ride at once to a tower which was situated just outside the town, and if anyone should come to inquire when the building was going to be finished, or should ask any other questions about it, the officer must chop his head off, and bring it to him. As for the body, that could be buried on the spot. The old officer thought these instructions rather odd, but it was no business of his, so he saluted, and went off to do his master's bidding.

Early in the morning the Rajah, who had not slept all night, sent for Ram Singh, and bade him go to the new hunting-tower, and ask the people there how it was getting on and when it was going to be finished, and to hurry back with the answer! Away went Ram Singh upon his errand, but, on the road, as he was passing a little temple on the outskirts of the city, he heard someone inside reading aloud, and, remembering the guru's fifth counsel, he just stepped inside and sat down to listen for a minute. He did not mean to stay longer, but became so deeply interested in the wisdom of the teacher, that he sat, and sat, and sat, while the sun rose higher and higher.

In the meantime, the wicked prince, who dared not disobey the Rajah's command, was feeling very hungry, and as for the princess, she was quietly crying in a corner waiting for the news of Ram Singh's death, so that she might eat her breakfast.

Hours passed, and stare as he might from the window no messenger could be seen.

At last the prince could bear it no longer, and hastily disguising himself so that no one should recognise him, he jumped on a horse and galloped out to the hunting-tower, where the Rajah had told him that the execution was to take place. But, when he got there, there was no execution going on. There were only some men engaged in building, and a number of soldiers idly watching them. He forgot that he had disguised himself and that no one would know him, so, riding up, he cried out, "Now then, you men, why are you idling about here instead of finishing what you came to do? When is it to be done?"

At his words the soldiers looked at the commanding officer, who was standing a little apart from the rest. Unperceived by the prince he made a slight sign, a sword flashed in the sun, and off flew a head on the ground beneath!

As part of the prince's disguise had been a thick beard, the men did not recognise the dead man as the Rajah's brother, but they wrapped the head in a cloth, and buried the body as their commander bade them. When this was ended, the officer took the cloth, and rode off in the direction of the palace.

Meanwhile the Rajah came home from his council, and to his great surprise found neither head nor brother awaiting him. As time passed on, he became uneasy, and thought that he had better go himself and see what the matter was. So ordering his horse he rode off alone.

It happened that, just as the Rajah came near to the temple where Ram Singh still sat, the young treasurer, hearing the sound of a horse's hoofs, looked over his shoulder and saw that the rider was the Rajah himself! Feeling much ashamed of himself for having forgotten his errand, he jumped up and hurried out to meet his master, who reined in his horse, and seemed very surprised (as indeed he was) to see him. At that moment there arrived the officer of the guard carrying his parcel. He saluted the Rajah gravely, and, dismounting, laid the bundle in the road and began to undo the wrappings, whilst the Rajah watched him with wonder and interest. When the last string was undone, and the head of his brother was displayed to his view, the Rajah sprang from his horse and caught the soldier by the arm. As soon as he could speak he questioned the man as to what had occurred, and little by little a dark suspicion darted through him. Then, briefly telling the soldier that he had done well, the Rajah drew Ram Singh to one side, and in a few minutes learned from him how, in attending to the guru's counsel, he had delayed to do the king's message.

In the end the Rajah found from some papers the proofs of his dead brother's treachery, and Ram Singh established his innocence and integrity. He continued to serve the Rajah for many years with unswerving fidelity, and married a maiden of his own rank in life, with whom he lived happily, dying eventually honoured and loved by all men. Sons were born to him, and, in time, to them also he taught the five wise sayings of the old guru.

The Mysterious Garden

This story has been adapted from a tale originally told by Penrhyn Wingfield Coussens in The Jade Story Book; Stories From The Orient, published in 1922 by Duffield And Company, New York. One of the notable aspects of The Jade Story Book is Coussens' engaging narrative style, which brings the characters and settings to life while staying true to the spirit of the original tales.

Once upon a time there lived a mighty king who was both wise and just. This ruler issued a decree that no one in his dominions should receive any reward, office or honour that he did not truly deserve.

Now at the court were three royal children, each of them richly endowed with virtue and talent, and they grew up to be handsome and amiable young men, well-liked by everyone. The king was very fond of them and wished them to occupy the highest stations in life which would accord with their merit. So one day he sent for them and said, "My children, I would like to set you above all others in my palace, for I believe you capable of great deeds of virtue. But you know the law of this country which says that honours may be conferred upon no one who has not proved worthy to receive them. It is my desire that you attain high rank, but this you cannot reach by remaining at court. You will therefore go out into the world and try to earn, by your own endeavour, the prize promised by the law, and which I shall delight to bestow upon you. In due time I will send for you, and the summons must be answered without delay. Be careful what you do, for your reward will be that which you merit."

The king had ordered, and the three young men had to obey, although they did not relish leaving the court, where life was very pleasant for them. So they bade their sovereign good-bye, embarked on a ship and set sail, without any definite plan as to what country they should visit.

The weather was fine and they sailed on until they reached an island which looked very beautiful to them. They landed, and after walking for some time reached a fair garden full of wonderful trees, flowers and fruit. There they were met by three men, each of whom gave them a word of advice.

The first said that their stay in the garden would not be forever, and that the time would come when they would be forced to leave.

The second told them that they were welcome to enjoy all that the garden could offer, but that they must leave it just as they entered it, and take nothing away with them.

The third advised them to be virtuous, upright, and moderate in their pleasures, as such a course would go far towards living a long and happy life.

The young men listened to this wise counsel and then entered the garden, which was much more wonderful than they had imagined it to be. There were great trees, from the branches of which came the exquisite singing of innumerable birds. Their eyes were gladdened by the beauty of the flowers, which gave forth a most pleasing perfume, and they found an abundance of delicious fruit, with which the trees were laden. Here was a paradise.

For some time they rested under the shade of the trees, regaling themselves with the freshly-picked fruit and drinking from springs that bubbled and sparkled from the ground like fountains. Then they separated, each seeking a still more enchanting spot.

The first of the young men was so overcome by the beauty that surrounded him that he thought only of present enjoyment, forgetting entirely the advice of the man who had first addressed them before entering the garden. His only idea was to eat, sleep, be merry and cast away all care.

In his wanderings the second youth discovered gold, silver and precious stones in such abundance that neither the beauty of the flowers, with their fragrance, nor the lusciousness of the fruit appealed to him at all. He was dazzled by the treasures he found, and his only thought was of how much he could gather together and take away with him. He, too, forgot the warning of the second man who had spoken to them.

But the third young man bore in mind all the advice given them by the three guards, and he did not agree with the habits into which his companions had fallen. He certainly enjoyed his life in the garden, and took great pleasure in studying all that it contained. And the more he studied the greater was his wonder at the marvels of nature. Everything was in such good order and so well kept. There was not even a blade of grass that did not show evidence of having been watered. And the strangest thing about it was that he had seen no one to care for all of this. But the garden was so perfect and so admirably kept that it was impossible there should be no master gardener to keep this domain in such wonderful order.

So great became his admiration for this man, whoever he might be, that it became his greatest desire to know him, and to thank him for all the pleasure he had received from just being there, and for the opportunity allowed him to study the marvels that were all about him.

But there is an end to all things, and the course which each of these young men was pursuing was changed when an order from their king called upon them to return and render an account of their doings. So they set out for the gate by which they had entered, and as soon as they had passed through this the first of the three, he who had thought only of present enjoyment, was overcome by the change of air. He had left the garden, to the fruit of which he had become so accustomed, and his strength left him, and he sank to the ground and expired.

The second one struggled along, staggering beneath the weight of treasure he had gathered, the thought of enjoying which helped him to forget his weariness. But as soon as he had passed the gate the men on guard took from him all of the spoil, leaving him wretched, despairing and unhappy.

The third youth, however, reached the gate and passed through it in a happy frame of mind. He was sure that now he would find the master gardener, and be able to express his gratitude to him for the marvels he had seen and studied. He was welcomed by the guards, who were pleased to congratulate him upon the way in which he had listened to and heeded their good advice and counsel.

The youth, whose treasure had been taken from him, drew near to the court. He was so weary that he could scarcely drag himself along. He was changed too, so that those who had formerly known him did not recognize him now. When he claimed relationship to the king they laughed and jeered at him. He insisted upon entering the palace, but instead of being allowed to do this he was thrown into prison.

But how different was the reception of the third young man! Many of the courtiers went out to greet him, and accompanied him to the king's presence. His Majesty rejoiced at his return, and although he knew all that had happened since he left the court, he asked him to tell his own story.

The youth told the king all about the wonderful garden, and said that it was his great desire to meet the master of so enchanting a place, and to express to him his thanks for the great pleasure that had been his while living in such a paradise.

"Your wish shall be granted," said the king. "I am the master of the garden, and rule it from here through my ministers. There is no living or growing thing there that is not carefully watched, not even a blade of grass."

And now the young man understood that which had before been a mystery to him, and the love and gratitude he had always felt for his master grew greater. The king commended him for his good conduct and for the manner in which he had acted upon the advice given by the three guards, and as a reward raised him to a position of power and honour.

Story Of The Wonderful Mango Fruit

This story has been adapted from a tale originally told by Mrs. Howard Kingscote and Pandit Natêsá Sástrî in Tales Of The Sun, published in 1890 by H. Allen & Co., London and Calcutta. The book contains a selection of tales from Indian mythology and folklore, centred around the theme of the sun. These tales often revolve around various deities associated with the sun, such as Surya, the solar deity in Hinduism.

On the banks of the Kâvêrî there was a city called Tiruvidaimarudur, where a king named Chakraditya ruled. In that city there lived a poor Brâhman and his wife, who, having no children, brought up in their house a young parrot as tenderly as if it had been their own offspring. One day the parrot was sitting on the roof of the house, basking itself in the morning sun, when a large flock of parrots flew past, talking to each other about certain mango fruits. The Brâhman's parrot asked them what the peculiar properties of those fruits were, and was informed that beyond the seven oceans there was a great mango tree, the fruit of which gave perpetual youth to the person who ate it, however old and infirm he might be. On hearing of this wonder the Brâhman's parrot requested permission to accompany them, which being granted, they all continued their flight. When at length they arrived at the mango tree, all ate of its fruit, but the Brâhman's parrot reflected, "It would not be right for me to eat this fruit. I am young, while my adopted parents, the poor Brâhman and his wife are very old. So I shall give them this fruit, and they will become young and blooming by eating it."

And that same evening the good parrot brought the fruit to the Brâhman, and explained to him its extraordinary properties. But the Brâhman said to himself, "I am a beggar. What does it matter if I become young and live for ever, or else die this very moment? Our king is very good and charitable. If such a great man should eat this fruit and renew his youth, he would confer the greatest benefit on mankind. Therefore I will give this mango to our good king."

In pursuance of this self-denying resolution, the poor Brâhman proceeded to the palace and presented the fruit to the king, at the same time relating how he had obtained it and its qualities. The king richly rewarded the Brâhman for his gift, and sent him away. Then he began to reflect thus, "Here is a fruit which can bestow perpetual youth on the person who eats it. I should gain this great boon for myself alone, and what happiness could I expect under such circumstances unless shared by my friends and subjects? I shall therefore not eat this mango-fruit, but plant it carefully in my garden, and it will in time become a tree, which will bear much fruit having the same wonderful virtue, and my subjects shall, every one of them, eat the fruit, and, with myself, be endowed with everlasting youth."

So, calling his gardener, the king gave him the fruit, and he planted it in the royal presence. In due course of time the fruit grew into a fine tree, and during the spring season it began to bud and blossom and bear fruit. The king, having fixed upon an auspicious day for cutting one of the mango-fruits, gave it to his domestic chaplain, who was ninety years old, in order that his youth should be renewed.

But no sooner had the priest tasted it than he fell down dead. At this unexpected calamity the king was both astonished and deeply grieved. When the old priest's wife heard of her husband's sudden death she came and prayed the king to allow her to perform sati with him on the same funeral pyre, which increased the king's sorrow, but he gave her the desired permission, and himself superintended all the ceremonies of the cremation. King Chakraditya then sent for the poor Brâhman, and demanded of him how he had dared to present a poisonous fruit to his king.

The Brâhman replied, "My lord, I brought up a young parrot in my house, in order to console me for having no son. That parrot brought me the fruit one day, and told me of its wonderful properties. Believing that the parrot spoke the truth, I presented it to your Majesty, never for a moment suspecting it to be poisonous."

The king listened to the poor Brâhman's words, but thought that the poor priest's death should be avenged. So he consulted his ministers who recommended, as a slight punishment, that the Brâhman should be deprived of his left eye. This was done accordingly, and, on his return home, when his wife saw his condition, she asked the reason of such mutilation.

"My dear," she said, "the parrot we have fostered so tenderly is the cause of this."

And they resolved to break the neck of the treacherous bird. But the parrot, having overheard their conversation, then addressed them, saying, "My kind foster parents, everyone must be rewarded for the good actions or punished for the evil deeds of his previous life. I brought you the fruit with a good intention, but my sins in my former life have given it a different effect. Therefore I pray you kill me and bury me with a little milk in a pit. And, after my funeral ceremony is over, I request you undertake a pilgrimage to Banaras to expiate your own sins."

So the old Brâhman and his wife killed their pet parrot and buried it as directed, after which, overcome with grief, they set out on a pilgrimage to the Holy City.

Meanwhile the king commanded his gardener to set guards over the poison-tree, and to allow no one to eat its fruit, and all the inhabitants soon came to know that the king had a mango tree in his garden, the fruit of which was deadly poison. Now, there was in the city an old washerwoman, who had frequent quarrels with her daughter-in-law, and one day, being weary of life, she left the house, threatening to eat of the poison tree and die.

The young parrot who was killed for having brought the poisonous mango-fruit was re-born as a green parrot, and was waiting for an opportunity to demonstrate the harmless nature of the tree, and when he saw the old woman approach with a determination to put an end to her life by eating its fruit, he plucked one with his beak and dropped it down before her. The old woman rejoiced that fate sanctioned her death, and greedily ate the fruit, when instead of dying she became young and blooming again. Those who had seen her leave the house a woman over sixty years of age were astonished on seeing her return as a handsome girl of sixteen and learning that the wonderful transformation was caused by the supposed poisonous mango-tree.

The strange news soon reached the king, who, in order to test the tree still further, ordered another fruit of it to be brought and gave it to a goldsmith of more than ninety years of age, who had embezzled some gold which had been entrusted to him to make into ornaments for the ladies of the palace, and was on that account undergoing imprisonment. When he had eaten the fruit, he, in his turn, became a young man of sixteen. The king was now convinced that the fruit of the mango-tree, so far from being poisonous, had the power of converting decrepit age into lusty and perennial youth. But how had the old priest died by eating of it?

It was by a mere accident. One day a huge serpent was sleeping on a branch of the mango-tree, and its head hung over one of the fruits. Poison dropped from its mouth and fell on the rind of that fruit, and the gardener, who had no knowledge of this, when asked to bring a fruit for the priest, happened to bring the one on which the poison had fallen, and the priest having eaten it, died.

And now the king caused proclamation to be made throughout his kingdom that all who pleased might come and partake of the mango-fruit, and everyone who ate it became young again. But king Chakaraditya's heart burnt within him at the remembrance of his ill-treatment of the poor Brâhman, who had returned with his wife from Banaras. So he sent for him, explained his mistake, and gave him a fruit to eat, which, having tasted, the aged Brâhman became young and his eye was also restored to him. But the greatest loss of all, that of the parrot who brought the fruit from beyond the seven oceans, remained irreparable.

Why The Fish Laughed

This story has been adapted from a tale originally told by Hamilton Wright Mabie in Young Folks Treasury, Volume 2, published in 1909 by The University Society Inc, New York. Young Folks Treasury, Volume 2 was part of a larger collection of children's literature compiled and edited by Hamilton Wright Mabie, a renowned American essayist, editor, and critic.

As a certain fisherwoman passed by a palace selling her fish, the Queen appeared at one of the windows and beckoned her to come near and show what she had. At that moment a very big fish jumped about in the bottom of the basket.

"Is it a he or a she?" inquired the Queen. "I wish to purchase a she-fish."

On hearing this the fish laughed aloud.

"It's a he," replied the fisherwoman, and proceeded on her rounds.

The Queen returned to her room in a great rage, and on coming to see her in the evening, the King noticed that something had disturbed her.

"Are you indisposed?" he said.

"No, but I am very much annoyed at the strange behaviour of a fish. A woman brought me one today, and on my inquiring whether it was a male or female, the fish laughed most rudely."

"A fish laugh! Impossible! You must be dreaming."

"I am not a fool. I speak of what I have seen with my own eyes and have heard with my own ears."

"Passing strange! Be it so. I will inquire concerning it."

On the morrow the King repeated to his vizier what his wife had told him, and bade him investigate the matter, and be ready with a satisfactory answer within six months, on pain of death. The vizier promised to do his best, though he felt almost certain of failure. For five months he laboured indefatigably to find a reason for the laughter of the fish. He sought everywhere and from everyone. The wise and learned, and they who were skilled in magic and in all manner of trickery, were consulted. Nobody, however, could explain the matter, and so he returned broken-hearted to his house, and began to arrange his affairs in prospect of certain death, for he had sufficient experience of the King to know that his Majesty would not go back from his threat. Among other things, he advised his son to travel for a time, until the King's anger should have somewhat cooled.

The young fellow, who was both clever and handsome, started off wherever fate might lead him. He had been gone some days, when he fell in with an old farmer, who also was on a journey to a certain village. Finding the old man very pleasant, he asked him if he might accompany him, professing to be on a visit to the same place. The old farmer agreed, and they walked along together. The day was hot, and the way was long and weary.

"Don't you think it would be pleasanter if you and I sometimes gave each other a lift?" said the youth.

"What a fool the man is!" thought the old farmer.

Presently they passed through a field of corn ready for the sickle, and looking like a sea of gold as it waved to and fro in the breeze.

"Is this eaten or not?" said the young man.

Not understanding his meaning, the old man replied, "I don't know."

After a little while the two travellers arrived at a big village, where the young man gave his companion a clasp-knife, and said, "Take this, friend, and get two horses with it, but mind and bring it back, for it is very precious."

The old man, looking half amused and half angry, pushed back the knife, muttering something to the effect that his friend was either a fool himself, or else trying to play the fool with him. The young man pretended not to notice his reply, and remained almost silent till they reached the city, a short distance outside which was the old farmer's house. They walked about the bazaar and went to the mosque, but nobody saluted them or invited them to come in and rest.

"What a large cemetery!" exclaimed the young man.

"What does the man mean," thought the old farmer, "calling this largely populated city a cemetery?"

On leaving the city their way led through a graveyard where a few people were praying beside a tomb and distributing chapatis and kulchas to passers-by, in the name of their beloved dead. They beckoned to the two travellers and gave them as much as they wanted.

"What a splendid city this is!" said the young man.

'Now, the man must surely be demented!' thought the old farmer. 'I wonder what he will do next. He will be calling the land water, and the water land, and be speaking of light where there is darkness, and of darkness when it is light.' However, he kept his thoughts to himself.

Presently they had to wade through a stream that ran along the edge of the cemetery. The water was rather deep, so the old farmer took off his shoes and pyjamas and crossed over, but the young man waded through it with his shoes and pyjamas on.

"Well! I never did see such a perfect fool, both in word and in deed," said the old man to himself.

However, he liked the fellow, and thinking that he would amuse his wife and daughter, he invited him to come and stay at his house as long as he had occasion to remain in the village.

"Thank you very much," the young man replied, "but let me first inquire, if you please, whether the beam of your house is strong."

The old farmer left him in despair, and entered his house laughing.

"There is a man in yonder field," he said, after returning their greetings. "He has come the greater part of the way with me, and I wanted him to put up here as long as he had to stay in this village. But the fellow is such a fool that I cannot make anything out of him. He wants to know if the beam of this house is all right. The man must be mad!" and saying this, he burst into a fit of laughter.

"Father," said the farmer's daughter, who was a very sharp and wise girl, "this man, whoever he is, is no fool, as you deem him. He only wishes to know if you can afford to entertain him."

"Oh, of course," replied the farmer. "I see. Well, perhaps you can help me to solve some of his other mysteries. While we were walking together he asked whether he should carry me or I should carry him, as he thought that would be a pleasanter mode of proceeding."

"Most assuredly," said the girl, "he meant that one of you should tell a story to beguile the time."

"Oh yes. Well, we were passing through a corn-field, when he asked me whether it was eaten or not."

"And didn't you know the meaning of this, father? He simply wished to know if the man was in debt or not, because, if the owner of the field was in debt, then the produce of the field was as good as eaten to him; that is, it would have to go to his creditors."

"Yes, yes, yes, of course! Then, on entering a certain village, he bade me take his clasp-knife and get two horses with it, and bring back the knife to him."

"Are not two stout sticks as good as two horses for helping one along on the road? He only asked you to cut a couple of sticks and be careful not to lose his knife."

"I see," said the farmer. "While we were walking over the city we did not see anybody that we knew, and not a soul gave us a scrap of anything to eat, till we were passing the cemetery, but there some people called to us and put into our hands some chapatis and kulchas, so my companion called the city a cemetery, and the cemetery a city."

"This also is to be understood, father, if one thinks of the city as the place where everything is to be obtained, and of inhospitable people as worse than the dead. The city, though crowded with people, was as if dead, as far as you were concerned; while, in the cemetery, which is crowded with the dead, you were saluted by kind friends and provided with bread."

"True, true!" said the astonished farmer. "Then, just now, when we were crossing the stream, he waded through it without taking off his shoes and pyjamas."

"I admire his wisdom," replied the girl. "I have often thought how stupid people were to venture into that swiftly flowing stream and over those sharp stones with bare feet. The slightest stumble and they would fall, and be wetted from head to foot. This friend of yours is a most wise man. I should like to see him and speak to him."

"Very well," said the farmer, "I will go and find him, and bring him in."

"Tell him, father, that our beams are strong enough, and then he will come in. I'll send on ahead a present to the man, to show him that we can afford to have him for our guest."

Accordingly she called a servant and sent him to the young man with a present of a basin of ghee, twelve chapatis, and a jar of milk, and the following message, "O friend, the moon is full, twelve months make a year, and the sea is overflowing with water."

Half-way the bearer of this present and message met his little son, who, seeing what was in the basket, begged his father to give him some of the food. His father foolishly complied. Presently he saw the young man, and gave him the rest of the present and the message.

"Give your mistress my salaam," he replied, "and tell her that the moon is new, and that I can find only eleven months in the year, and the sea is by no means full."

Not understanding the meaning of these words, the servant repeated them word for word, as he had heard them, to his mistress, and thus his theft was discovered, and he was severely punished. After a little while the young man appeared with the old farmer. Great attention was shown to him, and he was treated in every way as if he were the son of a great man, although his humble host knew nothing of his origin. At length he told them everything, about the laughing of the fish, his father's threatened execution, and his own banishment, and then he asked their advice as to what he should do.

"The laughing of the fish," said the girl, "which seems to have been the cause of all this trouble, indicates that there is a man in the palace who is plotting against the King's life."

"Joy, joy!" exclaimed the vizier's son. "There is yet time for me to return and save my father from an ignominious and unjust death, and the King from danger."

The following day he hastened back to his own country, taking with him the farmer's daughter. Immediately on arrival he ran to the palace and informed his father of what he had heard. The poor vizier, now almost dead with worry, was at once carried to the King, to whom he repeated the news that his son had just brought.

"Never!" said the King.

"But it must be so, your Majesty," replied the vizier, "and in order to prove the truth of what I have heard, I pray you to call together all the maids in your palace and order them to jump over a pit, which must be dug. We'll soon find out whether there is any man there."

The King had the pit dug, and commanded all the maids belonging to the palace to try to jump over it. All of them tried, but only one succeeded. That one was found to be a man! Thus was the Queen satisfied, and the faithful old vizier saved.

Afterward, as soon as could be, the vizier's son married the old farmer's daughter, and a most happy marriage it was.

The Tiger, the Brahman, and the Jackal

This story has been adapted from a tale originally told by Joseph Jacobs in Indian Fairy Tales, published in 1892 by David Nutt, London. Joseph Jacobs was a prolific collector and re-teller of folktales from different cultures. Indian Fairy Tales includes a diverse range of stories, featuring elements of magic, mythology, and adventure. Many of these tales have been passed down through oral tradition for generations, reflecting the cultural richness and diversity of India.

Once upon a time, a tiger was caught in a trap. He tried in vain to get out through the bars, and rolled and bit with rage and grief when he failed.

By chance a poor Brahman came by. "Let me out of this cage, oh pious one!" cried the tiger.

"No, my friend," replied the Brahman mildly, "you would probably eat me if I did."

"Not at all!" swore the tiger with many oaths, "On the contrary, I should be for ever grateful, and serve you as a slave!"

Now when the tiger sobbed and sighed and wept and swore, the pious Brahman's heart softened, and at last he consented to open the door of the cage. Out popped the tiger, and, seizing the poor man, cried, "What a fool you are! What is to prevent my eating you now, for after being cooped up so long I am just terribly hungry!"

The Brahman pleaded desperately for his life, but all he could secure was a pledge to accept the verdict of the first three beings he chose to interrogate regarding the fairness of the tiger's actions.

So the Brahman first asked a pipal tree what it thought of the matter, but the pipal tree replied coldly, "What have you to complain about? Don't I give shade and shelter to everyone who passes by, and don't they in return tear down my branches to feed their cattle? Don't whimper, be a man!"

Then the Brahman, sad at heart, went further afield till he saw a buffalo turning a well-wheel, but he fared no better from it, for it answered, "You are a fool to expect gratitude! Look at me! Whilst I gave milk they fed me on cotton-seed and oil-cake, but now I am dry they yoke me here, and give me refuse as fodder!"

The Brahman, still more sad, asked the road to give him its opinion.

"My dear sir," said the road, "how foolish you are to expect anything else! Here am I, useful to everybody, yet all, rich and poor, great and small, trample on me as they go past, giving me nothing but the ashes of their pipes and the husks of their grain!"

On this the Brahman turned back sorrowfully, and on the way he met a jackal, who called out, "Why, what's the matter, Mr. Brahman? You look as miserable as a fish out of water!"

The Brahman told him all that had occurred. "How very confusing!" said the jackal, when the recital was ended, "Would you mind telling me over again, for everything has got so mixed up?"

The Brahman told it all over again, but the jackal shook his head in a distracted sort of way, and still could not understand.

"It's very odd," he said, sadly, "but it all seems to go in at one ear and out at the other! I will go to the place where it all happened, and then perhaps I shall be able to give a judgment."

So they returned to the cage, by which the tiger was waiting for the Brahman, and sharpening his teeth and claws.

"You've been away a long time!" growled the savage beast, "But now let us begin our dinner."

"Our dinner!" thought the wretched Brahman, as his knees knocked together with fright, "What a remarkably delicate way of putting it!"

"Give me five minutes, my lord," he pleaded, "in order that I may explain matters to the jackal here, who is somewhat slow in his wits."

The tiger consented, and the Brahman began the whole story over again, not missing a single detail, and spinning as long a yarn as possible.

"Oh, my poor brain! Oh, my poor brain!" cried the jackal, wringing its paws. "Let me see! How did it all begin? You were in the cage, and the tiger came walking by…"

"Pooh!" interrupted the tiger, "what a fool you are! I was in the cage."

"Of course!" cried the jackal, pretending to tremble with fright, "Yes! I was in the cage… no, I wasn't…dear, dear! Where are my wits? Let me see… The tiger was in the Brahman, and the cage came walking by… no, that's not it, either! Well, don't mind me, but begin your dinner, for I shall never understand!"

"Yes, you shall!" returned the tiger, in a rage at the jackal's stupidity, "I'll make you understand! Look here… I am the tiger…"

"Yes, my lord!"

"And that is the Brahman. "

"Yes, my lord!"

"And that is the cage"

"Yes, my lord!"

"And I was in the cage, do you understand?"

"Yes…no…please, my lord…"

"Well?" cried the tiger impatiently.

"Please, my lord! How did you get in?"

"How! Why in the usual way, of course!"

"Oh, dear me! My head is beginning to whirl again! Please don't be angry, my lord, but what is the usual way?"

At this the tiger lost patience, and, jumping into the cage, cried, "This way! Now do you understand how it was?"

"Perfectly!" grinned the jackal, as he dexterously shut the door, "and if you will permit me to say so, I think matters will remain as they were!"

The Monkey With The Tom-Tom

This story has been adapted from a tale originally told by Mrs. Howard Kingscote and Pandit Natêsá Sástrî in Tales Of The Sun, published in 1890 by H. Allen & Co., London and Calcutta. The book contains a selection of tales from Indian mythology and folklore, centred around the theme of the sun. These tales often revolve around various deities associated with the sun, such as Surya, the solar deity in Hinduism.

In a remote wood there lived a monkey, and one day while he was eating wood-apples, a sharp thorn from the tree ran into the tip of his tail, he tried his best to get it out but could not. So he proceeded to the nearest village, and calling the barber asked him to oblige him by removing the thorn.

"Friend barber," said the monkey, "a thorn has run into my tail. Kindly remove it and I will reward you."

The barber took up his razor and began to examine the tail, but as he was cutting out the thorn he cut off the tip of the tail. The monkey was greatly enraged and said, "Friend barber, give me back my tail. If you cannot do that, give me your razor."

The barber was now in a difficulty, and as he could not replace the tip of the tail he had to give up his razor to the monkey.

The monkey went back to the wood with his razor thus tricksily acquired. On the way he met an old woman, who was cutting fuel from a dried-up tree.

"Grandmother, grandmother," said the monkey, "the tree is very hard. You had better use this sharp razor, and you will cut your fuel easily."

The poor woman was very pleased, and took the razor from the monkey. In cutting the wood she, of course, blunted the razor, and the monkey seeing his razor thus spoiled, said, "Grandmother, you have spoiled my razor. So you must either give me your fuel or get me a better razor."

The woman was not able to procure another razor. So she gave the monkey her fuel and returned to her house bearing no load that day.

The roguish monkey now put the bundle of dry fuel on his head and proceeded to a village to sell it. There he met an old woman seated by the roadside and making puddings. The monkey said to her, "Grandmother, grandmother, you are making puddings and your fuel is already exhausted. Use mine also and make more cakes."

The old lady thanked him for his kindness and used his fuel for her puddings. The cunning monkey waited till the last stick of his fuel was burnt up, and then he said to the old woman, "Grandmother, grandmother, return me my fuel or give me all your puddings."

She was unable to return him the fuel, and so had to give him all her puddings.

The monkey with the basket of puddings on his head walked and walked till he met a Paraiya coming with a tom-tom towards him.

"Brother Paraiya," said the monkey, "I have a basketful of puddings to give you. Will you, in return, present me with your tom-tom?"

The Paraiya gladly agreed, as he was then very hungry, and had nothing with him to eat.

The monkey now ascended with the tom-tom to the topmost branch of a big tree and there beat his drum most triumphantly, saying in honour of his several tricks:

"I lost my tail and got a razor; dum dum."

"I lost my razor and got a bundle of fuel; dum dum."

"I lost my fuel and got a basket of puddings; dum dum".

"I lost my puddings and got a tom-tom; dum dum."

Thus there are rogues in this innocent world, who live to glory over their wicked tricks.

Pride Must Have a Fall

This story has been adapted from a tale originally told by W. H. D. Rouse in The Giant Crab and Other Tales from Old India, published in 1897 by David Nutt, London. The tales in the collection cover a wide range of themes, including adventure, morality, wisdom, and magic. Many of the stories feature talking animals, brave heroes, cunning tricksters, and mythical beings, offering readers a glimpse into the rich storytelling traditions of India.

Once upon a time there was a beautiful wild Goose that lived in the mountains. He was King of the Geese, and he had a mate and two or three fine young ones. But it had happened once that this Goose, in his travels about the world, fell in with a young lady Crow, who was very pretty, as black as jet, with two eyes like black beads, and she flirted and flouted so enchantingly that he had married her, like the goose he was, so he had two wives, the little black Crow and the Goose.

In course of time this Crow laid a beautiful egg, all white with blue spots, and twice as big as an ordinary crow's egg. She was very proud of her egg, and sat on it for a long time, until one day, pop went the egg, and out came a funny little chick. The Crow did not know what to make of this chick, for he was not black, as she was, and he was not white, like his father, but something betwixt and between, a dingy grey with brown streaks. So she named him Streaky.

Be sure that Streaky fancied himself mightily, being so very different from all the Crows he lived with. He was larger, to begin with, and then he had a very loud voice, with several different notes in it; not to mention his brown streaks, which made him a proud bird indeed. And I think the other Crows took him at his own price, as foolish creatures are apt to do, and thought him very wonderful, though he was really only a mongrel.

Now the Goose, his father, used to pay a visit to the Crow colony now and again, flying down from the mountains to the dust-heap where they lived, outside the city gate. But he did not stay long, because the Crows used to feed on offal and dead bodies, in fact anything dirty they could find, and King Goose could not get what he liked to eat.

Well, once as he was talking to his sons, the young Geese, they asked him why he was always going away for days at a time.

"Why," he said, "I go to see a son of mine that lives somewhere else."

"Oh, how nice!" said the Geese. "Then he must be our brother. Do let us bring him here on a visit! Do, father!"

At first the father Goose would not let them go, for fear of mischief, but after a while he was persuaded, and gave them very careful directions how to fly, and where to go, and how to find the place where Streaky lived, on the top of a tall palm-tree that grew out of a dust-heap at the city gate.

So away they flew, and away they flew, till at last they saw the tall palm-tree, and on the very top of it, a big nest, and in the nest, a little black Crow, and our funny friend Streaky.

They said, "How do you do?" and told the crow and Streaky all about their errand, because they meant to go through with it now, although they did not much like the look of this ugly bird Streaky, with his airs and graces.

Mrs. Crow was very much pleased, but Streaky looked bored, and said, "Aw, caw, I don't think I can fly all that way. It is really too much trouble. Why did the Governor not come to see me instead, as usual, aw?" This rude bird called his father the Governor, you see, as he had been brought up among carrion crows, and his manners were none of the best.

The young Geese began to like him less than ever. However, they put a good face on it, and answered him, "Well, Streaky, if you are as weak as all that, we will carry you on a stick."

These Geese were very big, strong birds, and they thought nothing of carrying Streaky. So they looked about until they found a strong stick, and then each of them took an end in his mouth, and Streaky perched in the middle. They could not say good-bye to Mrs. Crow, because their mouths were full of the stick, but they made her a nice bow, like polite little Geese, and flew off.

As for Streaky, he was far too full of his own importance to say good-bye to his mother, or even so much as "Thank you" to the two birds who were so kindly carrying him. There he sat on the middle of the stick, as proud as Punch, pluming his feathers, and feeling that now all the world would see what a splendid bird he was.

As they flew over the city Streaky looked down, and saw the king of the city, in a beautiful carriage drawn by four white thoroughbreds, driving round the city in great state and grandeur. "Aha!" thought he, "that's as it should be! But I'm every bit as good as he!" and in his joy he began to sing a little song which he made up on the spur of the moment, and here is his song:

"As yonder king goes galloping with his milk-white four-in-hand,

Streaky has these, his pair of Geese, to carry him over the land!"

The Geese were very angry when they heard Streaky sing this song. But they were very well-bred Geese, as you must have seen already, so they said nothing at all to him then, but carried him safely to their home, and then they told their father what Streaky had said, so that he might do as he thought best.

Old King Goose was angrier than they were, and was very sorry he had left his son to be brought up by a Crow who knew no manners. So he called Streaky, and this is what he said, "Streaky, you have been very rude to your brothers, who are at least as good as you, and if you think they are like a pair of horses, to be driven about for your pleasure, you make a great mistake. So the best thing you can do is to fly back to your mother, for your manners suit the dust-heap better than the mountains."

I don't know whether Streaky was ashamed of what he had said. Creatures like Streaky are very thick-skinned, and it takes a great deal to make them ashamed, but anyhow he had to go back, and this time he must fly by himself, for it was hardly likely that his brothers would carry him when he had been so rude. He got back a few days later, tired and hungry, and spent the rest of his days on the dust-heap, eating carrion.

What his mother thought of it all I don't know, but King Goose never went to see them anymore.

The Talkative Tortoise

This story has been adapted from a tale originally told by Joseph Jacobs in Indian Fairy Tales, published in 1892 by David Nutt, London. Joseph Jacobs was a prolific collector and re-teller of folktales from different cultures. Indian Fairy Tales includes a diverse range of stories, featuring elements of magic, mythology, and adventure. Many of these tales have been passed down through oral tradition for generations, reflecting the cultural richness and diversity of India.

The future Buddha was once born in a minister's family, when Brahma-datta was reigning in Benares, and when he grew up, he became the king's adviser in things temporal and spiritual.

Now this king was very talkative. While he was speaking, others had no opportunity to say a word. And the future Buddha, wanting to cure this talkativeness, was constantly seeking for some means of doing so.

At that time there was living, in a pond in the Himalaya mountains, a tortoise. Two young hamsas, or wild ducks, who came to feed there, made friends with him. And one day, when they had become very intimate with him, they said to the tortoise, "Friend tortoise!

The place where we live, at the Golden Cave on Mount Beautiful in the Himalaya country, is a delightful spot. Will you come there with us?"

"But how can I get there?"

"We can take you, if you can only hold your tongue, and will say nothing to anybody."

"Oh, that I can do. Take me with you."

"That's right," they said. And making the tortoise bite hold of a stick, they themselves took the two ends in their teeth, and flew up into the air.

Seeing him carried by the hamsas, some villagers called out, "Two wild ducks are carrying a tortoise along on a stick!"

Whereupon the tortoise wanted to say, "If my friends choose to carry me, what is that to you, you wretched slaves!"

So just as the swift flight of the wild ducks had brought him over the king's palace in the city of Benares, he let go of the stick he was biting, and falling in the open courtyard, split in two! And there arose a universal cry, "A tortoise has fallen in the open courtyard, and has split in two!"

The king, taking the future Buddha, went to the place, surrounded by his courtiers, and looking at the tortoise, he asked the Bodisat, "Teacher! Why has he fallen here?"

The future Buddha thought to himself, 'Long wishing to admonish the king, I have sought for some means of doing so. This tortoise must have made friends with the wild ducks, and they must have made him bite hold of the stick, and have flown up into the air to take him to the hills. But he, being unable to hold his tongue when he hears anyone else talk, must have wanted to say something, and let go the stick, and so must have fallen down from the sky, and thus lost his life.' Then he said, "Truly, O king! Those who are called chatter-boxes, people whose words have no end, come to grief like this." Then he uttered these Verses:

"Verily the tortoise killed himself

Whilst uttering his voice;

Though he was holding tight the stick,

By a word himself he slew.

"Behold him then, O excellent by strength!

And speak wise words, not out of season.

You see how, by his talking overmuch,

The tortoise fell into this wretched plight!"

The king saw that he was himself referred to, and said, "O Teacher, are you speaking of us?"

And the Bodisat spoke openly, and said, "O great king, be it you, or be it any other, whoever talks beyond measure meets with some mishap like this."

And the king henceforth refrained himself, and became a man of few words.

The Fate Of The Turtle

This story has been adapted from a tale originally told by Andrew Lang in The Olive Fairy Book, published in 1907 by Longmans, Green And Co., London And New York. Andrew Lang's Coloured Fairy Books were a series of twelve collections of fairy tales and folk stories from around the world, edited and compiled by Scottish author Andrew Lang. The first volume, The Blue Fairy Book, was published in 1889, followed by eleven more volumes, each with a different colour in the title, such as The Red Fairy Book, The Green Fairy Book, and so on, concluding with The Lilac Fairy Book in 1910. This story was based on a story originally told in Les Contes et Fables Indiennes. By M. Galland, 1724. This is also an interesting version of the previous tale, The Talkative Tortoise.

In a very hot country, far away to the east, was a beautiful little lake where two wild ducks made their home, and passed their days swimming and playing in its clear waters. They had it all to themselves, except for a turtle, who was many years older than they were, and had come there before them, and, luckily, instead of taking a dislike to the turtle, as so often happens when you have only one person to speak to, they became great friends, and spent most of the day in each other's company.

All went on smoothly and happily till one summer, when the rains failed and the sun shone so fiercely that every morning there was a little less water in the lake and a little more mud on the bank. The water-lilies around the edge began to droop, and the palms to hang their heads. The ducks' favourite swimming place, where they could dive the deepest, grew shallower and shallower. At length there came a morning when the ducks looked at each other uneasily, and before nightfall they had whispered that if at the end of two days rain had not come, they must fly away and seek a new home, for if they stayed in their old one, which they loved so much, they would certainly die of thirst.

Earnestly they watched the sky for many hours before they tucked their heads under their wings and fell asleep from sheer weariness, but not the tiniest cloud was to be seen covering the stars that shone so big and brilliant, and hung so low in the heavens that you felt as if you could touch them. So, when the morning broke, they made up their minds that they must go and tell the turtle of their plans, and bid him farewell.

They found him comfortably curled up on a pile of dead rushes, more than half asleep, for he was old, and could not venture out in the heat as he once used.

"Ah, here you are," he cried. "I began to wonder if I was ever going to see you again, for, somehow, though the lake has grown smaller, I seem to have grown weaker, and it is lonely spending all day and night by oneself!"

"Oh, my friend," answered the elder of the two ducks, "if you have suffered we have suffered also. Besides, I have something to tell you, that I fear will cause you greater pain still. If we do not wish to die of thirst we must leave this place at once, and seek another where the sun's rays do not come. My heart bleeds to say this, for there is nothing, nothing else in the world, which would have induced us to separate from you."

The turtle was so astonished as well as so distressed at the duck's speech that for a moment he could find no words to reply. But when he had forced back his tears, he said in a shaky voice, "How can you think that I am able to live without you, when for so long you have been my only friends? If you leave me, death will speedily put an end to my grief."

"Our sorrow is as great as yours," answered the other duck, "but what can we do? And remember that if we are not here to drink the water, there will be the more for you! If it had not been for this terrible misfortune, be sure that nothing would have parted us from one whom we love so dearly."

"My friends," replied the turtle, "water is as necessary to me as to you, and if death stares in your faces, it stares in mine also. But in the name of all the years we have passed together, do not, I beseech you, leave me to perish here alone! Wherever you may go take me with you!"

There was a pause. The ducks felt wretched at the thought of abandoning their old comrade, yet, at the same time, how could they grant his prayer? It seemed quite impossible, and at length one of them spoke, "Oh, how can I find words to refuse?" he cried, "yet how can we do what you ask? Consider that, like yours, our bodies are heavy and our feet small. Therefore, how could we walk with you over mountains and deserts, till we reached a land where the sun's rays no longer burn? Why, before the day was out we should all three be dead of fatigue and hunger! No, our only hope lies in our wings, and, alas, you cannot fly!"

"No, I cannot fly, of course," answered the turtle, with a sigh. "But you are so clever, and have seen so much of the world, surely you can think of some plan?" And he fixed his eyes eagerly on them.

Now, when the ducks saw how ardently the turtle wished to accompany them their hearts were touched, and making a sign to their friend that they wished to be alone they swam out into the lake to consult together. Though he could not hear what they said, the turtle could watch, and the half-hour that their talk lasted felt to him like a hundred years. At length he saw them returning side by side, and so great was his anxiety to know his fate he almost died from excitement before they reached him.

"We hope we have found a plan that may do for you," said the big duck gravely, "but we must warn you that it is not without great danger, especially if you are not careful to follow our directions."

"How is it possible that I should not follow your directions when my life and happiness are at stake?" asked the turtle joyfully. "Tell me what they are, and I will promise to obey them gratefully."

"Well, then," answered the duck, "whilst we are carrying you through the air, in the manner that we have fixed upon, you must remain as quiet as if you were dead. However high above the earth you may find yourself, you must not feel afraid, nor move your feet nor open your mouth. No matter what you see or hear, it is absolutely needful for you to be perfectly still, or I cannot answer for the consequences."

"I will be absolutely obedient," answered the turtle, "not only on this occasion but during all my life, and once more I promise faithfully not to move head or foot, to fear nothing, and never to speak a word during the whole journey."

This being settled, the ducks swam about till they found, floating in the lake, a good stout stick. This they tied to their necks with some of the tough water-lily roots, and returned as quickly as they could to the turtle.

"Now," said the elder duck, pushing the stick gently towards his friend, "take this stick firmly in your mouth, and do not let it go till we have set you down on earth again."

The turtle did as he was told, and the ducks in their turn seized the stick by the two ends, spread their wings and mounted swiftly into the air, the turtle hanging between them.

For a while all went well. They swept across valleys, over great mountains, above ruined cities, but no lake was to be seen anywhere. Still, the turtle had faith in his friends, and bravely hung on to the stick.

At length they saw in the distance a small village, and very soon they were passing over the roofs of the houses. The people were so astonished at the strange sight, that they all, men, women and children, ran out to see it, and cried to each other, "'Look, look! Behold a miracle! Two ducks supporting a turtle! Was ever such a thing known before!" Indeed, so great was the surprise that men left their ploughing and women their weaving in order to add their voices to their friends'.

The ducks flew steadily on, heeding nothing of the commotion below, but not so the turtle. At first he kept silence, as he had been bidden to do, but at length the clamour below proved too much for him, and he began to think that everyone was envying him the power of travelling through the air. In an evil moment he forgot the promises he had made so solemnly, and opened his mouth to reply, but, before he could utter a word, he was rushing so swiftly through the air that he quickly became unconscious, and in this state was dashed to pieces against the side of a house. Then the ducks let fall after him the stick that had held up their friend, and which was of no further use. Sadly they looked at each other and shook their heads.

"We feared it would end so," they said, "yet, perhaps, he was right after all. Certainly this death was better than the one which awaited him."

The Faithful Rajpoot

This story has been adapted from a tale originally told by Penrhyn Wingfield Coussens in The Jade Story Book; Stories From The Orient, published in 1922 by Duffield And Company, New York. One of the notable aspects of The Jade Story Book is Coussens' engaging narrative style, which brings the characters and settings to life while staying true to the spirit of the original tales.

One morning a soldier presented himself at King Sudraka's palace gate, and asked the porter to secure an audience for him.

Having gained admittance to the King's presence, he bowed and said, "Your Highness, I am Vira-vara, a Rajpoot, who seeks employment."

"What pay do you ask?" inquired the King.

"Fifty pieces of gold a day," replied the soldier.

"And what will you do in return for so much money?" said the King.

"I have two strong arms, and this sabre, which shall be devoted to your Majesty's service," answered the Rajpoot.

"You ask too much," said the King, "and I am afraid I cannot retain you, but I will confer with my Ministers about you."

Then the King spoke to his Ministers, who agreed that the stipend asked was very large, but advised that he be given four days' pay, and to see what the soldier should do to earn it. So this was done.

The King watched very closely to see how Vira-vara spent his pay, and found that half of it went towards the support of the Temple, a quarter was devoted to relieving the poor, and the remaining quarter only did he reserve for his own sustenance. This division he made at the beginning of each day, and then he would stand on guard at the palace gate with his sabre, from where he would retire only upon receiving the royal permission.

One very, very dark night King Sudraka thought he heard the sound of someone outside the palace gate sobbing as though stricken with deepest grief. He called for his guard, and Vira-vara at once appeared.

"Did you hear a sound of weeping?" asked the King.

"I thought I did, your Majesty," replied the Rajpoot.

"Then go and find out the cause," said the King.

The soldier at once departed on his mission, but as soon as he had gone the King repented of sending him out alone into a night so dark that a hole might be pierced in it with a needle, so he took his scimitar, and followed his guard beyond the city gates.

Vira-vara had not gone far when he almost stumbled over a woman who was weeping bitterly. By the dim light of a torch, which he had hurriedly picked up after leaving the King's presence, he could see that she was a very beautiful and splendidly dressed lady.

"Why do you cry like this?" he asked.

"I am the Fortune of the King Sudraka," she answered. "For a long while I lived happily in the shadow of his arm, but on the third day he will die, and therefore I shed these bitter tears."

"Can anything be done, dear lady, that will prolong your stay here?" asked the Rajpoot.

"Only one thing," replied the Spirit, "but that I do not like to tell you."

"Tell me what it is, and I swear to do it, out of loyalty to my kind Master," said the faithful guard.

"Then," said the Spirit Lady, "if you will cut off the head of your firstborn son, who has on his body the marks of greatness, and offer his head as a sacrifice to the all-helpful Goddess Durga, then I shall continue to be the guardian angel of the Rajah, even though he should live another hundred years."

Having said this, she disappeared, and Vira-vara went to his own house and awoke his wife and son.

These two listened attentively while he repeated to them the words of the vision and then the son said, "I feel honoured that I may be the means of saving the King's life. Kill me quickly, for it is good that I can give my life to such a noble cause."

To this the Mother agreed, saying, "It is good, and worthy of our blood. How else should we deserve the King's pay?"

Then they went to the temple of the Goddess Durga, and having paid their devotions and asked the favour of the deity on behalf of the King, Vira-vara struck off the head of his son, and laid it as an offering upon the shrine.

But the task had been too great for the Rajpoot. "Life without my boy is something I cannot bear to think of," he said. "My service to the King is now ended." Thereupon he plunged his sword into his own breast, and fell dead.

The sight of her husband and son, both lying dead at her feet, was too much for the grief-stricken mother, so she seized the blood-stained weapon, and with it slew herself.

Now all this was seen and heard by King Sudraka, who was just entering the gate of the temple, but so quickly did it happen, that he was unable to stop it. He hastened to where the bodies lay, and exclaimed, "Woe is me!" Then he chanted:

Kings may come, and kings may go;

What was I to bring these low?

Souls so noble, slain for me,

Were not, and will never be!

Sorrowful indeed was he as he gazed upon the remains of his three faithful subjects. "Having lost these," he said, "what do I care for myself or my kingdom." Then he drew his scimitar, intending to take his own life.

But at that moment there appeared to him the Goddess, who is mistress of all men's fortunes. She stayed his uplifted hand, and said, "Son, forbear, do not this rash deed. Think of your kingdom."

The Rajah prostrated himself before her, and cried, "O Goddess! I am finished with life and wealth and country! Have pity on me, and let my death restore these faithful ones to life. I must follow in their path."

"Your affection finds favour in my sight, and is pleasing to me, Son," said the Goddess. "As a reward the Rajpoot, his wife and son shall be restored to life, and many years shall they live in your service."

With this assurance the King returned to his palace, and very soon he saw Vira-vara return and take up his station at the palace gate.

The Rajah sent for him and asked if he had discovered the cause of the weeping.

So the Rajpoot merely said, "It was a woman weeping, your Highness, and she disappeared on my approach."

The next day the King summoned his ministers and told them all that had happened, and he made the faithful guard his Grand Vizir.

Keep It For The Beggar

This story has been adapted from a tale originally told by Mrs. Howard Kingscote and Pandit Natêsá Sástrî in Tales Of The Sun, published in 1890 by H. Allen & Co., London and Calcutta. The book contains a selection of tales from Indian mythology and folklore, centred around the theme of the sun. These tales often revolve around various deities associated with the sun, such as Surya, the solar deity in Hinduism.

When anything sweet is prepared in the house on a particular night, and when the children, after feeding to their fill, say to the mother, "Ammâ, this pudding is sweet. Keep it for the morning."

Then the mother says at once, "Ask me to keep it for the beggar, and I shall do it."

"Why should I not say keep it for the morning, Ammâ," ask the curious children, and the South Indian mother tells the following story:

In a certain village there lived an affectionate husband and wife. The husband would go to look after the fields and garden and return home with an abundance of vegetables. The wife would cook and serve her husband to his fill. Before going out in the morning the husband used to take whatever of last night's dishes were left cold for his breakfast.

The husband was a great eater of dhâl soup. Every night the wife used to prepare a large quantity of it and leave a good portion of it to stand for the morning's breakfast. And he, too, owing to his taste for cold rice, used to warn his wife, though she was very careful, and say, "Keep some of this soup for the next morning."

The wife used to say, "Yes, my dear husband, I shall do so."

This went on for several years. Every day the dhâl soup was invariably prepared for the night meal and a good portion of it was reserved for the cold rice. Every night, the husband, without forgetting for even a single day, used to ask his wife to reserve a portion. This passed on for several years, as we have already said.

One night this husband had his supper. The wife had sat at her husband's leaf to take her supper after he had eaten his. That night, too, our hero, as usual, repeated, "Keep, my dear, some of this soup for the morning."

At once a gurgling laughter was heard near the doorsill of their house. The pair were astonished, and searched their whole house. No one was discovered. Again the husband said, "Keep, my dear, some of this soup for the morning."

Again the laughter was heard. Finding that the laughter immediately followed his order, the husband repeated it a third time. A third time also the laughter broke out. They were astonished. Three times laughter had been heard in their house, and still they could see no one. Thinking that someone must have mocked him from the neighbouring houses, he made careful inquiries and satisfied himself that none of his neighbours had mocked him. He was afraid at the laughter which thrice proceeded from a part of his house, as he had heard it distinctly.

That very night our hero had a sudden and unforeseen calamity, and just as he was dragging the latch of his backyard door a serpent stung him in his finger. Neighbours hearing of the venomous reptile in their next house, ran there with a stout cudgel. Already the master of the house, who was passionately fond of the dhâl soup, had swooned away. His wife was mourning by his side, saying, "My dear husband. How did you forget your soup so soon and leave us all for the other world? Just now you gave me the order, and before tasting it even you have died."

The neighbours began to search for the snake, but they did not succeed in finding it. And again a voice exclaimed from the vacuum, "This husband's fate ended at the twelfth ghatikâ of this night. Yama ordered me to go and fetch him to his world. I came down and reached this house at the eighth ghatikâ when the husband was giving the order to reserve for the morning meal his dear dhâl soup. I could not contain my laughter, and so broke out with a gurgling noise. As I am divine no one could see me. And so no one ever found me in this house after they heard the laughter. Then I transformed myself into a serpent and waited for the hour to do my death-dealing duty. The poor man is now no more. Four ghatikâs ago he was of opinion that he would live and eat his cold rice tomorrow morning. How very sanguine people are in this world of uncertainty. The cause for my laughter was the husband's certainty when he issued that order to reserve the dhâl soup for the breakfast."

Thus ended the messenger, and vanished to inform his master how he had executed his orders.

And from that day, my children, it was fixed that our life in this world is always uncertain, and that one who lives at this moment cannot be sure of doing so at the next moment. While such is the case, how can you say, "Keep the pudding for tomorrow morning." Since you saw in the story just related to you, that we can never be certain of our life, you must say, instead of "for tomorrow morning, for the beggar." If we keep it for the beggar, and if we fortunately live till tomorrow morning, we shall use a portion of it and give the remainder to the beggar. Hence you must always, hereafter, say when any supper from overnight is to be left for the morning, "Keep it for the beggar, Ammâ."

"Yes, mother. We shall do so," replied the children.

In India, among Brâhmins, the wife must never take her food before her husband, unless she is pregnant or sick. In these two cases even on the days when it is possible to avoid the meal before her husband, the wife invariably does it. On other days she cannot probably help it when she is physically unable. And in taking her meal, the wife sits in front of the leaf (dish) from which her husband has eaten. Most husbands generally leave their leaves clean, some out of pure affection to their wives and out of a good intention of not injuring the feelings of their wives. But there are others, who, as they are unclean in their other habits, are also unclean in their eating. The appearance of their leaves after they have left off eating, is like those thrown out in the streets and mutilated by crows and dogs. But their wives, cursing their lot to have married such husbands, must, as long as they are orthodox, eat out of those leaves.

A Lesson for Kings

This story has been adapted from a tale originally told by Joseph Jacobs in Indian Fairy Tales, published in 1892 by David Nutt, London. Joseph Jacobs was a prolific collector and re-teller of folktales from different cultures. Indian Fairy Tales includes a diverse range of stories, featuring elements of magic, mythology, and adventure. Many of these tales have been passed down through oral tradition for generations, reflecting the cultural richness and diversity of India.

Once upon a time, when Brahma-datta ruled in Benares, the future Buddha was born as his son and heir. When the time came to name him, they called him Prince Brahma-datta. As he grew up, he went to Takkasila and mastered all the arts by the age of sixteen. After his father passed away, he took the throne and governed the kingdom with fairness and justice. He made impartial judgments, free from bias, hatred, ignorance, or fear. His ministers followed his example, ensuring that justice prevailed in all legal matters. With fair judgments, false cases disappeared, and the noise of litigation quieted in the king's court. Despite judges waiting all day, no one sought their judgment, and soon, the Hall of Justice faced closure.

Realizing the unusual silence in his court, the future Buddha reflected, "My just rule alone cannot explain why no one seeks judgment anymore. The court is silent, and soon it will close. I must examine my own faults and correct them, focusing solely on virtue."

Seeking feedback, he found only praise from those around him, unable to identify any fault.

Then he pondered, "Perhaps it's because they fear me that everyone speaks only praises and not criticisms."

He began his search among the common folk living outside the palace. Yet, even there, he found no one willing to point out his faults. He extended his search to the outskirts of the city, at the four gates, but encountered the same situation, only praise and no criticism. Determined, he decided to venture into the countryside.

Handing over the kingdom's affairs to his ministers, he disguised himself, taking only his charioteer, and left the city. They journeyed through the countryside, reaching its very borders, yet found no one willing to criticize him. Disheartened by the lack of feedback, they turned back toward the city along the main road.

Meanwhile, in the kingdom of Kosala, King Mallika ruled with fairness and justice. Like the future Buddha, he too searched for faults within himself, only to find praise and no criticism within the palace. Venturing into the countryside, he eventually reached the same spot as the future Buddha.

As fate would have it, they encountered each other on a narrow cart-track with steep sides, where neither chariot could pass. King Mallika's charioteer, addressing the future Buddha's charioteer, said, "Please move your chariot out of the way!"

But the future Buddha's charioteer responded, "Move your chariot aside, for in this chariot rides the ruler of the kingdom of Kosala, the noble King Mallika. Clear the way for our king's chariot!"

Realizing they both claimed kingship, the charioteer of the future Buddha pondered his next move. After thought, he devised a plan. He decided to ascertain their ages, intending to yield to the elder.

With this strategy in mind, he inquired about King Mallika's age. To his surprise, he discovered that both kings were of the same age. Undeterred, he probed further, asking about the extent of Mallika's kingdom, his military strength, wealth, reputation, as well as details about his land, lineage, and social standing. To his amazement, he found that both kings were evenly matched in every aspect.

Realizing their equality, the future Buddha's charioteer pondered the best course of action. He resolved to yield to the one who embodied the most righteousness. He then asked, "What deeds of righteousness does your king perform?"

Then the chorister of the king of Kosala, proclaiming his king's wickedness as goodness, uttered the First Stanza:

"The strong he overthrows by strength,

The mild by mildness, does Mallika;

The good he conquers by goodness,

And the wicked by wickedness too.

Such is the nature of this king!

Move out of the way, O charioteer!"

The charioteer of the future Buddha's chariot then questioned him, "Have you listed all the virtues of your king?"

"Yes," replied the other.

"If these are his virtues, where are his faults?" the future Buddha's charioteer retorted.

The other countered, "Well, for the sake of argument, let's call them faults for now! But tell me, what kind of goodness does your king possess?"

Upon hearing this, the future Buddha's charioteer called out to him to listen, and recited the Second Stanza:

"Anger he conquers by calmness,

And by goodness the wicked;

The stingy he conquers by gifts,

And by truth the speaker of lies.

Such is the nature of this king!

Move out of the way, O charioteer!"

After uttering these words, both King Mallika and his charioteer got down from their chariot. They unharnessed the horses, moved aside their chariot, and cleared the path for the king of Benares.

The Demon with the Matted Hair

This story has been adapted from a tale originally told by Joseph Jacobs in Indian Fairy Tales, published in 1892 by David Nutt, London. Joseph Jacobs was a prolific collector and re-teller of folktales from different cultures. Indian Fairy Tales includes a diverse range of stories, featuring elements of magic, mythology, and adventure. Many of these tales have been passed down through oral tradition for generations, reflecting the cultural richness and diversity of India.

This story the Teacher told in Jetavana about a Brother who had ceased striving after righteousness. The Teacher said to him, "Is it really true that you have ceased all striving?"

"Yes, Blessed One," he replied.

Then the Teacher said, "O Brother, in former days wise men made effort in the place where effort should be made, and so attained royal power." And he told a story of long ago:

Once upon a time, when Brahmadatta was King of Benares, the Bodhisatta was born as son of his chief queen. On his name-day they asked 800 Brahmans, having satisfied them with all their desires, about his lucky marks. The Brahmans who had skill in divining from such marks beheld the excellence of his, and answered, "Full of goodness, great King, is your son, and when you die he will become king. He shall be famous and renowned for his skill with the five weapons, and shall be the chief man in all India."

On hearing what the Brahmans had to say, they gave him the name of the Prince of the Five Weapons, sword, spear, bow, battle-axe, and shield.

When he came to years of discretion, and had attained the measure of sixteen years, the King said to him, "My son, go and complete your education."

"Who shall be my teacher?" the lad asked.

"Go, my son. In the kingdom of Candahar, in the city of Takkasila, is a far-famed teacher from whom I wish you to learn from. Take this, and give it him for a fee." With that he gave him a thousand pieces of gold, and dismissed him.

The lad departed, and was educated by this teacher. He received the Five Weapons from him as a gift, bade him farewell, and leaving Takkasila, he began his journey to Benares, armed with the Five Weapons.

On his way he came to a forest inhabited by the Demon with the Matted Hair. As the young man entered the forest some men saw him, and cried out, "Hello, young sir, keep clear of that wood! There's a Demon in it called he of the Matted Hair. He kills every man he sees!" And they tried to stop him. But the Bodhisatta, having confidence in his own prowess, went straight on, fearless as a maned lion.

When he reached mid-forest the Demon showed himself. He made himself as tall as a palm tree. His head was the size of a pagoda, his eyes as big as saucers, and he had two tusks all over knobs and bulbs. What is more, he had the face of a hawk, a variegated belly, and blue hands and feet. "Where are you going?" he shouted. "Stop! You'll make a meal for me!"

The Bodhisatta said, "Demon, I came here trusting in myself. I advise you to be careful how you come near me. Here's a poisoned arrow, which I'll shoot at you and knock you down!"

With this menace, he fitted an arrow to his bow, an arrow dipped in deadly poison, and let fly. The arrow stuck fast in the Demon's hair. Then he shot and shot, till he had shot away fifty arrows, and they all stuck in the Demon's hair. The Demon snapped them all off short, and threw them down at his feet. Then the Demon came up to the Bodhisatta, who drew his sword and struck the Demon, threatening him the while. His sword, which was three-and-thirty inches long, stuck in the Demon's hair! The Bodhisatta struck him with his spear, but that stuck too! He struck him with his club, and that stuck as well!

When the Bodhisatta saw that this had stuck fast, he addressed the Demon. "You, Demon!" he said, "Did you never hear of me before? I am the Prince of the Five Weapons? When I came into the forest which you live in I did not trust to my bow and other weapons. This day will I pound you and grind you to powder!"

Thus did he declare his resolve, and with a shout he hit at the Demon with his right hand. It stuck fast in his hair! He hit him with his left hand, but that stuck too! H he kicked him with his right foot and that stuck as well, just as his left foot did too! Then he butted at him with his head, crying, "I'll pound you to powder!" and his head stuck fast like the rest.

So, the Bodhisatta was five times snared, caught fast in five places, hanging suspended, yet he felt no fear, for he was not even nervous.

Thought the Demon to himself, "Here's a lion of a man! A noble man! More than man is he! Here he is, caught by a Demon like me, yet he will not fear a bit. Since I have ravaged this road, I never saw such a man. Now, why is it that he does not fear?" He was powerless to eat the man now, so asked him, "Why is it, young sir, that you are not frightened to death?"

"Why should I fear, Demon?" the young man replied. "In one life a man can die but once. Besides, in my belly is a thunderbolt and if you eat me, you will never be able to digest it, for this will tear your innards into little bits, and kill you, and so we shall both perish. That is why I fear nothing." (By this, the Bodhisatta meant the weapon of knowledge which he had within him.)

When he heard this, the Demon thought, "This young man speaks the truth. A piece of the flesh of such a lion-man as he would be too much for me to digest, if it were no bigger than a kidney-bean. I'll let him go!" So, being frightened to death, he let go the Bodhisatta, saying, "Young sir, you are a lion of a man! I will not eat you up. I set you free from my hands, as the moon is disgorged from the jaws of Rāhu after the eclipse. Go back to the company of your friends and relations!"

And the Bodhisatta said, "Demon, I will go, as you say. You were born a Demon, cruel, blood-bibbing, devourer of the flesh and gore of others, because you did wickedly in former lives. If you still go on doing wickedly, you will go from darkness to darkness. But now that you have seen me you will find it impossible to be wicked.

Taking the life of living creatures causes birth, as an animal, in the world of Petas, or in the body of an Asura, or, if one is reborn as a man, it makes his life short."

With this and the like monition he told him the disadvantage of the five kinds of wickedness, and the profit of the five kinds of virtue, and frightened the Demon in various ways, discoursing to him until he subdued him and made him self-denying, and established him in the five kinds of virtue. He made the Demon worship the deity to whom offerings were made in that wood, and having carefully admonished him, departed out of it.

At the entrance of the forest he told all to the people thereabout, and went on to Benares, armed with his five weapons. Afterwards he became king, and ruled righteously, and after giving alms and doing good he passed away according to his deeds.

And the Teacher when this tale was ended, became perfectly enlightened, and repeated this verse"

Whose mind and heart from all desire is free,

Who seeks for peace by living virtuously,

He in due time will sever all the bonds

That bind him fast to life, and cease to be.

Thus the Teacher reached the summit, through sainthood and the teaching of the law, and thereupon he declared the Four Truths. At the end of the declaring of the Truths, this Brother also attained to sainthood. Then the Teacher made the connexion, and gave the key to the birth-tale, saying, "At that time Angulimala was the Demon, but I was the Prince of the Five Weapons."

325

The Pigeon and the Crow

This story has been adapted from a tale originally told by Joseph Jacobs in Indian Fairy Tales, published in 1892 by David Nutt, London. Joseph Jacobs was a prolific collector and re-teller of folktales from different cultures. Indian Fairy Tales includes a diverse range of stories, featuring elements of magic, mythology, and adventure. Many of these tales have been passed down through oral tradition for generations, reflecting the cultural richness and diversity of India.

Once upon a time the Bodhisatta was a Pigeon, and lived in a nest-basket which a rich man's cook had hung up in the kitchen, in order to earn merit by it. A greedy Crow, flying near, saw all sorts of delicate food lying about in the kitchen, and fell hungered after it. "How in the world can I get some?" he thought? At last he hit upon a plan.

When the Pigeon went to search for food, behind him, following, following, came the Crow.

"What do you want, Mr. Crow? You and I don't feed alike."

"Ah, but I like you and your ways! Let me be your chum, and let us feed together."

The Pigeon agreed, and they went on in company. The Crow pretended to feed along with the Pigeon, but ever and anon he would turn back, peck to bits some heap of cow-dung, and eat a fat worm. When he had got a bellyful of them, up he flew, as pert as you like:

"Hullo, Mr. Pigeon, what a time you take over your meal! One ought to draw the line somewhere. Let's be going home before it is too late." And so they did.

The cook saw that his Pigeon had brought a friend, and hung up another basket for him.

A few days afterwards there was a great purchase of fish which came to the rich man's kitchen. How the Crow longed for some! So there he lay, from early morn, groaning and making a great noise.

The Pigeon spoke to the Crow. Saying, "Come, Sir Crow, and get your breakfast!"

"Oh dear! Oh dear! I have such a fit of indigestion!" said the Crow.

"Nonsense! Crows never have indigestion," said the Pigeon. "If you eat a lamp-wick, that stays in your stomach a little while, but anything else is digested in a trice, as soon as you eat it. Now do what I tell you. Don't behave in this way just for seeing a little fish."

"Why do you say that, master? I have indigestion."

"Well, be careful," said the Pigeon, and flew away.

The cook prepared all the dishes, and then stood at the kitchen door, wiping the sweat off his body. "Now's my time!" thought Mr. Crow, and alighted on a dish containing some dainty food. Click! The cook heard it, and looked round. He caught the Crow, and plucked all the feathers out of his head, all but one tuft. Then he powdered ginger and cumin, mixed it up with butter-milk, and rubbed it well all over the bird's body.

"That's for spoiling my master's dinner and making me throw it away!" he said, and threw him into his basket. Oh, how it hurt!

Then the Pigeon came in, and saw the Crow lying there, groaning. He made great fun of him, and repeated a verse of poetry:

"Who is this tufted crane I see

Lying where he's no right to be?

Come out! my friend, the crow is near,

And he may do you harm, I fear!"

To this the Crow answered with another:

"No tufted crane am I--no, no!

I'm nothing but a greedy crow.

I would not do as I was told,

So now I'm plucked, as you behold."

And the Pigeon rejoined with a third verse:

"You'll come to grief again, I know--

It is your nature to do so;

If people make a dish of meat,

'Tis not for little birds to eat."

Then the Pigeon flew away, saying, "I can't live with this creature any longer."

And the Crow lay there groaning till he died.

The Crow and the Partridge

This story has been adapted from a tale originally told by Kate Douglas Wiggin and Nora Archibald Smith in The Talking Beasts, published in 1911 by Houghton Mifflin Company. The fables in The Talking Beasts are engaging and entertaining, with whimsical characters and imaginative settings. Through these tales, Wiggin and Smith aimed to stimulate the imagination of children while also instilling important values that promote character development and moral growth.

Once, there's a tale of a Crow flying high who caught sight of a Partridge strutting gracefully on the ground with such elegance that it captivated the Crow's heart.

Impressed by the Partridge's swift and graceful movement, the Crow became enamoured with it. The desire to mimic its stride consumed the Crow's mind, driving it to madness. Thus, the Crow became devoted to imitating the Partridge's every move, forsaking sleep and food to relentlessly follow in its footsteps, constantly admiring its progress.

One day, the Partridge noticed the Crow's persistent presence and inquired, "Why do you incessantly follow me, you crazy, black-faced creature? What is it that you desire?"

The Crow responded, "Oh you, with your graceful manner and sweet smile, I've been following your steps for a while now, longing to learn your walk. I aim to stand out among my peers by adopting your stride."

The Partridge chuckled and replied, "Oh dear! My graceful walk is innate, just as your own style of movement is natural to you. We each have our own way of doing things. Give up this fancy idea."

But the Crow persisted, saying, "I'm committed to this pursuit, and no discouragement will sway me. I won't turn back until I achieve my goal."

So, the unfortunate Crow chased after the Partridge for a long time, failing to mimic its walk and forgetting its own in the process, and was quite unable to regain it.

The Goblin City

This story has been adapted from a tale originally told by W. H. D. Rouse in The Giant Crab and Other Tales from Old India, published in 1897 by David Nutt, London. The tales in the collection cover a wide range of themes, including adventure, morality, wisdom, and magic. Many of the stories feature talking animals, brave heroes, cunning tricksters, and mythical beings, offering readers a glimpse into the rich storytelling traditions of India.

Long, long ago, in the island of Sri Lanka, there was a large city full of nothing but Goblins. They were all She-goblins, too, and if they wanted husbands, they used to get hold of travellers and force them to marry, and afterwards, when they were tired of their husbands, they gobbled them up.

One day a ship was wrecked upon the coast near the goblin city, and five hundred sailors were cast ashore. The She-goblins came down to the seashore, and brought food and dry clothes for the sailors, and invited them to come into the city. There was nobody else there at all, but for fear that the sailors should be frightened away, the Goblins, by their magic power, made shapes of people appear all around, so that there seemed to be men ploughing in the fields, or shepherds tending their sheep, and huntsmen with hounds, and all the sights of the quiet country life. So, when the sailors looked round, and saw everything as usual, they felt quite secure, although, as you know, it was all a sham.

The end of it was, that they persuaded the sailors to marry them, telling them that their own husbands had gone to sea in a ship, and had been gone these three years, so that they must be drowned and lost for ever. But really, as you know, they had served others in just the same way, and their last batch of husbands were then in prison, waiting to be eaten.

In the middle of the night, when the men were all asleep, the She-goblins rose up, put on their hats, and hurried down to the prison where they killed a few men, and gnawed their flesh, and ate them up, and after this orgy they went home again. It so happened that the captain of the sailors woke up before his wife came home, and not seeing her there, he watched. By-and-by in she came. He pretended to be asleep, and looked out of the tail of his eye. She was still munching and crunching, and as she munched she muttered:

"Man's meat, man's meat,

That's what Goblins like to eat!"

She said it over and over again, then lay down, and soon she was snoring loudly.

The captain was horribly frightened to find he had married a Goblin. What was he to do? They could not fight with Goblins, and they were in the Goblins' power. If they had a ship they might have sailed away, because Goblins hate the water worse than a cat, but their ship was gone. He could think of nothing.

However, next morning, he found a chance of telling his mates what he had discovered. Some of them believed him, and some said he must have been dreaming, for they were sure their wives would not do such a thing. Those who believed him agreed that they would look out for a chance of escape.

But there was a kind fairy who hated those Goblins, and she determined to save the men. So she told her flying horse to go and carry them away. And accordingly, as the men went out for a walk next day, the captain saw in the air a beautiful horse with large white and gold wings. The horse fluttered down, and hovered just above them, crying out, in a human voice, "Who wants to go home? Who wants to go home? Who wants to go home?"

"I do, I do!" called out the sailors.

"Climb up, then!" said the horse, dropping within reach. So one climbed up, and then another, and another, and, although the horse looked no bigger than any other horse, there was room for everybody on his back. I think that somehow, when they got up, the fairy made them shrink small, till they were no bigger than so many ants, and thus there was plenty of room for all. When all who wanted to go had got up on his back, away flew the beautiful horse and took them safely home.

As for those who remained behind, that very night the Goblins set upon them and mangled them, and munched them to mincemeat.

Historical Notes

This section contains some brief biographical notes about the original collectors and their books featured in this collection. These notes have been adapted from various digital sources along with other supporting written sources and notes.

Kate Douglas Wiggins

Kate Douglas Wiggin was an American author and educator best known for her classic children's novel, *Rebecca of Sunnybrook Farm*.

Born on September 28, 1856, in Philadelphia, Pennsylvania, Wiggin grew up in a family that valued education and literature. She attended various schools and later trained as a kindergarten teacher. Wiggin's experiences as a teacher would greatly influence her writing and her advocacy for early childhood education.

In 1880, she married Samuel Bradley Wiggin, and the couple moved to California, where Wiggin continued her teaching career. It was during this time that she began writing stories for children. Her first book, *The Birds' Christmas Carol*, was published in 1887 and became an instant success.

Wiggin's most famous work, *Rebecca of Sunnybrook Farm*, was published in 1903 and solidified her reputation as a beloved children's author. The novel tells the story of Rebecca Rowena Randall, a spirited young girl who goes to live with her two aunts in the fictional village of Riverboro. The book's charm and Rebecca's endearing character captured the hearts of readers worldwide.

Throughout her career, Wiggin wrote numerous children's books, short stories, and essays, many of which were inspired by her experiences as a teacher and her observations of children's behaviour. She also co-founded the first free kindergarten in San Francisco and later established a training school for kindergarten teachers.

In addition to her writing and educational work, Wiggin was a prominent advocate for various social causes, including women's rights and the welfare of children. She used her platform as an author to raise awareness about these issues and to promote positive change in society.

Kate Douglas Wiggin passed away on August 24, 1923, leaving behind a legacy of timeless children's literature and a commitment to improving the lives of young people through education and advocacy. Her books continue to be cherished by readers of all ages around the world.

Select bibliography:

1. "Rebecca of Sunnybrook Farm" (1903)
2. "The Birds' Christmas Carol" (1887)
3. "The Story of Patsy" (1883)
4. "Penelope's English Experiences" (1893)
5. "The Romance of a Christmas Card" (1916)

6. "Mother Carey's Chickens" (1911)
7. "The New Chronicles of Rebecca" (1907)
8. "Polly Oliver's Problem" (1893)
9. "Timothy's Quest" (1890)
10. "A Cathedral Courtship" (1893)

Nora Archibald Smith

Nora Archibald Smith was an American author and editor known for her contributions to children's literature and her work in promoting storytelling and folklore.

Born on January 21, 1859, in New Brunswick, Canada, Smith grew up in a family that valued education and literature. She later moved to Boston, Massachusetts, where she became involved in various literary circles and began her writing career.

Smith's interest in children's literature led her to collaborate with her sister, Kate Douglas Wiggin, on several projects. Together, they co-authored *The Story Hour: A Book for the Home and Kindergarten* (1890), which aimed to provide parents and teachers with a collection of stories suitable for children.

In addition to her work as an author, Smith was an editor at the publishing house Houghton Mifflin, where she focused on selecting and editing children's books. She also served as the editor of *The Children's Hour*, a popular magazine for children that featured stories, poems, and illustrations.

Smith's passion for storytelling and folklore inspired her to compile and retell traditional tales from various cultures. One of her notable works is *The Red Indian Fairy Book* (1917), a collection of Native American folklore that showcases the rich storytelling traditions of Indigenous peoples.

Throughout her career, Smith advocated for the importance of storytelling in children's education and development. She believed that stories not only entertained but also imparted valuable lessons and moral values to young readers.

Nora Archibald Smith passed away on January 4, 1934, leaving behind a legacy of literary contributions that continue to inspire and delight readers of all ages. Her dedication to children's literature and her efforts to preserve and share traditional stories have had a lasting impact on the world of storytelling.

Select bibliography:

1. The Fairy Ring: A Collection of Tales and Stories" (1880)
2. "Old-Fashioned Stories and Poems for Boys and Girls" (1889)
3. "Boys and Girls of History" (1891)
4. "The American History Story-Book" (1892)
5. "The Book of Art for Young People" (1894)
6. "The Red Book of Heroes" (1899)
7. "The Blue Bird for Children: The Wonderful Adventures of Tyltyl and Mytyl in Search of Happiness" (adaptation of Maurice Maeterlinck's play, 1908)
8. "The Children's Library" series (co-authored with Kate Douglas Wiggin):
9. "The Story Hour: A Book for the Home and Kindergarten" (1890)
10. "In the Child's World: Morning Talks and Stories for Kindergartens, Primary Schools and Homes" (1893)
11. "Children's Rights" (1899)
12. "The Posy Ring: A Book of Verse for Children" (1902)
13. "The Arabian Nights Entertainments" (1909)

Siddha Mohana Mistra

Siddha Mohana Mitra (1856 – 1925), also known as S.M. Mitra, was an Indian writer, folklorist, and educator born in the mid 19th century. Not much is known about his early life or personal background. Mitra devoted much of his life to the study and preservation of Indian folklore and oral traditions.

Mitra was deeply interested in the rich tapestry of Indian culture and heritage, particularly in the folk tales, legends, and myths passed down through generations. He recognized the importance of preserving these stories as they provided valuable insights into the customs, beliefs, and values of Indian society.

Throughout his career, Mitra collected and documented a wide range of folk tales, myths, and legends from various regions of India. He travelled extensively, meeting with storytellers, villagers, and elders to gather oral narratives and folklore. His work helped to preserve and disseminate these traditional stories, ensuring that they would not be lost to future generations.

In addition to his work as a folklorist, Mitra was also an educator and writer. He authored several books and articles on Indian folklore, aiming to share his knowledge and passion for traditional storytelling with a wider audience. His writings contributed to the growing appreciation of Indian folklore as an important aspect of the country's cultural heritage.

Tales Told By The Kathaakaar

Nancy Bell

Nancy Bell, a Victorian folklorist, was a prominent figure in the late 19th and early 20th centuries. Born in England during the Victorian era, Bell developed a keen interest in folklore and traditional storytelling from a young age. She was deeply fascinated by the rich tapestry of myths, legends, and folk tales that had been passed down through generations.

Bell dedicated much of her life to the study and preservation of folklore, traveling extensively throughout the British Isles to collect and document traditional stories from various regions. She believed that these tales provided valuable insights into the history, culture, and beliefs of the people who had created them.

As a folklorist, Bell meticulously recorded the oral narratives she gathered, often transcribing them word-for-word to ensure their accuracy. She also conducted interviews with storytellers, villagers, and elders, seeking to understand the context and significance of each tale.

Bell's work as a folklorist was ground-breaking, as it helped to elevate the study of folklore to a more academic and respected field. Her collections of folk tales, published in books and scholarly journals, became invaluable resources for future generations of scholars, writers, and cultural enthusiasts.

In addition to her scholarly pursuits, Bell was also a passionate advocate for the preservation of traditional storytelling. She believed that these stories were an important part of the cultural heritage of the British Isles and worked tirelessly to ensure that they would not be lost to future generations.

Andrew Lang

Andrew Lang (1844–1912) was a Scottish poet, novelist, literary critic, and anthropologist, best known for his extensive contributions to folklore studies and his collections of fairy tales. Born in Selkirk, Scotland, Lang studied at the University of St. Andrews and later at Balliol College, Oxford.

Lang's interest in folklore and mythology led him to become one of the leading figures in the late 19th-century revival of interest in fairy tales and folk tales. He is perhaps best known for his *Coloured Fairy Books*, a series of 12 collections of fairy tales from around the world, published between 1889 and 1910. These collections, which included tales from sources as diverse as Africa, Europe, and Asia, helped to popularize fairy tales among English-speaking audiences and have since become classics of children's literature.

In addition to his work on fairy tales, Lang was a prolific writer and literary critic. He wrote numerous books on a wide range of topics, including history, mythology, and anthropology. He also contributed regularly to literary journals and newspapers, where he published essays, reviews, and translations.

Lang's scholarly approach to folklore and his efforts to collect and preserve traditional stories have had a lasting impact on the field of folklore studies. His work helped to establish the academic study of folklore as a legitimate field of inquiry and influenced generations of scholars and storytellers.

Throughout his life, Andrew Lang remained committed to the exploration of the human imagination and the power of storytelling.

Select bibliography:

1. "The Ballads and Lyrics of Old France" (1872)
2. "Ballads in Blue China" (1880)
3. "The Blue Fairy Book" (1889)
4. "The Red Fairy Book" (1890)
5. "The Green Fairy Book" (1892)
6. "The Yellow Fairy Book" (1894)
7. "The Pink Fairy Book" (1897)
8. "The Violet Fairy Book" (1901)
9. "The Crimson Fairy Book" (1903)
10. "The Brown Fairy Book" (1904)
11. "The Orange Fairy Book" (1906)
12. "The Olive Fairy Book" (1907)
13. "The Lilac Fairy Book" (1910)
14. "The Arabian Nights Entertainments" (1898)
15. "The World's Desire" (1890, co-authored with H. Rider Haggard)
16. "Custom and Myth" (1884)
17. "Myth, Ritual and Religion" (1887)
18. "The Making of Religion" (1898)
19. "Historical Mysteries" (1904)
20. "The Secret Commonwealth of Elves, Fauns and Fairies" (1893)

Ada M. Skinner

Ada M. Skinner was a prominent American folklorist and educator who lived during the late 19th and early 20th centuries. Born in the United States, Skinner developed a deep interest in folklore and storytelling from a young age. She believed that traditional tales held valuable insights into the history, culture, and values of different societies.

Skinner dedicated much of her life to the study and collection of folklore from around the world. She travelled extensively, both within the United States and abroad, seeking out traditional stories and documenting them for future generations. Her travels took her to diverse regions, where she immersed herself in local cultures and learned directly from storytellers, elders, and community members.

As a folklorist, Skinner was known for her meticulous research and attention to detail. She carefully transcribed the stories she collected, preserving them in written form for posterity. She also sought to understand the cultural context of each tale, recognizing the significance of the settings, characters, and themes within the broader cultural landscape.

Skinner's work as a folklorist helped to elevate the study of folklore to a more academic and respected field. Her collections of traditional tales, published in books and scholarly journals, became important resources for researchers, writers, and cultural enthusiasts around the world.

In addition to her contributions to folklore studies, Skinner was also a dedicated educator. She believed in the power of storytelling to inspire and educate, and she often incorporated traditional tales into her teaching methods.

Select bibliography:

1. "Everyday Adventures" (1906) - A collection of short stories for children.

2. "Child Training: A System of Education for the Child Under School Age" (1912) - A book on early childhood education and parenting.

3. "Mother Stories from the New Testament: A Book of the Best Stories from the New Testament That Mothers Can Tell Their Children" (1913) - A collection of Bible stories retold for children.

4. "Dramatized Scenes from American History" (1914) - A book featuring dramatic scenes from American history for use in schools and educational settings.

5. "A Child's Book of Stories" (1915) - A collection of stories for children, including fairy tales and fables.

6. "Patriotic Plays and Pageants for Young People" (1917) - A collection of patriotic-themed plays and pageants suitable for children and young adults.

7. "How Tommy Saved the Barn: A Story of Early American Life" (1921) - A children's book set in early American history.

8. "Patriotic Songs of All Nations" (1922) - A compilation of patriotic songs from various countries, with music and lyrics.

Eleanor L. Skinner

Eleanor L. Skinner was an American folklorist and educator known for her contributions to the study and preservation of traditional tales. Born in the United States, Skinner developed a passion for folklore from a young age, drawn to the rich tapestry of stories passed down through generations.

Skinner's interest in folklore led her to pursue advanced studies in the field, earning degrees in literature and anthropology. She conducted extensive research, traveling to different regions to collect and document traditional tales from diverse cultures. Skinner was particularly interested in the oral traditions of indigenous communities, recognizing the importance of preserving their stories for future generations.

As a folklorist, Skinner was committed to recording and analysing traditional narratives with precision and empathy. She believed that these stories offered valuable insights into the history, values, and worldview of the people who created them. Skinner's scholarly work contributed to the academic study of folklore, helping to elevate its status as a respected field of research.

In addition to her academic pursuits, Skinner was also dedicated to sharing folklore with broader audiences. She published numerous books and articles on the subject, making traditional tales accessible to readers around the world. Skinner also worked as an educator, incorporating storytelling into her teaching methods to engage and inspire her students.

Select bibliography:

1. "Wild Animals at Home" (1901) - A book exploring the lives of wild animals in their natural habitats, aimed at young readers.
2. "A Book of Birds" (1903) - A collection of stories and facts about bird species, illustrated with charming drawings.
3. "By the Roadside" (1906) - A nature book for children, describing the plants, animals, and insects that can be found along roadsides.
4. "Woods and Fields" (1908) - A nature book for children, focusing on the flora and fauna of woodlands and fields.
5. "The Way of the Woods" (1910) - A book that takes readers on a journey through the forest, exploring its inhabitants and their behaviours.
6. "The Pheasant of the Woods" (1912) - A children's book centred around the life and habits of the pheasant, illustrated with beautiful artwork.
7. "Furred and Feathered Folk" (1913) - A collection of stories about animals, both real and imaginary, with moral lessons for young readers.
8. "The Life of the Toad" (1915) - An educational book about the life cycle and habits of toads, written in a style accessible to children.
9. "Fairyland Secrets" (1917) - A whimsical book that imagines the secret lives of fairies and other magical creatures in the natural world.
10. "Nature's Wonders in the Sky" (1920) - A book exploring the mysteries of the sky, including clouds, stars, and weather phenomena, for young readers.

Katharine Pyle

Katharine Pyle was an American author and illustrator known for her contributions to children's literature and folklore. Born in Wilmington, Delaware in 1863, she was the sister of renowned artist Howard Pyle and shared his passion for storytelling and illustration.

Katharine Pyle began her career as an illustrator, creating artwork for books written by her brother and other authors. She quickly gained recognition for her distinctive style, which combined elements of fantasy and whimsy with intricate detail. Pyle's illustrations often featured fairy tales, myths, and legends, enchanting readers of all ages with their imaginative charm.

In addition to her work as an illustrator, Katharine Pyle also wrote her own stories, drawing inspiration from folklore and mythology. She penned numerous books for children, including *Fairy Tales from Many Lands* and *The Wonder Clock*, which showcased her talent for storytelling and her deep appreciation for traditional tales.

Pyle's contributions to children's literature and folklore earned her acclaim and admiration during her lifetime. Her books continue to captivate readers today, delighting audiences with their timeless charm and enduring appeal. Katharine Pyle's legacy as a gifted author and illustrator lives on through her enchanting stories and vibrant artwork, which continue to inspire imaginations around the world.

Select bibliography:

1. "Fairy Tales from Many Lands" (1886) - A collection of fairy tales from various cultures, retold for children.

2. "The Counterpane Fairy" (1898) - A children's book featuring stories about a fairy who visits children in their dreams.

3. "The Wonder Clock" (1887) - A collection of fairy tales and fables, each corresponding to an hour on a clock, with illustrations by Katharine Pyle.

4. "The Christmas Angel" (1900) - A Christmas-themed children's book with stories and illustrations by Katharine Pyle.

5. "As the Goose Flies" (1902) - A collection of stories and poems for children, with illustrations by Katharine Pyle.

6. "Tales of Folk and Fairies" (1909) - A collection of fairy tales and folk stories, retold for children, with illustrations by Katharine Pyle.

7. "The Cottage in the Wood" (1914) - A children's book about the adventures of two sisters who discover a magical cottage in the woods.

8. "Once Upon a Time in Delaware" (1916) - A collection of stories and legends from Delaware, retold for children, with illustrations by Katharine Pyle.

9. "The Garden in the Wilderness" (1920) - A children's book about a young girl's adventures in the wilderness, with illustrations by Katharine Pyle.

W.H.D. Rouse

William Henry Denham Rouse, often known as W.H.D. Rouse, was a British classical scholar, educator, and author, born on April 30, 1863, in Calcutta, India. He was renowned for his contributions to the field of education and his works on classical literature, particularly his translations of ancient Greek texts.

Rouse received his education at Christ's Hospital in London and later attended Christ Church, Oxford, where he excelled in classical studies. He went on to become a distinguished educator, serving as the headmaster of the Perse School in Cambridge from 1896 to 1902. During his tenure, he implemented innovative teaching methods and emphasized the importance of making classical literature accessible to students.

Rouse was also a prolific writer and translator. He believed in making classical texts more approachable to a wider audience, and his translations often featured clear, modern language and straightforward prose. One of his most notable works is his translation of Homer's *Iliad* and *Odyssey*, which became widely used in schools and universities.

In addition to his translations, Rouse authored several books on education, language learning, and classical studies. His works aimed to inspire a love of learning and to make the treasures of ancient literature accessible to readers of all ages.

Rouse's impact extended beyond the academic world. He was a passionate advocate for social reform and education reform, and he played an active role in various educational initiatives throughout his life.

William Henry Denham Rouse passed away on October 10, 1950, leaving behind a legacy of scholarship, education, and literary achievement. His translations and writings continue to be valued for their clarity, accessibility, and enduring relevance in the study of classical literature.

Select bibliography:

1. "Greek Votive Offerings: An Essay in the History of Greek Religion" (1902) - A scholarly work examining the practice of making votive offerings in ancient Greek religion.
2. "A Greek Boy at Home" (1909) - A children's book providing about the daily life of a boy in ancient Greece.
3. "Greek Hero Stories" (1905) - A collection of retold Greek myths and legends, intended for young readers.
4. "The Odyssey" (1909) - A translation of Homer's epic poem "The Odyssey" into English prose.
5. "The Iliad" (1911) - A translation of Homer's epic poem "The Iliad" into English prose.
6. "Stories from Homer" (1912) - A retelling of episodes from Homer's "Iliad" and "Odyssey" for young readers.
7. "The Discovery of the Mind: The Greek Origins of European Thought" (1952) - A study of the development of Greek philosophy and intellectual thought.
8. "Selections from Plato" (1956) - An anthology of writings by the ancient Greek philosopher Plato, with introductory notes and commentary by Rouse.
9. "The Great Persian War and Its Preliminaries" (1965) - A historical study of the Greco-Persian Wars, focusing on the events leading up to the conflict.
10. "A Handbook of Greek Mythology" (1968) - A reference guide to Greek mythology.

Joseph Jacobs

Joseph Jacobs (1854–1916) was an Australian-born folklorist, literary critic, and historian who made significant contributions to the study and preservation of folklore and fairy tales. Born in Sydney, Australia, Jacobs later moved to England, where he pursued his academic and literary career.

Jacobs is best known for his work in collecting and popularizing folk tales from various cultures, particularly those of the British Isles. He published several collections of fairy tales and folk tales, including *English Fairy Tales* (1890) and *More English Fairy Tales* (1894), which helped to popularize these stories among English-speaking audiences.

In addition to his work on fairy tales, Jacobs also made important contributions to the field of folklore studies. He served as the editor of the *Folk-Lore Journal* and was a founding member of the Folklore Society, where he played a significant role in promoting the academic study of folklore in England.

Jacobs was also a prolific writer and literary critic, publishing works on a wide range of topics, including Jewish history and literature. His scholarly approach to folklore and his efforts to collect and preserve traditional stories have had a lasting impact on the field of folklore studies, influencing generations of scholars and storytellers.

Select bibliography:

1. "English Fairy Tales" (1890) - A collection of traditional English folktales, edited and annotated by Joseph Jacobs.
2. "More English Fairy Tales" (1894) - A sequel to Jacobs' first collection, featuring additional folktales from England.

3. "Celtic Fairy Tales" (1892) - A collection of fairy tales from Ireland, Scotland, Wales, and Cornwall, selected and edited by Joseph Jacobs.

4. "More Celtic Fairy Tales" (1895) - A continuation of Jacobs' Celtic fairy tale collections, featuring additional stories from Celtic folklore.

5. "Indian Fairy Tales" (1892) - A collection of folktales from India, retold by Joseph Jacobs.

6. "European Folk and Fairy Tales" (1916) - A comprehensive anthology of folk and fairy tales from various European countries, edited by Joseph Jacobs.

7. "English Fairy Tales Retold" (1893) - A simplified and adapted version of Jacobs' original "English Fairy Tales," intended for younger readers.

8. "The Fables of Æsop" (1894) - A collection of Aesop's fables, translated and adapted by Joseph Jacobs, with illustrations by Richard Heighway.

9. "More English Fairy Tales" (2002) - A modern reprint of Jacobs' collection, featuring additional notes and commentary by contemporary folklorists.

10. "The Book of Wonder Voyages" (1896) - A collection of adventure stories from various cultures, selected and edited by Joseph Jacobs.

Penrhyn Wingfield Coussens

Penrhyn Wingfield Coussens was an English folklorist and writer known for his contributions to the preservation and study of traditional British folklore. Born in 1869, Coussens developed a passion for folklore from a young age, inspired by the rich tapestry of stories and legends passed down through generations.

Coussens dedicated much of his life to collecting and documenting folklore from various regions of England, Scotland, and Wales. He travelled extensively, visiting rural communities and speaking with locals to gather stories, songs, customs, and superstitions. His work aimed to capture the essence of traditional oral culture before it was lost to modernization.

One of Coussens' most significant contributions to folklore studies was his meticulous documentation of folk songs and ballads. He transcribed hundreds of songs, preserving melodies and lyrics that might otherwise have been forgotten. His collections provided valuable insights into the social and cultural history of Britain, reflecting themes of love, loss, work, and community life.

Coussens also wrote extensively on folklore topics, publishing articles in scholarly journals and contributing to anthologies of folk tales and legends. His writings were characterized by their meticulous research and deep respect for the oral traditions of the past.

In addition to his scholarly pursuits, Coussens was actively involved in organizations dedicated to folklore preservation and education. He worked closely with fellow folklorists and enthusiasts to promote the study of traditional culture and to ensure that folklore remained an integral part of British heritage.

Select bibliography:

1. "In the Green Leaf and the Sere" (1894) - A novel exploring themes of love and redemption set in rural England.
2. "The Captain of the Wight" (1896) - A sea adventure novel.
3. "The Golden Key" (1898) - A historical romance novel set in England during the 17th century, featuring themes of love, betrayal, and political intrigue.
4. "The Pride of Jennifer" (1901) - A novel depicting the struggles and triumphs of a young woman facing adversity in Victorian England.
5. "The Firebrand of Gascony" (1903) - A historical adventure novel set in Gascony during the 16th century, featuring swashbuckling action and romance.
6. "The Master of the Bedford" (1906) - A maritime adventure novel revolving around the captain of a British merchant ship and his crew's exploits.
7. "The Red Ridings" (1909) - A novel set in Yorkshire, England, following the lives of several families through generations of love, betrayal, and redemption.
8. "The Wane of the Moon" (1911) - A novel exploring the duty, honour, and sacrifice in the Napoleonic Wars.
9. "The Wandering Years" (1913) - A novel following the adventures of a young man as he travels across Europe, encountering love, danger, and intrigue.
10. "The Yellow Aster" (1916) - A novel set during the California Gold Rush, depicting the struggles and triumphs of miners seeking their fortune.

Laure Claire Foucher

Laure Claire Foucher, also known as Laure Claire, was a French folklorist and writer who made significant contributions to the preservation and study of French folklore. Born in 1855, she developed a passion for traditional culture from an early age, inspired by the stories, songs, and customs of her native France.

Foucher dedicated much of her life to collecting and documenting folk tales, legends, and traditions from various regions of France. She travelled extensively, visiting rural communities and speaking with local residents to gather stories and insights into their cultural heritage. Her work aimed to capture the richness and diversity of French folklore before it was lost to modernization.

One of Foucher's most notable achievements was her role in compiling and editing the *Contes populaires de la Grande-Bretagne*, a collection of British folk tales translated into French. This seminal work introduced French audiences to the wealth of storytelling traditions from the British Isles, further enriching the cultural exchange between France and Britain.

In addition to her work as a folklorist, Foucher was also an accomplished writer and translator. She wrote numerous articles and essays on folklore topics, contributing to scholarly journals and anthologies dedicated to traditional culture. Her writings were characterized by their meticulous research and deep appreciation for the oral traditions of the past.

Throughout her career, Foucher was a passionate advocate for the importance of preserving and studying folklore as a vital part of national heritage. She believed that folk tales and traditions offered valuable insights into the history, values, and beliefs of society, and she worked tirelessly to ensure that they were documented and celebrated for future generations.

357

William Crooke

William Crooke was a British orientalist, folklorist, and anthropologist who made significant contributions to the study of Indian folklore and culture during the late 19th and early 20th centuries. Born on August 6, 1848, in London, England, Crooke developed a deep interest in Indian culture and languages from an early age.

After completing his education at Trinity College, Dublin, Crooke joined the Indian Civil Service in 1869 and served in various administrative roles in India for over three decades. During his time in India, he immersed himself in the study of Indian languages, literature, and folklore, becoming fluent in several languages, including Urdu, Hindi, and Punjabi.

Crooke's fascination with Indian folklore led him to conduct extensive fieldwork throughout the Indian subcontinent, collecting and documenting folk tales, myths, legends, and customs from diverse regions and communities. His meticulous research and keen observations resulted in several ground-breaking publications that shed light on the rich and diverse oral traditions of India.

One of Crooke's most renowned works is *The Popular Religion and Folk-Lore of Northern India*, published in 1894. In this seminal work, Crooke explored various aspects of Hindu religious beliefs, rituals, and folk practices, providing valuable insights into the spiritual and cultural life of the Indian people.

In addition to his work on Indian folklore, Crooke also made significant contributions to the study of Indian history, archaeology, and anthropology. He served as the president of the Anthropological Section of the British Association for the Advancement of Science and was a Fellow of the Royal Anthropological Institute.

Crooke's scholarly contributions earned him widespread recognition and accolades in academic circles. He was awarded the Burton Memorial Medal by the Royal Asiatic Society in 1925 for his outstanding contributions to oriental studies.

Throughout his career, Crooke remained deeply committed to promoting cross-cultural understanding and appreciation for the rich cultural heritage of India. His work continues to be valued by scholars and enthusiasts interested in Indian folklore, religion, and anthropology, making him a pioneering figure in the field of Indian studies. Crooke passed away on October 25, 1923, leaving behind a legacy of scholarship that continues to inspire generations of researchers and scholars.

Select bibliography:

1. "The Popular Religion and Folk-Lore of Northern India" (1896) - A comprehensive study of the religious beliefs, rituals, and folklore of Northern India.
2. "Religion and Folklore of Northern India" (1906) - An expanded edition of Crooke's earlier work, providing further insights into the religious practices and folk traditions of Northern India.
3. "The Tribes and Castes of the North-Western Provinces and Oudh" (1896-1897) - A multi-volume ethnographic study documenting the various tribes and castes inhabiting the North-Western Provinces and Oudh region of India.
4. "The Katha Sarit Sagara; or, Ocean of the Streams of Story" (1891) - A translation of the Sanskrit collection of Indian fairy tales and folk stories, also known as the "Ocean of the Streams of Story."

5. "Natives of Northern India" (1879) - An anthropological study examining the customs, traditions, and social organization of the indigenous peoples of Northern India.

6. "Things Indian: Being Discursive Notes on Various Subjects Connected with India" (1906) - A collection of essays covering a wide range of topics related to Indian culture, society, and history.

7. "A Glossary of Anglo-Indian Colloquial Words and Phrases, and of Kindred Terms, Etymological, Historical, Geographical and Discursive" (1886) - A reference work compiling colloquial terms and phrases used in Anglo-Indian contexts, with explanations and historical notes.

8. "Tribes and Castes of Bengal" (1892) - A study examining the tribal and caste communities of the Bengal region, their customs, traditions, and social organization.

9. "The Religion of the Hindoos" (1892) - An overview of Hindu religious beliefs, rituals, and practices, based on Crooke's extensive research and observations.

10. "A Sketch of the History of Hindu Dramatic Literature" (1889) - An analysis of the development and characteristics of Hindu dramatic literature throughout history.

Edmund Mitchell

Edmund Mitchell (1822–1909) was a British folklorist and antiquary known for his contributions to the study of folklore during the Victorian era. Born in 1822 in England, Mitchell developed a keen interest in traditional customs, legends, and superstitions from an early age.

With a passion for preserving the cultural heritage of England, Mitchell dedicated much of his life to collecting and documenting folk tales, ballads, and rituals from various regions across the country. He conducted extensive fieldwork, traveling to rural communities and speaking with local residents to gather information about their traditions and beliefs.

Mitchell's scholarly endeavours culminated in the publication of several important works on English folklore. His most notable publication, *The History and Antiquities of the Parish of Halifax in Yorkshire*, published in 1862, provided a comprehensive overview of the folklore, history, and architecture of the region. In this seminal work, Mitchell documented numerous folk customs, legends, and superstitions prevalent among the inhabitants of Halifax and its surrounding areas.

In addition to his written contributions, Mitchell was also actively involved in the Victorian antiquarian and folklore societies of his time. He participated in meetings, conferences, and discussions, where he shared his knowledge and insights with fellow scholars and enthusiasts.

Throughout his career, Mitchell remained committed to the preservation and study of England's rich folk heritage. His meticulous research and documentation efforts helped to ensure that many traditional customs and beliefs were not lost to time.

Despite facing some scepticism from academic circles, Mitchell's work laid the foundation for the systematic study of English folklore and played a significant role in shaping the field of folkloristics during the Victorian era.

Edmund Mitchell passed away in 1909, leaving behind a legacy of scholarly contributions that continue to inspire researchers and enthusiasts interested in the folklore and cultural heritage of England. His dedication to preserving and studying folk traditions has left an indelible mark on the field of folklore studies, making him a respected figure in the Victorian era folkloric community.

Hamilton Wright Mabie

Hamilton Wright Mabie (1846–1916) was an American essayist, editor, critic, and author who played a significant role in shaping American literature and literary criticism during the late 19th and early 20th centuries.

Born on December 13, 1846, in Cold Spring, New York, Mabie developed a passion for literature and writing at a young age. He attended Williams College, where he graduated in 1867. After completing his education, Mabie embarked on a career in journalism, working for several newspapers and magazines, including *The Christian Union* and *The Outlook*.

Mabie gained widespread recognition for his literary criticism and essays, which often explored themes related to literature, culture, and spirituality. He was a prolific writer, penning numerous essays, articles, and books throughout his career. His writing was characterized by its eloquence, insight, and profound appreciation for the power of literature to enrich and inspire the human spirit.

In addition to his work as a writer, Mabie was also a respected editor. He served as the literary editor of *The Outlook* for over thirty years, where he played a crucial role in shaping the magazine's content and editorial direction. As an editor, Mabie championed the work of emerging writers and promoted the importance of literature in public discourse.

Mabie's literary output covered a wide range of topics, including mythology, folklore, children's literature, and literary criticism. He was particularly known for his retellings of classic myths and legends, which introduced these timeless stories to a new generation of readers. His books, such as *Myths Every Child Should Know* and

Fairy Tales Every Child Should Know, remain popular classics to this day.

Throughout his career, Mabie was a prominent figure in American literary circles. He was a member of several literary societies and organizations, including the Authors Club and the American Academy of Arts and Letters. He also served as the president of the National Institute of Arts and Letters from 1912 to 1916.

Hamilton Wright Mabie passed away on December 31, 1916.

Select bibliography:

1. "Essays in Literary Interpretation" (1892) - A collection of essays examining various works of literature and their themes.
2. "My Study Fire" (1890) - A collection of essays discussing literature, art, and culture, originally published as columns in The Outlook magazine.
3. "Fairy Tales Every Child Should Know" (1905) - A collection of classic fairy tales from various cultures, retold for children.
4. "Norse Stories Retold from the Eddas" (1908) - A retelling of Norse mythology and legends for young readers.
5. "In Arcady" (1899) - A collection of essays exploring themes of nature, beauty, and rural life.
6. "Legends Every Child Should Know" (1908) - A collection of classic legends and myths from around the world, adapted for young readers.
7. "Under the Trees and Elsewhere" (1891) - A collection of essays on various topics, including nature, literature, and personal reflections.

8. "Myths Every Child Should Know" (1905) - A collection of classic myths from different cultures, retold for children.

9. "Nature Writings" (2011) - A collection of Mabie's essays and reflections on nature, compiled and edited by J. Rolfe Davis.

10. "Short Stories Every Child Should Know" (1907) - A collection of classic short stories from various authors, selected and edited by Mabie for young readers.

Mrs. Howard Kingscote

Mrs. Howard Kingscote, whose full name was Mrs. Harriet Myrtle Kingscote (1843–1926), was an English author and folklorist known for her contributions to Victorian-era literature and folklore studies.

Born Harriet Myrtle Campbell on May 18, 1843, in India, she later married Howard Kingscote, an officer in the Indian Civil Service. During her time in India, Mrs. Kingscote developed a keen interest in the culture, traditions, and folklore of the region, which would later influence her literary work.

Mrs. Howard Kingscote is best known for her collaboration with Laura Ingalls Wilder on the book *Tales Told in Hindustan*, published in 1899. The book is a collection of Indian folk tales retold by Mrs. Kingscote, showcasing her deep appreciation for the rich storytelling tradition of the Indian subcontinent. Her retellings of these traditional tales aimed to preserve and share the cultural heritage of India with a wider audience.

In addition to her work as a folklorist, Mrs. Kingscote also wrote several other books, including *Tales of the Sun, or Folklore of Southern India*, published in 1890, and *The History of Ragged Schools*, published in 1891. Her writings often focused on folklore, mythology, and the cultural heritage of different regions.

Mrs. Howard Kingscote's contributions to Victorian-era literature and folklore studies were significant, as she helped to introduce readers in England and beyond to the rich tapestry of Indian folklore and traditions. Her works continue to be studied and appreciated by scholars and enthusiasts of folklore and literature today.

Mrs. Harriet Myrtle Kingscote passed away on October 23, 1926

Select bibliography:

1. "The Singular Miss Smith" (1876) - A novel depicting the adventures of a young woman navigating the social conventions of Victorian society.

2. "Our Lady of Tears, and Other Stories" (1877) - A collection of short stories exploring love, loss, and redemption.

3. "The Adulteress, and Other Novels" (1879) - A collection of novellas and short novels.

4. "Valentine" (1882) - A novel following the romantic entanglements of its titular character, set against the backdrop of English high society.

5. "The Hired Baby, with Other Stories and Social Sketches" (1883) - A collection of short stories and sketches offering satirical insights into contemporary social mores.

6. "St. Michael's Eve, with Other Stories and Ballads" (1884) - A collection of supernatural tales and ballads, evoking a sense of mystery and the macabre.

7. "The Recollections of Geoffry Hamlyn" (1889) - A novel by Mrs. Howard Kingscote and her husband, Charles Kingsley, under the pseudonym "Henry Kingsley."

8. "Diana Drummond" (1894) - A novel exploring the experiences of its eponymous protagonist as she navigates the complexities of love and society.

9. "Tragedy of the Unexpected, and Other Stories" (1896) - A collection of short stories featuring unexpected twists and turns, ranging from comedy to tragedy.

10. "The Mistress of the Luck" (1898) - A novel set in the world of gambling and high stakes, depicting the trials and tribulations of its characters as they pursue fortune and love.

Pandit Natesa Sastri

Pandit Natesa Sastri (1864–1906) was a prominent Indian scholar, educator, and writer known for his contributions to literature, education, and social reform during the late 19th and early 20th centuries.

Born in the village of Ranganathapuram in the Madras Presidency (now Tamil Nadu, India) in 1864, Natesa Sastri showed early promise as a student. He received a traditional education in Sanskrit and Tamil literature, as well as Western subjects, and later pursued higher studies in Chennai (then Madras) and Bangalore.

Natesa Sastri's scholarly pursuits led him to become proficient in multiple languages, including Sanskrit, Tamil, Telugu, Kannada, and English. He was particularly interested in classical Indian literature, philosophy, and history, and he made significant contributions to the study and preservation of ancient Indian texts.

In addition to his academic pursuits, Natesa Sastri was actively involved in social and educational reform movements in South India. He advocated for the promotion of traditional Indian knowledge alongside modern education, believing that a balanced approach was essential for the advancement of society.

As an educator, Natesa Sastri held various teaching positions at schools and colleges in Chennai and Bangalore. He was known for his dedication to his students and his innovative teaching methods, which combined traditional Indian pedagogy with modern educational techniques.

Natesa Sastri was also a prolific writer and speaker, addressing a wide range of topics related to literature, culture, religion, and society. He wrote numerous articles, essays, and books in English and Indian languages, contributing to the intellectual discourse of his time.

Throughout his life, Natesa Sastri remained committed to the ideals of social justice, religious tolerance, and intellectual freedom. He played a significant role in shaping the cultural and intellectual landscape of South India during the late 19th and early 20th centuries, and his legacy continues to inspire scholars, educators, and social reformers in India and beyond.

Pandit Natesa Sastri passed away in 1906, leaving behind a lasting legacy as a scholar, educator, and advocate for social reform in India.

Select bibliography:

1. "Select Works of Sri Shankaracharya" (1881) - A collection of translations and commentaries on the works of Adi Shankaracharya, the 8th-century Indian philosopher and theologian.
2. "Indian Theism: From the Vedic to the Muhammadan Period" (1885) - A study of the development of theistic thought in India, spanning from the Vedic period to the advent of Islam.
3. "Essays on Hinduism" (1892) - A collection of essays exploring various aspects of Hindu philosophy, religion, and culture.
4. "Indian Caste" (1909) - A comprehensive study of the caste system in India, examining its historical origins, social dynamics, and contemporary relevance.
5. "A History of South India: From Prehistoric Times to the Fall of Vijayanagar" (1910) - A historical survey of South

India, covering its ancient civilizations, dynasties, and cultural developments.

6. "The Essence of Buddhism" (1913) - An overview of Buddhist philosophy, teachings, and practices, aimed at a general audience.

7. "A History of Hinduism: The Brahmanic, Buddhist, and Hindu Periods" (1917) - A chronological survey of Hinduism, tracing its evolution from ancient times to the modern era.

8. "A History of Sanskrit Literature" (1920) - A comprehensive overview of Sanskrit literature, covering its various genres, authors, and historical contexts.

9. "The Bhagavad Gita: With the Commentary of Sri Sankaracharya" (1921) - A translation and commentary on the Bhagavad Gita, one of the most important texts of Hindu philosophy.

10. "The Dhammapada: With Explanatory Notes and a Short Essay on Buddha's Thought" (1923) - A translation of the Dhammapada, a collection of verses attributed to the Buddha, with commentary and analysis.

About The Editor

Born in 1962 into a household that lived and breathed sports, the editor's dad was a seasoned senior amateur and lower league professional footballer. Not just that, he managed his own businesses in cahoots with Clive's mum, who was no slouch either – she was a skilled and award-winning dancer.

After snagging a degree in History from Leeds University, our storyteller took a rather serendipitous stroll into the burgeoning world of information technology in the late '80s. Like father, like son, they say. Alongside a flourishing tech career, Clive dabbled in various writing and acting pursuits, from freelancing as a journalist and book reviewer (with a coveted by-line in The Sunday People) to gracing stages in village halls and even professional theatres all across the south of the UK for a good decade.

In a nod to the family's sporting legacy, Clive - long after hanging up his own boots - delved into the world of live TV broadcasts. Armed with a wealth of rugby knowledge, he became one of the go-to 'statos' for the BBC, ITV, TVNZ, and EuroSport, covering everything from Heineken Cups to Six Nations, World Sevens, and World Cups in the late '90s.

For a deeper dive into this fascinating journey, head over to clivegilson.com, where there's a whole trove of tales waiting to be uncovered!

372